THE SCENT OF ROME

LISE GOLD

Edited by Claire Jarrett

Cover Design by Irvine Design

To Elena Vilalta

'Long after one has forgotten what a woman wore, the memory of her perfume lingers.'

— CHRISTIAN DIOR

1

Nadine Costa was waiting at the bar of the St. Regis in Rome. Her red silk dress, black stiletto heels, long dark hair and elegant physique made her the center of attention and she knew it. People's eyes were always drawn to her, wherever she went, especially when dressed the way she was tonight. She scanned the opulent space as she inhaled the scent of luxury. It was hard to define the ingredients that made up the hotel's signature scent, but she picked up on a hint of rosewood and leather, no doubt carefully selected to leave a lasting impression on its guests.

It wasn't the first time she'd been here, but the grandeur of the hotel always impressed her. The marble floor of the meticulously renovated palazzo sparkled like it had just been polished, reflecting the light of the crystal chandeliers in the ceiling. Even though this wasn't Nadine's scene, she looked like she belonged here as she waited for the man who would be her date for tonight while sipping a glass of champagne. She was early as always because she liked getting acquainted with her stage, as she thought of it, taking her time to prepare for her performance.

It was pretty simple, but the rules were strict. All meetings happened in public places, no exceptions. Touching was not allowed, unless it was a hand on her back while leading her to a table or opening a door, or maybe a peck on the cheek to convince others of their affection. Possible topics of conversation had been sent through prior to their meeting, so she could make herself familiar with the material. She also had a file with information on the man she was meeting, including a basic script on how they'd 'met'. His name was Flavio Russo, a Rome-based investor and tonight, she was playing the role of a wealthy American on holiday in Rome, who had recently met Flavio in a café. After dinner, during which she would charm the hell out of his business partners, her agency would send a limo to pick them up, as she never got into private cars. The driver would drop off her client first before she went back to her own apartment in Trastevere.

Her privacy was protected by the high-end escort company she worked for, and sleeping with the clients was against the agency's policy within their contracts. They often asked her out on a real date by the time the night was over, but it was purely a job to her and she had no interest in dating.

Nadine wasn't afraid of anyone finding out what she did for a living. Her mother was back home in New York, and she didn't have any close friends in Rome. What she did was innocent in her opinion; making the men and women who booked her look good for others. Sometimes it was fun, sometimes it was boring, but it was always strictly business.

"I love your dress."

Nadine turned upon hearing the distinct American accent and smiled at the woman standing next to her at the bar. "Thank you. You look pretty great yourself."

The woman frowned for a moment, clearly not expecting her to be American too. "Thank you back I guess," she finally said. "I never know how to dress for meetings, it's not my strong point."

Nadine studied the petite woman, taking in her blonde bob, striking blue eyes, black knee-length pencil skirt and black top. She was carrying a simple leather envelope file and a small black purse hung from a silver chain over her shoulder. Her legs looked great in the high heels, but Nadine noted that just like her purse, they were designer replicas, which told her the woman was pretending to be wealthier than she actually was. "I'll have to disagree on that." She winked. "What are you drinking?"

"I was going to join you and order a glass of champagne."

"Then please allow me." Nadine gestured to the bartender to order another drink. "I'll put it on my date's tab."

"No, that's not necessary, I…"

"Please." Nadine smiled as she handed her the glass. "I'm Nadine."

"Rome. It's nice to meet you."

Nadine laughed. "Rome? Are you kidding me?" She studied the woman's delicate features for a hint of humor, but she seemed serious.

"No, I'm not joking." Rome laughed too. "I've never had that reaction to my name before but now that I'm here, suddenly everyone seems to think it's funny. There's no connection; my parents just thought it sounded exotic, and it's actually my first time in Rome. I only arrived this afternoon."

"Then you're in for a treat. How long are you staying in town, Rome?" Nadine repeated her name because she liked the sound of it. It was unusual but cute and bold, full-bodied like a good Bordeaux.

"Depends. If my meeting goes well, a couple of days to round up the contracts, then for a considerable stretch of time after I've gone back home to Portland to pack my things. If it doesn't go well, I'll be flying back tomorrow."

"Let's hope this evening is a success, then. It would be a waste of the long-haul flight if you don't get to see anything." Nadine took a sip of her champagne, careful not to smudge her red lipstick. "What is it that you do?"

"I'm an app developer." Rome shot her a goofy grin. "It's very nerdy; I won't bore you with the details but I'm here to meet a potential investor. I arrived early so I could take on some liquid courage and mentally prepare for my pitch."

"Then I shouldn't be distracting you."

"No, it's fine. It's nice talking to you; it settles my nerves a little." Rome tilted her head, then looked Nadine up and down. "Where's your date?"

"He'll be here soon. I came early too."

"Oh. First date?"

Nadine thought about her answer for a moment, then decided to be honest. "All my dates are a first. It's a paid date," she said, lowering her voice, then clarified: "I'm an escort." Rome's wide-eyed reaction amused her. The response was to be expected but it wasn't like they would ever see each other again and Nadine felt no need to defend what she did to make ends meet.

"So... he's taking you out to dinner and then you go home with him?"

"Gross, no. I don't sleep with them, it's only dinner." Nadine grimaced. "Wealthy men tend to like a younger woman on their arm to impress their business partners. I occasionally sleep with my female clients though, but only if I really want to and when I initiate it. Free of charge of course as that's purely for my own pleasure. I have needs too, and it's not exactly easy to maintain a relationship when you're in this business."

Rome seemed even more stunned now as a blush appeared on her cheeks. "Oh... So you only sleep with women? Because you're..."

"Because I'm gay, yes." Nadine locked her eyes with Rome and saw a hint of nervousness in them. "What about you? Men or women? Or both?"

"Men," Rome answered almost immediately.

"Husband? Boyfriend?" Nadine was surprised to feel a little flicker of disappointment at Rome's reply. Not that she expected anything to happen between them, but she liked flirting with women, and it was clear that she was not going to get anywhere with this one. A beautiful stranger who might only be in Rome for one night would have been perfect, because it had been a while since she'd had some action between the sheets.

"No, I'm single. Too busy with my nerdy stuff to meet people, and anyway, I'm not that bothered." Rome hesitated for a moment. "Can I ask you something? Just out of curiosity..."

"Anything."

"How much do you get paid to have dinner with your clients?"

"You mean how much does it cost to spend time in my company?" Nadine chuckled. "I don't normally disclose that but as you have the best name I've ever heard and the best ass I've ever laid my eyes on, from what I can see in that skirt..." Inching closer, she decided to flirt with her anyway. She wasn't doing anything wrong and besides, she liked how Rome blushed when she looked at her. Nadine was

5

good at reading people and there was definitely something there, straight or not. "I'm seventeen-hundred Euros a night. Out of the seventeen hundred, I get twelve hundred and my agency takes five hundred. The duration of the date is flexible but as a general rule, I like to be home by midnight. That's harder in Rome, though. People tend to stay up later than in New York and Paris, where I did this before."

"Jesus." Rome frowned as she processed the information. Or maybe she was processing the comment about her ass, Nadine wasn't sure. Either way, she looked flustered. "So, you get twelve-hundred Euros just to have dinner with someone? Nice, fancy dinners in the best places in town?"

"I wouldn't call them the best places. My personal tastes are a little more authentic than this, but yes, that's the deal."

"And your agency takes five-hundred? That seems like daylight robbery to me."

"It's not unreasonable." Nadine shrugged and smiled. "They do a background check on the clients and make sure it's safe for me to go out with them. They also protect my privacy and prepare an information pack, so I know exactly what I'm getting myself into. They've been good so far, so I'm not complaining."

"Well, it doesn't sound so daunting now that you've explained it." Rome leaned against the bar and sighed. "Maybe I should look into it. Then I wouldn't have to drag my presentation around the world while maxing out my credit cards." She finished her champagne and shook her head. "But I couldn't, I'd feel dirty." As soon as she realized what she'd said, Rome slammed a hand in front of her mouth. "Oh God, I didn't mean it like that." Regret was written all over her face and it was endearing how her gaze kept shifting to the ceiling, trying to think of something to pull her out of the hole she'd dug for herself. Nadine didn't mind the comment so much; she was used to it, and her line of work wasn't for everyone. "I didn't mean to insult you, I..." Rome's clumsy stammering stopped when a big, bald man in a sharp, black suit came walking up to them, eyeing Nadine.

Nadine realized she'd lost track of time and turned to him with her most charming smile. *Damn it. I never make mistakes.* He looked extremely wealthy in his Brioni suit and patent leather shoes. A gold Rolex peeked from underneath his right sleeve, and his wedding band was still on his ring finger; it was something men often forgot. Or perhaps he simply didn't care.

"Nadine, there you are. I've been looking for you everywhere." He eyed her up and down, then pointed to her dress. "You look beautiful as always."

"Flavio." Nadine kissed him on both cheeks and patted his shoulder. "I'm sorry, I got distracted talking to this lovely lady here." She turned to Rome. "Flavio, this is Rome. Rome, this is Flavio." She noticed Rome looked even more uncomfortable now as they shook hands.

"Flavio Russo, the CEO of *Nero*," Rome said. "It's great to finally meet you in person. I'm Rome Foster."

Flavio's gaze nervously shifted from Rome to Nadine and back and Nadine cursed herself as it clicked. An investor... of course. How could she have been so stupid? She was clearly not thinking straight, too immersed in flirting with the captivating woman who was apparently going to be at her table for the rest of the night.

"Rome was just telling me all about her app," Nadine lied, trying to put him at ease. She knew it was vital for him that their secret was safe, yet she'd just told Rome about their arrangement. "It sounds like a great opportunity." She gave Flavio another smile and knew that she had him then, as his shoulders relaxed and he smiled back, checking out her cleavage.

"Yes, we're looking forward to hearing all about it." Flavio put a hand on Nadine's back and led them to their table, where another two men were waiting.

Nadine took a deep breath and braced herself for the evening ahead, then introduced herself and sat down next to Flavio.

2

_____

Rome watched Nadine immerse herself in the conversation with the confidence and flair of someone who was used to mixing in wealthy circles. The beautiful dark-haired woman who had been shamelessly flirting with her only five minutes ago knew exactly how to wrap men around her little finger; that much was clear. Nadine's comment about her ass still lingered in the back of her mind. Women never flirted with her, and it was both exciting and distracting. For some reason she couldn't explain, she was just as worried about what Nadine thought of her as the men around the table who were making the decisions. She could tell Flavio was happy with his 'date' by the way he kept looking at Nadine, as if she was the only thing that mattered in the room. Knowing that he'd hired an escort for the evening made Rome secretly loathe him, but she needed his money badly, so she tried not to think about it. She was down to the last of her savings, after dragging her presentation from one side of the world to the other, and he was her last hope. Other investors had been interested, but most of them were worried about privacy issues. So, she'd spent months adjusting her program and here she was again with the latest update of her app, which she was hoping would change the world for the better. It was now or never.

"I apologize for bringing a date to our meeting," Flavio said. "But Nadine is only here for another two weeks and we wanted to spend as much time together as we could." He shot his hired girlfriend a creepy grin and the two men nodded their agreement, looking a little envious as Flavio put an arm around Nadine and squeezed her shoulder. Nadine flinched for a moment, but immediately corrected herself and gave him a playful look. Rome found herself unable to take her eyes off the escort when her bright red lips stretched into a wide and infectious smile, showing perfectly straight, white teeth. *God, she's gorgeous.*

"I understand. Young love is precious," Rome improvised as her eyes locked with Nadine's for a brief moment, letting her know that her secret was safe. "So, would you like to order first or shall I just go right ahead and tell you about my product?"

"Let's eat first," Flavio's dark and handsome co-investor, who had introduced himself as Rob, said. "I can't think on an empty stomach."

"Me either," Matteo, his chubby neighbor agreed. "I haven't even had time for lunch today and that's a crime in Rome, so thank God for the St. Regis' sirloin and the two beautiful women at our table." The men laughed, and Rome and Nadine laughed along half-heartedly. She realized then, that although they were there for different reasons, they were both in a similar position. They both needed something from the men in their company, and now she was the one who felt dirty.

Rome waited for her hosts to pick up their menus, then opened her own. If there was one thing she'd learned from boarding school, it was manners. "I must admit, I like how you do business here in Rome. I can't say I've ever done a pitch in a restaurant before, but it sure beats a boardroom." She didn't mind eating first and was silently hoping the men would be more impressionable once they had a couple of glasses of wine in their system. She'd make sure not to drink more than one glass herself though, as she needed to stay focused.

"Hey, you've come all the way here to tell us about your app. Taking you out for dinner first is the least we can do," Matteo said, then mumbled something in Italian to his friends.

The way they chuckled told Rome he was referring to the women at their table, but she pretended not to notice. *Don't say anything rude, Rome. You need this.* "Well thank you, I appreciate it." She scanned the menu and became internally outraged when a few moments later Matteo took it upon himself to order for her and Nadine.

"The ladies will have the artichokes, followed by the Sicilian red prawns, then the polenta with summer vegetables," he said to the waiter in English so they could clearly hear what he'd ordered. "And we need champagne of course, and the best red wine on your list." After that, Flavio, Rob and Matteo ordered for themselves in Italian.

Rome was shocked when she realized Matteo had not just only decided what she was going to eat, but he'd also ordered all the low-calorie dishes on the menu for her and Nadine. If they'd been on a date tonight, she would have waited for the food to arrive and then thrown it at him. Nadine's eyes met hers for a moment and they exchanged a knowing look, acknowledging they were on the same page about his misogynistic behavior. It was a small comfort, knowing she wasn't the only one appalled by his actions.

. . .

"So, as I explained, the Carbon app is connected to the Carbon Card. Think of it as a credit card," Rome said after discussing the practicalities of her pitch. It had been a long dinner, but the espresso was doing its work and keeping her alert. "It's an app to measure your carbon footprint, so before you start using it, you have to answer around two hundred questions. Various things like the type of car you drive, whether your house has double-pane windows or not, your utility usage, etcetera. Then, every time you purchase something, and you pay with the card, the estimated carbon footprint of the purchased items is stored in your profile. If you take a bus to work for example, you can enter that manually and Google Maps will pick up your location and measure your journey accordingly. Public transport gives you positive credit, of course, and walking is even better. The system can be connected to your health app too, so it tracks your physical journey. You can also use the app to scan products in grocery stores or anywhere you want really, and it will give you better alternatives in terms of mindful products and packaging. The Carbon platform is the future; it will change the way people think about consuming and living in general. It's simple, like a calorie app. Every single thing you do in your day to day life counts." Rome looked smug as she always did when she finished her pitch. She was proud of her product, even though it was surprisingly hard to physically get the idea out there. "I've patented the analytical part of the platform. Copycats are obviously still a risk, but they won't be able to extract the data the way my program can."

"Okay..." Flavio took his time to think about it, but it was Matteo who came up with the first question.

"I believe you when you say consumers are changing. You explained the shopping behavior of the new generations and I can see that. But, as far as I can see, the demographic that makes up the truly conscientious 'green' consumers still only represents a small percentage of the population and quite frankly, I think it's too early to invest in this. People aren't ready yet."

"That's where you're wrong. People just need a catalyst." Rome looked at all three men, then rested her eyes on Nadine, who appeared to be the only one captivated by what she had to say. For a moment, she almost lost her train of thought, but she quickly pulled herself back together and answered just like she had over a hundred times before. "Not everyone cares about the environment. But everyone cares about what others think of them. Humble bragging is real and showing the world you're doing good online is the new status symbol, even if it's for all the wrong reasons." She gave them a confident smile. "Imagine major influencers and stars using the app to tweet their progress on cutting back on their carbon footprint. It will be the most positive trend the world has ever seen, and I'm giving you the opportunity to be at the forefront of this huge universe of information that is not only immensely valuable, but also world-changing."

"Why are *you* doing this?" Nadine studied Rome intently and seemed genuinely interested in the answer. She looked caught out as soon as she'd asked the question, like she only then realized then that her role was just to sit there and look pretty. Flavio seemed to be curious about the answer too though, his eyes flicking to Nadine as she spoke.

"Yes, why *are* you doing this?" He repeated the question, studying the file containing the financial details of Rome's global roll-out proposal. "It's a huge risk; sixteen million is a lot of money. And it's not only risky for us, but for you too. If this goes wrong, no investor will ever touch you again."

"And sixteen million is a bottom guestimate," Matteo added. "We would have to put a team of experts together to work with you, and that will add significant investment too."

"I know there's a considerable risk. But I believe in this, and I'm doing it because I genuinely care about the environment and worry about global warming. I'm invested, and it's been my life-long mission to make the world a better place. You may find that naïve, but it's the only honest answer I can give you." Rome focused on Nadine as she passionately answered the question, then remembered she was addressing the wrong person and turned to Flavio instead. Besides the fact that he was the biggest shareholder in their tech investment company, she'd already figured he was their main negotiator too. "But for you, it's also an opportunity to make a lot of money. And I mean a lot. It is for all of us."

Matteo cleared his throat. "What about user privacy?"

"Well, I'm glad you asked because I've been working on that. The products that are bought or consumed do not register to individual accounts. Once they're processed, they move to the main database and only leave a code on the user's app which is then converted into the ever-changing percentage of their own carbon footprint as they continue to use it. The history is deleted, so to speak. Therefore, it would not be possible for me to see what you, Rob and Matteo have purchased this week but I would be able to see how many combined quarts of milk have been purchased by all the people using this app, or how much gas they've gone through while driving. Although the data is not personal, and therefore direct marketing is not an option, the data is still very valuable because the people who will be using this app are the consumers of the future and the insights are pretty precise. The data can be used to predict how popular certain consumer goods will be before they're even launched, and as a result, companies will be willing to pay a fortune for such lucrative information."

"Hmmm..." Flavio scratched his chin and let out a deep sigh. To Rome's surprise, it was Rob, who had been fairly quiet so far, who voiced his opinion first.

"I think sixteen million is a lot for something that's never been trialed before. *Nero* tends to follow proven formulas, we don't lead, and that's been the key to our success so far."

Rome sank back listless in her chair as she watched her life fall apart. She was pretty sure she wasn't going to secure their investment tonight. She'd put all her bets on this app, confident that no one in their right mind would say no to it. How could she have been so stupid? *I'm so fucked.*

"Excuse me. I'm going to visit the restrooms while you gentlemen discuss business." Nadine stood up and walked away with the sexiest sway in her hips Rome had ever seen. Despite the outcome of her meeting dampening her mood, she suddenly felt an urge to follow her and seize the opportunity to apologize in case she'd insulted her earlier. She sensed Nadine was fun and even though she was playing a role tonight, Rome had a feeling she was a lot smarter than she was letting on. Maybe she would have some advice on how to rope these guys in, because if they didn't invest in the app, she might need an escort job of her own, soon.

"I'll be right back." Rome stood up too and rushed after her. Her heart rate accelerated when she saw Nadine reapplying her red lipstick, stretching forward as she looked into the mirror above the marble basins.

Nadine smiled at her through the mirror, then pursed her lips and ruffled a hand through her dark hair that fell over her back in long waves. "How do you feel the meeting is going?"

"I'm not sure," Rome said, a little deflated. "But if my gut is anything to go by, it's not looking good."

"No, they're not going to bite, I can tell. Believe me, I'm good at reading people." Nadine turned, put a hand on Rome's shoulder and gave her a wink. "But maybe I can help you. I can't promise anything, though." She headed for the door without waiting for a reply.

"Wait." Rome watched her turn back and her stomach felt funny as Nadine's dark eyes flashed back at her. "I wanted to apologize for what I said. I don't think you're dirty." She rolled her eyes and let out a nervous giggle, then raised a hand to her temple, shaking her head. "Okay, that came out wrong."

Nadine laughed too and walked back to her, then did something so unexpected that Rome froze on the spot. Closing her eyes, she leaned in and inhaled deeply against Rome's neck, taking her time as if drinking in her scent. Rome's pulse raced when she felt the woman's breath on her neck. "You smell amazing," she whispered, bringing her mouth close to Rome's ear. "And the comment... don't worry about it. I'm plenty dirty."

Rome tried to compose herself after Nadine had left. *Fuck.* Her hands were visibly shaking as she opened the top three buttons of her top to get some air. She leaned against the wash basin and splashed cool water on her face as she focused on taking one deep breath after another. What was this woman doing to her? Shaking her head, she told herself not to get distracted by the unexpected turn of events. Nadine was a woman and her reaction to her made no sense. *Go back and do what you do best. You need that money.*

3

When Nadine returned from the restroom, she knew she'd been right. The three men seemed keener to have another couple of drinks with their female companions than they were to discuss investment opportunities. Flavio put a hand on her back when she sat down, and she suppressed the urge to shrug it away.

"What would you like my dear?" he asked her in a sickening endearing tone. "More wine? Another glass of champagne, perhaps?"

"Just another espresso would be wonderful, honey. I've already had way too much alcohol," she answered, giving him a saccharine smile. Her eyes followed Rome as she joined them a moment later and for the first time in months, she felt a little flutter in her belly. The woman was beautiful and sexy, and smart, too. Extremely smart. And that, in Nadine's eyes, was a total turn-on. Not only was Rome able to put together a world-changing proposal and make it sound simple and understandable, she was also clearly passionate about her idea, and for those reasons, she desperately wanted to help her.

"Well gentlemen," she said, after their last round of drinks had arrived. "If you're not interested in getting involved in this gem of a plan, I'd like to introduce Rome to my very good friend Harold Gardner. I understand your concerns as, unlike Harold, you tend to follow, but this sounds like it's right up his street." Suddenly all eyes were on her and the mood took a nervous shift. "In fact, I'll call him right now if you don't mind," she continued, pulling her phone out of her bag in a fake-tipsy state. Nadine never drank more than two glasses of wine, but her companions rarely noticed. "He's always up late and I know he's still in Europe; I spent a couple of days on his yacht in the South of France before I came here." She managed to hold back a chuckle at their perplexed expressions.

"You're friends with Harold Gardner?" Flavio asked, studying her for any signs that she was bluffing.

"Yeah. Didn't I tell you last time we went for dinner? We met a couple of years ago at a charity event." Nadine knew there was a plausible chance Flavio would believe her. Harold, the world-famous tech-investor was also a well-known ladies' man and it was likely Flavio would suspect she was his regular companion. She watched his right eye twitch, enjoying the game. Flavio's weakness was now her strength because she knew Harold Gardner was his nemesis. Nadine never went anywhere without doing some research herself, simply because she found people intriguing.

"You can't do that," Matteo said then. "We haven't decided yet, so the first offer still lies with us." Flavio and Rob nodded in agreement.

"Of course. I apologize, I was just trying to help out this lovely lady." Nadine looked at them innocently, a little apprehensive about overstepping her boundaries. "How about you think about it for twenty-four hours, so Rome doesn't have to leave her namesake just yet?" She had no idea why she'd suggested it, but it seemed like a good idea, even if she was treading on dangerous ground. If her agency found out she'd been toying with one of their clients and interfering in his business matters, she'd never work for them again. Why was she taking such a risk? Maybe she cared less, now that she was nearing thirty and approaching the end of her escort career. Or maybe she wasn't ready to say goodbye to Rome. She liked how the woman had been thrown off her game by her flirtations and even though Rome would never admit it, she could see that she'd been affected more than she had let on.

"Fine. Let's speak in twenty-four hours," Flavio agreed. By now, Nadine had a feeling she could get him to do anything and she liked that. He would probably book her again this week, if his wife was still out of town like she assumed.

Matteo and Rob nodded and mumbled something along the lines of it giving them time to discuss funding and timing.

They stayed for a little longer—Nadine and Rome drinking espresso and the men sharing another bottle of red wine. Matteo was desperately trying to impress Rome, but she was vaguely aware it had more to do with her looks than her brain. It was obvious that Rome was keeping her distance but her replies were clever and witty and she pulled them in with her charms without even so much as a flirty glance. She'd also noticed Rome's top was unbuttoned after returning from the restrooms and the idea that it might have something to do with her, pleased her. The men were getting tipsier now and she decided to call it a night, saving Rome from more hungry glances.

"Maybe if we're done here, you'd like to go home soon?" Nadine batted her eyelashes at Flavio. "After all, as you said, we only have two weeks left."

Flavio's cheeks turned red hot as he looked at her. He knew he wasn't going to get any more than a cab ride out of this, but he clearly liked that his friends didn't know that. Or maybe he was hoping she'd fallen for him already. They were all suckers like that.

"Of course, my dear. As you wish." He stood, reached into his pocket for his wallet and slammed a pile of cash on the table without bothering to count it. When Nadine arched a perfectly sculpted eyebrow at Rome, an amused look passed between them. She was glad she'd told her about her situation tonight; she'd be terribly embarrassed if Rome actually believed she was dating a man like him.

"Gentlemen, have a good night." Nadine stood up too and gave Matteo and Rob a kiss on each cheek, before turning to Rome. "Rome, it was an absolute pleasure to meet you. I wrote down my number, let me know if this doesn't work out and I'll put you in contact with Harold." She shot her a conspiratorial wink and saw Rome's hand trembling as she took the slip of paper and put it in her purse.

"Thank you. That's very kind of you, and it was great to meet you too." She held Nadine's gaze for a couple of beats, and Nadine was so captured by her blue eyes that she almost fell out of her role, but she quickly composed herself, remembering she was leaving with Flavio, and not with Rome. "Enjoy the rest of your stay," she said, casting one last glance over her shoulder as they walked away.

4

Rome shut her eyes tight and shook her head in an attempt to rid herself of the memory that kept haunting her. Nadine inhaling against her neck was all she'd been able to think of during the taxi journey back to her hotel. She turned on the bedside lamp and stared up at the ceiling, wondering why her mind was with Nadine, rather than with her pitch. The slip of paper with her number was still in her hand, even though she'd already saved it into her phone. Nadine's handwriting was beautiful; swirly and cursive, like her grandmother's used to be, which was unusual for someone her age.

Should she send her a message to thank her tonight? Or would tomorrow be better? Nadine was probably asleep by now. *Why am I making such a big deal out of this?*

After much deliberation, Rome finally typed a message, deciding she'd rather get it over with. *'Hey, it's Rome. It was lovely to meet you tonight and thank you so much for your help. It was very kind of you.'* She didn't mention Harold Gardner. Nadine had done enough for her, buying her time with potential investors, and all she wanted to do was thank her.

Biting her fingernails, she waited for a reply, but it didn't take long for Nadine to get back to her.

'Hey, Rome. It was great to meet you too. The Harold Gardner thing was bluff, by the way. I apologize for that, but I think it might have worked. Let me know if it did.'

Rome smiled, because she did have a feeling Nadine had been bluffing. *'Well, I really appreciate it, and I'll let you know if your bluff worked.'* She put her phone on the nightstand and pulled the covers over her, feeling wide awake and strangely disappointed their exchange was over. Her heart jumped when her phone suddenly rang, and Nadine's name lit up on her screen. Caught off guard and a little panicky, Rome let it ring a couple of times before she picked up.

"Nadine?" She rolled her eyes at herself for stating the obvious.

"Yeah, it's me." There was a pause while Nadine cleared her throat. "Sorry, I know it's late." She hesitated. "I'm not even sure why I'm calling, I guess I just wanted to wish you luck. You have a great product and I really hope it works out for you."

"Thank you." Rome smiled at her kind words and the sound of her voice. "Why did you do that for me? Why did you help me?"

"Because I like you," Nadine said. "And because you seem passionate about what you do. It's fascinating to watch your face light up while you pitch and I know more than anyone how important it is to do what you love." She chuckled. "You're probably wondering why an escort would say something like that, but there's more to me than my job," she continued. "And us women need to stick together when our livelihoods depend on men like Flavio, for whatever reason."

"That's very kind and so true," Rome agreed. "And

although I desperately need their money, I'm not sure how I feel about them. I couldn't believe it when Matteo ordered for us. Is that an Italian thing?"

Nadine laughed. "Most certainly not. But you'd be surprised how many men think it's perfectly normal." There was another pause, and all Rome could think of was how strange and exciting it was to talk to Nadine on the phone. She felt like she was doing something forbidden, something secretive, even though that made no sense. "Hey, do you want to have a coffee with me tomorrow morning?" Nadine asked.

The question came out of nowhere and Rome fell silent as her pulse started racing. It would have been a perfectly normal question, if it wasn't for the fact that Nadine had been sniffing her neck and commenting on her ass only a few hours ago.

"Come on, it's just a coffee," Nadine insisted when she didn't answer immediately. "Even if nothing comes out of this trip at least you will have had the best coffee in the world."

"The best coffee in the world? That's quite a promise," Rome joked, and managed to relax a little. "Sure. I'd love that." She could picture Nadine smiling on the phone, and closed her eyes for a moment, imagining her full lips and perfect, white teeth.

"Great. Message me where you're staying, and I'll pick you up at eight."

"Wait... eight? In the morning?"

"Yeah. The city is beautiful when it wakes up. Unless that's too early?"

"No, no, eight is fine." Rome's eyes darted over her open suitcase in the middle of the floor, already wondering what to wear tomorrow. "Are you sure you don't want me to meet you somewhere?"

"No, I'll pick you up, otherwise it will take you forever to get here."

"Okay. I'll see you tomorrow then. I'm looking forward to it."

"Me too. Sweet dreams, Rome."

Rome stared at her phone long after she'd hung up. "Sweet dreams," she repeated to herself. Wasn't that a weird thing to say to someone you barely knew? She let out a long sigh and once again, tried to think of nothing at all because the way her mind was spinning, she'd get no sleep tonight. There was still a chance she'd get the funding. A small chance, but a chance, nevertheless. Curiously though, it wasn't the funding that had her tossing and turning.

5

When her alarm went off at seven, Rome was already awake, and that was strange because she wasn't really a morning person and did most of her best thinking at night. It was during the dark hours that her brain worked at full capacity and ideas and solutions came to her. Her brain had certainly worked overtime last night, but she hadn't fallen into the deep sleep that normally gave her a good rest.

She groaned as she dragged herself out of bed and headed for the bathroom. The shower adjacent to the small, stuffy bedroom was moldy and worn-out but the hotel was cheap and cheap was a necessity right now. It took her forever to decide what to wear, suspecting Nadine would probably rock up in glamorous attire sporting big, Italian shades.

It was a beautiful warm spring day in early April, so she decided on a navy and white floral thin-strap summer dress and white Converse. Not too dressy, not too casual, she thought, studying herself in the mirror. Her blonde bob was blow-dried into a messy do, the way she'd worn it for years, but suddenly she was questioning everything about her appearance. There was no more time to change her hairdo or her outfit though, as she got a message that said: *I'm here! X*, then heard a horn honk several times outside her window. When she grabbed her purse and rushed downstairs, Rome noted that she felt more nervous than she had last night.

"Hey, over here!" Nadine yelled, waving at her from the other side of the street. Rome didn't recognize her at first with her helmet on, sitting on a mint green Vespa. She was wearing denim shorts and a tie-dyed black and white T-shirt and couldn't have looked more different to last night, free of makeup and heels. Even in the white sneakers, her legs looked never-ending, and Rome did her best to keep her gaze at eye-level.

"Are you the same person I met last night?" She asked, laughing as she took the helmet Nadine handed her.

"It's me, all right." Nadine tilted her head. "What, you expected me to wear a ball gown and be in the back of a limo or something? Driving makes no sense in Rome. We'd never get anywhere in a car; there's too much traffic."

"Honestly, I don't know what I expected, just not this." Rome gestured toward the back, then looked down at her dress, a little hesitant to get on.

"You'll be fine," Nadine assured her. "It's totally okay to show off your legs here. And those are great legs."

"Thank you." Rome chuckled at the compliment and climbed on the back before tucking the front hem of her dress between her legs.

"Closer." Nadine looked over her shoulder. "I'm not hitting on you, Rome. Not right now, anyway. Your dress will blow up if you don't." She laughed, and Rome felt a stir deep in her core, totally caught off guard by her body's reaction to seeing Nadine again. Hesitantly, she scooted closer and was surprised to feel another reaction skitter in her stomach as she pressed her body against Nadine's own. Nadine reached behind her, took her hands and pulled them around her waist. "Hold on tight. I don't know why the hell you decided to stay at this god-awful hotel in the worst part of town, but this is going to be a long ride."

Rome cursed herself for feeling the way she did when Nadine drove off. *Jesus.* Why did it feel like such a big deal having her arms around this woman's waist? She tried to relax as they drove through the busy morning traffic, over-taking cars like all the other thousands of multi-colored scooters. The roads were chaos, and even though she was slightly terrified, it was also fascinating to see the city this way. Despite Nadine's breakneck speeding and constant beeping, somehow managing to avoid hitting cars and other road users on many occasions, Rome actually started believing that she wasn't going to die today. Nadine took lots of shortcuts, zooming through narrow alleyways with bikes and scooters parked on either side against the façades where people were drinking coffee on fold-out chairs outside their homes. They passed under low arcades covered in ivy and vintage posters, drove past ornate churches, old ruins with frescoes, and courtyards with Baroque fountains and orange trees in a more resi-dential area that looked charming and bohemian. The roads were cobbled, the corners sharp and Rome held on tight each time they levitated after hitting a bump. She had mixed feelings when Nadine finally parked the scooter in front of a small coffee shop in a cute courtyard. On the one hand, she was glad to still be alive but on the other, she found herself missing sitting on the back snug-gled against Nadine, which was a particularly interesting development. With one swift movement, as if she'd done it a thousand times before, Nadine chained the scooter to a drainpipe.

"Best coffee in the world here, I promise."

"I believe you. I hope it lives up to its hype as you almost killed us getting here."

Nadine laughed and ran a hand through her hair after taking off her helmet. "You sit down honey; I'll get you a cappuccino like you've never tasted before. That's my apartment by the way". She pointed skyward, to the top floor above the café.

Rome took off her helmet and looked up. It was a beautiful building. Old, with cracks in the yellow painted stone façade, and ivy growing up on one side, crawling over the railing of Nadine's balcony, where a small table and a cast-iron bench were placed. It looked ridiculously charming.

"I see you're living like a local. How long have you lived here?"

"Almost four years. Best years of my life." Nadine beckoned for Rome to sit down before opening the door to the coffee shop, causing an intoxicating waft of baked cookies and freshly ground coffee beans to fill the air. "I'll be right back."

Rome took a seat at one of the tables and looked around, trying to imagine herself living here as a fellow American but it was so different from what she was used to that she couldn't picture it. The streets were narrow, the houses were built close together and everything around her was old and authentic, like she'd travelled back in time. An old man who was drinking coffee in front of his door, waved at her from the other side of the street and she waved back. There was a small bakery next to his house, and another even smaller grocery store next door to that. She hadn't seen many chain-restaurants or fast-food places outside the tourist area.

Instead, the cobbled streets of the working-class neighborhood she found herself in were lined with quaint restaurants, trattorias, artisan shops, quirky bars, independent businesses and galleries.

"One cappuccino for you..." Nadine placed the coffee in front of Rome. "And one for me." Then she went inside again and came back with a plate full of cookies. "You need to try the biscotti too. They're amazing."

Rome took a careful sip of her coffee and moaned. "You weren't joking. This really is great coffee." She watched Nadine dip one of the biscotti in her coffee and then close her eyes as she took a bite. It was almost erotic to watch, the way she licked the milky foam off her lips and enjoyed the small mouthful like it was all she cared about in that moment.

"Mmm... so good." She took another biscotti, reached over the table and held it in front of Rome's mouth.

Rome felt herself blush but parted her lips anyway and took a bite. "It's delicious," she admitted. Her face then pulled into a grin and she couldn't help but laugh. "Tell me Nadine, what are you doing here with me? I get the feeling you're flirting with me and although I love this coffee and these cookies and I'm forever grateful for what you did for me last night, I already told you I'm not into women."

Nadine shot her an amused look, clearly not fazed about her comment. "Right. You just keep telling yourself that." She sat back and crossed one leg over another, resting her ankle on her knee. "So, how are you feeling about the investment thing?"

Changing topic now, are we? "I honestly don't know." Rome pursed her lips and took another sip of her coffee. "My gut is usually a good indicator and at the moment it's telling me no—I don't think they're going to take on my project. However, I'm still hopeful," she added. "I have to be. Everything depends on this. If I don't find an investor soon, I'll have to look for a day job to pay my rent and the interest on my credit cards, and I'll have to say goodbye to my dream for the foreseeable future because I just have too much to pay back."

Nadine shook her head. "Don't be so negative, I think you stand a good chance."

"Why do you think that?"

"Because I've been booked to go to dinner with Flavio again tonight. Men never waste money on an escort who's not going to sleep with them unless there are going to be other people around. So, I have a good feeling about this."

"You do?" Rome's heart started racing and although she'd already told herself not to get too excited, Nadine's tiny glimmer of hope made her feel better already. Once more, she found herself staring at Nadine, wondering how it was possible that the glamorous escort from last night had transformed into this beautiful but casually dressed woman who was flirting with her like a man. Nadine was a total mystery, not to mention highly confusing.

"Yes, I do. But as I said, I can't promise anything. It's just my intuition." She batted her lashes and reached for another cookie. "And my intuition is usually pretty great, too."

Rome wasn't sure how to reply to that because there seemed to be an underlying innuendo to the comment. She wanted to know more about Nadine though, after lying awake for most of the night, thinking about her. "How long have you been doing the escorting?" she asked.

"Eight years. Since I was twenty-one. I started out in New York for two years, then did two years in Paris and this is my fourth year here." Nadine shrugged. "It's not so bad as it seems, really. It allows me to travel and to live where I want, providing my agency has an office near me. It gives me the income I need to do what I love most and work on my future. I'm turning thirty next year, so I'll stop then. Even if I wanted to carry on, that's where my agency draws the line."

"Really? Thirty is too old? That's ridiculous." Rome frowned. "So, what is it that you love the most?" Before Nadine had a chance to answer, two young men on a scooter zoomed past and whistled at them. She shot Nadine a confused look when she waved at them and yelled something back in Italian. "Are you okay with that? Or do you know them?"

Nadine shrugged it off and laughed. She had a great laugh, Rome thought. Deep and loud and hearty. "Okay, Rome. If you want to do your name justice, here's rule number one while you're here. If someone winks at you or smiles or even whistles, it's a compliment, okay? People think you're pretty and you are, so enjoy the attention. You smile and wave. Or at least acknowledge the compliment politely. If men or women do that, it doesn't mean they're hitting on you, they're simply appreciating your beauty. I do it all the time myself."

"You do?" Rome grinned. "Are you serious?"

"Yeah. I'd whistle if I saw you walking by."

Rome rolled her eyes. *Here we go again.* "I guess it makes sense when you put it like that. You're right; there's nothing wrong with a compliment." She finished her coffee and noted Nadine was watching her intently when she licked the foam off her upper lip again. *God, that intense stare.* "You were about to tell me about yourself. About what you're passionate about."

"Oh yes, that." Nadine stood up and waved at the man

behind the bar inside. "I'll tell you about that later. We have a lot to do today."

"What do you mean?"

"Well, if you don't seal the deal, you'll be leaving tomorrow morning, right? And you can't leave without seeing Rome." She didn't wait for an answer as she unlocked her scooter and jumped on, then gestured for Rome to get on the back.

Rome hesitated and shuffled on the spot, a little taken aback by Nadine's directness. The woman was persistent, but she was enjoying herself and it wasn't like she had anything else to do. Shaking her head with a smile, she took the proffered helmet and climbed on.

6

_____

Nadine maneuvered through the traffic once again, thoroughly enjoying Rome's arms around her waist. It had been a while since a woman had held her, even though the contact was entirely innocent. The way Rome reacted to her flirtations told her there was definitely something there. *She just doesn't know it yet.*

She wasn't sure why she felt the need to show Rome the city. Maybe because as a fellow American, she wanted her to see Rome for what it really was, see it like she had experienced it when she'd first arrived and fell in love with the place. Rome's hands shifted, tightening against her stomach when she drove over a bump in the road, and Nadine tried to shake off the stir of arousal she felt. Flirting was one thing, but she wasn't going to fall for a straight woman, even if that straight woman wasn't as straight as she thought she was. Besides, Rome didn't seem like a one-night stand type and Nadine didn't do relationships of any kind. It wasn't an option with her job, and even if she quit tomorrow, she simply loved her freedom too much. No, this was fun. Just a bit of flirting with the cutest and smartest woman she'd met in a long time, nothing more. It was starting to get warmer now, and she could feel the clamminess between their bodies as she steered the vehicle into Via Tagliamento in the northern part of the city.

"This is Quartiere Coppedè," she said in her convincing Italian accent as she parked and helped Rome off the back. "The smallest, cutest and strangest neighborhood in Rome. Are you up for a short walk?" She felt proud as she watched Rome take in her surroundings. The area was picturesque— even she herself was still impressed by the wonderfully odd buildings and whimsical feel of the streets and the small square.

"What is this place?" Rome's expressive eyes widened as she looked around, clearly overwhelmed when they passed under the archway that led into the main square. It was adorned with crests and animals, and a huge wrought iron gothic-looking chandelier hung from the arch.

"This whole area was built by and named after the architect Gino Coppedè, who lived here and worked on it until his death. It's a jumble of different styles; Art Nouveau, Medieval, Baroque, Ancient Greek... There may be more influences but I'm no expert. Normally mixing up building styles would be frowned upon, but it works, don't you think? It's like someone's brilliant mind designed it during a surreal dream, then decided to make it a reality." They entered a courtyard, surrounded by homes that looked like they came straight out of a fairy tale. Floral, medieval and mythological details decorated the façades of the buildings, some with randomly placed towers and odd out buildings.

"They're like bizarre castles." Rome took her phone out of her purse and snapped a few pictures. "It's so cool." She was quiet while they wandered the streets, passing buildings that incorporated crazy combinations of materials like brick, marble, stone and wood, covered in frescos and with psychedelic patterns in their entryways. After putting away her phone, she stopped under the shade of a tree and turned to Nadine. "Now, tell me about your passion because I'm awfully curious."

"I'm not sure where to start," Nadine said. Deciding it was easier to just demonstrate her skill, she stuck her nose up in the air, then dragged Rome along to a bakery on the corner of the street. "Smell that?" she said. "It's fresh ciabatta."

"It is," Rome agreed. "And? You love bread?"

Nadine laughed. "I do, but that's not the point. There's garlic in it and rosemary, of course, but also a hint of orange peel to bring out the sweetness in the dough."

"Clearly your favorite bakery. Did they give you the recipe?" Rome asked.

"No, I can smell it."

Rome stared at her in surprise. "You can smell the orange peel in the bread that is baked in the back of that building? I don't even get a hint of it."

"Yes, I can smell everything."

"Hmm…" Rome looked up at her, clearly not convinced. "What else do you smell?"

"Are you sure you want to know? Because I'm going to start with you." Rome didn't answer, so Nadine continued. "The fragrance you wear daily is Pure Grace by Philosophy. You're loyal to the brand, no exceptions. Its trace is incredibly pure on your skin, so I'd know if you wore a different perfume last week. It's an interesting choice in my opinion because although it's not expensive or fancy, it's very clean and elegant and it really suits you. Not many people get it right with fragrances. Your face cream is possibly Japanese because it contains cucumber essence but I suspect you put it on last night, not this morning. Your shampoo has traces of pine which is unusual for shampoos, and the fabric conditioner you use on your clothes has the same undertones, which makes me think you like being outdoors, love walking in the woods?" She frowned. "Or maybe you just like the idea of the scent of the woods because it makes you feel calm. You actually strike me as more of a city girl."

"Are you serious?" Rome looked shocked.

"Am I right?" Nadine shot her a self-satisfied look. "Don't even answer that, I know I am. But best of all is your own scent. I wish I could bottle it; it's sweet and feminine and so innocent because you don't use any artificial crap on your body, but rather natural and organic products. You smell like the sun. It's rare and extremely arousing."

Rome was silent for a long moment, her lips parting as she processed Nadine's words. "Is that why you sniffed me in the restrooms last night?"

"Uh-huh." Nadine moved closer and nuzzled against Rome's hairline inhaling along her temple. She liked how goose bumps appeared on Rome's arms when she was close, but she also knew she was pushing it now, and didn't want to scare her away. "I'm sorry." She tried to compose herself. "That was intrusive." A smile played around her lips. "But so good, though."

Rome blushed profusely as she sniffed her arm, then shrugged casually, although she couldn't have looked more disoriented. "Sorry, I don't get it."

"That's because you can't smell yourself. I mean you can, when you sweat. That's a different thing because it's an out of the ordinary state. But the pureness of you, you'll never get to experience, and I'm so terribly sorry to tell you that because it's divine." Nadine proceeded to walk toward a square with a big fountain, surrounded by benches, and Rome followed. "What's your favorite natural scent?"

Rome had to think about that. "I'm not sure, no one's ever asked me that question before... After it rains, I guess."

"Interesting." Nadine smiled. "Pine, woods, the smell of nature after rain... see? You like calm things and you don't even realize it. You instinctively pick the fragrances you're drawn to and they all merge well together."

"You're right, I do. So, what's your favorite?"

Nadine sighed. "I have so many. Sea breeze, the smell of trees in a forest—like you—burning wood, old books, freshly cut grass, citrus, sex..."

"Sex?"

"Yeah. I like scents that make me feel something. All in all, I prefer pure scents but right now, my favorite one is you." God, she couldn't help herself. *You just had to say it again, didn't you?*

"You're lying. You're just turning on the charm again and I already told you, that's not going to work on me. I'm as straight as an arrow."

Nadine quirked her brow. "Okay, maybe I am turning on the charm but I'm not lying when I say you actually are my favorite scent right now. I've never smelled anything quite like you."

Rome chuckled and shook her head. "Well thank you, I'm flattered. So, what do you do with it? With your gift? It is a gift, right?" she asked, moving the conversation away from herself.

"I guess you could call it that. I'm highly sensitive to my surroundings because of my unique sense of smell and it enables me to read people." Nadine sat down on a bench and closed her eyes as droplets from the wet breeze wafting from the fountain blew in her face, cooling her down a little.

When Rome sat down next to her, she fought the urge to put her arm over the bench's backrest behind her. "I develop perfumes. It's an expensive hobby, hence my lucrative side business. It's also a slow process, as I won't settle for anything less than perfection and there's a lot I'm trying to bottle. Hopefully, I can go to market in the near future."

"That's impressive. So you're a perfumer?"

"Yes. I don't have a chemistry degree. I'm self-taught, but I'm probably as good as any, if not better than most master perfumers. I've got what's known as a *Nose*." Nadine rolled her eyes. "I know I sound cocky now, but it's true; I can bottle the essence of just about anything." She turned to Rome and grinned. "Anything but you, I guess. Although technically I might be able to bottle you too."

"Now you're creeping me out," Rome said, nudging her. "I assume you're familiar with the book *Perfume: The Story of a Murderer*? Am I safe right now?"

Nadine gave one of her deep, lyrical laughs. "Of course I'm familiar with it. Don't worry, I'm not a serial killer who wants to kidnap you to extract the essence from your skin. I just want to sniff you," she joked.

Rome joined in her laughter. "Good. So what do you love about creating perfumes? Apart from the fact that you can put your natural talent to use?"

"Everything." Nadine turned to her, pleasantly surprised that Rome seemed interested and maybe even a little intrigued. She looked gorgeous with the sunlight on her hair and her skin shimmering from the condensation from the fountain. "Everything from the science to the emotion it evokes. A fragrance should perform a function or take you somewhere; make you want to travel, make you dream, cause attraction or bring forth memories... If it doesn't do any of that, it's not the right one for you."

"That makes sense... And beautifully said," Rome added. "What are you working on?"

Nadine hesitated. "Can you keep a secret? I'm really private about it because I'm terrified of someone stealing my idea."

"Of course," Rome said, and Nadine believed her.

"Okay, well, I'm creating a set of twelve perfumes." Nadine was a little unsure about telling Rome more as she never talked about her creations—especially with strangers —but for some reason, she really wanted to share her concept with Rome. Following their meeting, where Rome had pitched her app, she could see that Rome was as ardent as she was about what she did and talking about her enterprise with another creative person felt like too good an opportunity to miss. "You seem too much of a logical thinker to be into horoscopes. Do you hate that kind of stuff?"

"No, I don't actually. I find it interesting." Rome grinned. "Doesn't mean I believe in it, though."

Nadine smiled as she gave her a slow nod. "So, what's your star sign? Is it Libra?" It was just a hunch—she tended to gravitate toward Libras—and she felt a wave of victory when Rome's face pulled into a baffled expression yet again.

"Jesus, how do you even know that? Are you some kind of mind reader? And what has that got to do with perfumes?" Rome frowned and Nadine could almost hear her analytic brain ticking over. "Wait... twelve perfumes, you said. I get it now. Clever."

"It's only clever if it works and I'm not quite there yet. But yes, you guessed right. I'm creating a unique perfume for each star sign. It's all about attraction, you see. Certain star signs are generally speaking naturally attracted to each other because the universe tells them they make a good fit.

The perfumes are unisex and very subtle—barely notice-able—yet in theory you, as a Libra, would be likely to be attracted to an Aquarius, like me." She smiled when she saw Rome blush, then added: "Hypothetically speaking of course, if you weren't quite clearly straight. And the idea is that if I wear my Aquarius enhancing perfume, you'll have a greater chance of noticing me and the other way around if you wear yours."

"But it only makes sense if a lot of people actually wear it," Rome argued. "Otherwise the chances of meeting someone through attraction of scent is very small."

"Right. The attraction part of that is true. But the perfume will still be the perfect fit for you, enhancing your personality no matter what. And when I say perfume, it's not necessarily floral or anything that stands out. It's delib-erately subtle and registers in the subconscious rather than in the direct sense of smell. I've done a lot of research into this, and I can back it all up."

Rome nodded. "I like it, it's a fantastic idea. It sounds super commercial and I have no doubt you'll be able to pull it off if it's marketed well but being a nerd and all, I have to see the test results before I believe it will actually work."

"Of course." Nadine sighed and sank further down on the bench, crossing her legs. "But it will work. It has to."

7

"Okay, you've convinced me, I love Rome already." Tucking into a delicious seafood pasta, Rome felt relaxed and happy despite the underlying nerves as she waited for a phone call from Flavio. They were in another old and beautiful non-touristy neighborhood, sitting among locals who all seemed to know Nadine. Rome was impressed by her Italian since she'd told her she'd only lived here for four years and to her untrained ear she sounded as fluent as everyone around them. Lunchtime was a busy affair in the small establishment where the red cloth covered tables were placed so close together that they might as well have been attached. Waiters were running around with bottles, topping everyone's glasses up with the house wine, and the tables were decked out with baskets of freshly baked bread and plates of steaming hot food. It was brightly lit, and both the background music and the chatter were really loud, yet she was pretty sure it was one of the most charming places she'd dined at.

Nadine looked like she was in her element, joking with the people sitting to their left as she joined in with their conversation. Being a woman with interesting passions, Nadine was fascinating to talk to, but she also made a really great listener. As she sat there watching Nadine playfully tease the older couple, Rome knew she liked being around her and she really wanted Nadine to like her back.

"Why did you come here?" She asked. "Why didn't you stay in France? Wouldn't that be the obvious choice, since it's all about perfume there?"

Nadine took a sip of her white wine and nodded. "Yes, you're right. It would be the obvious choice. I was in Paris, mainly. However, the escort work that I do to provide the funds to finance my goal is only available in certain cities, at least through my current agency, and it was unlikely that I'd be able to find clients in Grasse, where most perfume factories are based. Also, the laboratory in Paris I worked with was crazy expensive. It's much cheaper here and they're just as good. Italians speak the language of passion, so they understand perfume. It's easy to communicate with them, they just get it. Besides that, I've grown to love Rome and I never want to leave." She paused, swirling her linguine around her fork. "Before I came here, I wasn't sure how long I'd stay, but it only took me a week to realize this was the place for me. My father was Italian, so I knew the basics of the language, and it felt like coming home, even though I'd never been here before."

"So basically you're half Italian," Rome said. "That's where your dark and mysterious features come from..." She straightened herself, realizing she sounded a little flirty. "I just meant that it all makes sense now that you've told me," she hastily added. "And it also explains how you picked up speaking Italian so quickly."

Nadine studied her, a small smile playing around her lips. "Yes, I look like my dad, and have dual citizenship. And yes, it also helped that I spoke Italian with him when I was little. Language fades if you don't practice, yet somehow it sticks too. It made it easier to learn it properly when I came here, even though I hadn't spoken Italian in twenty-one years."

"So what happened to your dad? Do you mind me asking?" Rome looked at her while she pushed her plate to the side. She couldn't possibly eat any more and wondered how Nadine stayed so slim, living here.

"No, I don't mind. He died when I was eight. Heart attack." Nadine paused, clearly reluctant to carry on the topic. "But enough about me, I want to know more about the passion project you've dedicated your life to." She dabbed her mouth with a napkin so elegantly that Rome wondered if she was raised like that or if it was a result of her many years of escorting. But then again, now that she was getting to know her a little, everything Nadine did seemed effortlessly elegant, even hitting on women and driving like a maniac.

"Sure. I'll tell you more about it, but I can't promise you I won't bore you."

"Bore me?" Nadine slowly shook her head as she locked her eyes with Rome's. "You could never bore me. Just hearing you read the dictionary would be fascinating." At that moment, Rome's phone rang, and she gasped when she saw it was an Italian number.

"Excuse me, I need to take this." Her heart sank to her stomach when she heard Matteo's voice say her name. *Shit. Flavio sent his minion. It's bad news.* "Yes, it's me," she said, trying to keep the tremor out of her voice. "How are you, Matteo?"

"Excellent, thank you." Matteo cleared his throat. "I'm happy to inform you that we'd like to go ahead with the funding for your app and that we're accepting the terms stated in your proposal."

"Seriously?" Rome wanted to jump on the table and scream to release the adrenaline that was rushing through her. She couldn't quite believe what he was saying because she'd been picturing this moment for over two years, hoping, praying that it would happen, but it hadn't felt nearly as good in her fantasies as it did right now. Trying to tone down her excitement, she took a long drink of her wine and calmed herself before continuing. "That's great news, I'm very happy."

"So you'll be ready to sign in a couple of days?" Matteo asked. "I'll email you the contracts and supporting documents, so you can forward them to your lawyer. In the meantime, we'd like to take you out for dinner again to go over some further details. Are you free tonight?"

"Absolutely." Rome grinned as she gave Nadine a thumbs-up, then tried not to laugh when Nadine stood up and did a victory dance, almost knocking over their neighbor's wine. "Just let me know where and when and I'll be there."

"Great. My assistant will contact you and she'll also arrange a cab to pick you up at eight."

"Thank you, I'll see you later." After she'd hung up, Rome needed a moment to process what was happening. Her precious idea, her lifelong dream, was about to become a reality after she'd just about given up all hope.

"Well, looks like I'm your lucky charm" Nadine said, sitting back down. "You should seriously consider spending a lot of time with me."

"I think you are lucky for me." Rome sank back in her chair and let out a long sigh. "I thought it was over when

Matteo called. I expected Flavio; I thought he was the one calling the shots."

"Nah. Flavio is probably busy having his back waxed in the hope of getting some action tonight."

"I owe you big time," Rome said. "I don't even know how I can repay you."

"I can think of a way or two." Nadine grinned. "Just kidding." She held up her hand to high-five Rome. "Who would have thought I'd be sitting here having lunch with the smart and gorgeous woman that I was hitting on last night without even knowing I was about to have dinner with her, huh? Coincidences don't exist, this was meant to happen. It was written in the stars."

Rome laughed and felt heat rise to her cheeks, but she didn't care. Nadine had been her knight in shining armor, buying her time with her investors, perhaps even pushing them over the edge to make a decision and today, she'd saved her from a nerve-racking waiting game. The distraction had not only helped calm her down, but it had also been incredibly fun to see such an amazing city through the eyes of a captivating and interesting local. "I assume you'll have to go soon, then?" she asked. "To get ready for tonight?"

Nadine shook her head and smiled, keeping her gaze fixed on Rome while she pushed her own plate to the side. "No. I only need half an hour and we haven't even had dessert yet. And you really need to try the tiramisu because this place is famous for it."

8

The choice of venue for tonight's dinner was significantly better than yesterday's, Nadine decided as she walked the red carpet that led to the dimly lit courtyard. Round tables were elegantly laid out under blossoming orange trees, and burning torches were placed along the wall of the old building where the inside dining space and the kitchen were situated. Classical music was playing softly in the background, and the waiters were immaculately dressed in white uniforms. The setting was way too romantic for a business affair, but still, she preferred dining outside when she was working. It made her feel less trapped in a way and there was more distraction to save her from boredom over the sometimes dull conversations. She doubted tonight would be dull though, since Rome would be joining them.

"Flavio, darling. You're looking devilishly handsome tonight." Nadine kissed her client on the cheek when she reached the table, fashionably late, then turned to Matteo and Rob before greeting Rome who looked beyond stunning in a bright blue off-the shoulder cocktail dress. The color brought out her eyes in the most incredible way, their shimmering blue illuminated by the candles on their table. Resisting the urge to take her hand and kiss it, she still let her eyes linger on her for a little longer than necessary, letting her know she appreciated her beauty. There was nothing wrong with a little flirting, but now that it looked like Rome would be getting the funding for her app and staying in the city for longer, which meant they might see more of each other, she would have to let go of her pursuit after tonight. Anything past flirtation wasn't an option anymore and she liked Rome way too much to give her up for a meaningless night. "Rome, it's so nice to see you again," she said at last, leaning in to kiss her on the cheek. She lingered for a moment, inhaling deeply, taking in the scent that she loved more than anything. Human scent was really hard to describe as it was made up of DNA rather than separate components, and so she tried to take it all in so she could analyze it later. "I love your dress." Sitting down next to Flavio, she noticed a hint of apprehension in Rome's expression.

"Thank you. I love yours too." Rome smiled at her and gave her a quick wink, which put Nadine at ease again. It was only natural that Rome would be a little anxious tonight; it was the biggest deal of her life after all.

Before dropping her back off at her hotel in the late afternoon, Nadine had asked her to keep their meet-up private as she didn't want Flavio to think they were some kind of tag-team. Spending private time with her client's new business partner would not only look bad on her, but it could even get her fired. Of course, the oblivious Flavio was beaming as he talked to Rome, wildly gesturing with one hand while the other was steadily resting on Nadine's thigh. He was well aware that touching wasn't part of the deal unless she initiated it, but she let it slide just for now, not wanting to ruin Rome's big night. Carefully making sure no one saw what she was doing, she took his hand and placed it back onto his own lap.

The look that crossed his face for a split second told her that he was mildly irritated by her dismissal, but she gave him a sweet smile and that seemed to mellow him.

It was crazy how easy it was to manipulate men when showing off a bit of cleavage. The black dress the agency had sent her was low-cut, both at the front and the back, but not too revealing, and she'd managed to wash and blow-dry her hair in the little time she had left once she was back at her apartment. She'd had a great day and had completely lost track of time as she and Rome wandered through different neighborhoods in the north of the city together. She knew she looked more than presentable though, at least when it came to her client, who clearly had a soft spot for her.

Her eyes darted back to Rome and she watched her smile forcefully when Matteo whispered something in her ear. There was a tiny flinch in her eyes that came as fast as it went. Very few people would have noticed, but Nadine knew her intuition was usually right, and something came over her then. A hunch, a feeling...

Just to be on the safe side, she gave a nod to her friend Angelo, who was sitting a little farther down, at one of the drinking tables. Technically, they weren't friends, but she considered him a confidant. For fifty Euros a night, he'd discreetly hang around for the first half hour of her date, blending in somewhere in the background. Angelo worked for a couple of her colleagues too, and she really liked how he never tried to chat her up. It was always strictly business and cash with him. The subtle look that passed between them then was a sign for him to do what he was hired to do and leave right after.

"So, what are we celebrating?" she asked innocently, running a hand over Flavio's forearm. As she touched him, she felt his hairs rise and tried not to think of him being aroused. "Do we have a deal?"

"We do." Flavio leaned in to kiss her on the cheek and in that moment, she gave in, just a little, and smiled.

"Excellent. It's time for champagne then, isn't it, gentlemen?"

"It's always time for champagne when there are beautiful women involved." Matteo put his arm on the back of Rome's chair, upon which Rome cautiously moved away from him. It was subtle, but Nadine made a mental note to keep a close eye on Matteo during the evening.

"How about we discuss the details first?" Rome proposed. "Leave the fun for last?" She smiled at both men, then opened her menu.

"Very well, details first, but why don't I order for you?" Matteo said, taking the menu from her. To Nadine's amusement, Rome pulled it back.

"If you'd like me to run one of the biggest and most promising projects you've ever funded, I'm sure you'll trust me to make a decision about what to have for dinner." Her tone was playful, but it was clear she wanted to put him in his place.

"As you wish." Matteo seemed to like her feistiness as he grinned and shamelessly looked her up and down again.

Nadine balled her hands into fists under the table, refraining herself from punching him. He hadn't been like this last night, and she was disappointed in herself for failing to see through him. She didn't like the idea of Rome working with him one bit, now. Even though he was unlikely to interfere in the developmental process and her day-to-day duties, she was pretty sure he'd manage to make up excuses to have her to himself every now and then.

Trying to shake off that disturbing thought, she turned the conversation to Rome's app, asking questions that she by now already knew the answers to. Flavio and Matteo weren't overly engaged, which confirmed her growing suspicion that both she and Rome were purely here for entertainment purposes. She understood that was the case with *her* of course, but with Rome, it felt like an insult to the woman's intelligence and it made her furious. Suppressing a need to roll her eyes at one of Matteo's tasteless jokes after their appetizers, she dabbed her mouth and stood up.

"Excuse me, I need to powder my nose. Rome?"

Rome nodded and stood up too. "I'll come with you." She followed Nadine inside, through the lavishly decorated restaurant and into the bar at the back, so they would have some privacy. Neither of them actually needed the bathroom, so Nadine leaned against one of the barstools as she tilted her head and looked Rome over.

"What's bothering you tonight? Is it Matteo?" she asked with a frown. "You look stunning by the way."

Rome gave her a small smile. "Thank you..." She hesitated. "Matteo sent me a dress to wear for tonight. I felt incredibly insulted and a little worried because he seems to have this idea in his head that I'll give him something in return for that contract. I want nothing to do with him of course, so I sent it back. He made a snarky remark about it when I arrived and it was just him and me, but I made it clear that I don't appreciate such behavior."

"Jesus, the audacity..." Nadine closed the distance between them and put her hands on Rome's shoulders. "You did the right thing, for sure." She brushed a lock of hair away from Rome's face, then lifted her chin to look at her. "He thinks he can use his power to get to you, and you can't let that happen, no matter what. I know men like him; he won't stop until he gets what he wants." She tried to calm her voice, not wanting her rage to upset Rome even more. "You have to be careful with him."

Rome nodded, and Nadine felt helpless at seeing the worry in her gaze. "I really need their funding, but I have a bad feeling about him. I don't know what to do."

Nadine took a firmer hold of her. "Listen to me. Don't sign anything until you've thought this through. Your contract is still with your lawyer, right?" She continued when Rome nodded again. "Good. We'll meet tomorrow and we'll talk about it in the morning when we're fresh. The fact that he doesn't know the difference between business and pleasure doesn't have to stand in the way of your dream but it's important to be prepared, because if you go through with this, you're going to have to deal with him in the foreseeable future."

"I know." Nadine could tell that Rome was fighting to pull herself together as she looked up at her. "Why are you being so nice to me? So sweet?"

Nadine gave her a smile. It was a good question. She wouldn't normally be so invested in her client's business partners, but Rome was different. She'd been drawn to her from the minute they'd met and now, all she wanted to do was protect her. It was strange, she realized, as she rubbed her temple, a little confused herself. "Because I really like you," she finally said. "And because I want this to work out for you. You deserve it." Her eyes darted toward a small mole on Rome's neck and she felt an overwhelming urge to kiss her right there. *And I clearly want other things too.* Deciding this was not the moment to have such thoughts, and even feeling slightly ashamed for most likely having similar fantasies to Matteo, she took a step to the side and let go of Rome.

"I'm so grateful to have you here," Rome said then, locking her eyes with Nadine's. "I need you to know that. It's nice to have someone by my side during the biggest deal of my life. I don't know what I would have done if I was alone in this. You probably have better things to do than babysit me, but I can't thank you enough for everything you've done."

"Hey, I like spending time with you so there's no babysitting involved here. If I don't want to do something, I won't; it's as simple as that." Nadine bit her lip, pondering over the next steps. "Let's go back in there and pretend that we're having fun. Don't let him touch you and make it very clear that you have no interest in him romantically. I'll pick you up at eight again tomorrow and we'll figure out what to do."

"Don't you have work?" Rome asked.

"No. It's Sunday and anyway, I'm in charge of my own schedule." Nadine's eyes softened as she squeezed her hand. "Don't worry, it's going to be okay."

9

Rome rushed to get ready, frantically searching for something appropriate to wear in her small suitcase. She wanted to look good, and although she hated to admit it, she knew Nadine was the reason for that. Her fascinating new friend had gone through great lengths to help her and she was incredibly grateful and excited to spend more time with her.

The gnawing feeling that had settled in the pit of her stomach ever since Matteo sent over the dress had subsided. It was a new day—a beautiful sunny day—and she could hardly wait to see Nadine again. Her dream of getting her app out there to users all over the world would come true, and nothing could stop her now, especially not some creep who was trying to get into her pants, even though that very same creep was one of the financers. She hadn't signed yet and reminded herself to keep her cool, because the situation was still fragile, and she wasn't going to mess up the opportunity of a lifetime.

She settled on a pair of jeans and her cutest top, then reconsidered and changed back into a white, cotton dress, remembering Nadine's comment about her legs. She felt a flash of excitement at the familiar beep and ran over to the window to wave at her. For a moment, she found herself staring down at Nadine, taking her in. She was graceful, even on a scooter, wearing denim shorts and a white T-shirt, and she blended in seamlessly with the elegant locals who, just like her, didn't seem to go through much effort at all to look stylish.

"Good morning." Rome could kick herself for the sheepish grin that settled over her features when she crossed the road, but she couldn't help it. Nadine made her smile.

"Good morning, beautiful," Nadine said as she got on the back and put on her helmet. "You know the drill. Hold on tight."

"You know all the best coffee places." Rome sank back in her chair, feeling happy and comfortable in the shade of a large parasol on a beautiful square in the old center.

"It's not hard. Everyone does good coffee in Rome, it's a crime to serve anything less than excellent." Nadine stretched her legs out and took a sip of her cappuccino. "It's a little touristy here but I thought you might want to see some of the famous sites, so we can go for a walk later if you're up for it?"

"I'm up for it. I just don't want to take up so much of your time. I'm sure you've got a life and..."

"And I'll live my life the way I want to," Nadine interrupted her. "Right now, I want to have coffee and spend time with a gorgeous woman. Even though she claims she's straight," she added with a chuckle.

Rome laughed and averted her gaze. Apparently, she was a sucker for a compliment, especially when it came from Nadine. "Well thank you. I appreciate it."

Nadine smiled and shamelessly looked her over before locking her eyes with Rome's again. "So... Matteo. Do you think he's going to be a problem?"

"I hope not. I think I've been clear with him." Rome shrugged. "I felt better about the situation this morning; he must know I'm not interested now."

"I'm pretty sure he sent it with the intention of making you feel like you owed him in return for the funding, so whatever he does or says, just remember that you don't owe him anything," Nadine said.

"I know. But once I've signed, I've signed, and that's that. I won't have to be so polite with him anymore."

"Yeah... Just make sure you're never alone with him." Nadine bit her lip, contemplating how much to share. What she did—hiring Angelo to effectively act as her bodyguard during her dates—was in principle illegal and if her agency found out she had someone shadow her and take pictures of her clients, she'd be out of a job. "You know Matteo is married, right?"

"Yes, he mentioned his wife over dinner." Rome huffed. "Although you wouldn't think so from the way he behaves."

"No, but still. He's married on paper. I have no doubt he fools around behind his wife's back all the time, but he's careful because a divorce would be very expensive for him." Nadine paused. "This needs to stay between us, but I always have someone looking out for me, hovering discreetly in the background, when I'm on a date. And he takes pictures when I ask him to."

"Right..." Rome narrowed her eyes, a worried frown

appearing between her brows. "Why? So that you can use them for blackmail purposes?"

Nadine pursed her lips as she tilted her head from side to side. "Technically, yes. But I'd never blackmail them unless I had no other choice. I've only done it once, when one of my clients found out where I lived and started stalking me." She shrugged. "It was in Paris, a long time ago, and it helped me get rid of him, so I don't regret it. I never asked for money or anything, I just wanted him to back off."

"But Matteo didn't really do anything last night."

"Maybe not. But I have some pictures of him whispering in your ear and they look pretty intimate. I also have pictures of Flavio kissing me on my cheek, so if needs must, we could use it as ammunition." Nadine held up a hand. "But as I said, these pictures should never be used unless there's an emergency situation."

Rome was silent for a moment, then straightened her back and shook her head. "It's never going to come to the point where I'm so desperate that I'd even consider black-mail. I'm confident Matteo will behave, and even if he doesn't there are other ways to deal with him. I appreciate your help, but I can take care of myself."

"I know you can." Nadine sighed when Rome finished her espresso and put some money on the table, letting her know the conversation was over. "I apologize, I shouldn't have brought it up. Just forget I ever told you this, okay?"

"Okay." Rome told herself to get over it. Although the idea of blackmail was disturbing to her, in Nadine's world, she imagined the pictures gave her a sense of safety and security.

"Good." Nadine gave her a big smile, and her carefree expression was back as if they'd never had a serious talk.

"Now, would you like to go and see some pretty places with me?"

"Absolutely." Rome burst out in laughter when Nadine stood up and held out her hand. "But I'm not going to hold hands with you. My God, don't you ever give up?" By now, she was over the shock of Nadine's constant flirtations, but this was a whole new level. She couldn't deny that she felt flattered though, and in some weird way, she liked it.

"Are you sure? My hand feels really nice."

"I'm sure it does."

"Your loss." Nadine winked playfully and tucked her hands in the back pockets of her shorts. "Don't panic if you get lost in the crowds, though. It's very busy where we're going."

"I'm a big girl; I'm sure I can find my way home." Rome shot a quick glance at Nadine's long, toned legs and her perky ass in the short denim shorts and for a split second, she wondered what it would feel like to touch her. She'd never had thoughts like that; not with a woman, but as they walked side by side, she couldn't seem to rid herself of the seed Nadine had planted in her mind the first time she'd flirted with her.

They wandered through narrow streets with cute shops and busy restaurants, crossed squares with Baroque fountains, overflowing terraces and passed beautiful buildings and churches, one more opulent than the other. It was heaving with tourists, and just like Nadine had predicted, Rome did indeed have trouble staying close to her in the crowds. One small street felt like a funnel, and when she got on her tiptoes and saw the sea of people pushing their way through, she changed her mind and grabbed Nadine's hand before she disappeared in the crowd. Nadine took a tight hold and shot her a smug smile over her shoulder. It was the look of victory, and it made Rome laugh despite the butter-flies that suddenly started flapping around in her stomach at the feel of her warm skin. She didn't realize they were butterflies at first, as she'd never felt anything like this before, but there was no other explanation for the crazy flutter and her accelerating heartbeat. She couldn't help but wonder if Nadine had taken her to the busiest street in Rome on purpose, but when they turned the corner onto a small piazza, she was faced with an incredible fountain, so grand and beautiful that she stopped in her stride to take it in while people bashed against her from all sides.

"Come on, let's go a bit farther, otherwise you'll lose me." Nadine pulled her along toward the front where it was a little less crowded. They walked down the marble steps onto a platform that formed a half circle around the spectacular fountain and looked up at enormous sculpted roman gods and horses, rising from the water. Rome felt sweat dripping down her back, but she wasn't sure if it that was caused by the heat or the fact that Nadine was now standing close behind her. She was alarmingly aware of her visceral reaction, as if suddenly she had zero control over her limbs—every synapse in her body on high alert.

"This is the famous Trevi Fountain. It's beautiful, don't you think?" Nadine's voice was low and sultry, as if she was sharing a secret. "It's one of the oldest water sources in Rome."

Trying to steady her breathing, Rome hoped Nadine couldn't feel her sudden shift in energy as her body did crazy things. She told herself to create some distance but for some reason she did the opposite, leaning back against Nadine, who in return, put her hands on her hips and rested her chin on her shoulder. Minutes passed as they stood there in silence; Rome pretending to take in the wonder of the fountain, which by now was the last thing on her mind, and Nadine perhaps doing the same. Fueled with adrenaline, she almost jumped when Nadine spoke again and pressed something into the palm of her hand.

"Here. Turn around and throw this over your shoulder."

Rome looked down at the Euro in her hand. "Why?"

"Because it's a tradition and it ensures a safe return to Rome." Nadine pointed at dozens of other people who were doing exactly that. "And I really want you to come back."

"I think most of all, you just want me to turn around." Rome could have kicked herself for the tremble in her voice when she spoke. She felt Nadine's body shake against hers as she chuckled, knowing she'd been caught out.

"Maybe. But I'm also a little superstitious, so I think you should do it regardless."

A lot of things went through Rome's head in that moment. She was scared to turn around, to come face to face with Nadine who was standing so close to her but at the same time, an urge to do so tugged at her. Nadine had her curious, fascinated, and right now, Rome wanted to see the look in her eyes. Slowly, she turned around, her arm brushing against Nadine's stomach and breasts before they were facing each other. She felt Nadine's chest heaving as her soft breasts pressed against hers when a tour group arrived, pushing them even closer together. Looking up, Rome met her eyes that now had an amused twinkle in them.

Nadine tilted her head and smiled. "Are you scared of me?" She grinned and licked her lips when Rome didn't answer. "Don't worry. I'm not going to kiss you." Her smile widened. "Not unless you want me to."

Rome froze and was unable to stop her gaze from lowering to Nadine's mouth. White teeth behind wide and full peachy lips, the top one curling up, just a little. The coin in her hand reminded her of what she was doing, and she threw it over her shoulder without taking her eyes off Nadine. "I don't want you to kiss me," she said, knowing that was a lie.

Suddenly, it was all too much. The crowd, the heat, Nadine so close, looking at her in a way that stopped her from thinking clearly. She tried to leave the platform and was close to panicking when no one would move out of the way.

Nadine noticed her distress, grabbed her arm and started yelling in Italian for people to let them through as she dragged Rome out of the crowd and onto the steps of a church by the piazza. "I'm so sorry," she said, handing Rome a bottle of water from her purse. "I didn't mean to scare you and I shouldn't have flirted with you like that."

"It's fine. It was just a little too busy for me there. I get claustrophobic sometimes," Rome lied. She took a sip of water, cursing herself for being out of control.

"Are you sure it was just that?" Nadine bit her lip and looked regretful as she continued. "I really will stop flirting with you regardless; I don't want you to feel uncomfortable around me in any way. I just thought you liked me flirting with you."

Rome remained silent as she had no idea how to reply to that. She didn't want to chase Nadine away. In fact, she loved being around her, and she loved the sexy teasing more than anything. But she wasn't ready to admit that she was physically attracted to her because that would make everything she thought to be true about herself a lie. Rome wasn't into women. She'd never been attracted to one before and therefore it just didn't make sense. Why now, at the age of thirty-two? When Nadine took a step away though, she realized she wanted her close. "Wait." She took her hand and pulled her back. "You weren't wrong. I like that you're flirtatious with me, even though I don't understand why as I'm not..." She shook her head. "Never mind."

"You're not gay, I know." Nadine sat down next to her and leaned back on her elbows, raising her face toward the sun. "You're not gay and I don't do relationships, so don't worry. Nothing more than a bit of fun can come from this." Her laid-back attitude had returned, and it put Rome at ease. Nadine made everything sound so simple, as if their undeniable attraction was no big deal and completely normal and natural. "Let's just go with the flow and see where this day takes us, okay?"

"Okay," Rome heard herself say. "But maybe we could go somewhere less busy?"

Nadine nodded, then finished the rest of her water. "You got it, babe."

10

"**C**an I take you out for dinner to thank you?" Rome asked as they were at the end of their tour. They were standing by the beautiful and iconic Spanish Steps, not far from where Nadine had parked her scooter.

"Yes, you can. I'd hate to say goodbye already, I'm having fun."

"Me too." Rome looked around, trying to spot somewhere quiet. There were hundreds of restaurants in close proximity, but they were all overflowing with tourists. "Any recommendations?"

Nadine pointed toward the top of the steps, where little lights were twinkling in the pergola on a long roof terrace. "I've never been there, but someone told me they do good pizzas."

"Perfect." Rome smiled. "I can't believe I didn't see that."

"You should look up more. The most amazing sites are high up in this city. Take for example the colors of the buildings against the blue sky, it's simply stunning. People just tend to look at their phones and they miss so much." Nadine took her hand as they walked up the steps and Rome didn't resist. She'd stopped resisting hours ago and had been wandering around in a dreamy haze, enjoying the charming woman's company so much that she didn't want to go back to her hotel yet. Apart from two calls to her lawyer, who had assured her everything was in order, she'd ignored her phone all day, which was something that would have been unthinkable last week. It had all gone so fast, and she was still trying to get her head around the new life she was about to lead. She was so full of energy at the prospect of her dream coming true and finally having an income, that the hundred-and-thirty-eight steps they were climbing seemed like nothing.

"Do you need to go into the *Nero* office to sign?" Nadine asked.

"No, we're using electronic signatures. They've signed their end, and I'm signing tomorrow afternoon through my lawyer. I'm flying back on Tuesday to pack my things."

"Are they arranging an apartment for you for when you get back?"

"No. Matteo offered to help me with it, but I kindly declined." Rome chuckled. "Technically, I'm not employed by *Nero*; I'll be there as a consultant with shares in the project. I'm sure the HR department would help me out though, if I asked them."

"I can help you," Nadine suggested.

Rome shook her head. "Thank you, but you've done more than enough for me already."

"But it's not a problem. I can read the ads, you can't. And yes, you could go through an English-speaking realtor, but you'd still want someone to see it, right? I know the neighborhoods, convenient places close to the metro, and I can go over and take some pictures for you if we have a look online together and narrow down your selection."

Rome thought about that. If anyone would be able to find her something nice, it would be Nadine, who seemed to know the city inside out. "Are you sure it's no trouble for you?"

"I'm sure." Nadine squeezed her hand. "I'd love to do it."

"Okay. But you definitely need to let me thank you properly when I'm back."

"That's a deal." Nadine's small smile told Rome she wasn't thinking of dinner or a present, and she ignored the innuendo as she simply couldn't handle that thought. "So, I take it you're not on a tight budget anymore? For the apartment, I mean."

"No. I'll have a very nice lump sum in my bank account by tomorrow afternoon, and I'll also have ten percent of the Carbon app share after roll-out." Relief washed over Rome as she said it out loud. There would be no more debt, no more juggling credit cards, paying one off with the other, and she was going to live in a decent apartment in a nice neighborhood, instead of a tiny studio on the outskirts of town.

"Ten percent doesn't seem like much."

"Well, it's normal in cases like this. Without investors, my product would never see the light of day, and *Nero*'s the one taking a risk with a huge investment upfront. The intellectual property still belongs to me; it always will. Our contract stands for seven years following the launch and after that, I can renegotiate with them."

"Sounds like you know your stuff."

"I do." Rome followed Nadine through the ornamental cast-iron gates and onto the roof terrace. "And my lawyer is one of the best in his field. I'm glad I'll finally be able to pay him."

"You haven't paid him yet?"

"No, he's an old friend." Rome shook her head. "Actually, we're not even friends, we just went to college together for a year. But I asked him for advice one day, and he was genuinely excited about my product and offered to help me out until I had funding. I doubt he expected it would take two years, though, so I'm sure he's just as happy as I am right now."

"I'm sure he is. Anything else you need to do while you're back home, apart from packing, paying people and deciding on an apartment?" Nadine asked as they were led to a table by the edge of the terrace. They were lucky to be early, as places with a view in the city center usually had a long queue.

"Not really." Rome shrugged. "I need to say goodbye to my father, but it's not like we see much of each other as it is. I don't have any siblings, and I'm not close to anyone else, apart from one childhood friend."

"That sounds like a lonely life."

"I guess so." Rome paused as the waiter put down the bottle of red wine she'd asked for and handed them the menus. "But I never saw it that way. I mean, I never felt like I missed out on anything socially."

"Do you think it will be strange for you to lead a team, after working by yourself for so long?"

"Yeah, it will take some getting used to, I think. But I'm also looking forward to it. I've spent ten years of my life behind a desk, trying to figure this out, then another two pitching the product. The last time I interacted with people on a daily basis was in college, and that was a long time ago."

"You've been on a one-woman mission."

"Exactly. And now that I'll have my own team, I'll also have time to do more fun stuff." Rome poured the wine and sat back, enjoying the beautiful view that stretched over the roof tops of the historical city center. The sun was low, and the warm light enhanced the earthy tones of the buildings, resulting in a beautiful sepia palette. Below them were the Spanish Steps and Piazza di Spagna with crowds gathered around Bernini's charming boat fountain centered in the long, triangular square. Behind them was the huge Trinità dei Monti church, and a big park, where they'd walked earlier. There was so much rich history here, and she could even see Shelley House, John Keats' old home, from where they were sitting. "I wasn't sure if I was capable of relaxing," she continued, keeping her gaze fixed on the view. "But it's easy with you."

"Well, I happen to be an expert when it comes to that." Nadine held up her wine in a toast. "I learned it from the Italians, and so will you."

11

———

"**D**o you want to come up?" Nadine asked when they were back at her apartment. They'd ridden back to her neighborhood, where she'd chained up her scooter before they'd walked to a bar close by.

"I ehm... I don't know." After the wine over dinner and the Campari cocktails they'd just enjoyed, Rome was feeling a little tipsy, and she wasn't sure if sticking around was the best idea right now.

Nadine leaned seductively against the doorpost and shamelessly raked her eyes over her. "Or I could give you a ride back... it's up to you."

Rome's heart started beating so fast that she was worried it would fly out of her chest. Taking a deep breath, she tried to clear her mind before deciding, aware that this wasn't just an innocent coffee invite. There had been sexual tension between them all day, and although the idea of going upstairs with Nadine scared her, it also set her body on fire. *Why won't it just go away?* She kept looking at Nadine's lips, imagining what they would feel like on hers, and if she was honest with herself, she really, really wanted to kiss her. Of course, it was possible that Nadine just wanted to talk over coffee, but their intense chemistry told her otherwise. "Thank you, but there's no need to give me a ride back; I can take a cab," she said with a tremble ringing through her voice. She hesitated for a moment before she added: "I'd love to see your apartment first, though. I'm curious."

"You're curious, huh?" The double meaning in Nadine's comment did not go unnoticed, and neither did the look in her eyes when she held her gaze for a few electrifying moments, making Rome shiver with anticipation.

"Yes..." Rome felt like clarifying her statement, but there was nothing left to say. She simply had no choice. Nadine was gorgeous, captivating, seductive and had something about her that made her irresistible, like she had the ability to take away her free will.

"Excellent... follow me." Nadine opened the door and walked upfront as they climbed the four flights of stone stairs. The hallway was dark and chilly, the smell of damp and mold rooted into the old, cracked walls. On the top floor, she let them in and turned on the lights, exposing a large space with a dark wooden floor and a beautifully painted ceiling, the old plaster showing a scenic panorama of an Italian landscape.

"This is incredible." Rome forgot about her nerves for a moment, astonished by what she saw. She felt like she'd walked into a different world, and in a way, she had. This was Nadine's world and it was mind-blowing. The eclectic and bohemian apartment was spectacular in every way, filled with antique furniture and chandeliers, rich tapestries and disheveled looking footstools and cushions that only added to the charm. The deep red of the wallpaper subtly resonated with the color of the cushions and the vintage

Persian rugs, but nothing about it was contrived. There was an abundance of exotic plants too; large and bold, placed in ornate ceramic pots. In front of a large quilted velvet couch stood a low coffee table with chunky, half-burned candles and a pile of books. An enormous gold framed mirror hung above a marble fireplace, with a pair of life-sized golden lions on each side. Anywhere else, they would have looked ridiculous but here, they blended in seamlessly. "Did you create this amazing room?"

Nadine smiled proudly. "Creation is a strong word. The beautiful ceiling, the floor and the wallpaper were already here. I fell in love with this place the first time I walked in to view it because well, how could I not?" She gestured to the couch for Rome to sit down. "All the rest, I found at flea markets throughout the city. I love visiting them at the weekends, you should come with me some time. Now that you'll be spending more time here..."

"I'd love that." Rome sat back against the cushions, taking in the palatial surroundings, and only then noticed the floor-to-ceiling doors that opened onto the balcony. It looked so much grander from the inside than it did from the street. "I'm sorry if I took up your flea market time this morning."

"Nonsense." Nadine left the room and came back with a bottle of red wine and two glasses. "I'd much rather spend time with you than strolling the markets by myself. Wine? Or would you rather have a coffee?"

Rome swallowed hard and nodded, her pulse racing. "Wine is fine, thank you." She was in Nadine's apartment and it wasn't hard to figure out where this was heading. Her hand was trembling as she reached for the glass, and she took a small sip while Nadine lit the candles and put on some music.

"My Alexa is the only modern thing in this room; I don't even have a TV. But I can't live without music, so something had to give," Nadine said as she sat down next to her. She put her glass on the table, kicked off her shoes and propped one leg under the other, turning to Rome as she draped her arm over the backrest. "Are you okay?" she asked, reaching out and running her fingers through Rome's hair.

Rome shivered, unable to hide her intense physical reaction. Knowing it was intentional, just that simple gesture was enough to drive her wild with desire. She leaned into Nadine's touch, deciding now was not the time to think because there was no explanation for how she made her feel. "I think so," she whispered, gathering the courage to turn and face Nadine. "I don't know what's going on between us..."

"Come on, Rome. You know exactly what's going on. You want me... and I want you. It's simple." Nadine's voice was a near whisper as she spoke over the soft classical music in the background. "But you don't strike me as the impulsive type."

"You're right. I don't do one-night stands. Certainly not with women." Rome had to concentrate on speaking, because Nadine was playing with her hair and it made her a little crazy. "But I haven't been in many relationships either."

"So, it's been a while?" Nadine flicked her tongue over her lips as she continued to stare at her. "Since you've had sex?"

"It's been two years, perhaps even longer."

"And when was the last time you had good sex?" Rome took in a quick breath, and when she didn't answer, Nadine smiled. "That says enough to me. I think you should let me take care of that problem." She put her glass down with purpose, the light thump on the wooden table acting as both a promise and a warning.

Rome didn't dare move as Nadine inched closer, but she didn't want to stop her either. Trying to calm her racing heart was pointless, and whatever happened next was out of her control because her body was drawn to Nadine like a magnet and she was highly aware of her own parted lips and lust-filled eyes, giving away her raging desire.

"Can I kiss you?" Nadine's lips were almost on hers now, their shared breath flowing between them. Her hand trailed down Rome's cheek, her other moving to her knee.

Rome's muscles tensed under her touch as she trailed her hand up her thigh and rested it there. A delicious twitch shot through her core and settled in her center that was already wet and throbbing with need. "Please." Her voice didn't sound like her own as she uttered the plea.

Nadine tilted her head and cupped her neck to pull her in as their lips met in a featherlight kiss. Rome felt like she was floating as her core fluttered and an overwhelming craving took hostage of her body. It felt incredibly good, almost too good. Not until she moaned, did Nadine press her lips harder against hers, parting them to claim her mouth with her tongue.

Rome heard herself moan louder and sank into the kiss that grew more urgent and intense as their tongues melded together, the surge of warmth leaving her limp against Nadine's breasts. The sound of alarm bells in the back of her mind, reminding her that she was kissing a woman, slowly faded until there were only her hunger and her instincts telling her this was nothing but right. Her hands started leading a life of their own then, as she finally allowed herself to touch the thick dark hair she'd imagined the feel of so many times during the day. It was silky soft and endlessly long as it slipped through her fingers.

Nadine pulled out of the kiss and slowly trailed a finger down her cheek and her neck. "Are you okay?" Her eyes were hazy and lust-filled, promising so much more.

Rome nodded, out of breath and overwhelmed in the moment. Her body did things she wasn't familiar with, things she wasn't prepared for and she desperately needed to satisfy the need inside of her that was growing to boundless proportions. "I want this," she said, never having been surer of anything. This time, she didn't wait for Nadine to kiss her again. She wrapped her arms around her neck and pulled her in, taking what she wanted. It was feverish and sexy and when Nadine's hand disappeared under her dress and grazed her waist, she was pretty sure she never wanted it to end. Nothing could have dragged her away from Nadine, who made her crazy with lust. Rome had no idea what she was doing but it didn't matter; it felt good and she wanted more. She pulled the hem of Nadine's T-shirt from her shorts and lifted it so she could run a hand underneath it. Shivering at the feel of soft skin, she explored her back, scraping her nails over her spine as Nadine deepened the kiss and pushed her back into the cushions that were stacked against the armrest.

The moment Nadine lowered herself on top of her was something Rome knew she'd never forget. Nadine's weight, her hands, still roaming under her dress, moving up to her breasts, and her mouth on hers, so insistent. She moved like a panther; seductively, arching her back and pulling out of the kiss to trail her lips down Rome's neck. Rome could barely breathe when Nadine started unbuttoning the front of her dress. The first, the second, the third, and the fourth button came undone, baring her black, lace bra. Nadine sucked and bit at the side of her neck, the faint pain shooting a rush of delight between Rome's legs. She hadn't seen this coming; not how good it would feel, how incredibly thrilling and arousing. Every touch felt like an explosion, no matter how soft.

"Jesus, are you trying to kill me?" she whispered, and she felt Nadine's mouth pull into a smile against her neck as she opened her dress and slipped a hand inside.

"Why would I want to kill you? I want to enjoy you," Nadine mumbled between kisses. She chuckled. "You're so into this... I think I can make you come without even touching you there."

Rome gasped and barely had time to process what Nadine had said as her mouth was on hers again, kissing her fiercely while her hand disappeared under her bra, her fingers strumming her hard nipple. It all went so fast, and Rome wallowed at the delicious tension that started building in her core. Nadine shifted her weight and wedged a knee between her thighs, thrusting into her as she kissed her. The pressure against her center, combined with the all-consuming kiss and Nadine's hand cupping her breast made Rome cry out and buck her hips against her. It was only a matter of seconds before she exploded into a million pieces, shaking and moaning against Nadine's mouth. Nadine never stopped kissing her, and as she held her tight, Rome felt like she was sucking every last bit of tension out of her, relieving her from all the pent-up sexual frustration she'd carried with her in the past years. When she came down, she couldn't move at first, shivering at the aftershocks that still buzzed through her.

"Hmm..." Nadine pulled out of the kiss and ran a hand through Rome's hair, lifting her head to look at her. "I was right."

"You were." Rome gazed up at her in disbelief, not sure if she should feel euphoric or embarrassed at her obvious desperate need for sexual stimulation. No human being had given her an orgasm before; she could only do that to herself. Nadine had done it without even touching her. The smug and satisfied look in Nadine's eyes told her that shame was not an option, so she let out a deep, contented sigh and accepted her need for what it was. "How did you do that?"

"I hardly did anything. Your body just needed attention." Nadine bit her lip and tilted her head. "Will you stay here tonight?"

Rome didn't have to think twice about that invitation, because she was already on fire again. "If you want me to..." She swallowed hard and continued in a shaky voice. "I want more."

"Soon..." Nadine crawled off her and picked up their wine glasses, pointing to the balcony. "Come watch the full moon with me first."

Rome stared at her for a moment, trying to gauge if she was serious. She didn't even know it was full moon; she'd never been aware of stuff like that and if she wasn't mistaken, they were about to get undressed.

Nadine looked over her shoulder and raised a brow. "Why not? It's beautiful." She turned up the volume on the music and opened the balcony doors. A female voice sounded through the speakers, so pure, it sent a shiver down Rome's spine.

As if lost in a trance, Rome got up and followed Nadine outside, the wind baring her black lingerie each time her dress blew open. Her body felt incredibly relaxed and her mind cleared itself from further thoughts as she sank into a state of simple bliss.

Nadine patted the space next to her on the cast-iron

bench. Rome sat down and let out another deep sigh as Nadine wrapped an arm around her shoulders and pulled her in. Above them was an unobstructed view of the moon, bright and beautiful, but it seemed a lot bigger than normal, almost within reach.

"It's a supermoon," Nadine explained, handing Rome her wine. "Makes people a little crazy sometimes because it amplifies emotions." She grinned. "I know you don't believe in things like that, but I still think you should take a moment out here and process what just happened, so you don't regret anything tomorrow."

"Somehow I don't think I'll regret anything." Rome took a sip of her wine and stared up at the beautiful moon. "What's a supermoon?"

"It's the closest the moon comes to the earth in its elliptic orbit and, as you can see, it appears to be abnormally big and bright. It only happens a couple of times a year and in my opinion, it's a crime to miss it. Oceans feel the pull, so tides are extremely high, and they plunge extremely low, too. If its energy does that to oceans, imagine what it does to people."

"So according to astrology it's an excuse to indulge?" Rome arched an eyebrow. Yes, she was feeling a little impulsive, but she was pretty sure that had everything to do with Nadine and nothing to do with the moon.

Nadine chuckled and shook her head. "No, it should never be used as an excuse. But people tend to pursue their desires during a supermoon, no matter what the consequences because the pull to do so is stronger than normal." She shrugged. "Why am I even telling you this? You think I'm talking nonsense."

"Does it bother you that I don't believe in things like that?"

"No. Does it bother you that I do?"

"No." Rome smiled. "I think it makes you charming and I love to listen to you talk about it, whether I believe it or not." She rested her head on Nadine's shoulder, cherishing their closeness and the rush of adrenaline that it stirred in her. "And you were right; the moon is beautiful. I'm glad we came out here."

"We've all become so busy that we often forget to look and so we miss so much," Nadine said. "But if you just put five minutes a day aside to take a couple of deep breaths, observe what's happening in your body and around you, you'll be surprised at what you find." She bit her lip and turned to Rome. "I've been observing you and I must say, you're quite fascinating."

"Oh?" Rome lifted her chin, so their lips brushed. Her heart was doing that million beats per hour thing again, and her body gravitated toward Nadine as if she had no control over it. If she believed in magic, she'd almost suspect Nadine had put some kind of spell on her. "Well I happen to think you're pretty fascinating too. I don't think I've ever met someone so passionate and..." The rest of her words were lost against Nadine's mouth as she claimed hers with force. Being kissed by Nadine was like being swept away in a storm, the world around them vanishing instantly as their locked lips connected them on all levels.

Nadine's hand slipped down to the curve of Rome's hips, then worked its way up her back and in her hair. Heat radiated from everywhere she touched her, spreading through the rest of her body. Rome became light-headed, drunk on endorphins as the quickening of her breath matched Nadine's. She didn't know how long they kissed for. It could have been minutes, or hours. All she knew was that she would die with the memory of this. When they broke apart, her lips were sore, and she felt like all her secrets had been laid bare.

Nadine's eyes were dark when they looked into hers, and the moon lit up her face as she lifted her chin. "Come to bed with me," she whispered.

12

———

Nadine knew it was a bad idea but right now, she didn't care. She was doing the opposite of what she'd just preached, using the moon as an excuse. It was also Rome's fault, she decided, because she was so damn attractive that she simply had to have her. The long and sensual kiss had set her alight, and she tried to temper her steamy thoughts as she led Rome to her bedroom. Her body was flushed with heat, every inch of her saturated with need. She told herself to slow down once again, to take her time tonight. Normally, she would have been naked by now, but Rome was different, like a special treat, and she wanted to enjoy and savor her.

She waited for Rome to take in the room as she switched on the ornate marble bedside lamp. It cast a soft red light over the room that was decorated in gold and yellow tones, with heavy silk drapes and rich bedding. Knowing Rome needed time to get comfortable with her surroundings, she stepped back as she watched her appraise the furniture and paintings on the walls. Just like the living room, her bedroom was an eclectic concoction of things she'd found on her Sunday treasure hunts, and she was immensely proud of how it had come together. A mixture of Italian Baroque and romantic Gothic made for a dramatic scene in the spacious room. The music was softly playing through the speakers she'd installed in here too, as she loved waking up to classical music, and it was on whenever she was home.

Nadine loved drama, but only in the form of pretty things like antiques, art, music, and dance. Whenever there were people involved, she avoided drama at all times, and she just hoped spending the night with Rome wouldn't end in just that. She smiled when Rome fixed her gaze on her and stifled a moan at seeing the need in her eyes. Her natural beauty rang through in her smile, lifting her high cheekbones and brightening her blue eyes. She was like a perfect portrait, but there was so much more to Rome than what met the eye. It was her brilliant mind that attracted Nadine to her mostly, her intelligence and desire to make the world a better place. In a way, she was a dreamer too, just like her. She just didn't know it.

"Is this real?" Rome arched a brow and tilted her head, studying Nadine. "I feel like I've walked into a fantasy. This apartment, the moon, you..."

"If you appreciate history and detail, you can create anything you want." Nadine suppressed the urge to walk up to Rome and rip her dress off, because the way it was hanging open, giving her a peek of the body underneath, slayed her. "You really have no idea how stunning you are."

Heat rose to Rome's cheeks and she shook her head. "I don't know about that. I'm really very plain."

"You're not. You walk into places and set people on fire with your blue eyes, that cute ass of yours and your amazing ideas, and you don't even realize how others perceive you."

"I could say the same for you." Rome whispered. She opened her mouth to continue, but Nadine closed the distance between them, cupped her face and kissed her again.

Rome's smell flooded Nadine's senses as she grabbed her by her waist and pulled her in, crushing Rome's body to hers. The mixture of her natural scent, traces of pine in her hair and a hint of wine on her breath was intoxicating. She heard Rome take in a quick breath and it made her heart race, knowing how much she wanted this. "God, I want you," she whispered. "Please don't be afraid."

"I'm not." Rome's voice trembled, and although Nadine knew she was lying, she also knew she didn't want her to stop. Slowly, she opened Rome's dress and let her eyes roam over her body. The black, lace bra and panties looked incredibly sexy against her pale skin. Rome's small breasts were heaving fast, giving away her nerves, and Nadine felt her hands tremble against the small of her back. She ran her hand over the smooth skin of her stomach and her back, softly at first, then with more urgency as Rome's breath hitched. She loved being a woman's first, and it had been a long time since she'd had the privilege to introduce someone to her wonderful world.

Rome's eyes turned hazy as Nadine unclasped her bra, and when she gently pushed it down her shoulders and it fell to the ground along with her dress, she closed her eyes and leaned in, desperate for her touch. Nadine stroked her fingers over her nipples, around the curve of her breasts and down her rib cage while Rome's hands disappeared under her T-shirt. The nails scraping over her skin gave her goose bumps, and when Rome tugged at her T-shirt, she lifted her arms so she could take it off.

"You're so..." Rome swallowed her words, raking her eyes over Nadine's full breasts, enveloped in a champagne colored bra. Her gaze lowered to Nadine's toned stomach, then her sculpted arms and shoulders before she met her eyes again. "Fuck. You're so beautiful."

Nadine unbuttoned her shorts and let them fall down. The small smile that played around Rome's mouth told Nadine she liked what she saw. Pleased to know her intuition had been right, she pulled Rome against her and watched her let out a soft sigh when their warm bodies came together. Their hearts were pounding rapidly in rhythm as she walked them toward the bed and nudged Rome down on it. When she lowered her panties and stepped out of them, Rome crawled back, gazing up at her naked form. She looked gorgeous lying there with a hint of fear spilling through the need and anticipation that radiated off her, and Nadine couldn't tear her eyes away. Her soft curves, the blonde hair tousled around her heart-shaped face, her gray-blue eyes that were unusually light and her high cheekbones and cushiony lips that were undoubtedly the most kissable lips in the world. Something so haunting was sure to harm her, Nadine thought. Everything desirable had a price in life, but she didn't want to think about that now. She didn't want to analyze why she was feeling different with Rome, why she cared so much. Hell, why she even cared at all...

"Can I remove these?" she asked in a whisper, hooking her fingers under the sides of Rome's panties.

Rome hesitated for a moment, then nodded. There was a fragile shyness to her that made Nadine want to put her at ease, but at the same time, the fire in her eyes didn't lie. Rome had clearly not been blessed with good sex in her life, and Nadine wanted to be the one to pleasure her over and over again, because she craved it as much as Rome did.

She saw a fascinating shift in Rome's energy as she peeled the panties down and crawled on top of her, as if she'd stopped thinking and decided to just go with it. "I'll make sure you won't regret this," she said in a low voice, lowering her body over Rome's. "And I'll make sure you'll never forget this moment either."

Rome squirmed underneath her at the contact, and she wrapped her arms around Nadine's waist, brushing her hands over her back down to her behind. Nadine felt them linger there before moving up and down over her hips, exploring her curves. She kissed the small mole on Rome's neck, and encouraged by the wonderful sounds of her pleasure, she moved to her breasts. Rome's skin tasted as good as it smelled; fresh, natural and innocent, but most of all, Nadine loved the hint of adrenaline-fueled sweat that glistened off Rome's body in the dim light. She devoured her breasts, smiling at Rome's moans, while her hands travelled over her pale waist, her hips and her legs, teasing the inside of her thighs just high enough to make her gasp and buck her hips in need of more.

"What do you like?" Nadine asked, moving back up to meet her lips. "When you have sex. Tell me."

Rome looked at her and opened her mouth to speak, then shook her head. Her breaths were quick against Nadine's lips, her body jerking with carnal desire. "I don't know."

"You don't know?"

"No..." Rome hesitated. "I've never had sex like this before but I love everything you're doing."

Nadine ran her tongue over Rome's bottom lip, then sucked it into her mouth. "Do you like this?" she whispered, moving her thigh between Rome's legs. The pool of wetness she felt caused a flash of arousal to course through her, and she ground her hips down and kissed her hard.

"Uh-huh." Rome mumbled against her mouth. She was

having trouble lying still and was moaning softly, a sound so beautiful Nadine vowed to make her do that all night long.

"Good." Nadine shifted her weight and moved her hand down, reaching between Rome's legs. "What about this?" She carefully ran a finger through her wet and swollen folds, causing her hips to jerk again. "Does that feel good?"

"Fuck, yes," Rome said in a strangled voice, and she gasped when Nadine moved to her clit and started circling it. "Yes..."

Nadine watched Rome's expression with wild fascination. Her eyelashes fluttered, her smiling lips were parted, and she looked like she was about to scream any moment. "And what about this?" She brought a finger down and gently entered her, pushing deeper when Rome opened her legs. Nadine groaned at how ready she was and although Rome didn't answer, the guttural sounds she was making told her she loved having her inside her. Claiming Rome's mouth, she started thrusting into her as she moved her body in sync, then carefully added another finger and pushed deeper and faster when Rome wrapped her legs around her hips and started moving with her.

Nadine pulled out of the kiss, wanting to see Rome's face when she exploded again because it was all she'd been thinking of since they'd been on the couch. She indulged in the sight of Rome holding her breath and tensing up, throwing her head back before her walls clenched around her fingers, drawing her in deeper. A loud cry echoed through the room, and Nadine held her while she trembled and shook. Rome held onto her in return, one arm around her neck, her hand fisting her hair, the other clenched tightly around her back. The closeness Nadine felt worried her for a fleeting second, but she let go of her thoughts and instead, concentrated on drawing every last bit of pleasure out of Rome until she was spent and limp, looking up at her through hazy eyes.

Nadine rolled off Rome and lay down beside her, stroking her cheek while Rome stared at the ceiling. She looked like an angel; beautiful, calm and serene, but there was also something else that Nadine couldn't put her finger on. It was like she felt it herself, even though she was unable to give it a name. She wasn't used to feeling things after sex, but maybe that was because she knew her partners were using her, just like she was using them. This was also the first time she'd had a woman in her own bed, someone she'd let into her personal space—someone she'd let into her private life. She couldn't leave or ask Rome to go, and she didn't want to. When Rome turned her head to look at her, a strange sensation started swirling around in her belly, reminding her that this was dangerous.

"I'm..." Rome swallowed hard, then cleared her throat. "I don't know what to say." She looked so deadly serious and pale that Nadine was suddenly worried.

"Are you okay?"

"Yes." Rome chuckled. "It's not that. I'm just..." She let out a deep sigh as she furrowed her brows in the cutest way. "I'm... You're... well, you're the first person to ever give me an orgasm, and you did it not only once but twice. You're amazing."

Nadine smiled at Rome's clumsy stammer and wrapped her arms around her. "No. you're amazing. But we're not done." She shot her a flirty grin. "I told you I'm plenty dirty and I plan to take full advantage of you tonight"

Rome blushed and smiled back. "Yeah, you did say that." She laughed. "And I don't mind getting dirty with you at all."

13

The music couldn't have been more perfect. Lara Fabian's *'Caruso'* was filling the room and Rome's soul as she lay beside Nadine, resting her head in the crook of her arm. They'd been silent for a while, enjoying the breeze that came through the windows, cooling the heat that radiated off them. Her hand was resting on Nadine's chest, which was in stark contrast to what she was used to; creamy and smooth, not rough and hairy, and she couldn't get enough of her full breasts and her nipples that rose to attention each time she circled her fingers over their tips. Her smell was different too; feminine and sweet instead of sweaty and drenched in heavy, spicy cologne, and her voice was soft when she spoke.

"What are you thinking about?"

"I'm just thinking how nice this is." Rome whispered, turning to meet her eyes. "And that you're a woman."

"I am a woman." Nadine chuckled and kissed her temple. "And so are you, just the way I like it." She shot her a wicked grin. "And from what I gathered; I think you like it too."

Rome returned her smile and ran her hand through Nadine's long, dark hair that was draped around her shoulders in soft layers. She could have graced any magazine cover and was probably the kind of woman other women love to hate, yet to Rome she was one of the sweetest people she'd ever met. Her brown eyes looked like they'd swallowed heaven, and Rome allowed herself to drown in them while her hand traced Nadine's belly down to the thin strip of hair between her legs. She hadn't dared to touch her there yet, but it was all she wanted now, and seeing Nadine's reaction as she shivered and let out a soft moan gave her courage. She continued her exploration farther down, watching Nadine's face closely as her fingers reached their destination, her center so wet it made her breath hitch. It felt incredible to touch her and hear her whimpers, knowing she was making her feel good. "What do *you* like?" she asked.

Nadine looked at her with a hint of amusement shining through her lustful gaze as she cupped Rome's face and kissed her. "What you're doing now is perfect," she whispered. "This is..." Her voice trailed away when Rome increased the pressure and moved on top of her, kissing her breasts while she circled her clit. The sounds Nadine made and the way she moved underneath her was so sensual, so immensely intense and beautiful, and Rome could feel her getting closer with each stroke of her fingers and touch of her lips.

Desperate for release, Nadine took her hand and pushed it farther down, pressing it harder against her sex while she bucked her hips. Rome kissed her and slid a finger inside her, delirious with lust now, her only mission to make Nadine come hard and fast because she looked like she needed it. Nadine went wild, her loud moans filling the room, and she jerked her hips up, arching her back as she grabbed Rome's hair and kissed her deeper. "More," she whispered through quick breaths, then kissed Rome again with so much conviction it left her dizzy.

Fueled with confidence, Rome added a second finger and pushed deeper. Fucking her slowly at first, then faster, she drew another long and throaty cry from Nadine, who was taking and meeting each thrust, her luscious lips parted in delight.

"Rome... yes... Oh God, yes."

Never before had her name sounded so sweet, and Rome smiled against her lips as Nadine let go and tensed in her grip. Feeling her climax was awe-inspiring and Rome didn't want it to end. She stayed inside her until Nadine let out a long sigh, intermittent shudders still surprising her every few seconds. A satisfied grin spread across her face while she shifted on top of Rome and lazily traced her hips and waist, kissing her softly.

"Who's amazing now, huh?" She grinned mischievously. "I'm going to have to step up my game."

Rome wanted to answer, but Nadine was already making her way down her body, showering her with kisses and trailing her tongue over her breasts. When Nadine reached her belly, she felt a twitch between her legs at knowing what was coming. The first touch of Nadine's tongue against her drenched center was electrifying and sent Rome through the roof. Her eyes blinked rapidly as she fisted the sheets and held her breath, unsure if she was going to be able to handle so much pleasure. Finally, she looked down, and the sight of Nadine's mouth between her legs, her fingers splayed wide on her thighs, squeezing them hard, as if she needed an outlet for her own passion, was a sight so arousing that she knew it would stay with her forever. When

Nadine's tongue flicked at her clit, then darted inside her, Rome's quivering muscles soon started clenching around it, sucking her in as she buckled and squirmed, peaking to new heights again and again. The curtains blew wildly as the wind picked up, matching the tornado that was raging inside her, and the cool air on her damp skin made her shiver. When Nadine had wrung ever last tremor out of her, she came back up and covered her with her warm body, tenderly stroking her face while she tried to breathe again.

"Are you okay?" she asked again, placing a soft kiss on the corner of Rome's mouth.

"Yes, I'm more than okay." Rome smiled at her and kissed her back, every part of her still basking in an endorphin rush as she tasted herself on Nadine's lips. She had a lot of thoughts running through her normally organized mind, but none of them were clear. One thing was certain though; tonight, her life had changed on so many levels, and she wondered if she'd ever be the same again. The red light in the room covered their skin in a surreal and sensual glow, and Nadine looked stunningly sexy with her tousled hair and her lips glistening from her juices. "I'm just trying to understand what's just happened to me," she whispered.

Nadine nodded and was silent for a moment as she watched Rome, deep in thought. "Don't try to overanalyze this." She took her hand and laced their fingers together. "It takes away the magic."

14

A gentle whisper and a soft kiss on her forehead woke Rome up. "I'm going to the lab."

"The lab?" Rome frowned as she looked up at Nadine, who was showered and dressed and looked curiously refreshed for someone who hadn't slept much at all.

"Yes, I'm working with a lab on the other side of town. They help me with the logistics of producing my perfumes in volume and I have a meeting with them so I might be a while."

"Okay." Rome sat up and looked for her clothes. "If you give me five minutes I'll be gone. Why didn't you wake me earlier?"

"Because I want you to stay." Nadine shot her a dazzling smile and threw a set of keys on the bed. "Please make yourself at home. I'd love to see you again tonight." Then she disappeared, and Rome cursed herself for not setting her alarm. Here she was, in Nadine's bed, and Nadine was gone.

Sleepily she sank back into the pillows and reflected on last night, every single emotion on the spectrum hitting her as she remembered their love making. First came shock, then confusion, followed by arousal and finally a curious mix of excitement and fear that made her stomach flip. *What have I done? Was it the wine? No...* It wasn't the alcohol or the romantic setting, and it certainly wasn't the moon. She'd wanted this for longer than she'd been willing to admit, and if she was entirely honest with herself, she still wanted it.

She felt light-headed, her body doing things it never did first thing in the morning. Arousal still lingered as she lay there for minutes, obsessively trying to recall every delicious moment. God, what was happening to her? This was a time to make her life-long dream come true, to work on her career, not to mess around with a woman. But then again, Nadine wasn't just any woman.

Always focused on her mission and never looking for instant satisfaction, it had been a long time since Rome had felt so alive. In fact, thinking back, she couldn't remember a time she'd felt like this at all. Was it a crush? Was this what it felt like to lust after someone? To physically indulge until you had nothing left to give? Many men had asked her out over the years, but she'd never been that interested. Was she into women? And if she was, why had she never looked at women the way she looked at Nadine now, in that outrageous, sexual manner? Of all the questions that ran through her head, clouding her thinking, one thing she was sure of; the sex had been amazing, and it had been right. Maybe because deep down, she'd wanted Nadine from the moment they'd met.

Rome smiled dreamily as she turned to the nightstand, where a cappuccino and a fresh croissant had been placed next to a single rose. *Such a charmer.* If she left now, it would be a while before she'd see Nadine again and even though this was just a fleeting thing between them, Rome wasn't ready to say goodbye. She wanted more. As she turned to pick up her cappuccino, the ache in her muscles reminded her of what she'd been up to and a soft moan passed her lips, just thinking about it.

Slowly, she sipped her coffee, waking up in the magical bedroom that reflected Nadine's classical beauty and passionate soul. The windows were still wide open, and she could hear birdsong, church bells ringing and people talking in the courtyard below. She suddenly felt curious about daily life here, and the need to go for a walk and explore Nadine's neighborhood sealed her decision to stick around. If all of this turned out to be a bad idea, the harm was already done, so what difference would another night make? Besides, Nadine didn't seem like the kind of person to offer the keys to her apartment if she wanted her gone. Convincing herself that it was no big deal, Rome jumped out of bed, grabbed the towel Nadine had left for her at the end of the bed and headed for the shower.

The sun greeted Rome as she stepped outside, following the sounds and smells that drew her from courtyard and into the narrow streets behind it. Bakeries and coffee shops were open, old ladies were walking up the hill with trollies full of groceries and there was a lot of small talk going on. Besides the groups of people chatting on the street, sitting on low walls or in folding chairs, a passionate conversation between a woman on the pavement and a woman hanging out of the window on the third floor of one of the old buildings seemed to be getting louder and more aggressive with each exchange. Rome realized she couldn't have been more wrong when both women burst out in laughter and waved at each other, before the one below attached the leash to her poodle's collar, and left. The language was a mystery to her, but she vowed to learn at least the basics while she was here. Two nuns walked past and smiled at her, then said something to a man who was putting fresh flowers on the ridge of a building, under a shrine. She got the impression most people knew each other in the neighborhood, and she hadn't expected that in such a big city.

Rome passed a handful of churches as she followed the street downward, some small, some surprisingly large considering how densely built it was. Their impressive entrances drew her inside each time, and the doors were always wide open, bringing a little light into the dark but extraordinary decorated interiors with beautiful frescos, colorful oil paintings and lavish altars. As she wandered farther, there were surprises around each corner. The quaint little alleyways with restaurants—their crooked tables placed underneath overflowing clothes lines—seemed endlessly connected. Beautiful fountains and small parks made her smile every few minutes, but what struck her most were the colors of the city. Remembering Nadine had told her to look up, she raised her eyes upward making sure not to miss a thing. The palette of the buildings, all in sun-bleached earthy tones were indeed stunning against the bright blue sky, and she loved the small balconies and roof terraces that were full of plants and flowers.

It was an exciting neighborhood, and Rome liked the idea of hanging around for the day. And yes, part of that was an excuse to see Nadine again tonight, she knew that. But she was leaving tomorrow, and what was wrong with enjoying herself while she still could? Soon, she'd be responsible for a multi-million-dollar project that would require all her focus and attention and there wouldn't be time to do anything as pleasant as strolling through the streets of Rome on a Monday morning.

A waiter at one of the cafés waved her over, and as she couldn't think of a reason not to, Rome sat down in the sun and ordered an espresso. The smell of roasted coffee beans and the chatter around her made her giddy, something about the scene telling her that life was only just starting for her. She checked her emails on her phone and her smile widened when she saw the contract was ready to sign. Logging onto her lawyer's website with the details he'd provided, she checked the documents one last time before she signed and pressed 'send'. It almost made her laugh, how quietly the biggest moment in her life had come and gone. *Just like that.* Sitting by herself on a terrace in a strange city that would soon be her new home, her whole life had changed in a matter of seconds. She took a moment—a very happy moment—to get used to the idea, but it was still impossible to picture herself as successful and wealthy. Only seconds later, her phone rang.

"Hi Michael."

"Hello Miss Millionaire-at-thirty-two. Congratulations."

"Thank you." Rome beamed as she took a sip of her espresso. "It feels surreal."

"I can only imagine after all those years of hard work..." Michael paused. "I knew you'd manage eventually."

"Well, I couldn't have done it without you." Rome meant if from the bottom of her heart. Michael had taken a chance on her. He'd believed in her when no one else had, and for that she couldn't thank him enough. "I'm so glad I can finally pay you."

Michael laughed. "Yeah, me too... Just kidding," he added. "There's no rush, just great to see things coming together. Are you having a good time in Rome?"

"Yes, I love it here." Rome sank back in her chair and raised her face toward the sun. "Can't say I'm going to mind moving here for a while. But I'm coming home first, so I'll stop by your office next week, if you're going to be there."

"That would be great." Michael cleared his throat. "Well, I'm going back to bed, don't want to wake up the household, but I'm looking forward to catching up when you're back."

Giddy with happiness and elated beyond control, Rome's first thought after she'd hung up was to call Nadine, but she knew that was ridiculous. They hardly knew each other and surely there would be other people she could tell instead? She messaged her father, as they weren't very close and never had much to discuss on the phone, then contemplated calling her best friend Barbara, but decided to message her instead. It was still really early in Portland, and she didn't want to wake Barbara's kids. It was a little shocking to realize there really was no one else in her life who she stayed in regular contact with, and although she had her reasons for that, it was mildly frustrating having to celebrate her moment alone when all she wanted to do was talk about her new future. Rome was used to that, though. She'd worked alone, traveled alone, pitched alone... But tonight, she wouldn't be alone, and she wanted to do something nice for Nadine, who had been so helpful and kind to her.

After a casual stroll, Rome reached a market square with stalls displaying an incredible selection of fruits, vegetables, cheeses, pastas, meats, oils and condiments. The stallholders greeted her, and she was a little shy at first, but finally gave in and walked up to one of them when he beckoned her over. The old man rattled off a monologue in Italian, and although she didn't get a word of what he was saying, she understood he wanted her to try his produce. The others joined in and before she knew it, she was presented with a selection of nuts and cheeses, all too good to resist. They weren't pushy, just proud of their merchandise, and it was refreshing to see people caring so much for the food they sold. One of the stallholders spoke a little English and explained how to prepare the food, which sounded too simple to be true.

Walking away with paper bags full of vegetables, walnuts, mozzarella, pecorino and fresh pasta, Rome felt a surge of excitement at the idea of living here. She could do this on her weekends; stopping off for coffee at every corner and exploring everything there was to see.

Admittedly, she wasn't a great cook, but something about Rome made her want to give it a go, and she hoped Nadine wouldn't mind if she used her kitchen. The market was inspiring compared to the massive grocery store in Portland that she normally visited or ordered from, and although Portland was a lovely city, there wasn't much choice on the outskirts, where she lived. She realized she'd bought way too much for two people as she carried the heavy bags back up the hill to drop them off at Nadine's apartment, and she noticed older people used trolleys for their groceries. It took forever to get back, as she'd taken another route and got side-tracked every few steps, unable to resist stopping at the interesting boutiques and beautiful churches. Rome was a wealth of beauty, and she'd have more than enough time to see everything once she'd moved here and started her new life. *My new life.*

15

———

B ack in Nadine's courtyard, an old man was shouting at another man in a truck and this time, Rome was sure the conversation was getting heated. He cast her a suspicious glance as she opened the door to the communal staircase, then continued his rant while the other man yelled back at him. She quickly made her way upstairs, not wanting to get in the middle of a fistfight. When she let herself into the apartment, she was surprised to see Nadine in the living room.

"Hey. You're here already." Rome glanced at her watch and noted it was only three pm.

"Yeah, I came straight back after my meeting; I was hoping you'd still be here. I had to brief the lab team on the last formula for one of the twelve perfumes I've been working on. They turn it into an official recipe, so it's easy for the factories to replicate my creations. I saw your things when I came in, and I thought I'd wait for you." Nadine walked up to her and kissed her as if it was the most natural thing in the world. It wasn't a welcoming peck, but a slow and sensual kiss that left Rome limp against the doorpost.

"Did you have a nice day?" she asked, taking the bags from Rome.

"I did..." Rome needed a minute to catch her breath after the kiss had taken it away. "It was really nice," she stammered, unable to hide her grin. "But something else— there are two guys fighting downstairs. Should we be worried?"

Nadine walked over to the window and looked down at the courtyard. "There's no one out there now; they must have left. But let me guess. You're talking about an old man with a flat cap?"

"Yes. And a guy in a truck."

Nadine laughed. "That old man is my neighbor, Luca. And he's always angry about something, but since the new mayor's been elected, his rage has escalated. Our garbage hasn't been picked up regularly, so I'm guessing that's the garbage truck you saw. There was some scandal between the mayor's office and the garbage collection service and so they're under investigation. The previous mayor was a crook too, but this woman has been bribing people left right and center, so it's been a little unstable when it comes to council services."

"Right." Rome laughed too. "He seemed pretty upset about it."

"Well, so am I, but there's nothing we can do but run down the stairs when the truck finally shows up." Nadine went into the kitchen and placed the groceries on the dining table. "What did you get?"

Rome sighed as she stared at the bags because she'd already forgotten how to prepare them. "I was actually planning on cooking for you. Or at least I was going to try," she added with a chuckle. "You've been so nice and helpful, and I thought about taking you out tonight, but then I walked past this wonderful market nearby and I couldn't resist buying lots of food even though I have no idea what to do with any of it."

"You went to Trastevere market? It's where I go, too. They have some great produce there."

"Yes, but..." Rome felt foolish for coming in with groceries, as if she'd expected Nadine to help her. "I didn't think you'd be back already..."

"That's okay. We'll do it together, I love cooking."

"Are you sure?" Rome pursed her lips. "You must be tired and hungry after getting up early, especially since we didn't get much sleep."

Nadine shot her a flirty smile. "Tired? No, I barely had a full day. Hungry? Yes." She traced her thumb over Rome's mouth as she licked her lips. "But not for food. I rushed back in the hope of seeing you before you left."

Rome shivered, her chest heaving against Nadine's. "I guess I'm a little hungry too," she whispered, parting her lips when Nadine kissed her again. Before she knew it, she was pushed up against the kitchen table and Nadine's hands were under her dress and on her behind, squeezing her while she deepened the kiss. "I also signed the contract," Rome continued in a breathless pant.

"You did?" Nadine's eyes widened, and she lifted Rome up and spun her around like she weighed nothing. "Congratulations, we need to celebrate."

Rome chuckled as Nadine put her back down. She was surprisingly strong for her build. "I get the feeling you celebrate a lot."

"Any excuse. Life needs to be celebrated." Nadine shot her a mischievous look. "And there are many ways to do that." She turned Rome around, then moved her hands to her breasts as she stood behind her, kissing her neck.

Rome closed her eyes, tilted her head to the side and leaned back against her. It felt amazing for someone to crave her so much. Nadine's hands cupped her breasts over her dress and held her possessively as her tongue trailed up her neck. Rome reached behind her to lace her fingers through Nadine's hair, but she took them and placed them palms-down on the table.

"Bend over and spread your legs," she whispered in her ear, and at that moment Rome needed the support of the table because hearing those words suddenly made her legs give way. She bent over the surface, supporting herself on her lower arms and gasped when Nadine's feet spread her legs apart. Her hand slipped between them, cupping her center from behind until Rome let out a groan and pushed herself back against Nadine's hips. This woman knew exactly what she needed to drive her to the edge before she even knew it herself.

"Yes!" She threw her head back and gasped when Nadine's fingers moved inside her panties, squeezed her ass hard, then moved lower, finding her wet and ready. Her touch sent a jolt of lightning through Rome, making her hips jerk. When Nadine pushed inside her, Rome cried out and met her fingers, moving back with every stroke. The way Nadine took control was beyond sexy, and Rome didn't think she would last long as she felt her core tighten with each thrust. Nadine wrapped her other arm around her and lowered her hand into her panties at the front, circling her clit until Rome collapsed over the table and moaned louder. She fell into a strange state, as if she was both in her body and watching herself from above, shuddering at the explosive orgasm that Nadine drew out of her while she bent over her, moaning softly into her ear.

"I'll say it again..." Nadine shot Rome a grin as she clumsily turned back around; unsteady on her feet, still catching her breath and looking baffled. "You are so into this."

Rome laughed, then shook her head. "You have no idea. Even better; I had no idea." She pulled Nadine close and ran her hands under her T-shirt, scraping her nails over her back. "It's like you take away my inhibitions; I have no shame with you. I feel free."

"Free is good. That makes me happy." Nadine lifted her arms when Rome took off her T-shirt, then ran a hand through her hair. "How about we continue this in the shower?" She raised a brow and shot her a mischievous smile. "There are a lot of fun things we can do in the shower."

16

Rome rolled up the sleeves of the yellow kimono-style dressing gown she'd borrowed from Nadine and unpacked the abandoned groceries. After more mind-blowing sex in the shower, they'd made out under the running water until they were too hungry to continue. She felt relaxed, happy, invigorated even. Her short stay had not only changed her life in terms of her career, but it had also woken her sexually, and made her realize there were more things to life than just work. That was a lot, and even though she was reluctant to go back, she sensed she might need the five weeks away to process everything.

Rome was a beautiful, fascinating city, full of rich history and she loved the vibe, the food, the wine, the weather and the way it made her feel inside. She understood why Nadine loved it and she felt lucky for being able to spend more time here. Rome had been her last call, her last chance, but now it hit her that each previous rejection she'd suffered had been worth it—coming here was her destiny.

Of course, Nadine had something to do with her fond-ness for the city, too. The striking creature beside her, dressed in a satin, black dressing gown that made her look a little gothic with her long, dark hair, had messed her up like no one else ever had, and right now, Rome didn't know up from down. It was just a fling of course, because how could it ever be anything more? She'd never been into women, and Nadine didn't date because she was an escort. It was all too ridiculous for words, but it didn't stop her from wishing she could stay in this wonderful bubble for a little longer.

Just like her apartment, Nadine belonged to another world; one she would never fit into. Her philosophies on life, her carefree spirit, her timeless beauty and her sexy nonchalance were surely too inspiring to settle for a boring app developer like her. Rome shook it off, because right now, she didn't want to think about it and besides, if it wasn't going anywhere, none of that mattered.

"What do I do?" she asked, looking at her purchases. "I can count the times I've cooked on one hand, and none of the attempts were a success." She chuckled. "I don't know what I was thinking; it was the market, I guess. Seeing all the fresh stuff and being able to taste it was fantastic, but actually putting it together is another thing."

"Don't worry, it's very, very easy." Nadine picked up a tomato and closed her eyes as she smelled it. "You've got some great ingredients. Put the mozzarella on a plate with some sliced tomato, sprinkle with rock salt and just drizzle olive oil over it. We can quickly fry up the radicchio with crushed garlic and throw some walnuts on top, and the pasta is easy too. We're just going to boil it for a couple of minutes, then keep some of the boiling water and add pecorino and black pepper. Trust me, it's delicious." She started cleaning the radicchio with care and ease, almost elegantly. But then everything Nadine did was elegant, and

Rome tried to keep her eyes on the tomatoes so she wouldn't cut her fingers while distracted.

The old blue-tiled kitchen with wooden surfaces and an enameled sink was fitted with copper taps and shelves full of cookbooks and dried herbs. Plants intertwined with string lights were hanging from the ceiling above the dining table in crocheted baskets. It was fairly dark in the apartment with the lowering sun, but Nadine clearly loved dim lighting and candles, and the latter were burning on the windowsills and on the mid-century sideboard that held vintage porcelain tableware.

"Do you cook a lot?" Rome sliced the tomatoes and plated them.

"A couple of times a week. Just when I feel like it." Nadine handed her a big bottle of olive oil. "And when I do, I usually cook for Luca too. You know, the grumpy old man you saw outside earlier."

"Really?" Rome thought Nadine was joking at first, but her expression held no sign of that. "Why?"

"Because he's lonely. His wife died four years ago, just before I moved here, and ever since, I have dinner with him twice a week, if my schedule permits." She grinned. "He loves my melanzane alla parmigiana."

"That's so sweet of you." Rome didn't think it was possible to like Nadine even more, but she'd just gone up in her estimation once again. There weren't many people who would go to the trouble of cooking and having dinner with their grumpy old neighbors, and she admired her for being so kind.

"It's not, it's just the decent thing to do." Nadine handed her the bag of pasta to throw into the boiling water. "He's also becoming a little forgetful, so I like to keep an eye on him, and sometimes we go to church together. His son is

LISE GOLD

building a house in Sicily and he can move in with his family once it's ready, but he doesn't want to leave Rome, and he hates his daughter-in-law for no reason other than that she's Sicilian..." Nadine shook her head and rolled her eyes. "But I'm glad he's going to be looked after properly soon, whether he wants it or not."

"Should we invite him?" Rome asked.

"No, absolutely not." Nadine chuckled. "I'll check on him when you're gone. Tonight is all about us."

Half an hour later, they were sitting on Nadine's balcony, watching the sun go down and eating delicious food. "How is it possible something so simple tastes so good?"

"Simple, fresh and local ingredients taste the best." Nadine twirled some pasta around her fork and held it out for Rome, who took the bite.

"Mmm... so good. And so easy to make."

"This is called caccio e pepe. It's the traditional pasta dish of Rome and you'll find it on most menus. Artichokes are also pretty popular. I like the deep-fried ones, but I can't do that here as the smoke from the fat might impact my ventilation system."

"You have a ventilation system in this old apartment?"

"Best of the best, it cost me a fortune to have it installed. Haven't you noticed it doesn't smell 'old' in here, like on the staircase and in the hallway?" Nadine asked.

"I guess now you've mentioned it, yes, it does smell neutral in here. But why?"

Nadine hesitated as she twirled more pasta around her fork. "I'll show you after dinner."

Rome narrowed her eyes, then slowly shook her head as

she stared at Nadine. "Could you be any more intriguing?"

"You think I'm intriguing?" Nadine seemed genuinely surprised at her statement.

"I do. You're stunning, funny, intelligent, you have this amazingly talented nose and you create your own perfumes. You're cultural and live in some kind of dreamworld, yet you're also very grounded. You're sexy as hell and incredible with people—you know how to play your clients but you're sincere in real life..." Rome hesitated. "You're also kind and caring, which totally contradicts the air of nonchalance you gave off the first time we met." She raised a brow. "And for some mysterious reason, you have a top-notch ventilation system in your apartment."

A softness took over Nadine's features as she processed Rome's words. "Thank you. That's the nicest thing anyone's ever said to me." She smiled. "But I happen to think you're pretty intriguing too, Miss Foster. You give the impression of an Icelandic fae; hauntingly gorgeous, cute and petite with eyes like the waters around winter fjords. You're the smartest person I know, and you've come up with an idea that is going to change the world. You're someone who will make a real difference and you don't even brag about it because you're genuine about your cause and incredibly modest." Her smile widened, and a naughty sparkle appeared in her eyes as she lowered her voice. "That, and you make this really sexy noise when I make you come."

Rome grinned sheepishly and took a sip from her wine. "Okay... but so do you."

"I do not."

"Yes, you do. And it's the most wonderful sound in the world." Rome spooned some more pasta onto her plate. "And you know what's even more wonderful? Knowing I made that happen. It's like I've discovered this thing that I'm really into and now I can't get enough and..." She rolled her eyes. "God, I sound pathetic, don't I?"

"Not at all. I'm glad I could introduce you to the wonderful world of same-sex delights." Nadine bit her lip and gave Rome a stare that she recognized too well by now. "I might not do relationships, but that doesn't mean this thing going on between us isn't special to me. Because it is."

Rome nodded, a warm buzz settling over her. It was comforting to hear that it meant something to Nadine too, because to her, it didn't feel the way she'd expected casual sex to feel. "It's special to me too," she said, noting Nadine had used the present tense. She was grateful they still had another night, but she also worried what spending more time with Nadine would do to her. Luckily, she'd have five weeks to recover from her sudden crush. Surely it would fade?

"Follow me," Nadine said after dinner as she crossed the living room. She stopped at a grand fitted floor-to-ceiling bookcase that covered most of the side wall, filled with classics and books on chemistry and biology. She pushed at one end of the bookcase, and it creaked as it turned inward, creating a small opening they could squeeze themselves through. "Secret rooms used to be popular in Italy. It's where the rich hid their money in times when the banks were in trouble, or during the war," she said, using the handle on the inside to close the door before flipping a switch that turned on the lights and set off a roaring ventilation system. "Sorry about the noise, I have to do this each time I've opened the door as I don't want any smells to get in here." She waited for a minute, then switched it off again.

"My God..." Rome looked around the large room that, in

contrast to the rest of the house, looked as sterile as a hospital ward. "I assumed your neighbors lived behind that wall; this was the last thing I expected." The walls were white, the floor was rubberized, and the only original pieces of furniture in the room were a large old teak desk and a matching chair. In a corner stood something that looked like a dishwasher and on top were metal racks holding an assortment of test-tubes, glass flasks and beakers, and several sets of scales. Sliding frosted glass doors covered the entire back wall behind the desk. They were lit from the inside, and Rome could see the silhouettes of hundreds of bottles. Nadine opened the doors, revealing rows and rows of oils. The lights that shone from underneath, highlighting the names written on them, made for an impressive sight.

"This is my fragrance organ."

"Your fragrance organ..." Rome repeated, casting her gaze over the bottles.

"Yeah, I have just about anything here. Three-hundred-and eighty-nine core oils. Everything from the most basic to the very, very rare ones."

"I thought you did everything in the lab," Rome said.

"No, as I mentioned before, the lab just helps me to work out formulas so that factories can produce it in bulk." Nadine pointed to a selection on the left. "These are the natural and fresh ones that you like; pine, wet soil, cucumber, lemon..." She picked a bottle from the back of the shelf and held it up. "I travelled halfway across the world to get my hands on this, but sadly, I rarely use it. It just doesn't mix well with other oils as it's best in its purest form." She opened it and held it out for Rome to smell.

"It's kind of floral but not overwhelming. Like a natural scent."

"Yes, it's Bulgarian rose. Pricey and rare in its purity. And this one..." She picked another one and opened it. "This is neroli, also very rare, and it's actually from Italy. It comes from the bitter orange tree and has a honey-ish undertone."

"I like it," Rome said, after smelling it.

"You would. It suits your preferred fragrances."

Rome ran a hand across the bottles, studying the labels one by one. "This is amazing. What's your favorite one?"

Nadine thought about that, then took the stepladder that was leaning against the wall, got up on it and reached for a bottle in the top corner. "To work with, I like good old simple jasmine. It's supremely sensual, and it also affects emotional balance and the hormonal system. It blends well, and it's very feminine without being too sweet." She held it out for Rome, who nodded in agreement.

"I like it. It's a little leafy too."

Nadine looked impressed. "It is. Seems you have a good nose." She picked another bottle. "And this is champaca absolute essential oil, the most expensive oil in the world. It's fresh, citrussy and floral at the same time. It's also said to be a powerful aphrodisiac, although I've never tested it on myself."

"I doubt you've ever needed an aphrodisiac." Rome shot her a flirty smile and wafted her hand over the bottle Nadine held out. "Hmm... it's good, but I preferred the previous one. How expensive are we talking?"

"Over two thousand dollars an ounce."

"What?" Rome's eyes widened. "Then this cabinet must be worth a fortune."

"It is. That's why I needed a well-paying job to fund my passion." Nadine reached for the next. "This one is pretty exclusive too, I'm sure you'll recognize the scent."

"It's very familiar," Rome said, inhaling over the bottle. "But I can't put my finger on it."

"Frangipani." Nadine carefully put it back. "It blends well in perfumes, but it also reduces stress and inflammations. If you're ever feeling anxious, just dab a little behind your ear and believe it or not, it works. And this is agarwood, also known as oud, and it's used a lot in the Middle East. The perception is that it smells of money and it's also used to treat the digestive system, the kidneys and used as pain relief. The tree it derives from is currently a threatened species so I'm not using it anymore." She gave Rome a knowing smile. "Because that wouldn't look good on my Carbon account now, would it?"

Rome laughed. "No, it wouldn't, so thank you for that. So, all of these oils have medicinal qualities too?"

"Most of them. Take this one for example. Just be warned; it's very strong."

Rome grimaced when Nadine opened the bottle and laughed when she realized what it was. "Cannabis?"

"Yes. Proven to work against inflammations, skin irritations and hormonal imbalances. And again, it's great for pain management of course, but some countries or states would argue with that. I can't actually use it as it's illegal in many parts of the world, and also, it wouldn't make you smell great, but I like my collection to be as complete as possible, so I added it anyway."

"Incredible. You really do have everything."

"Everything apart from one thing." Nadine leaned in to absorb the aroma emanating from Rome's neck, causing a shiver to run down her spine. "God, you smell so good. I really, really want to bottle this."

Rome laughed. "I don't think my neck is classified as a fragrance."

Nadine kissed her mole and smiled against her neck. "It is now. It's called the scent of Rome."

17

"I bet you did a lot of thinking after I left yesterday morning." Nadine stroked Rome's hair, cherishing the closeness while she could. It was four am, and Rome would leave in a couple of hours. Although that was perfect, since it might get too serious for Nadine's liking if she stayed any longer, she didn't like the prospect of saying goodbye. Rome was lying on top of her, and they were both spent after indulging in each other for hours. They didn't feel the need to sleep, both aware that this would come to an end soon. "American girl comes to Rome in the hope of getting funding for her super smart invention. She gets the deal of her life, then ends up sleeping with a woman for the first time two nights in a row..."

"You guessed right, I have been thinking a lot." Rome smiled lazily at her, tracing a finger over Nadine's lips.

"There was no guessing involved, you're about as straightforward as they come."

Rome chuckled "I'm not sure how to take that. I wouldn't mind having some of that mysterious air about me that you have."

"No, I like that about you. That there's ambiguity." Nadine met her gaze and hesitated. "Anything you'd like to share?"

"No, nothing to share." Rome shrugged. "I have no answers to my out-of-character behavior. Maybe you were right; maybe it was the moon," she joked, unwilling to go any deeper and admit that she felt more than she had in a very, very long time. "Do you have anything to share?"

Nadine shook her head. "Only that I want you to know that I like you, and that I hope we'll see each other when you're back. As friends," she added. "And maybe a little more every now and then."

"Every now and then as in during a supermoon?" Rome asked with a grin.

"We could do that." Nadine sighed. "Or any full moon. Supermoons are quite rare so that might not be enough because someone as irresistible as you should be sampled regularly."

"Full moons work for me." Rome moved down and kissed Nadine's breasts that she just couldn't get enough of. "In fact, I'm starting to think it's an excellent excuse."

"Getting a little drawn to astrology after all, are you?"

"Maybe a little." Rome circled her finger around Nadine's nipple and smiled when it rose to attention. "So, tell me something about the Aquarius star sign."

Nadine shot her an amused look. "Okay, let's see... Aquarius is an air sign, despite the 'aqua' in the name. People born under the Aquarius star sign are generally rebels at heart; non-conformist, eccentric, often with unusual hobbies and jobs."

"Is that all true?" Rome chuckled. "Or are you making it up?"

Nadine nudged her. "Hey, I'm not making anything up.

Whatever source you use to research signs, they're all very consistent, and I know a lot about this stuff. Anyway, Aquarius people are also stubborn," she continued. "They appreciate their own space and time to dream, and they need their independence."

"That could also be true. I don't know you well enough to be sure, but I can imagine you're stubborn. What else?"

"No, enough about me." Nadine waved a finger in front of her. "Let's talk about Libras." She narrowed her eyes and smiled. "Libra is an air sign too. The scales associated with Libra stand for balance and symmetry. People born under this sign like to learn, and to put their knowledge to use. Generally, others are attracted to their air of intelligence and they use that to their advantage. Libras love the outdoors, hate chaos and mess and will do just about anything to avoid conflict."

"Not bad," Rome said. "But that can be applied to a lot of people. What else?"

Nadine let out a dramatic sigh and laughed as she shook her head. "God, you're the worst. It doesn't matter what I say, because you're just going to tell me that's all general too. What I will tell you, is that Libras are best matched with Gemini and Aquarius because they're all big thinkers and they inspire each other."

"What are you saying?"

"Just that we're well-matched."

"I have to agree on that. You certainly inspire me." Rome wished she could stop her goofy grin from spreading, but that didn't seem to be an option when she was with Nadine. "On so many levels."

"Oh yeah?" Nadine pulled Rome's face down and sucked her bottom lip into her mouth, making Rome moan and shift on top of her.

"Uh-huh. So many." Rome swooned as she looked down on what could only be described as the most gorgeous and charismatic woman she'd ever encountered and realized there was so much more that she wanted to know about Nadine. "Do you ever go back to New York?" she asked.

"Sometimes. To visit my mom. Why?"

"No reason, I was just wondering about your family."

"I don't have much family, apart from my mom. No one that I'm particularly close to, anyway." She hesitated. "My mom doesn't like to fly, so she's never been here. We're close in the sense that our relationship is good, but she doesn't know what I do for a living. I could never tell her about the escorting."

"What did you tell her?" Rome asked.

"My mom thinks I manage a store." Nadine let out a sarcastic chuckle. "A fashion boutique. It's good enough for her to be proud of me but not big enough for it to be a terrible lie. I will tell her about my perfumes though, as soon as I get the business off the ground. She knows I'm creating perfumes but she doesn't know I'm about to commercialize them. I used to boil rose petals in the kitchen when I was younger and bottled the water for her to wear. It didn't really smell of much, so sometimes I'd steal a couple of drops from her perfume or my father's cologne to mix with it. They always turned a blind eye and dabbed some on, even if it smelled horrible."

"That's so adorable."

"Yeah, they were good like that. My dad even wore it to work if I insisted."

"Did your mom meet someone else after your father passed away?" Rome asked.

"Yes, she remarried seven years after he died, then got divorced, and now she's dating someone again. He's a nice guy and knowing she's got company makes me feel less guilty about being so far away from her." Nadine paused while she played with Rome's hair. "What about your parents?"

A serious frown appeared between Rome's brows as she pondered over how to answer. "It's complicated, I guess. As I mentioned before, I'm not very close to my dad but we're okay. We go for lunch once a month, if we're both around, and we see each other at the occasional family gathering."

"What about your mom?" Nadine asked, immediately regretting her question when she saw Rome flinch.

"I don't want to talk about her."

"I'm sorry, I didn't mean to upset you."

Rome shook her head. "No, it's fine, it's just..."

Nadine silenced her then, kissing her as she cupped her face. She sensed that Rome was looking for a way out of the conversation, and it was the only thing she could think of to distract her. Her kiss was met with a moan, and Rome gratefully reciprocated, lacing her fingers through Nadine's hair until they were entangled in a fierce make-out session. Nadine pulled the covers over them and cherished the wonderful feeling of Rome's bodyweight. Her mouth felt so perfect, her skin warm and soothing, and for a moment, she wondered what it would be like to have this every night. To have someone by her side who just simply was right for her. Someone who made her smile and laugh and who loved her... As quickly as that thought came, she shook it off, remembering she didn't do any of that stuff, and neither did Rome. No, this was the perfect arrangement, and it was more than she'd ever had before. It was enough.

18

———————

"This is for you." Nadine felt herself blush as she gave the small bottle to Rome.

Rome studied it and smiled, reading the label that only said: *'For Rome'*. "Is this the scent of Rome?"

Nadine laughed. "No, it's definitely not your scent, but I think you'll like it. I threw it together while you were in the shower. It's not perfect and it might be a little overbearing on some of the ingredients, but I just wanted to give you something to take home."

"Thank you, that's incredibly thoughtful." Just as she was about to open the bottle, Nadine took it back, pulled the glass stopper from the top and sensually ran it along her neck and wrists. She shivered as she took a deep breath, not sure if she was reacting to Nadine's touch or the intoxicating perfume now pervading her senses. "I love it."

"You do?" Nadine had no idea why she was feeling insecure all of a sudden, but she was. The woman she'd been a little too obsessed with for her liking was leaving and for some dumb, inexplicable reason, she was worried Rome would forget about her. In a moment of panic, she'd gone into her hidden perfume room and fueled by inspiration, she'd instinctively mixed oils together, creating something she thought Rome might like. The result was far greater than anything she'd achieved before in such a short amount of time, and it mattered to her what Rome thought of it. She leaned in and inhaled against her skin one more time, running her nose along her neck and her hairline.

"You've got to stop sniffing me, woman," Rome joked.

"Come on, you've got to indulge me, I'm not going to see you for a while." Nadine bit her tongue before saying something she might regret later. Something along the lines of 'I'll miss you' or 'I'll be thinking of you', because the truth was, she really was going to miss Rome. What had started out as an innocent flirting game had ended in passion and a sense of closeness that was entirely new to her. It felt dangerous, and so she said nothing more as Rome cupped her face.

"Thank you," Rome whispered as she got on her tiptoes and kissed her one last time. "Take care, Nadine, I'll see you when I'm back."

"Yeah. I'll see you soon." A hint of sadness flashed over Rome's face before she turned and made her way down the stairs, and Nadine realized Rome was having a little trouble saying goodbye, too.

She closed the door behind her and walked over to the window where she watched Rome get into the cab that would take her back to her hotel, so she could check out and pick up her luggage before heading to the airport. Surprised at the lump that settled in her throat, she quickly made her way to the kitchen and focused on the coffee machine, cursing herself for feeling the way she did. It was ridiculous to get emotional over someone she'd only spent two nights with, and she figured she was just a little tired. She contemplated going to sleep, then changed her mind and made herself a double espresso. Luca was probably wondering if she'd forgotten about him.

"Melanzane di Nadine," Nadine said, holding up the oven dish when Luca opened the door. It was lunchtime, but as she had to work tonight, lunch would have to do.

He shot her a beaming smile as he grabbed the bottle of wine she had clenched under her arm and walked ahead into his kitchen. Although Luca was usually at home, she'd checked with him first and brought him some groceries as he never seemed to have much in the house. "You're late," he mumbled in Italian, then shot her a wink.

"I'm not late." Nadine rolled her eyes at the first of undoubtedly many more stabs to come. She'd neglected him, and now she was going to pay. That was fine though; she knew arguing was Luca's favorite pastime and their feisty discussions always had a friendly undertone. "How have you been?"

"Hungry," he grunted, looking at the food.

Nadine ignored his comment and plated the food while Luca laid the table in the worn-out kitchen that hadn't been updated since he'd bought the apartment in the seventies. She'd offered to paint it for him many times, but he liked things to stay the same, and wasn't even using the new pans she'd bought him.

"There was a stranger in the building," he said as he sat down and poured them wine.

"That was my friend Rome, she's been staying with me." Nadine prepared herself for a stream of curses. She'd had trouble understanding him when she was first learning

Italian as he mumbled and swore a lot, using old curse words and a lot of slang, but now, their conversations flowed effortlessly. Luca's ignorance to how predictable he was amused her, and so she could only laugh when he started on a new rant that centered around Rome.

"That's the most ridiculous name I've ever heard."

"It's not ridiculous. I think it's a nice name," Nadine retorted in an equally harsh tone as she sat down opposite him.

Luca huffed and chewed his food slowly. He always did that when he needed time to come up with a reply. "I bet she's American." He narrowed his eyes at her. "Is she?"

"Yes, she is and I'm American too, so watch your words."

"You're not. You have dual nationality and while you're here, you're Italian. Why was she staying at your place? Can't she afford a hotel?"

"We're dating," Nadine lied, purely to wind him up. She'd told him she was gay after he kept trying to set her up with his son, but he always pretended he didn't recall that conversation.

"You're lying. You can't date a woman, that's not God's way. I've told you many times, my son is a good man, but you refuse to give him a chance."

Nadine let out a sarcastic chuckle and shook her head incredulously. "Your son is married with three kids. Just because you don't like his wife doesn't mean he doesn't." And just to get back at him for being nasty about Rome, she added: "I think your daughter-in-law is a lovely woman."

Luca's eyes darkened, and he looked like he was about to explode. He knew exactly how far he could go with Nadine though, as she'd walked out on him on multiple occasions, so he changed the subject and asked her about work. Nadine's story was that she worked at a restaurant as she was often away at night, and although that didn't exactly line up with the expensive apartment she rented or the dresses she wore when she left, he'd never questioned it.

Nadine made some stuff up about her recent shifts and they talked and ate, entirely comfortable around each other. What had started as a near fistfight, had turned into a weird kind of friendship, and Nadine always smiled to herself when she thought back to her first meeting with her incredibly rude neighbor. He'd accused her of pushing the previous tenant—who she'd never met—out of her house and called her a charlatan. Nadine had thought about shouting back at him, but instead, she'd cooked him a meal and knocked on his door that same night, figuring he was lonely and missed his old neighbor and his wife, who she'd learned had recently passed away. Luca would have probably thrown it in her face back then, if it wasn't for the fact that he really loved food, and he wasn't a very good cook himself. So, he'd put the empty dish back in front of her door with a 'thank you' note, and that was when she'd started cooking for him regularly. She'd almost fainted when he invited her in for the first time. Although they generally argued a lot, she knew he appreciated her company and in some strange way, she liked hanging out with him.

Lately, she'd been worried about him, though. Throughout their conversation, the frown between his brows came and went as he fell back into thoughts. Memories, maybe? It happened more frequently now, and sometimes he forgot what they were discussing. Nadine never commented on it, but she called his son every two weeks to let him know how his father was doing, as the old man would never admit to becoming forgetful himself.

The deep grooves in his face spoke of a hard past, but all

she knew about Luca, was that he used to own a bar, as he blatantly refused to talk about himself. When his only son, who was supposed to take over the business fell in love with a Sicilian girl and moved there, his heart was crushed and that had triggered his unreasonable hatred for his daughter-in-law.

"When will you be moving?" she asked him, knowing his son wanted to collect him in roughly six months' time.

"I won't be moving. I'm staying right here," Luca said, pounding his fist on the table. "That damn woman wants to sell my house and take the money."

Nadine shook her head and sighed. His son had asked her to mentally prepare him as she seemed to be the only one who could get through to him sometimes, but so far, Luca wasn't having any of it. "She's not going to steal your money. And it will be nice to be with your grandkids, right?" she tried, knowing that was his soft spot.

Luca, gave her a small smile, then pushed his plate to the side. "I think I'm going to take a nap now. Thank you for lunch, it was delicious. You're a great cook and you're going to make some man very happy one day."

19

"Finally, babe. You did it." Barbara, Rome's childhood friend, was going through the clothes Rome was planning on getting rid of after clearing out her closets. "If I'm honest with you, I wanted to tell you to give up a couple of times. After all those rejections I was worried you were going to work yourself to death and get into tons of debt over something that would never happen." She smiled, finger combing her strawberry blonde hair back behind her ears. "But I was wrong, and you were right. You're about to become the next Bill Gates or Zuckerman or..."

"Stop it!" Rome threw a T-shirt at her. "There's still no guarantee it will pass the test stages once it's rolled out on a small scale, but I have high hopes. Doesn't mean it will make me an app tycoon, though; that's just ridiculous."

"Well, tycoon or not, I'm sure you'll be able to afford a place with a spare bedroom now because I'm going to miss you." Barbara jutted out her bottom lip. "Even though I barely see you as it is."

"Of course I'll have a spare room for you. And I'm sorry I

LISE GOLD

haven't been around much." Rome folded up the last T-shirts she would take and piled them into her third suitcase.

"You should be sorry about this instead," Barbara said, holding up the Buffy T-shirt Rome had thrown at her. "It's about time this was thrown in the garbage."

Rome laughed and stopped her from putting it into the charity pile. "Hey, that's my favorite T-shirt."

"Exactly, that's what worries me." Barbara teased her by going on her tiptoes and holding it high up. "Sucks being short, huh?"

Rome jumped up and snatched it out of her hand. "I don't care what you think; I like to sleep in it."

"You're never going to find an Italian boyfriend if you wear that in bed."

"I don't need a boyfriend," Rome was quick to retort. The truth was, since her nights with Nadine, she couldn't picture her future with a man at all, but she kept that to herself.

"Everyone needs someone to love." Barbara picked up a scarf from the 'go' pile, wrapped it around her neck in front of the mirror, then put it in her own bag. "And don't you want kids at some point?"

"Not again." Rome shot her a warning look. "Spare me the kids talk, I'm not even in the headspace to date, let alone think about kids." She shook her head and sighed. "I'm sorry, I didn't mean to snap."

"It's fine, I shouldn't keep bringing it up. I just don't want you to be lonely, and your life seems so incredibly lonely."

"Well, that's sweet of you, but my life is about to change drastically, so you can stop worrying." Rome gave Barbara's arm a squeeze. "I really appreciate you coming over and helping me pack. I know I said I didn't need help, but it's really hard to plan if I don't know how long I'll be away.

And since you're the Queen of Planning, I really appreciate it."

"With three kids you learn how to run a smooth operation," Barbara said with a chuckle. "And it's not like I've been available much in the past years either. I've missed you, and I'm looking forward to a little trip to Rome. If Terry is willing to have the kids for a week," she added, rolling her eyes.

"I'd like that," Rome said. "You'll love Italy, there's no way you couldn't." With Barbara being a full-time mom, and Rome solely focused on her career, they couldn't have been more different, yet their bond felt more like one of sisters, and so it didn't really matter how often they saw each other.

"I'm glad you'll be living in a place you love. Who would have thought you'd ever be in Rome, right? Your nametown? I'd expected you to move to Silicon Valley, or Tokyo, not Rome. But hey, that's Silicon Valley's loss." Barbara winked. "So, tell me more about this new friend you haven't shut up about since I got here."

"Nadine?" Rome felt heat rise to her cheeks as she said her name. She'd thought of little else over the weeks she'd been back in Portland, and although their communication was mainly concentrated on the apartment hunt, there had been some flirty messages back and forth, too. "I haven't talked about her that much, have I?"

Barbara let out a sarcastic chuckle as she shot her an amused glance. "You've mentioned her like five times since I got here. And I've only been here for two hours."

"Okay." Rome felt busted, but she managed to keep her cool. "Well, Nadine's great fun. She lives in this amazing bohemian apartment in an incredibly charming neighborhood. She's American-Italian, and she's the most passionate person I've ever met."

"Passionate?" Barbara laughed out loud, pointing to Rome. "I've rarely heard you say that word before. You're a nerd; you don't do passionate. You get off on statistics and…" She paused, noticing the blush on Rome's cheeks. "Wait… what has she done to you? And where did you meet?"

"We ehm… we met at my pitch." Rome bit her lip, wondering whether to share the whole truth or not. "It was in a restaurant and she was with one of the investors as his escort…" She waited for Barbara's reaction that was as predictable as the time.

"What the fuck?" Barbara laughed even harder now. "You're friends with a hooker?"

"She's not a hooker," Rome said, a little too sharply for her own liking. She was surprised at the stab she felt at Barbara even calling Nadine that, but she tried not to get worked up about it. "She goes out with people to make them look good; she doesn't sleep with her clients. Unless they're female and she wants to sleep with them…" She reached into her purse and held up the small bottle Nadine had given her. "And she's only doing it to fund her perfume business. Nadine's a perfumer and she's incredibly talented. She made me this."

Barbara glared at her while opening the bottle. "Jesus, Rome."

"What?" Rome arched a brow as she zipped closed her suitcase and opened the next.

"You're defending her like your life depends on it. And you keep talking about her." Barbara dabbed a little of the essence on her wrist and sniffed it. "Mmm… God, this smells good."

"But you asked me!" Rome crossed her arms and widened her stance. "I was only answering your question."

"Yeah, but you kept bringing her up before, and now

that you've told me she's gay—I mean, I assume she is, if she sleeps with her female clients... Do you have a crush on her or something?"

"Of course not." Rome started rooting through her toiletries, barely registering what she was throwing into her toiletry pouch. She couldn't look at her friend, because Barbara knew her too well and she was sure her swooning expression would give her away. Yes, she was smitten with Nadine. But only a little, she told herself. "She's a woman."

"You don't have to remind me of that. But it's not unthinkable, right?" Barbara walked around Rome to face her again when she didn't answer. "Do you have a picture of her?"

"No." Rome picked a couple of random nail varnishes from her box and added them to the pouch.

"Liar. Come on. I know you have a picture. Show me."

Rome let out a deep sigh and reluctantly reached for her phone. She opened one of the few pictures she had of her and Nadine—a headshot of them in bed—and tried not to stare at it while she held it out.

"Fuck me, she's pretty." Barbara frowned.

"Pretty is an understatement," Rome said without thinking.

Barbara's gaze shifted from the picture to Rome and back. "I was right, I knew it. You should see yourself." She tilted her head as she studied the image closer. "And why are you lying down? Is that a pillow? We've never taken pictures like this together. And why is your hair all messy?"

Rome took her phone back and threw it in her purse, then sat down on the bed, deciding to confess. "I slept with her." A strange sensation settled in her core as she said it out loud, and in that moment, she knew that telling someone would change everything, because it made it real. Barbara had already figured her out, though, so there was no point denying it. This time, there was no laughter, and Rome was grateful for that.

"You did not..." Barbara bit her lip and hesitated before she continued. "Was it a drunken thing or..."

"No, it wasn't. I stayed for two nights, actually." Rome let herself fall on her back and stared up at the ceiling. "She's addictive, Barb. She drags me along in her passions, and I can't help but get sucked in. The fact that she's a woman..." Her voice trailed away, and she continued in a near whisper. "I don't care because no man could ever live up to her. No woman either. She's incredible."

"And she's also an escort."

"I told you, she's only doing that to fund her..."

"It doesn't matter," Barbara interrupted her. "You have a crush on her and she's an escort. I don't want you to get hurt."

"I won't. It's not serious and it never will be." Rome had told herself that a million times. As a true analyst, she'd dissected the situation and concluded that A; it was unlikely that she was gay because if she was, she'd surely have known sooner. Nadine was just an exception because she was, well... Nadine. B; it could never get serious as Nadine didn't do relationships and Rome always made sure never to get close to anyone either. C; she was likely to be overexcited because the whole woman-thing was new to her and so her pheromones were likely playing up. As soon as they'd settled, she'd be free from her infatuation and everything could go back to normal. Until that happened, there was nothing wrong with indulging in the memories. Despite her attempts to rationalize her feelings, her heart started racing just at the thought of seeing Nadine again. "Please stop worrying about me."

"Okay. Just be careful." Barbara sat down on the bed and leaned over her, forcing Rome to look at her. "So... how was it?" Her lips pulled into a smirk, lifting her freckled cheeks. "I don't get much action these days, but now that you do, I can finally start living vicariously through my best friend."

Rome met her eyes and couldn't help but laugh. "It was insane."

"Insane?"

"Yeah, insanely good. Like I didn't know it was possible to be so good-good."

"Oh..." Barbara's voice went up a notch as she stared down at her. "Better than with a man-good?"

"Absolutely. A different league entirely."

"Fuck..." Barbara swallowed hard, hanging onto her every word, now. "What did you guys do?"

Rome looked up again, her face taking on an even brighter shade of red. "Do you really want to know?"

"Hell, yeah! Tell me everything."

"Okay. Rome scooted to the middle of her bed and crossed her legs, then poured them both a large glass of wine from the bottle on her nightstand. "Here, take this. you're going to need it."

20

Nadine was fidgeting with her napkin while trying to refrain from drinking her nerves away. She was usually the one to be late, but tonight, she'd been early. She didn't like that her reunion with Rome would take place during one of her escort dates, but it was the way it was. Besides, Nadine had told herself to stop getting carried away. Their passionate nights had been great, but now she needed to refocus and so did Rome. As soon as Rome walked in though, her resolve crumbled.

"Hey." She smiled as she kissed Rome on both cheeks and caught a waft of the perfume she'd made for her. Rome looked incredible in a simple, black dress that reached her knees, and a black, silk scarf draped around her shoulders. Her blonde bob was immaculately straightened, and the elegant designer heels told Nadine she'd been shopping for tonight. Had she been shopping with *her* in mind?

When she met Rome's gaze, the look of longing in her eyes made Nadine's breath hitch, and as hard as it was, she fought to hide her desire and refocused on Flavio, who was sitting next to her. He kept trying to place his hand on her thigh, and she repeatedly brushed it away, thinking it wouldn't be a bad thing when this job came to an end. It was rare that she went on more than two or three dates with the same person, exactly for this reason. They got sucked into the fantasy and almost started believing it was real sometimes, as seemed to be the case with Flavio tonight. He was looking at her like he was about to propose any minute now, and his infatuation might become a problem if she wasn't careful.

Nadine's story tonight was that she liked the city so much that she'd decided to stay for longer, and she'd only agreed to go out with Flavio once more because she knew Rome would be here, and because Matteo would be here too. She didn't like the idea of Rome being in the company of the creep who'd kept eyeing her up during their previous dinners, and her protective streak flared up once again when she watched him slide his hand down Rome's back while he greeted her. Rome quickly pulled out of his embrace and turned to say hello to Rob, and then Flavio, looking mildly irritated. She didn't seem threatened by Matteo anymore, now that contracts had been signed, and the power balance was restored, but Nadine still wanted to throw her glass of wine in his face for even touching her that way. *Stay professional. You still need this job*, she silently reminded herself.

"Well isn't this nice?" Flavio shot them a wide grin. "All reunited like old friends." He waited for the waiter to pour Rome a glass of champagne, then held his own glass up in a toast. "Here's to Rome, who's going to make us a lot of money. Welcome to team *Nero*."

Rome toasted with them and gave them a charming smile, locking her eyes with Nadine's for a beat before she spoke. "Thank you. I promise you I will work very hard to make you even wealthier, but most of all, I'm proud that we will be working together to make this world more environmentally friendly."

The three men snickered, then composed themselves when they realized the women weren't laughing.

"Why is that funny, honey?" Nadine asked Flavio. "Aren't you going to test the app yourself, considering you have such a high stake in it?"

"Me?" Flavio chuckled. "Absolutely not. I fly first class twice a week and take private limos everywhere; I don't think my carbon score would look good on my social profile."

"Of course." Nadine managed an indulgent smile, then fixed her attention back to Rome. "Well I for one, can't wait to try it. In all honesty, I'm not the most conscientious person either, so I really think the app would help me consider everything I do more carefully."

"Do you drive a car?" Rome asked her, pretending she knew nothing about Nadine.

"No."

"Okay. Do you use plastic bags?"

"No. I get my groceries from the market and take my own bag."

"Then you're already doing a lot better than most people," Rome said. "And besides, it's not about being perfect because there is no such thing and we all need our comforts in life. It's about the little things we can do every day, because if millions of people join in with the little things, big changes will happen."

"I like that." Nadine tried not to swoon over Rome, whose eyes lit up when she spoke about her mission.

"Yes, it's fascinating, but let's order food now, shall we?" Matteo chuckled as he unfolded his napkin and opened the menu. Nadine gritted her teeth while she took a sip of her champagne, but noted Rome wasn't getting worked up about his attitude. They'd both met their fair share of assholes over the course of their career and, just like her, Rome understood that sometimes you needed to let things slide in order to get things done. Things that mattered.

"Sure," she said, giving Nadine a subtle wink.

Nadine felt a rush of arousal and without thinking, she stretched out her leg under the table to rub her heeled foot against Rome's calf. Rome's reaction pleased her, and she studied the blonde woman whose cheeks turned a cute shade of pink as her lips pulled into a small smile. Conscious that someone might notice, she straightened herself again and mumbled something about the appetizers to Flavio. By now he was so smitten with her that he even asked for her opinion on things.

"How about the oysters, honey? Would you like to share?"

"That would be nice," she said in a sultry voice, even though she wasn't a big fan of oysters.

"You know what they say about oysters..." He licked his lips and leaned in to kiss her on the cheek. Nadine let him as there was no way she could subtly fend him off. Disgusted by the feel of his wet mouth against her skin, she immediately turned to her other table companions and started firing off a story about a time she found a pearl while oyster diving in the Maldives. Only half of it was true, but she really needed to take the conversation away from aphrodisiacs. The men laughed, but she felt a shift in Rome's demeanor. Although she was laughing along, the sparkle was gone from her eyes, and Nadine saw her hands were balled into fists. It made her worry, and she had trouble following the conversation after that.

"Nadine and I like to have brunch in bed on Sundays, don't we, sexy?" Nadine vaguely registered Flavio saying something while she studied Rome, who avoided eye-contact with her after they'd ordered.

"I'm sorry honey. What did you say?" she asked, feeling more confused than anything. Nothing of consequence had happened, at least not anything she was aware of.

"I was saying how much we love to have brunch in bed on Sundays." Flavio covered her hand with his own. "The hotel where Nadine is staying does very good eggs Benedict."

"Yeah, they're great," Nadine mumbled, forcing a smile. She followed Flavio with her eyes as he stood up. "Where are you going?"

"Rob is just going to show us his new car before the food arrives. Would you ladies like to join us?"

"No thank you. I'd rather just stay seated in these heels and anyway, what do I know about cars?" She chuckled and looked at Rome, begging her with her eyes to stay.

"I think I'll stay here too," Rome said. "Same thing, high heels. Take a picture for me though, I'd love to see it."

"Everything okay?" Nadine asked when they were alone.

"Yeah. I'm fine." Rome shrugged and put on a brave smile. "Why?"

"Well, because I'm really happy to see you again and I get the feeling it's not mutual. At least it hasn't felt like that in the past half hour. What happened?" Nadine leaned in and at the same time, Rome shifted back as if she was scared of being close to her. "I was hoping we could meet up tonight. There's no full moon, but it's been a while," she joked.

"I can't tonight; I'm feeling a little jet lagged." Rome sounded flat and avoided her gaze.

"Jet lagged," Nadine repeated with a puzzled frown. "Somehow I don't believe you." She waited for Rome to speak, but she remained silent. "Come on, Rome, please tell me what's wrong."

"It hurts," Rome finally whispered. "It hurts to see you with someone else and I know it's stupid because we're not together and this is your job, but it still stings. I can't stand it when he touches you." She shook her head. "I don't know what I was thinking. I'm not yours and you're not mine. I clearly got carried away, and we should never have taken it as far as we did because I don't like how I'm feeling. I've managed to live my whole life without self-inflicted drama, so I don't see why I should start now."

"But..."

"No, wait." Rome stopped Nadine. "I'm starting work on Monday, and I need to be on top of my game. I don't have space for these..." she patted her belly and sighed. "Feelings. It's too much. I guess I didn't realize how much I liked you until I saw you with him tonight."

"But Rome, it means nothing. I don't even like men that way."

"No, you don't, but next week you might be on a date with a woman, and that will be even worse for me." Rome's gaze shifted to the sky, her mind spinning as she searched for words. "I thought I could do casual and I really like you, Nadine. But right now, I'm about to start the most important project in my life and I can't get distracted by things I don't understand. I need to keep my head screwed on. It's not like we're in a relationship, but it's already messing me up and that's not a good sign."

"You're right. We're not in a relationship, and I'm not a fan of those in general." Nadine paused. "But please hear me out. What I wanted to say is that I really missed you when you were away and I've spent the whole day thinking of you, wishing time would speed up, because I couldn't wait to see you again." She surprised herself with her own honesty, because she rarely spoke about her feelings like this.

A sadness settled over Rome's features as she met her eyes. "Honestly, I was looking forward to seeing you too. I just didn't expect to feel this stabbing pain each time he touched you and pretended you were his girlfriend. Those two nights... they changed me, and they might just be casual to you, but to me, they meant so much more because I'd never been with a woman before. You made me want you and it's not fair; I was fine before I met you."

"You mean you were fine feeling nothing at all?" Nadine frowned. "I don't see how that's fine. How can you live like that?"

"How can I live like that?" Rome repeated, looking irritated now. "How can you live like this?" She took a long sip of her wine, then refilled her glass. "Look, I didn't mean it that way. I understand why you do what you do. It's your job and you need the income. But you have to admit that it's better if we stop sleeping together because someone's going to get hurt. You, me, or both of us, and I don't want that. I had a taste of it tonight and I just can't do whatever it is we're doing anymore."

Nadine nodded. She felt horrible, seeing Rome like this. "I'm so, so sorry, I never meant to hurt you. We can leave now if you want and..."

"No," Rome interrupted her again. "You need to stay here and do your job, and I need to do the same."

Nadine suppressed a sigh. She knew Rome was right, but the rejection still hurt. She'd longed for Rome for weeks, and she'd missed her like she'd never missed anyone before. "Can we at least still be friends?"

Rome's expression softened, and she gave her a small smile. "Yeah, I'd like that." She shrugged. "I can't imagine not seeing you anymore. I just need to try and get rid of these damn feelings."

"I sense you don't like 'feelings' very much," Nadine said, making quote marks in the air.

"I don't. Feelings are what make me turn away from people, especially painful feelings, and I don't want to lose you." Rome paused. "Don't ask me why, I'm just a little messed up like that."

"That's okay. We're all a little messed up." Nadine reached for her hand over the table, and Rome took it. It scared her how good it felt to touch her, but she kept that to herself. If this was hurting Rome in any way, she'd keep her distance, and being just friends was fine. After all, it was what she wanted too, wasn't it?

21

———

Rome folded up the cardboard box she'd just unpacked and flung it into a corner of the room. Her apartment in Monti in central Rome was starting to look like home, now that she'd bought some flowers and her personal items were displayed. Everything about the place Nadine had found for her was perfect: it was furnished, close to the metro, she could see parts of the Forum and the Colosseum from her bedroom window, and it was far enough from Nadine's apartment not to go wandering there on a whim. It was nice not to worry about being able to pay the rent for once and to simply pick something that she liked, and Nadine had provided her with an amazing selection. She hadn't gone overboard; it was still only a two-bedroom apartment, but it cost more than she'd ever spent on rent before. She had money in her account, her credit cards were paid off, she was debt-free and that felt really, really good.

She'd settled on six months with the rental agency as she wasn't sure how long she would be here, and that was the other thing that had held her back from staying at Nadine's last night. She'd realized how much she liked her, and she didn't want to get too attached if she'd be leaving again. If it already hurt seeing her with someone now—someone who didn't mean anything to Nadine—it would be impossible not to get her heart broken when she went back to the US, or perhaps much sooner, when Nadine got bored with her because she didn't 'do' relationships.

Nadine might be the most mysterious and intriguing woman Rome had ever met, but when it came to relationships, she wasn't hard to figure out. She recognized the signs; Nadine used her job as an excuse not to get close to anyone and even though she'd been the one who'd wanted Rome to stay over, she'd realize soon enough that it was getting too serious. No, it was best to remain friends and have fun together while she was here, nothing more. She wondered how Nadine had become this way. Was it a result of years of escort work, or was her escort work a result of a deep-rooted detachment that was already there? Whatever it was, they were more alike than they'd initially realized.

Her eyes were drawn to a box with her old photo albums and she opened it and picked one out. She wasn't sure why she'd brought them all the way here because she could have easily left them in storage in Portland, or at her father's house. Each time she'd moved, she'd brought them with her, literally carrying the burden of painful memories. Why was she still doing this to herself?

The old, brown and ochre yellow albums were torn at the edges and most pictures had faded over time. It was all Rome had left of her mother, and even though she hated her for leaving her and her father, she couldn't help but look through them every now and then as she tried to recall memories of happier times in her youth. She opened one of her favorite albums and allowed herself to feel angry and hurt at seeing her mother's smiling face.

Her sudden departure had destroyed her world when Rome was twelve. Although she'd suffered from light depression from time to time, she'd never given Rome any reason to believe she was unhappy with the life she led. Fathers were the ones who left if they couldn't handle mundane family life, not mothers. Fathers had affairs, started new families, or simply disappeared, at least that was what she'd witnessed with some of her friends throughout her youth. Mothers were supposed to stick by you, no matter what. They were supposed to see their children grow up and love them unconditionally.

A stupid note was all that was left of her when Rome had returned from school that day, twenty years ago. Her clothes were gone, her shoes, her makeup, her diary on the kitchen counter, and her glasses that were always on the coffee table. Even her hairbrush was gone, and when Rome broke down and needed it most, there wasn't even a towel left with her scent on it. Her mother had cleared away every trace of herself as if she'd never been there.

I'm so, so sorry. I love you both very much, but I can't do this anymore.

There had been no explanation, no excuse, and they'd been unable to contact her. Her father had called the police, but as her mother had left a note, and meticulously packed all her things, they'd carefully tried to break it to them that it looked like her mother had indeed, just left them.

It had been a normal Thursday afternoon, no different from any other day. After letting herself in through the backdoor that was always open, Rome had walked into the kitchen, expecting to see her mother there. She was always in the kitchen, cooking, when Rome came out of school. They would share a drink together and talk about their day. But she wasn't there, and it wasn't until Rome realized things like the coats and shoes in the hallway, and the makeup bag in the bathroom were missing, that she started to get worried.

Mom? Rome still remembered the sound of her own voice as it echoed through the house. It was just an uncomfortable feeling at first; her intuition telling her something was wrong. As soon as she started to scan the rooms though, it was clear that her mother was gone. Her father hadn't believed her when she called him at first, and to this day, she was pretty sure he was telling the truth when he said he hadn't seen it coming either.

Those first months without her mother were incredibly hard. It wasn't just the loneliness she felt, and the hurt of missing her when she came home to an empty house each day. It was the raging anger that threatened to choke her each time she envisioned seeing her again when she changed her mind and came back. Rome had rehearsed what she'd say to her so many times, but the reunion never happened, and she'd genuinely believed then, that it would have been easier if her mother had just died.

It broke her father too, and he buried himself in work. Rome's grandmother moved in with them and took care of Rome until she started boarding school the following year. She didn't blame her father for sending her there. He had to work, her grandmother was old and struggling with her health, and it was just easier that way. Besides, she and her father had never been close, not like she'd been with her mother, who had always been a stay-at-home mom. Looking back, she still didn't understand how her mother could have faked it with her all those years, because she looked genuinely happy in the pictures.

Rome didn't look like her mother, who was tall and dark-haired, but she didn't look like her father either, with his ginger beard and Irish features. One of the pictures showed them as a family, having Christmas dinner at her grandmother's house, another one was of her sitting between her parents on a bench in a park, eating ice cream. But most pictures were just of her and her mom; at home, on daytrips together, and even on holiday when her father was too busy with work. The pictures made her feel sick, but she still forced herself to look at every single one of them each time she opened the albums, endlessly wondering what was hidden behind that wide smile. It was generally just the two of them, and so Rome suspected Maggie Foster had been so bored of her own child that she simply had to get away. She'd looked for similar stories online but only found a few. Not knowing if her life had been based on a lie or not had been the hardest thing to comprehend, and she couldn't think of a greater betrayal, a greater pain, than what her mother had done to her.

Flipping the page, she wiped away a tear as she got to the last picture, taken by her grandmother, a month before her life fell apart. It was her twelfth birthday, and she was celebrating with her school friends. They were gathered around a table in the big yard of their beautiful house in the suburbs of Portland. Her mother held out a cake for her, and she was blowing out the candles while her father and her friends clapped and cheered. It was such a happy scene; the epitome of the American dream, but beneath it all, everything was rotten to the core.

Years later, they found out her mother had moved to Nashville, and that she was singing in a country band. The private investigator her father finally hired after Rome had been begging him to do so, also informed them that she'd lived in New York and San Francisco for a while. Rome had stopped tracking her after that. She'd thought of visiting her mother when she was younger, of showing up unannounced, but was glad she hadn't. Maggie had thrown her daughter to the curb like a piece of garbage and it was too late now for any excuse to make her feel better.

A number of therapists she'd seen in her teens had told Rome she'd become emotionally detached, and although she'd tried to work on it, her job had always been her priority and eventually she'd given up, because it was easier to throw herself into her life's work than to deal with the pain she'd buried so deep that she couldn't feel it anymore. *Apart from last night.*

There were many scars she hadn't dealt with, and throughout college she'd been so afraid of anything more than a superficial friendship that she'd been a loner. Her lonely life had been comfortable to her, and the solitude protected her from the risk of getting hurt again. Barbara was her only good friend, perhaps because she'd always been there, living next door since Rome was eight. Now, it seemed that a second person had managed to dig her way in. Why had it bothered her so much, seeing Nadine with Flavio? Was it because she'd trusted her, and felt betrayed? She knew that was ridiculous, because what she and Nadine had shared was nothing more than a two-day fling at this stage, but it hurt nevertheless. It had been a long time since she'd felt so emotional, and although these feelings toward Nadine were barely a scratch on the surface, it felt like a dam was about to break. Still, she desperately wanted to stay in touch with Nadine, and she told herself to get over her silly infatuation and get a grip. Nadine was the first person who'd made her feel really good in a long time, and maybe it was time she started letting people in a little. As long as she avoided intimacy, she'd be fine.

. . .

Rome had made herself a chamomile tea and pulled herself together after shoving the photo albums under her bed. It was getting late, and tomorrow she'd have an early start, meeting and briefing the roll-out team that *Nero* had hired for her. Always having worked by herself, she was nervous to be in charge of fourteen extremely smart people, but she figured that as long as she was respectful and nice to everyone, they would all get along. Matteo was sure to make things a little uncomfortable now and then, but he had no business getting involved apart from their monthly board meetings in which Rome would update the board members on their progress.

She wiped the sweat off her forehead after making the bed and plugging in her chargers. The apartment was warm, but she didn't like to use the air-conditioning unit as she loved the breeze, the noise and the smells pouring through the four open windows. It would cool down later, and she only needed her thin cotton sheets to sleep under. *Naked.* She'd never considered sleeping naked before but since spending those two nights with Nadine, she hadn't worn her pajama shorts and Buffy T-shirt once. The small bottle of perfume was on her nightstand and she sprinkled some over her pillows, then put some on her wrists. It was all she needed to wear to bed.

22

Nadine put the last bottle back in the box after examining the samples for over an hour. They looked and smelled great, and the sampling and packaging process that had been carried out in a factory in the north of Italy had been a smooth operation. Her twelve perfumes were ready to be tested, beautifully presented in a simple test-tube inspired bottle, each displaying a handwritten label that had been reproduced for the finished product as she wanted it to look as authentic as possible. The boxes were white with a subtle silver foil illustration of the star sign they represented, every image and word meticulously designed by herself. The samples came with a stainless steel test-tube holder for the retailers to present the twelve testers in store. They looked perfect together, and seeing the finished product should have excited her, but instead, she felt a choking dread. Her work was done, and now what?

She had a plan, of course, and she'd already booked the agency that would run the consumer tests, enabling her to make claims on the product, if it worked. She'd had a long meeting with them three months ago, and even then, it had seemed so far away. Just like Rome, this was her life's work, and she felt panicky at the thought of pushing through to the finish line now. Next year she'd turn thirty, would have to give up escorting, and would have to live without the security of her generous income, only relying on her perfumes and her business sense, which she wasn't sure she even had. If her perfumes didn't sell, she'd have to give up her apartment, her lifestyle, and she wouldn't be able to continue making more perfumes either. Nadine realized then that she was afraid, and fear wasn't an emotion she was familiar with.

Burying her head in her hands behind her desk in her perfume room, she took a couple of deep breaths in an attempt to stop the nausea that threatened to take over. Eight years ago, this moment had seemed like a distant dream, but one she loved to build on, nevertheless. Now, playtime was over, the pressure was on and she would have to make it count. She suddenly felt warm, even though she was naked under the white lab coat. Being naked made her feel free when she worked, and she liked to sample the oils on her own skin in the final steps of the process.

Her phone lit up and grateful for the distraction, she picked it up and read the message from the escort agency, requesting a last-minute booking for tonight. She checked the client's details and immediately accepted, thinking the elegant woman she'd been on two dates with previously, was exactly what she needed to distract herself from her fears, and to get Rome out of her head. It was clear that Rome wanted nothing more than friendship right now, and she would respect that. She'd missed Rome during the time she'd been back home, and her rejection Saturday night had hurt way more than expected, so it would be better to get back on the horse now, rather than suffer through worse later.

Nadine gave her consumer testing agency a ring to pick up the boxes containing five full sets of samples. The three sets on her desk she'd keep for herself, and she made a mental note to give the Libra perfume to Rome next time they met as she was curious to see if she liked the fragrance and whether she felt it suited her personality. Whether they were sleeping together or not, Nadine was still immensely attracted to her; nothing could change that, and she wanted her to be one of the first people to test her product.

'How is your first day going?' she texted Rome. She'd been able to refrain herself from contacting her for thirty-six hours, but that had been hard because she just loved talking to her. A smile lit up her face when she got a reply, almost immediately.

'It's going great actually, nice team. How are you?'

'Also great,' she lied. *'Just looking at my final samples and I'd like to give you a bottle.'*

'That's kind of you. I would love that. How about we meet up for dinner later?'

Nadine groaned in frustration. God, she would love to go for dinner with Rome. She wanted to hear about her team, her plans for the app, and she wanted to know if she liked the apartment she'd found for her. *'Can't, sorry. Working tonight. How about tomorrow?'*

'I can't tomorrow. Matteo wants to go for dinner. Not happy about it and not sure what the deal is. He says we still have some loose ends to tie up. Can you do Wednesday?'

'Sure.' Nadine felt her stomach sink at the thought of Rome going out with Matteo. She didn't like the idea of him preying on her and she didn't trust him one bit. Before she could enquire further, another message came in.

'Man or woman?'

Nadine frowned. 'What do you mean?'

'Your date. Are you going out with a man or a woman?'

"Fuck," she cursed out loud. It bothered her to tell Rome she'd been booked by a woman, but she didn't want to lie to her. 'Woman.' She expected Rome to ask her if she was a regular, or if she was attractive, but none of that happened. Desperate to hold onto their exchange, she asked: 'So I'll see you Wednesday?'

'Yeah. I'll let you know when I finish. Have to go.'

Nadine realized her hands were trembling, and she felt like throwing her phone against the wall. This, between her and Rome, was messing with her head and she hated being out of control. She flung her lab coat over the chair and walked out of the room, barefoot and naked, and stepped under the shower, even though she'd already had one a couple of hours ago. The second blow of the day arrived when the water turned cold after only three minutes. It happened more frequently lately, but today she couldn't seem to shake off her annoyance. She was craving a stiff drink, but couldn't leave the house as she had to wait for the delivery of her dress for tonight, so she rummaged through her cupboards and found an old unopened bottle of Chianti. "That will do," she mumbled, and poured herself a generous amount, before she put on a robe and went out onto the balcony to calm herself.

23

The meeting space at *Nero's* headquarters was nothing like the meeting rooms Rome was used to in the US. Comfortable couches, La-Z-Boy recliners and designer chairs were set up in a semi-circle around the digital board she could operate from her iPad. The room smelled of coffee —the quiet espresso machine constantly working to fuel the energy of the commercial masterminds in front of her.

Rome had spent the morning demonstrating her app and answering questions, and now they would need the rest of the week to scope out their road to market and tackle potential obstacles. The manufacturing part was straightforward and didn't come with any issues; the actual credit card was the only tangible item that needed to be produced, and they had an expert on board who promised to create a bidding war between several major banks who were interested in collaborating.

They'd decided to take the same collaborative approach when it came to the full roll-out; big department stores, supermarket chains, fashion brands or any other brands who prided themselves in being consciously driven would get the first chance to work with them on the marketing side and show the world they were revolutionary by endorsing such a forward-thinking concept. The small but powerful PR-team headed up by a woman called Eliza Ricci, was hired to approach celebrities; both global and local, from pop stars to athletes to general influencers. Rome's team members were some of the best in their field, who respected not only the brilliant product she'd created, but also her analytical ability to bring together every aspect of the launch, creating a logical platform that enabled them to reach as many people as possible within their given budget.

Rome noted it was five pm and decided to wrap it up. Although she could have easily continued for another couple of hours, she wanted to keep the team happy and driven, and longer workdays were proven to be ineffective in the long run. "I think that's it for today," she said, smiling at each and every one of them. "Unless there's something urgent I've forgotten?" She was pleased to see the faces of her team members light up. Apart from a couple of locals who spoke English, most of them had moved from abroad to be on the project, and she was pretty sure the newcomers were eager to explore the city in their free time.

A young man in one of the recliners held up his hand. "I don't know how everyone else feels about this, but maybe we should go out for drinks? Get to know each other better? We're a new team after all, and I for one don't know anyone in this town." He looked around the room. "My guess is a lot of you don't either."

"Sounds like a great idea." Rome narrowed her eyes, digging though the list of names she'd memorized. "Jonathan, right?" She also remembered he was only twenty-three, and already considered a branding and design genius. He'd been hired to work on the house style Rome had created for the brand, perfect the logo and the app visuals, and to design the Carbon Card, the website, and all other graphics-related materials. "Okay, Jonathan, why don't you set up a WhatsApp group, so we're all connected and perhaps one of you locals can suggest a good place to meet?"

T wo hours later, Rome was on her second beer of the night and enjoying the animated conversation that was flowing between the groups of people in the supplì bar in Trastevere. The bar with standing tables outside sold beer, cocktails and deep-fried rice balls to soak up the alcohol and although it was a Monday night and quiet, their party had livened up the quirky little place tucked away in an alleyway. They weren't far from Nadine's apartment, but Nadine was 'working' tonight, and Rome tried not to think about that as she felt a stab each time her mind went there. *Sometimes I sleep with the women.* Wasn't that what Nadine had said? *But only for my own pleasure and free of charge, of course.* Their first conversation had apparently impacted her so much that she remembered it word for word. Was she flirting with her client right now? Would she have sex with her? Rome shook it off and took a long drink of her beer, turning back to Eliza, the head of her PR team. Eliza had worked for some of Italy's biggest fashion brands, a couple of global sports brands and a cosmetics brand. She knew everyone who mattered and was a master in networking, but she was also surprisingly down to earth and funny, and Rome liked her a lot.

"Are you married? Kids?" Rome asked her.

"No. To my mother's horror, I'm single and very, very happy to mingle."

"Your mother's not happy about that?"

"No. Believe me; being single at thirty-eight in an Italian family is a challenge. They're convinced I'm about to pass my sell-by-date soon, and they try to set me up at any given opportunity." Eliza rolled her eyes. "But my brothers are married and have kids so luckily they take some of the pressure off me." She paused, clearly contemplating on how much to share, then continued in a whisper. "I don't ever want to settle down, but they don't need to know that."

Rome laughed. "And why is that?"

"Because I'm addicted to the excitement of meeting someone new and live for the feeling of oxytocin ruling my system." Eliza shrugged. "As soon as the first wave of euphoria fades, I bolt, in search of the next hit. I know it's not fair to my boyfriends, but I can't help myself; I just love being in love."

"You're not just passionate in your job, then?" Rome studied the tall woman, who was very pretty despite her unconventional looks and extravagant dress style. She had lilac hair, pale skin and wore lilac colored contact lenses that made her look a little alien. Her tight, black dress and enormous platform shoes made her even taller, and she guessed Eliza might be intimidating to some, but that she could also mingle with famous and influential people without blinking an eye.

"What can I say? I'm Italian; passion is in my blood." Eliza waved her hands as if to emphasize the fact. "So, are you married? Boyfriend?"

Rome shook her head. "I'm married to the Carbon app."

Eliza snickered. "I figured as much. You wouldn't be where you are if you hadn't given it everything."

"Yeah, it's been an intense ten years, but I could say the same for you."

"I work hard," Eliza said. "But fun always comes first.

Because without fun, what are we doing it all for, right? Don't forget that now is the time to enjoy the fruits of your labor, so go out and live your life to the full."

"Yeah, I haven't exactly been a social butterfly. In fact, I don't remember the last time I had a casual drink with someone back home."

"Well, it's not just you anymore. You have a whole team to support you, and although these six months will be crucial, I promise you, it's going to be a huge success and we're going to have a lot of fun along the way." Eliza's animated tone and wild hand gestures were infectious, and Rome had a feeling she was right about the fun part.

"I know. I'm just so used to working twenty-four-seven that I need a little time to get used to this." Rome thought of Nadine again, and how she'd made her forget about everything during those two nights. How she'd only been aware of her senses, feeding her lust in the most primal of ways.

"You know, the Italian men are charmers. It would be a shame not to drown yourself in romance while you're in *the City of Love*, right?" Eliza held up her beer and took a sip.

"Isn't Paris supposed to be *the City of Love*?" Rome asked with a chuckle.

Eliza waved a dismissive finger in front of her. "No. It's what they say, but they're wrong. Rome is the epicenter of love and romance, trust me. Right here is where people flirt like crazy, and where couples make out on park benches, in squares and on the steps of ancient fountains while the sun sets. It's the place where people serenade each other, share ice cream, and sometimes go a little crazy with passion. You can wake up next to a stranger in Rome and leave with a smile on your face instead of feeling ashamed."

"You're really selling it. I take it you're from Rome?"

"I am." Eliza couldn't have looked prouder. "I was actually born in a small village outside Rome, but I've lived here since I was nineteen. My job has taken me just about everywhere in the world, but I always love coming back." Something dropped on her head and they both laughed as she held up a pair of white panties that had fallen from the clothing line above them. She walked over to the front door under the line and stuffed it through the mailbox. "Anyway," she continued, as if it happened to her all the time, "as I said, you should be open to dating while you're here. Who knows? You might fall in love..."

Rome was getting sucked into their conversation, and suddenly felt an urge to talk about Nadine. As much as she'd tried not to think of her in any other way than merely a friend, she'd been on her mind the whole day, the delicious memories of their nights haunting her mind. "Can you keep a secret?" She looked around, making sure no one was listening in.

"Of course." Eliza's intense eyes widened with curiosity.

"There's this woman I met." Rome wondered for a moment if it would be unprofessional to discuss it, but she didn't consider herself to be their boss. She was simply the person who pulled everything together and working with such talented people, she didn't want them to feel like there was hierarchy.

Eliza gasped. "A woman? I would never have guessed you were gay, although that's a pretty lame statement to make in this day and age, I suppose."

"Well, that's the thing... I'm not."

Eliza laughed out loud. "Well in that case, this city has already rubbed off on you. Is she local?"

"Kind of. She's half Italian, half American and she's lived here for a while. It's over though. At least the physical part; we're still friends.... I hope," Rome added. "I behaved weird on Saturday night." She let out a deep sigh. When she woke up this morning, the whole thing had felt like an overreaction. Maybe she really had been jet lagged, or hormonal, or just a little emotional over starting a new chapter in her life. "But thinking of her still makes me a little crazy."

"Then I take it you're not happy being just friends?"

Rome pursed her lips and thought about it. "Let's just say I'm not the only person in her life, and I've discovered I get really jealous. It's something I didn't know about myself and I don't like it, especially as it wasn't serious in the first place. So, it's better if I keep a distance, at least emotionally."

"Hmm... Yeah, I get the jealousy thing. It's a horrible disease of the mind." Eliza waved at one of their colleagues who came out with a tray of beers and took two off for herself and Rome before thanking him in Italian. "And is there any chance she'll get rid of the third party anytime soon? Have you considered a threesome?"

Rome almost choked on her beer and chuckled. "No, and no. I may be going through a phase of exploring my sexuality, but I'm not that open-minded. Besides, it's way more complicated than that. I..." Their conversation was interrupted by flirtatious whistling, and one of their colleagues yelled something in Italian at a woman who was passing through the alleyway.

"Fuck..." Rome's heart started racing as she saw it was Nadine, dressed in a navy blue sequined dress and high heels. Her hair danced loosely around her shoulders as she walked with a sway in her hips, her small, black purse dangling from a gold chain on her arm. She gave the boys a dazzling smile and yelled something back that made them laugh. Rome would have given anything to speak Italian in that moment, and she also would have given anything to change the way she looked. As her team members had gone straight to the bar, she hadn't bothered getting dressed up either, but seeing Nadine now, she wished she had.

Nadine's eyes narrowed as she spotted her, and Rome could tell she was shocked to see her here. "Rome?" Her eyes darted from Rome to Eliza and back, a hint of something Rome hadn't seen before flashing over her features.

"Hey," Rome said, trying to look confident and relaxed, while all she wanted to do was run to the bathroom to check her hair and makeup. Whatever she'd said on Saturday night flew straight out of the window, and she shivered when Nadine walked up to her and gave her a soft kiss on her cheek. "What are you doing here? I thought you'd be out enjoying your evening by now."

"No, my meeting isn't until eight, and my limo is picking me up on the bridge. Apparently it was too long to make the turns around here." Nadine rolled her eyes. "Fucking show-off." Again, her curious eyes met Eliza's before she turned back to Rome. "But on the upside, I'm looking forward to Wednesday."

"Yeah, me too." Rome thought about introducing Nadine to Eliza, but she seemed to be in a hurry and something about the way Nadine looked at Eliza made her think that maybe now wasn't a good time. "Let me know where to meet you."

"No need, I'll pick you up." Nadine shot her a dazzling smile before she walked off. "Have a great night, Rome."

"Thanks, you too." Rome's eyes lowered to her behind, then realized that it had gone quiet around her. When she snapped back and looked at her colleagues, conversations picked up again as if they had never been interrupted. Even Eliza seemed a little impressed by Nadine, as she was still staring at her until she disappeared around the corner.

"Okay... That woman is smoking hot. Angry, but still

smoking hot." Eliza flipped her lilac hair to one side, her mouth opening, then closing again as if she was lost for words. "Was that her?" She finally asked in a whisper.

"Yeah." Rome bit her lip and winced, worried Eliza might think she was way out of Nadine's league.

"And you were saying *you* were jealous?" Eliza laughed and fanned a hand in front of her face. "Mama Mia. Did you see how she glared at me? And what's the limo for? Is she dating a celebrity, or some movie mogul?"

"Something like that."

"Well, whoever it is, you're clearly her number one, so I wouldn't worry too much. She'll come around."

24

"Hi Louise, it's good to see you again." Nadine scanned the hotel bar where she was meeting her client, Louise Spencer-Ayre, an in-the-closet English heiress, married to a wealthy investment banker. Running her own exclusive shoe emporium, Louise was a businesswoman herself, and was always jetting around to meet with manufacturers and retailers. "Where's the rest of the party?"

"Nadine." Louise batted her long eyelashes and chuckled. "No one else will be joining us, it's just you and me tonight. I hope that's not a problem?" She gave Nadine a kiss on her cheek and took her hand.

"Of course not." Nadine gave her a sweet smile and followed the older lady to their table where a bottle of Barolo was waiting for them. The lavish hotel was out of town, which was an unusual choice for Louise, who tended to stay central for her meetings. Nadine didn't feel entirely at ease tonight, and perhaps that was because it was just the two of them. The problem wasn't that they were short of things to talk about; they both loved Italian opera, traveling and art among many other things, but the absence of others made it feel very intimate all of a sudden.

Then there was also the run-in with Rome, of course. Although Nadine was happy that Rome was making new friends, the woman she'd been talking to had been stunning, and she couldn't seem to shake the feeling that something might be brewing between them. Perhaps she'd awoken something in Rome that she now wanted to explore, and that thought made her feel even worse. It was crazy to get worked up over it; she knew that. Fake or not; she was on a date herself tonight, and even if she wasn't, she still wouldn't be able to give all of herself to someone and sustain any form of intimate relationship. It had just always been that way.

"You're looking beautiful as always." Louise looked as if she was about to jump Nadine any minute as her eyes raked over her cleavage in the tight dress. "I'm glad I got your size right. Do you like it?"

"I do. Thank you." Nadine cleared her throat and tried to relax. "Why are you here by yourself?" she asked, keen to get to the bottom of Louise's motives, although she had a pretty good idea. "And why are we so far out of town?"

"No specific reason, I just felt like a change." Louise waited for the waiter to pour their wine and clinked her glass against Nadine's. "I checked up on my samples in Rome last week and the head of production there told me this was a nice place to stay, so I moved hotels and booked an extra couple of nights." She shrugged. "My husband is in Cape Town until next month, so he won't care that I'm away, and I'm getting to an age where I deserve some time off."

Her hand landed on Nadine's thigh, and although that wasn't allowed, Nadine hadn't exactly followed the rules with Louise on their previous dates, as she found her attractive. She'd slept with her twice but for some reason she wasn't feeling it anymore. "Well, good for you," she said, trying to sound casual. Then she stood up again and grabbed her purse. "Please excuse me for a moment. I need the restroom; I'll be right back."

She headed for the other end of the room and disappeared around the corner. In the toilet, she steadied herself against the sink and looked at her reflection. The sequined dress she was wearing tonight was by an expensive brand, and the fact that Louise had bought it for her to wear made her think that she might have come to expect certain things in return by now. Nadine had always been the one to suggest they'd take it further, and although she'd told herself she wanted to earlier, now she felt like she was being bought like never before. She'd taken advantage of Louise twice, but now Louise was taking advantage of her, and it would be hard to explain why she wasn't interested in sex as she didn't really understand it herself. The dress felt too tight, as if it was squeezing the life out of her, and a couple of broken sequins were poking into her skin. "Get a grip," she mumbled to her reflection, and topped up her lipstick. Her job was the only stable thing she had, and she was going to use the remainder of her time as an escort to build up a buffer, no matter what.

"Why do I get the feeling something is bothering you tonight?" Louise asked as she sat back down. She trailed a finger over Nadine's shoulder and arched an eyebrow. "Are you okay?"

"Yeah, absolutely." Nadine put a hand on Louise's in an attempt to put her at ease. "Just feeling a little light-headed tonight, that's all."

"Then maybe we should eat before you have more wine." Louise beckoned the waiter over and told him they were ready to be seated. When she reached out to take the glass from her, Nadine pulled back her hand and held onto it. It was a harsh realization that Louise was no different from the men she dated. She was convinced she had the right to make her do whatever she wanted, just because she was paying her, and taking the drink from her was simply rude and disrespectful.

"I'm okay finishing my drink, thank you." The words sounded harsh and she quickly painted on a smile to hide her annoyance.

"As you wish." Louise stood up and put an arm around her as they followed the host to their table. "I've been told they serve excellent orzo here."

"Orzo sounds good." Nadine tried to sound upbeat as she took a seat opposite Louise, but it was like a spell had been broken. Faking it had always been her thing; she was very, very good at it. She'd sat through thousands of hours of mind-numbing conversation, pretending to be interested and engaged, and she'd convinced every single one of her dates that she was charmed by them, no matter how much she disliked them. One place where she'd never faked it though, was in the bedroom, and she wasn't going to start tonight. Just as she tried to think of a way to subtly break it to Louise that nothing was going to happen between them, Louise's heeled foot caressed her calf under the table.

"I have the suite booked," she said in a sultry voice, lifting her foot a little higher, until Nadine took a hold of it and stopped her.

"I'm sorry, Louise, I can't do this."

"Do what?"

"You know what I mean. I can't sleep with you tonight.

Things have changed in my personal life. I... I have a girl-friend now," she lied, thinking of Rome. It was the first thing that sprung to mind, and even though they weren't in any kind of relationship, Rome was the main reason why she didn't feel like sleeping with Louise.

"Right... You have a girlfriend." Louise looked irritated as she let her words sink in. "And what does your girlfriend think of your job?" Sarcasm was dripping through her voice as she uttered the word 'girlfriend', like it was a dirty thing. "Does she even know?"

"She knows." Nadine met Louise's eyes and tried to remain calm. "And I'm faithful to her, so I don't sleep with any of my clients anymore." She swallowed hard and hesitated before she continued. "I apologize if I gave you the wrong idea the last times we met up. As per our contract, this will be nothing more than dinner tonight."

Louise stared at her as if she couldn't quite believe what she was hearing. The silence between them was palpable, but Nadine refused to explain herself further. She didn't have to, and she wouldn't. She was an escort, not a prosti-tute, and she'd do what she was hired to do, which was look pretty, sit through dinner and be polite, nothing more.

"Do you have any idea what that dress cost me?" Louise asked in a cold tone. Her smile was gone.

Nadine winced at the stab she felt, when Louise's words confirmed exactly what was happening here. "I'll bring the dress back to the agency; you can have it picked up there." She shrugged. "I never asked for it, and you shouldn't have made assumptions and lured me all the way out here. It's put me in a very uncomfortable position."

"Oh, you're uncomfortable, are you? What about me?" The graceful and composed woman was showing her true colors. Louise was not used to hearing no, and it clearly brought out the worst in her as her face pulled into a disgusted grimace. "You're the biggest disappointment since my daughter brought her last boyfriend home. I thought you were better than this."

"I am better than this." Nadine stood up and looked over her shoulder before she walked off, making sure to raise her voice enough so the diners around her could hear her. "That's why I'm leaving. Don't worry, they'll give you a refund if my services weren't satisfactory."

Louise slammed her fist on the table. "Good luck with making your own way back."

Nadine shot her another glare before she stormed out. She felt awful and disrespected. Here she was, an hour out of town, and she could only hope there would be a cab waiting outside the hotel. Angelo wasn't here to drive her back, because stupidly, she'd trusted that everything would go smoothly with Louise. She let out a sigh of relief when she saw a cab waiting. The driver would undoubtedly see the desperation in her eyes and charge her a fortune, but she didn't care because she really, really wanted to go home.

25

Rome rubbed her temples as she ventured outside on Tuesday morning. The five beers she'd drank last night hadn't seemed like much, but now she was paying the price. She walked up a steep hill toward the nearest Metro stop, and despite the headache, she couldn't help but smile at the bustle around her. It was a beautiful spring day and May was coming to an end. Cafés were already open, and there were long queues outside the most popular ones. She stopped and lined up too because the smell was amazing, and she wanted to do what the locals did. If she was going to be here for a while, she might as well embrace the morning rituals of the city and become a part of it. It was heaving with people when she finally squeezed her way toward the counter and ordered a cappuccino to take away. The small yellow cup looked so precious that it made her smile, and she sipped it while she continued up the hill, fueled by the seriously strong brew and the sun shining down on her. She passed the neighborhood's main square where the local dog walkers congregated in the morning. They were sitting on benches, catching up over coffee while the well-behaved dogs played, and the naughty ones chased cyclists, resulting in a lot of back-and-forth shouting. There was a bakery selling artisan flatbreads, an antique jewelry store and an assortment of vintage boutiques dotted among the restaurants that were just opening up for the day.

She was delighted with her new neighborhood and the apartment Nadine had found, and her second morning went a lot smoother, now that she knew how the ticket machines worked, and which metro line she needed to take. As she sat down on the train, she tried to concentrate on the emails on her phone, but it was hard after seeing Nadine last night. She'd looked so beautiful on her way to meet her dinner date, and despite Eliza assuring her Nadine was more than interested in her, she couldn't help but picture Nadine and her no-doubt beautiful and elegant date together. Maybe they were still in bed. Maybe they'd ordered room service. Maybe Nadine was doing that amazing thing to her... *Stop it*, she told herself. This was all her own doing, and if she was going to stand by her word, they could be nothing more than friends. Even if Nadine wanted more, Rome didn't think she could commit, simply because she'd never been able to.

Rome never crushed on people. Not like she had with Nadine, but occasionally, she'd met men she liked, and sometimes they liked her back. She knew that technically these men would make excellent life partners as they shared the same values and interests. Sometimes she even found them a little attractive, although that usually had more to do with their character than with their looks. But never once had she committed to a relationship. Rome was predictable that way; as soon as they told her they wanted more, she'd apologize, walk off without explanation and break off all contact. It was a terrible thing to do, but time after time, she'd been unable to fight the urge to do so. Why would this be any different?

She was pulled out of her thoughts when her stop was called, and she looked down at her first email that she hadn't even read yet. Walking out of the station and up another hill toward the office, she replied to Matteo's assistant, confirming their dinner plans for tonight, before scrolling through the rest of the messages.

N ero's headquarters comprised of a large, modern cube-like building on the outskirts of town, its glass exterior a stark contrast to the old buildings that surrounded it. A straight concrete path leading to the entrance divided the pristine lawn upfront into two sections; an outside lunch area to the left, with picnic tables and benches, and an outdoor gym to the right, where some of the employees were getting their morning exercise in before starting their day. So far, it seemed like a friendly company that looked after its staff, and Rome was happy with her new workplace. Downstairs was a reception area, the mail room, the canteen and a recreational area, and the first floor was taken up by experts who handled short-term investments, consisting mainly of start-ups. The second floor was taken by the finance department and HR, and the temporary teams were housed on the third floor, which was used for the occasional big project, such as hers. The board's offices were on the fourth floor, but apart from their assistants, she was told it was rarely occupied unless a meeting was planned.

Rome greeted the receptionist and the security guard and stepped into the elevator. Apparently, it was quite a big deal when a new team took over the third floor, which was now off-limits to the rest of the company, as *Nero* wanted to keep the project top-secret until its launch. Rome's team members had signed non-disclosure agreements, prohibiting them from talking about the Carbon project with anyone outside their circle of business-related partners.

Curious glances were cast her way as they went up, along with good mornings and smiles. Rome greeted her fellow passengers back and wished them a nice day in Italian, like she'd practiced before she came here. Thankfully, her team was international, so all their meetings were in English.

"Good morning, guys," she said to the ten people sitting behind their desks, feeling entirely comfortable around them after last night's drinks. Another four were already in her office, and her assistant handed her a coffee when she walked in. "Wow, thank you. I'm sorry, am I late?"

"Nope," Jonathan said as he connected his iPad to the screen behind her desk. "We're all just eager. First week and all," he joked. "Although my head is a little sore from last night."

"Yeah, mine too." Rome chuckled and sat down on the couch next to Eliza and the two marketing executives. "So, I've heard you're quite the genius, Jonathan, and I'm excited to hear about your ideas. Are we going to run through the timelines and set some dates for presentations?"

"We can do that." Jonathan grinned as he opened a presentation on the screen, the first page showing a 3-D rendering of an exclusive looking black credit card, its logo changing each time it flipped around. "But I've already been working on some ideas, so I've asked the other creative members to join us in case there's anything that excites you."

Rome stared at the screen, open-mouthed. "What is this? I mean, when did you do this?"

"Overnight, while I was slightly drunk. I haven't slept yet." His smile widened. "I can't stop once I start; it's both a curse and a blessing."

"It looks amazing." Rome was silent for a long moment, still baffled by the slick visual and the wide selection of fantastic logo varieties.

"It's just a rough mock-up," Jonathan said, holding up a hand. "Once you've narrowed down your selection, I'll do some more in-depth designs, but that will take more time."

At that, Rome and the others laughed. "I'm sorry." Rome sat back, resisting the urge to hug him. "Just so we're clear, these are 'rough mock-ups' you did while you were drunk?" She shook her head incredulously when he nodded.

"Hey, they weren't lying when they said the boy's a genius," Eliza said.

"No, most certainly not. I'm seriously impressed." Rome could hardly believe how lucky she was with people like Jonathan who were able to make her vision become a reality. He'd taken her clumsy scribbles and made them ten times better and more commercial, respecting the original idea. "Okay. I love everything I see, so please talk us through your designs." She turned to the others. "I'm by no means a creative so I'll trust you guys and I'd like Jonathan to take the lead on this."

26

"*Ciao*, Angelo." Nadine sat down in front of the shabby trattoria where Angelo had suggested they meet.

"*Ciao bella.*" He put down two espressos before taking a seat opposite her, crossing one leg over the other as he looked at her quizzically, rubbing his thumb over his rugged jawline.

They'd never met up like this before and Nadine shifted in her chair, conscious of their strange relationship and a little uncomfortable with the vague proposal she was about to lay out for him. *"Come stai?"*

"I'm good. But let's talk in English, please. I don't want my family to listen in." Angelo's brows furrowed, clearly confused as to why Nadine was here. "What's going on? Do we have a problem?" He wedged a hand under his beanie and scratched his head, looking worried.

Nadine shook her head, eyeing the shady looking figures at the neighboring table on the terrace and wondering if he was related to them. "No, we don't. But a friend of mine might."

"Okay." He stirred two bags of sugar through his brew before meeting her gaze. "Tell me."

"My friend Rome..." Nadine added sugar to her espresso too, then sipped it carefully, moaning at the full-bodied flavor. "Damn, this is good stuff."

"Yeah, it's the best." Angelo chuckled at her unexpected enthusiasm, then went straight back to business. "So, your friend...?"

"Yes, you saw her a few weeks back when I was out with that big, bald Italian man. The woman in the blue dress."

"I know who you mean. You wanted me to take pictures."

"That's right. And I probably won't need them, but please don't delete them either." Nadine paused, still not sure where she was going with this. She'd come completely unprepared and hadn't thought her plan through properly. "Anyway, Rome will be going out again with the man who was sitting next to her that night. His name is Matteo Romano. I don't know the details, but I have her address and it's likely he'll send a car over around eight. I'd like you to follow her to the venue and keep an eye on him during their dinner, make sure he doesn't do something he shouldn't." She bit her lip and looked longingly at Angelo's cup. For a place that looked like it was about to fall apart, the coffee was exceptional. "I think he might be a bit 'grabby' if you know what I mean."

Angelo smiled as he noticed her envious stare. He leaned back in his chair to open the door and shouted over his shoulder for someone to bring out another espresso. "And if he gets grabby?"

With a smile on his face, Angelo didn't seem so intimidating anymore, Nadine thought. His prominent nose scrunched, and dimples appeared in his cheeks that were partially covered by a dark stubble. "If he does..." Nadine felt sick at the thought of Rome getting hurt in any way. "Then maybe you could stop him and rough him up a little?" She lowered her gaze to Angelo's big biceps. "Pretend that you're mugging him? I'll pay you more of course, assuming that's how it works?"

Angelo shook his head and laughed out loud. "I can't do that. Who do you think I am? Taking pictures is one thing, physically hurting people is another. That's not my business."

"I apologize." Nadine tilted her head and hesitated as she regarded him. "But you know people in that business?"

Again, he shook his head. "Trust me. You don't want to get involved with people like that. Only trouble will come from it."

Nadine sighed, her mind spinning with potential risks and doom scenarios. "Then could you just keep an eye on them, and let me know where they are? If anything happens, call me, okay?" she finally said. "At least if I'm close by, I can take care of it myself."

Angelo gave her a confused look, then shrugged. "Okay, I can do that. But what if he hurts you?"

"He won't."

"Whatever you say. Just be careful. Is Rome a good friend?"

"Yeah, she is." Nadine wasn't actually sure if they were good friends. They hardly knew each other, and it had felt a little strange between them since their last dinner with Rome's investors. But no matter how much she analyzed their strange yet passionate relationship, she knew one thing for sure: she cared deeply for Rome and she felt protective of her.

"It's nice of you to look out for her." Angelo shot up and straightened when an elderly lady in an apron came out and started yelling at him after putting down Nadine's second espresso. His relaxed demeanor was gone, replaced by something that looked closer to fear, Nadine thought with an amused smirk as she watched the big man before her shrink like a wilting flower. The woman yelled some more, then went back inside, slamming the door shut behind her.

"So that was your mom...," she concluded, after overhearing the conversation. "And she wants you to peel the potatoes?" Nadine snickered, barely able to stop herself from bursting out in laughter. Here was big, scary Angelo—the man the other girls from her agency had recommended but assured her not to get personally involved with as he could be dangerous—being given an earful by his mother. The men at the table next to them were laughing too and told him in Italian to get his ass inside.

Angelo blushed and ignored them. "Yep. That was my mom," he grunted. "I'm supposed to help out in the kitchen today; our chef is at a wedding." He stood up and waved his phone at her. "Text me her details. I'll be done by six; my brother will be taking over from me so I'm available tonight." He lingered on the spot, hesitating.

"Do you like food?"

Nadine spread her arms in a dramatic gesture. "Do I like food? What kind of question is that? Of course I like food, who doesn't?"

"Never mind. I know you do; I've been watching you eat for years." He laughed. "That's why I asked. We do great gnocchi. Want to try some?"

Noting she was feeling hungry, Nadine nodded and smiled. "I do. But please let me pay for it. And for the espressos."

"Absolutely not, this is my family joint. It might not look the part, but our food is great, and I want you to try it."

"Okay. Thank you, I'd be honored to try your mom's gnocchi." Nadine waved as he disappeared inside, then sat back to enjoy the sun and her delicious brew. It was strange that in all the years they'd known each other, they'd never actually had a real conversation, and she decided she liked Angelo. Going on the smell that wafted from the kitchen window, she knew she was going to like the food, too.

27

"This is a rather..." Rome looked around as they followed the waiter. "...cozy place to discuss business, don't you think?" She'd read up on the intimate restaurant in the city center before she left the office. It was not only known for its three Michelin stars, but also for its reputation as a popular place to propose.

"Maybe. But the food is good, and we all need to eat, right?" Matteo pointed at her blazer. "Aren't you warm?"

Rome shook her head. "I'm fine, I think I'll keep it on." She'd purposely not dressed up and insisted she meet him straight from work. Perhaps her jeans and blazer would make it clear she wasn't interested, although she was pretty sure she'd been very clear all along.

"Whatever you want." Matteo discussed something with the waiter, then pulled out a chair for her. Rome hadn't objected when Nadine had done that. In fact, it had made her giddy, and she'd felt special. But with Matteo, she didn't like the chivalry. "You look beautiful tonight."

Rome gave him a polite smile. "Come on, Matteo. I've come straight from work. And although I'm happy to take a compliment, I have a feeling all this..." She gestured around the small dining room where candlelight flickered, and a pianist was playing romantic tunes. "Well, I don't want you to get the wrong idea. This will always be a purely professional relationship."

"Of course." Matteo stared at her for a moment, clearly taken aback by her directness. Then he tilted his head and shot her a puzzled look. "Rome... I think you're the one who's got the wrong idea here, not me. I'm a happily married man."

Rome sighed. This was not going well. Now he'd managed to make her look silly for defending herself which, of course, had been his intention all along. *And I walked right into that trap.* "Great," she finally said. "Then there must have been a misunderstanding. I suppose I didn't get why you wanted to go for dinner tonight as there's nothing left to discuss. The team is fantastic, we're going full steam ahead, and you'll get your update at the monthly board meeting."

"But I'm putting all my faith in you, Rome. I know nothing about this technology, and I prefer more detailed updates, that's just how I work. I may not be part of your team, but I put that team together for you, and I'm within my rights to ask questions. Besides that, I thought you could do with a friend, being here by yourself. Moving to another country can be lonely; I spent two years in Japan myself, so I know how it feels."

"Yes, of course you're entitled to ask questions at any time." Rome tried not to sound irritated. She knew exactly what he was doing; turning the tables on her so she'd feel bad for accusing him of wanting to sleep with her. He had backed her into a corner yet again and now she had to apologize, even if it was just out of politeness. "And I'm sorry; I didn't mean it like that. It's very kind of you to take me out but believe me, I have no problem being on my own. I'm sure your wife misses you enough as it is, with all those networking dinners you have to attend."

"My wife has many friends and keeps herself busy with our family. She's used to me being away." Matteo looked over the wine list and ordered a bottle of champagne to share and a double Scotch for himself.

"I suppose so." Rome didn't really feel like drinking champagne, especially not with Matteo, but she let it slide. "So, you lived in Japan? How was that?" she asked.

"What can I say?" He grimaced. "I'm from Rome. I like the good life and love wine, music, real food. I don't do raw fish and warm alcohol."

"Right." Rome thought back to her week in Tokyo, where she'd pitched her app last year. She'd loved the city and although the investors had kindly declined the collaboration, they'd been courteous, polite and they certainly hadn't tried to hit on her. She quickly decided to focus on a more positive subject matter. "Do you have kids?"

"Yes, my wife and I have two children. Two daughters; they're twelve and sixteen, and I also have a twenty-eight-year-old son from my first marriage. He grew up with his mother in Japan, but he visits sometimes."

"That's nice." Rome thought if safest to keep the conversation around Matteo's family to remind him of them. "And do you visit him in Japan?"

Matteo shook his head. "No. As I said, I'm not a big fan of Japan. I only went there for work and ended up staying longer because of Yoki. Yoki is my ex-wife," he clarified. "But it's long in the past, now." He nodded to the waiter, who brought over his Scotch and downed half of it while their flutes were being filled. "What about you? Boyfriend? I noticed you're not wearing a wedding ring."

"No, I'm single." Rome opened her menu. "I don't have time to date, especially not now." She cleared her throat and straightened herself before she got down to business. "So, tell me. What did you want to know?"

Their conversation felt forced over dinner, with Matteo clearly making up questions as he went along while drinking way more than he should, and Rome answering everything in detail while he zoned out, occasionally looking at her cleavage. He kept bringing the subject back to Rome and dating, with inappropriate remarks about the absence of sex and intimacy when single, and Rome kept going back to the Carbon app. He was slurring his words a little now, and as she put her spoon down next to her tiramisu, she was grateful the night was almost over. Dinner was never a short affair in Italy, and although the food was delicious, sitting through four courses with Matteo had felt like she'd entered an endurance contest. She was glad she'd been clear from the beginning, because even though he was still unprofessional, there was no way there could be any misunderstanding now. Although the night had been a pain in the ass, at least it was unlikely he would ask her out again. She'd had a glass of champagne and a glass of red wine, and Matteo had polished off the rest of the bottles, after two more large glasses of Scotch. When he ordered espresso and grappa, she suppressed a sigh, knowing she'd be here for another twenty minutes at least. It wasn't up to her to comment on his drinking though; she'd leave that to his wife.

"I'll call a cab for us," Matteo said after he'd paid. "We can drop you off home first."

"There's no need. I live close by, so I'll just walk back. I like walking." Rome stood up. "Thank you for dinner. I hope I've managed to clear things up for you." She seriously doubted he'd taken in a word she'd said.

"Yes, this was very helpful." Matteo put his hand on her lower back as they walked out into the alleyway where the restaurant was situated. "Let me at least walk you to the main street. It's not safe here for a woman on her own."

Rome wanted to say she'd felt nothing but safe since the day she'd arrived in Rome, but she had no energy left for a discussion. It was late and she just wanted to get home, run a hot bath and soak off the nasty aftertaste of Matteo's company. "Sure. Thank you."

They passed a man who was smoking a cigarette while talking to someone on the phone, and she followed him with her eyes, trying to remember if she'd seen him before. There was something familiar about him, but then again, he also looked like a typical Italian, so she could easily have mistaken him for someone in the office, or one of her neighbors. When Matteo's hand pressed harder into her back and his fingers curled around her waist, Rome had had enough. After all her efforts, he was not giving up and it was making her furious.

"Please take your hand away," she said sternly, turning to him. "It makes me feel uncomfortable and you have no business touching me like that." Matteo narrowed his eyes as if he couldn't quite believe what she was saying. When he made no effort to remove it, Rome took his hand and removed it herself, then stepped away from him.

"You American girls," he said with sarcasm dripping through his voice. "You all think you're so precious."

"Not wanting to be touched has nothing to do with being precious. Just keep your hands off me and we won't have a problem." Rome walked away from him, but he caught up and took her wrist, forcing her to turn back around. "Let go of me, Matteo, or I swear you'll be in trouble." She tried to free herself, but he was stronger and much bigger than her. Panic hit her when she realized she wasn't prepared for this, and she wouldn't be able to get away unless she kicked him where it hurt.

Matteo shook his head. "I think we need to have a talk, Rome. You're forgetting that you're here because of me, so if you're rude, there will be consequences." His bloodshot eyes raked over her, and he pulled her in closer. "If you go spreading rumors about me, you'll be very, very sorry. Do you hear me?"

Rome felt her heart beat wildly in her chest. She'd never been in a situation like this before, and had always expected to be in control and fighting back if it ever happened. Instead, she was paralyzed by fear and just couldn't seem to move. His unpleasant alcohol-drenched breath on her face, and his hand making its way down to her behind sent a surge of adrenaline through her, and she realized now was the time to kick him and scream for help. Just as she was about to lift her knee, someone came up behind him and pulled him away by his hair.

"You fucking pig!" a woman's voice yelled. It all happened so fast that Rome couldn't work out what was going on at first. "You think this is okay, do you?"

Matteo bent over, grabbing his crotch that was undoubtedly hurting after her knight in shining armor landed a fierce and well-positioned blow. Then the baseball cap wearing figure in dark clothing turned her way, and Rome gasped when she saw that the woman currently pounding him was Nadine. "You just couldn't help yourself, huh?" She pushed him violently away and Matteo fell to the ground, protecting his face with his hands.

"Stop!" he yelled. "Please stop."

"I believe that's what this woman just said to you." Nadine looked down at him sniveling on the ground. "I'm sick of people like you and Louise who think they can have anything they want as long as they throw enough money around." She planted her foot on his stomach now, making him yell even louder.

"This is a misunderstanding," Matteo yelled. "I don't know who Louise is and I was only walking Rome home."

Afraid she might actually harm him, Rome tried to stop Nadine and pull her away, but she was saved when a man took hold of her from behind and lifted her up. Nadine sharply elbowed him in the face and continued her rant, only stopping when two waiters from the restaurant came out and dragged her back. She shouted at the waiters, pointing at Matteo who was lying in a fetal position, his hands still covering his forehead. It wasn't until Rome took Nadine's face in her hands and forced her to look at her that she calmed down a little. She said something else to the waiters, shook herself out of their grip and then gained her composure, putting a protective arm around Rome. "Let's get out of here," she said in a breathless whisper. "You need to go to the police."

Rome was shaking as she let Nadine guide her away from the scene. She had no idea what might have happened if Nadine hadn't shown up and thinking of it made her nauseous. She heard Nadine thank someone in Italian and when she looked up, she saw it was the smoking man they'd passed. He gave her a nod, then lit another cigarette and disappeared into a courtyard.

"Thank you," she said as they stopped in front of Nadine's scooter. "How did you know where I was? You came out of nowhere."

"I'll explain everything later. Let's get to the police station first." Nadine cupped Rome's face with both hands, stoking her thumbs over her cheeks. "Are you okay?" she asked, her expression softening.

"Yeah, I'm okay. Just very shaken." Rome stopped her when she searched for the key to the chain lock in her pockets. "But so are you. You went crazy back there, and I don't think you should ride your scooter right now. Can we just walk? Will you come with me?"

"Of course I'll come with you, I'm your witness."

Rome looked at Nadine's hands, lifted one and kissed her knuckles. "You need to put some ice on that. It's swelling up, and it looks sore."

"Don't worry about it, I'm fine." Nadine took her hand, then changed her mind and put an arm around her instead. She held her close as they walked in the direction of the police station.

28

Nadine took in Rome's spacious apartment that she'd viewed three weeks ago. It was really nice, now that it looked inhabited, but it needed some personal touches. Not that any of that mattered now; Rome might not want to stay here after what had happened tonight. She passed the bedroom and went into the bathroom, where she ran a bath with some bath salts she'd found in the cabinet.

Rome had been quiet on the way back from the police station, and Nadine hadn't wanted to drag it all up again by asking more questions. She wished she'd gotten to her sooner, but it had all happened so fast. Angelo had called her when Rome and Matteo left the restaurant. The place was too intimate and small for him to blend in, so he'd waited outside for them to finish. "He's drunk," was all he'd said, and that was enough for Nadine to run, rather than walk over from the bar where she was waiting.

"Do you want to take a bath?" She asked, walking over to Rome, who was hunched on the couch, holding the mint tea she'd made for her. She sat down next to her and stroked her back. "Or would you rather just go to bed?"

"No, a bath would be nice. Will you join me?"

"If you want me to."

R ome leaned back against Nadine, quietly crying. "I'm so angry," she said between sniffs. "I never thought something like that would happen to me, ever. I don't know what he would have done if you hadn't shown up."

Nadine wrapped her arms around Rome and pulled her closer. "Matteo deserved every bit of pain he got." She stroked Rome's hair and kissed the top of her head. "I should have just killed him when I had the chance."

Rome shook her head. "I should have stopped you sooner. He's a powerful man with many connections, and he could make your life really hard if he finds out it was you."

"No, he won't. If anyone's life is going to be hard, it's Matteo's." Nadine paused, sensing Rome's hesitation. "Going to the police was the right thing to do. You might think he can make or break your career right now, but you have rights, and even within the shady system in Italy, people get punished for doing stuff like this."

"I know." Rome let out a deep sigh and Nadine could feel her calm down a little. "I just don't know where to go from here. There's no handbook that tells you how to deal with powerful perverts who pay your bills. It's my life's work we're talking about here. I can't just walk away."

"You don't have to walk away. He will."

Rome sat up and turned to her. "The police weren't very helpful. Why didn't they just arrest him right away? I mean, who needs proof, you're my eyewitness." She huffed. "I can't believe they asked if there could have been a misunderstanding."

"I know that doesn't seem fair, but they have to ask these

things, and they will question him tomorrow, hopefully when he's in the office, or at home with his wife, because people need to know what kind of person he is." Nadine stroked her hair and kissed her temple. "You need to talk to the HR department, too."

"I know." Rome sank back again and closed her eyes at the reassuring caress, grateful for Nadine's presence. There was nothing sexual about taking a bath with her tonight. It was just warm and comforting, and Rome felt safe with her. "What happened to you? You totally flipped and didn't even hear me yell. It was like you were so enraged that you had no idea what you were doing."

Nadine sighed. "I don't know what came over me. I just wanted to protect you." Nadine wrapped her arms around Rome. "I've never been so angry in my life."

Despite her blue mood, Rome's heart filled with something beautiful and warm, something she hadn't felt since her youth. Nadine cared about her. She'd be in her life in one way or another, and Rome knew that she would let her. Clinging onto Nadine's arms, she hesitated before she asked the question that had been on her mind for hours. "Who is Louise?"

Nadine rested her chin on Rome's shoulder and was silent for a moment, remembering what she'd said to Matteo. "Louise is the woman who hired me as her escort yesterday." She took a couple of deep breaths, getting worked up again at the memory. Where did all this rage come from? She'd never had a problem with her anger before. "I've slept with her a couple of times. As I told you before, I did it because I wanted to, and she didn't pay me for it. But I guess she'd come to expect it, so she bought me this hideously expensive dress and lured me out to a secluded hotel outside the city..." Nadine's voice broke as she continued. "It made me feel ashamed and for a moment, I really, really hated myself. She made me hate myself."

Now it was Rome's turn to take Nadine in her arms. She shifted and straddled her in the spacious bathtub, wrapped her arms around her and pressed Nadine's face against her chest. She could feel warm tears trickling down her skin. "What happened?"

"Nothing physical happened, but I left during dinner after she said things to me that made me feel cheap. I've never felt like that before." Nadine lifted her chin and locked her eyes with Rome's. "I didn't want to have sex with Louise because I couldn't stop thinking of you." She held up a hand. "Don't get me wrong, I know you prefer to be just friends and I respect that. I thought I wanted that too..."

Rome tilted her head and looked at her intently as she felt her heart racing. "But?"

Nadine shrugged. "But now I'm not so sure anymore."

Rome nodded slowly as she let Nadine's words sink in. Even after the horrible night she'd had, she could feel the bond between them, and hearing her say that meant the world to her. Nadine looked beautiful; naked and free of makeup, her hair casually pulled together in a lose top knot, her damp skin shimmering in the dim light of the candles she'd lit. "How did you know where I was? You still haven't told me."

"I had you followed." Nadine swallowed hard. "Please don't be mad, I just didn't trust Matteo. I've spent years going out with men like him and I just had this feeling about him. I didn't want you to see me and so I asked my friend Angelo to follow you and let me know where you were."

"I can't believe you had someone follow me..." Rome was silent for what seemed like an eternity, and Nadine was worried she'd lost her. Admittedly, she'd gone too far. It was a controlling thing to do, and Rome didn't seem like a woman who appreciated being checked up on.

"Please say something," she begged.

"I don't know what to say." Rome bit her lip and winced. "You should have told me about Angelo. You can't do that to me, ever again. Do you understand?"

"I understand." Nadine nodded.

"But then if you hadn't..." Rome continued, and Nadine shivered at that thought. "Thank you for caring. You saved me tonight."

Nadine let out the breath she'd been holding and pulled Rome into a hug. "Please promise me you won't ever go near that creep again."

"Of course not. I'll make sure I don't have to be in the same room with him, from now on." Rome kissed her lightly on the lips. She didn't mean to, it just seemed natural, the way they were sitting, so intimately. "Fuck," she said, biting her lip as she winced. "I shouldn't have done that. I..."

"Hey, it's fine." Nadine kissed her back and smiled. "Do you want me to stay here tonight?" She wiped her thumbs under Rome's eyes, removing the mascara stains. "I just want to hold you and make sure you're okay."

"Yeah, I'd like that." Rome didn't just say it; she felt the need to keep Nadine close deep in her core. Perhaps that thought was even more frightening than what had happened tonight, but she wasn't in the mind space to psychoanalyze herself right now. "Let's go to bed," she whispered.

29

"Hey, wake up."

Rome opened her eyes and blinked, relieved to see it was Nadine stroking her face, rather than her mother trying to choke her. She felt clammy and wiped her forehead, then realized she was lying in a pool of her own sweat. "Fuck…" She sighed. "I'm sorry, did I wake you?"

"I think you had a nightmare," Nadine said.

"Yeah, I did." Rome wanted to wrap her arms around Nadine but was afraid she'd feel her trembling. She hadn't had the nightmare in years. In fact, she didn't dream much at all anymore, or at least her dreams weren't memorable, and she cursed herself for going through the photo albums on Sunday, reawakening sad memories.

"Do you want to talk about it?"

Rome sat up and threw the covers off her. "No. I just need a shower."

Nadine nodded, and Rome was grateful that she didn't enquire further. "Want me to make some coffee? It's five am, so we might as well get up…"

"Thank you, that would be really great." Rome felt a

lump in her throat when she looked at Nadine. She was so kind and caring, so intuitive, and she said all the right things. Not once had she felt trapped in her presence. "Are you sure it's not too early for you?"

"Not at all." Nadine got up and shot her a sweet smile. "I like seeing the sun come up." She pointed to a robe that was hanging from a hook on the door. "Can I borrow that?"

"Of course." Rome followed Nadine with her eyes as she crossed the room, in awe of her beautiful, naked body, and just like that, the dream was forgotten. Even last night's events didn't weigh on her so heavily anymore, and she felt like she could breathe again. They'd slept naked, wrapped in each other's arms. Nadine had held her until she fell asleep and although it was strange to have her here in the morning, it was also wonderful.

She jumped under the shower for a quick wash and could smell the coffee as she dried herself off. It was still dark outside but there was a slight shimmer over the skyline, and from the cloudless sky she guessed it would be another beautiful sunny day. Coming from Portland, where sunny days were a gift rather than a given, the morning here felt like a blessing when she opened the curtains. She didn't bother getting dressed but wrapped herself in a fluffy towel instead as she walked into the living room, where the balcony doors were wide open. Nadine had made herself comfortable out there, her long legs resting on another chair as she sipped her coffee.

Rome poured herself a cup from the pot and sat down next to her.

"Better?" Nadine asked.

"Yeah." Rome drank her coffee in silence while they watched the city come to life. Something about sitting here as the sun came up made her want to talk, or at least explain why she'd acted so strange over dinner with her investors. "I have extreme detachment issues," she suddenly said. She could feel her pulse racing at the realization she'd just blurted out something so personal.

If Nadine was surprised by her random statement, she didn't let it show. "Okay. Can I ask why?"

Rome was quiet as she watched the shadows on the Colosseum and the Forum fade, the old ruins slowly coming into sharp focus as if rising up from the earth. She felt good here, both in her new space and in Nadine's company, and for the first time in her life, she answered without thinking. "My mother left me when I was twelve." She locked her eyes with Nadine's. "She left me and my father for no reason other than that she wanted out of her domestic life. I never saw it coming, neither did my father. She was always fun and caring before that."

"Jesus, Rome. I'm so sorry you had to go through that." Nadine's voice was genuine, but there was no trace of pity, and Rome appreciated that.

"It's in the past." She put her cup down, pulled her legs up and hugged her knees. "But it left me a little dysfunctional in the dating department. I don't trust people, and I generally don't let anyone get close to me. Frankly, it's unheard of that you're here in my space, and that I'm talking to you about this."

Nadine nodded. "Okay. But you are."

"I am." Rome paused. "I trust you and... I like you. And because I've never let people in, I've never felt jealousy before." She shrugged. "So, when I saw you with Flavio, I felt hurt, even though that was silly, and I'm sorry that I overreacted."

"It's not silly." Nadine smiled. "I was jealous when I saw you with that lilac-haired woman too."

"You were?" Rome felt her lips pull into a smile. "Well, there's no need."

"I know." Nadine paused. "Do you know where your mother is?"

"Yes." Rome frowned. "I mean, I knew. I haven't kept track of her lately, but I used to be obsessed with her whereabouts when I was younger. I think I was desperately trying to understand something I couldn't, or maybe I was looking for excuses to justify why she did what she did. She moved around a lot and made sure to stay under the radar at first but after a while, she stopped covering her tracks and I discovered she'd moved to Nashville and was singing with a band. It was as if she didn't even care that I would see a picture of her on social media, smiling in a bar somewhere and having fun with her new friends from her new life."

"So she just started over?" Nadine asked.

"A couple of times. But the other times never involved leaving a child behind. She remarried twice as far as I'm aware, and she left them too."

"That's harsh." Nadine put a hand on Rome's thigh. "Do you ever feel the desire to see her again?"

Rome shook her head. "Not anymore. I wanted to see her when I was younger but thankfully, my father stopped me. She would have only hurt me again."

"Yes, that's likely." Nadine reached for her hand and laced their fingers together. "Thank you for telling me."

"I just thought you should know, so you understand why I get scared when I start feeling things, because I do have feelings for you." Rome could hardly believe how forward she was being, talking about matters she hadn't even processed herself.

Nadine gave her a slow nod, her eyes softening with tenderness. "I have feelings for you too. And if I'm honest,

I'd like to see where this goes, but I can't make any promises. Neither of us has experience with relationships; I have trouble on that front, too."

"Why is that?" Rome asked.

"I don't know." Nadine fell silent and stared down at her hands. "I think because of my job. I started fairly young, and I guess I liked that I never had to work hard for anything. Not for money, not for relationships... The couple of times I tried—and with tried I mean that sometimes I dated someone for a week or two—it always ended in arguments about my job, so I just stopped dating altogether and told myself it wasn't for me without ever really trying."

"I think you've been lonely too," Rome said, meeting her eyes.

"Maybe." Nadine let out a deep sigh. "So, what are we going to do?" There was another long silence as neither of them had an answer to that question.

"How about we go out, see how we feel and take it from there?" Rome said in a soft voice. "I have to cancel tonight as I have to speak to HR and go back to the police station, but maybe we can meet up later this week?"

"I'd like that." Nadine looked resolute as she hesitated. "I have to work Friday and Saturday night. But I can promise you I won't sleep with any of my clients or anyone else for that matter. I don't want anyone but you."

"Okay." Rome put on a brave smile. "That helps."

"Can I pick you up at seven am on Sunday? I'll take you treasure hunting at the flea market if you don't mind getting up early. We could get you some stuff for your apartment?" Nadine suggested.

"That sounds like fun."

"Great. Sunday it is. Do you want me to come to the police station with you later today?"

Rome shook her head. "Thank you, but I'll be fine. I'm not so shaken anymore, mostly furious."

"So am I." Nadine pulled Rome out of her chair and onto her lap. "Will you be okay at work?" she asked, wrapping her arms around her from behind.

"Yeah, I'll be fine. I doubt Matteo will show his face anytime soon; he's rarely in the office as it is." Rome sunk back and buried her face against Nadine's shoulder. "Thank you," she said, swallowing down a lump in her throat. "Thank you for being here."

30

"Mom!" Nadine's face lit up when she picked up her phone.

"Nadine, honey. How are you?"

"I'm okay." Nadine put on her faux cheerful tone; the one she always used when her mother called. Not that she wasn't feeling cheerful, but it was just one of those things she did without thinking. Just like the way some people talked to their kids, or their pets, her voice seemed to go up a notch when she spoke to her mother. Aware of it, she rolled her eyes at herself in the mirror, releasing the curling iron from her hair as she wedged the phone between her chin and her shoulder. "Just got home from work," she lied.

"Good day at the store?"

"Yeah, fairly busy." Nadine never elaborated unless her mother specifically asked, as she didn't like lying to her. "How are you?"

"Oh, you know, this and that. I went to my morning yoga class, and I thought I'd give you a call before I go to work. Xander and I are seeing a play tonight on Broadway, but I can't remember what it's called. It's some small production he's been involved with."

"That sounds fun. Everything good with you and Xander?"

"Yes, we're great. He's getting close to his retirement date now, but you know Xander; he doesn't want to hear about it." Her mother cleared her throat. "What about you, honey? Are you seeing someone?"

"No." Nadine wasn't sure why her mother kept asking her the same question, since she always got the same answer. "But..." She quickly swallowed her words, shocked by the 'but' that had slipped from her tongue. She was so used to lying to her mother that telling the truth seemed unthinkable.

"But what?"

Nadine switched off the curling iron, put it to the side and sat down on her bed. "I met someone." She pursed her lips, carefully considering her words. "I don't know where it's heading, but I really like her."

"Sweetie..." Her mother fell silent, clearly surprised. "That's wonderful."

"Well, as I said, it's still very early days, but I care about her a lot." She smiled. "Whatever happens, I know we'll always be friends. We just click in the most amazing way, even though we couldn't be more different."

"Tell me about her. Where did you meet?" her mother asked eagerly.

"Her name is Rome, and we met in a hotel bar. She's American, and she's here to roll out an app she's developed. She's incredibly smart and driven and beautiful."

"Rome, that's a nice name and very appropriate considering where you are."

"Yeah." Nadine suppressed a swooning sigh. "I'm taking her to the flea market on Sunday to find some stuff for her new apartment."

"That's sweet. I'm so happy for you, and the way you talk about her is so unlike you." Her mother sounded emotional. "I was starting to think you'd be by yourself forever."

"Yeah... I don't really know what I'm doing as I don't have much experience with relationships, and I'm scared that I'll hurt her," Nadine admitted. It felt liberating to finally be open and honest with her mother. For once, she could just say what was on her mind without being careful with her words or making up excuses. "I've been scared of a lot of things lately, and... well, it's made me realize that maybe I've been living in a bubble, that I've never actually dealt with real life before."

"Oh honey, you were always in a bubble, even as a kid," her mother said in a sweet voice. "Remember your bedroom in our old house? After your father passed away, you spent weeks turning it into something out of a fairy tale, with Christmas lights and white organza draped over the broomsticks attached to your bed. You even covered the lampshades in white feathers; I had to take you to the doctor because you'd superglued your fingers together."

Nadine shook her head and groaned. "Oh God, I remember that. I haven't touched superglue since."

"I let you, because you needed something to focus on," her mother continued. "And I think it helped you to get through that difficult period. You spent all your time in there, reading your father's old art books and making perfumes that you bottled in small spice jars and handed out at school. The parents complained their kids smelled like oregano and cinnamon."

LISE GOLD

"I think I've come a long way from oregano." Nadine chuckled, but her smile didn't reach her eyes. It still hurt to think about her father's death, and she generally avoided talking about that time.

"I'm sure you have. Are you still working on those perfumes you told me about?"

"Yeah. it's going well, I'll fill you in next time we speak."

"Okay." Her mother paused, and Nadine could picture her smiling in her recliner while she was on the phone to her. "I'm glad we're finally talking."

"What do you mean?" Nadine asked, knowing very well what her mother meant. "We talk every week."

"We do, but we don't *really* talk, like this. About things that matter. You're always so confident and everything is always perfect when I ask you about your life. This is the first time you've admitted that you're scared, and that's a big deal to me because I finally have the chance to be there for you, and to help you as your mother."

"You're right. I don't know why I feel the need to talk now, I guess there are just some things that aren't in my control anymore."

"Like love."

"Yeah, like love."

"You never dated," her mother said. "Not even in high school. Kids that age didn't understand art the way you did, they weren't touched by music the way it touched you. God knows where you got that cultural streak from because your father and I were about as ordinary and working-class as people come." She chuckled. "I hoped that would change once you grew up, that you'd meet someone with the same interests, but no one was ever good enough to live in the beautiful world you'd created for yourself. Your first apartment was like a palace compared to our small house, and I still don't understand how you were able to afford it, but you made it work, somehow."

Nadine had no idea how to reply to that because she couldn't tell her mother she'd been dating men and women in return for a lot of money. "I just never met anyone I liked enough to take it further," she finally said, remembering the first girl who walked out on her as soon as she found out what she did for a living.

"Maybe. But I'm glad you've met someone now. I want you to be happy."

"I am happy, Mom. You don't have to worry about me."

"I know. Just remember that it might be comfortable to live in a bubble, but it's not real. Life isn't always smooth sailing and sometimes you have to bite the bullet and deal with things that are difficult or challenging. Relationships can be tough, but don't give up, just because it isn't perfect. Will you promise me that?"

"It's not a relationship," Nadine said, terrified by that word. Or was it? They had agreed to date and to be monogamous. Wasn't that exactly what a relationship was? She sighed before she continued, suddenly unsure if they were even dating. Did going to the flea market count as a date? "But yes, I promise I'll try. I want to try."

"Good girl. Now go take that woman out and if it feels right, don't let her go, do you hear me?"

"I hear you. I have to go; I'm meeting someone."

"Okay. Bye, honey. I love you. Take care."

"Love you too, Mom." Nadine hung up and noted that for the first time, she felt calmer after speaking to her mother, and she realized she'd missed feeling close to her. They were always joking and gossiping on the phone, but she never talked about her feelings. Her mother was right; she had to fight for Rome, and somehow conquer her own fear of commitment at the same time. Sunday couldn't come soon enough but first things first. Rome would be going to the police station soon, and although she'd said she'd be fine by herself, Nadine knew it would be better to have an Italian speaker there with her, just to make sure there were no misunderstandings with such a delicate case.

31

"Are you saying I'm lying?" Rome felt like she was about to burst with anger as she slammed her fist on the desk at the police station. Nadine had surprised her by showing up unannounced, and together they'd waited in the busy station for over three hours, only for someone to tell her the case was about to get closed due to lack of evidence. "Because I'm not fucking lying. My eye-witness is right here with me."

"No, that's not what I'm saying." The police officer opposite her looked genuinely regretful as he shook his head. "But the waiters we interviewed after speaking to Mr. Romano confirmed his story that you had a fair amount to drink, and that your memory might be a bit muddled."

"She was not drunk," Nadine said. "I can vouch for that, and so can the police officer who was on duty when we reported this." She continued in Italian, raising her voice at the officer until he managed to silence her.

"Don't you get that he bribed them?" Rome held her breath and counted to ten, afraid she might do something she regretted if she didn't calm down right now. "This man is swimming in money, and those waiters earn minimum wage. I already told you five times in my statement that he was the one who was drunk, not me. And what about *my* eyewitness?"

"We have your statement too," the officer said, turning to Nadine. "But the waiters claim to have witnessed the incident too, and they say..." He narrowed his eyes as he looked over the paperwork. "... that it looked like it was a misunderstanding resulting in an argument."

Rome leaned in and glared at him. "They weren't even there when it happened. So that's it? Mr. Romano gets away with sexual assault? Why didn't your team interview him right away and give him a breathalyzer test? And why didn't your officer on duty give me a breathalyzer test when I was here? I mean, what the fuck is going on?" She continued, despite Nadine pinching her hand, letting her know she was going too far. "Has Matteo Romano got the police in his pockets too?"

"You need to calm down, Miss Foster. Think about what you're saying, accusations like that are not taken lightly here." The officer leaned in too and cleared his throat. "I am terribly sorry, but there's nothing more I can do for you. Your statement is on file, so if this happens again, we will have the records, but this case will be closed."

Nadine argued some more with him in Italian, slamming her hand on the paperwork in front of him, but he kept shaking his head and pointing to the dozens of people waiting behind them.

Rome huffed. "So he needs to harass more women before something gets done?"

"I'm not in a position to advise you on anything beyond police business," the young man said. "But if I may give you some friendly advice, you could always hire a lawyer, if you can afford that." He looked around the station and lowered his voice. "Mr. Romano is a powerful man. It will take more than one case to take him down. If he is guilty, and he did this to you, he might have done it to others."

"Right." Rome nodded, grinding her teeth in exasperation. It wasn't the junior officer's fault; he was just the messenger and he hadn't even been at the police station when she'd reported the assault last night, but she still needed to vent her anger. "So only people who can afford a lawyer might get justice, is that how it works?" She tilted her head and frowned when he didn't answer. "And hypothetically speaking, how would I find these 'others' without help from the police?"

"I can't answer that, but perhaps your lawyer will have some ideas." He moved his chair back and stood up, letting Rome and Nadine know the conversation was over.

Rome shook her head as she grabbed her purse and got up too. "I guess I'll just have to find myself a lawyer then." She took Nadine's hand and walked out, tears of frustration stinging her eyes as she sat down on a bench in front of the station. Bella, the head of the HR department, had listened to her story and taken it seriously, but she'd also told Rome it was a case for the police, and that she could only provide mediation between Matteo and her, as no previous cases of sexual harassment against him had been reported. Rome was not looking forward to dealing with fake apologies and nonsense regarding a misunderstanding from her side, and she'd told her she wasn't ready for mediation yet because she needed a plan first.

"I can't believe that just happened," Nadine said, looking deflated as she wiped the tears from Rome's cheeks.

"It's so incredibly unfair." Rome took a deep breath and tried to compose herself as she looked at Nadine.

"It is." Nadine paused. "He's right. Your only option would be a lawyer now. I'm so sorry I couldn't help you more."

Rome shot her a sad smile. "I'm just glad you're here, it really helped." She searched for her phone in her purse. "There's no way I'm going to avoid the office; it could take months until this is settled with a lawyer."

"Of course not. Matteo will have to stay away, and if you make a case against him, the judge might give him a restraining order while you battle it out in court." Nadine shrugged. "I have no idea how these things work, but I can't imagine they would let him work with you under these circumstances."

"I hope so." Rome looked up the number of her American lawyer. "Now that we're so close to launching the app, they won't take back my funding, that's for sure. People have been hired, investments have been made and the stakes would be too high for them, even if I attack Matteo personally."

"Exactly. This has nothing to do with *Nero*, main investor or not."

Rome let out a long sigh as she closed her eyes and rested her head on Nadine's shoulder. "God, this is so messed up. For the first time, I really don't know what to do." Normally, Rome was good at problem solving. It was what she'd done since she'd started with the Carbon app; perfecting a system over and over until it was good enough to change the world. Rome couldn't count the amount of times she'd been stuck so badly she thought she'd never get over the hurdles, but she had eventually. It was crazy how getting justice for a straightforward crime with an eyewitness was more complicated than solving worldwide privacy issues on a commercial platform.

"You do know what to do," Nadine said, pulling her closer. "You're going to call your lawyer, explain the situation and ask him for advice. And then, you're going to fight this bastard, and I'll do anything I can to help you, okay? I'm here for you." She kissed Rome's temple and ran a hand through her hair. "It's no doubt true that if he's done this to you, he's probably done it to others. We'll just have to find them."

"Yeah, you're right." Rome tried to clear her mind and told herself to solve this problem the way she usually would at work—in a calm and analytical manner while anticipating potential obstacles. There was no easy solution, because Matteo was good at covering both his tracks and his own ass, but Rome was confident she was going to find other victims and together, they would make him pay. Being specialized in intellectual property law, Michael was unlikely to take on the case or even be able to represent her in Italian court, but she trusted him and he'd be the best person to talk to first.

32

"Okay, I love them," Rome said, staring at the enormous electric blue enameled plant pots. And I could definitely do with some greenery in my apartment but how are we going to get them there? I can barely lift them." Then her eyes darted to the Persian rug she'd been admiring. "There's so much nice stuff here, but if I'm not going to stay for that long, I'm not sure if there's any point."

"Of course there is. You need to surround yourself with things that make you happy and feel at home, and it's not like any of it is expensive." Nadine inspected the rug. "That stain will come out and it will look great with your furniture." She scrolled through her phone and smiled. "And I think I've got someone who can help with the transportation, so pick whatever you want."

"Really? You have a friend with a van?"

"Something like that." Nadine laughed. "The milkman. He only works in the mornings and uses his van to make some extra cash in the afternoon. I always call him when I have something big that needs transporting, and if you pay him a little extra, he'll bring his son and they'll carry it upstairs for you. I'll text him now."

Rome laughed. "That's great. In that case, maybe you can help me find something for my walls, too. The apartment is wonderful, but very minimalistic and I feel like it needs an injection of color."

"I agree with you, it needs a bit of soul." They continued their scavenger hunt, going through every stall at the outdoor market that was bustling with locals, of which most of them looked like they were just there to socialize, sitting on the merchandise while talking over coffee and cigarettes. Nadine found some copper candlesticks and a big vase for Rome too, and made a mental note to buy her a bunch of red roses. Was that too much? Going from casual to red roses? If it was confusing before, it was even more confusing now. They hadn't seen each other since they'd left the police station as Rome had been busy liaising with Michael, her lawyer, but they had spoken on the phone and messaged back and forth. Their exchanges had been serious, with Rome informing her about the selection of Italian law firms Michael had recommended to her, and so there had been no flirtations from either side. She felt the pull though, and she saw the desire in Rome's eyes too, every time she glanced at her. Nadine felt her heart beat violently when Rome casually reached for her hand as she pointed to a rattan daybed.

"How about that for my balcony?"

"It's nice. I think it will look great." Nadine hoped Rome couldn't see how flustered she felt. She'd never had a problem with women, and she'd certainly never had a problem flirting with Rome before, but now she just didn't know how to act anymore. Should she have kissed her when she picked her up? She'd wanted to, but by the time Rome got on the back of her scooter, it had been too late.

"Hey, are you okay?" Rome turned to her and took her other hand, a hint of insecurity flashing across her features.

"Uh-huh." Nadine hated the tremble in her own voice.

"No, you're not." Rome pulled her toward a bench and sat down, then patted the space next to her. "You've been acting strange all morning, like you don't know what to do with yourself." She studied Nadine as she slumped down. "And since you're usually this overly confident and charming Casanova-type, I get the feeling there's something you're not telling me."

Nadine pursed her lips and stared at her like a deer caught in the headlights. She was so aware of her body and her hands, and the new sensation made her feel clumsy. "I... I don't know," she stammered, picking at a fingernail. "I guess I just don't know how to behave around you anymore."

"Why?"

"Because I don't know what's going on between us. I mean, I said I wouldn't sleep with anyone else, there's this crazy attraction between us and I deeply care about you... And I know you like me too... So, is this a date?"

Rome noticeably relaxed as she shot her an endearing smile and put a hand on her thigh. "If it's a date, it's the best date I've ever had."

Nadine smiled too. "Really? The flea market? Then your past dates must have been pretty shitty."

"Yeah, you could say that." Rome turned and draped an arm over the bench behind Nadine. "But I'd have a good time with you anywhere." She took a deep breath, looking tense as she blurted out the question that had clearly been on her mind, too. "So, are we dating? Because I'd like to date you."

"I'd like to date you, too." Nadine ran a hand through

Rome's hair, breaking the awkwardness. "I'm just worried because we're both terrible dating material and I don't want you to get hurt."

Rome tilted her head, leaning into her touch. "Look, I understand this is new and confusing. It is for me, too. But just be yourself, do what feels natural. If it doesn't work out, I promise I won't break. And if I panic..." She shrugged. "Well, I'll try not to, because I don't want to hurt you either."

"It sounds like a recipe for disaster." Nadine couldn't help but laugh, because the two of them together really were a mess when it came to relationships.

"True," Rome agreed. "So let's just take it one day at a time and keep in mind that we're friends first." She shot Nadine a sexy smile. "And dating isn't all scary. You know what the best thing is?"

"No, but now I'm eager to find out." Nadine could see where Rome was heading with this, but she needed to hear it because her body was on fire.

"We can have sex or make out anytime and anywhere we want without having to overthink it. It's simple, really."

"Anywhere?" Nadine arched a brow and looked around. "I seriously want to kiss you right now, but I don't see anyone under the age of sixty here, and I'm not sure how the traditional Roman Catholics wandering around would feel about two women making out in front of them."

Rome laughed and gave her a quick kiss on her cheek. "Then this will just have to do for now." She gestured to Nadine's phone that she was still holding. "So, is the milkman available?"

Nadine grinned sheepishly as she checked her phone. "Yeah. He says we need to take everything we've bought to the coffee shop..." She scanned their surroundings, then pointed to a small coffee house at the end of the market.

"That would be that one over there. And if we tip the owner, he'll keep it in the back for the milkman to pick up later this afternoon. He says he can drop it off at your apartment any time after that."

"That easy, huh? You have amazing contacts."

"I do." Nadine stood up and held out her hand. "What do you want to do after we've stored your purchases?"

"I don't know. What do you suggest?"

"Well, since this date is a little unconventional and started out at the flea market, I feel like we need to continue with more totally random activities. How about church? It's Sunday, so if we hurry, we can make it for mass."

"Church?" Rome frowned, trying to work out if she was serious. "If you try to convert me it will officially be the most awkward date in history."

"No, I'm not trying to convert you." Nadine gave her an amused look. "I actually think you'll enjoy it."

"Okay, I'm open to anything." Rome chuckled. "But we can't make out in church either."

"Then we'll just have to wait." Nadine winked. "All the best things are worth waiting for."

33

The basilica of Santa Maria Maggiore was an impressive sight, and Rome stared up at its huge structure while Nadine parked her scooter.

"They have a mass in Latin at ten am every Sunday," Nadine said as they walked toward the security gates together. "Even if you're not religious, it's an incredible experience so I thought you might appreciate it. Bernini is also buried here. You know, the famous Roman sculptor and architect," she continued. "This is one of the four Papal major basilicas, which means it's part of the Vatican, even though it's on Italian grounds, hence the security." She put her purse through the X-ray machine and walked through the gates, then waited for Rome to follow. "Each year on the 5th of August, white petals fall from the ceiling, to celebrate the Miracle of the Snow, a legend surrounding the miraculous summer snowfall which marked the spot for the foundation of the basilica."

"That sounds amazing. Have you seen it?"

"Yes. I went last year. It was incredible. Thousands of people waiting for the petals to come down, everyone praying..." Nadine looked up and Rome followed her gaze toward the bell tower. "This church was built in the 5th century but it's been altered throughout time, and so it's got a really interesting mix of styles. It's got eighteenth century exterior, a medieval bell tower, the chapels and domes are Baroque, the ceiling decorations are Renaissance, and there are 5th century mosaics in the triumphal arch and nave." She turned to Rome and winced. "I'm sorry, am I boring you?"

Rome shook her head and smiled. "You couldn't bore me if you tried."

"Good. Anyway, the main reason why I brought you here today is the choir." Nadine opened the huge door and they quietly squeezed through as the service had already started.

Goose bumps appeared on Rome's arms as soon as she walked in. Perfectly harmonized voices echoed off the high walls and immensely impressive ceiling as the choir sang 'Gloria in Excelsis', and incense filled the church with a pungent, sweet smell.

Nadine dipped three fingers in the marble basin by the door and made a cross before walking to the back of the main, wide nave—an enormous and impressive space supported by columns on either side. Carried away by all the glorious beauty surrounding her, Rome looked at the basin and contemplated doing the same, then shook her head and rolled her eyes. She was many things, but hypocritical wasn't one of them, and she wasn't going to start now.

Her eyes were drawn toward the apse, where a high altar stood, framed by colorful mosaics in the arch behind it. Chairs were placed all the way to the front of the aisle, where cardinals and bishops were seated among locals, tourists and pilgrims. The roof was adorned with gilded ornaments and bright oil paintings of angels, and there was so much to see that she could have spent days taking in the wonder of it all.

She sat down next to Nadine on one of the pews in the back and when the male choir started singing louder, she reached for her hand and squeezed it, genuinely moved by the harmonious, low Gregorian chants. The organ music, the choir and the grandness of the church, filled to the brim with believers was an incredible experience, and she understood why Nadine had taken her here.

As someone who was not religious, it was strange to feel anything at all in a church, but she had to admit it was making her a little emotional as she sat there, listening and taking it all in while holding Nadine's hand. Even the Latin sermon was impressive, from the brief total silence before, to the deep voice of the bishop that gave her shivers even though she didn't understand a word of what he was saying. At the end of the mass, the priest, the deacon and the altar boys walked around the church while everyone sang along with the choir, the full sound of the music moving her to tears. The ritual was entirely alien to her, yet somehow comforting, too, and as the voices grew louder, she even found herself humming along.

"Do you believe in anything?" Nadine asked when they were back outside and ordering a coffee from one of the trucks parked on the square in front of the church.

Rome shook her head and shielded her eyes from the bright sun. "Not in anything that hasn't been proven to exist."

"Right. Of course not."

"Hey, what does that mean?" Rome's eyes widened as she nudged her. "I heard that sarcastic undertone."

"Okay..." Nadine grinned. "Maybe it was a little sarcastic. What I meant to say is, that your world must be pretty small if you don't believe in anything at all."

"My world is fine, thank you very much. It's exactly the right size for me, which is the span of the Earth, and I'll even add in the solar system for good measure." Rome looked up at Nadine and narrowed her eyes. "So are you religious?"

"Not really. I was raised Catholic, but I don't pray or go to church on a regular basis, apart from when I take Luca. But I do believe there's more out there, and that gives me comfort."

"More as in..."

"As in something, anything. The universe, a higher power, other dimensions, other planets with intelligent life forms, the likes of a God or maybe multiple... If you think of the universe, the original matter must have come from somewhere, right? So yeah, I'm spiritual on a lot of levels. I love astrology, as you know, but I also love churches, mosques, temples, and pilgrimage sites. They're places with a strong energy because people who believe in the same thing come together to focus on that, and I think that's beautiful."

"You have a point." Rome hooked her arm through Nadine's as they left the scooter by the church and walked downhill to have lunch. "It touched me when we were in there and I saw all those believers and heard the music. When everyone sang along at the end, a part of me wanted to believe too. It must be wonderful to be able to convince yourself there's something more out there; a God that guides us and makes sure everything will be all right in the end." She shrugged. "I just can't go there."

"Then don't," Nadine said, not in the least accusing. "Just

know that there are small miracles in everyday life and once you start paying attention, you can't help but notice them." She pulled Rome into an alcove when they turned a corner and pushed her against the brick wall as her lips pulled into a smile. "Enough spiritual talk." She paused, leaning in. "We're finally alone."

"Finally." Rome whispered as Nadine's lips brushed over hers, desire hanging thick between their shared breath. She'd longed for her like crazy, and not being able to kiss her all morning had been a challenge. Her hands slipped around Nadine's waist and continued down to her behind, drawing her tight against her. Nadine let out a soft moan, cupping her face as she parted her lips and kissed her hard, letting her know how much she'd longed for this, too. Her hands were firm, her kiss hungry and fueled with need as she pressed her body into Rome's.

They broke out of the kiss when things started to get too heated for public display, composing themselves and straightening their clothes while they giggled and shot each other longing looks.

"I needed that." Nadine bit her lip as she looked Rome up and down like she was ready to jump her. "Are you hungry?"

"Can't you tell?" Rome joked, taking her hand again with a huge grin on her face.

"I can tell all right." Nadine pointed to an old building where the paint was peeling off. There was a long queue of people waiting for their take-outs and inside it looked packed, too. "But we need to fuel a different kind of hunger first, otherwise I won't be able to perform." She waved at a muscular, rugged looking man who was smoking a cigarette outside on the terrace of the worn-out trattoria. "Angelo!"

Rome greeted him too, and when she was face-to-face

with him, it finally clicked who he was. "Hey, I'm Rome. Nice to meet you, Angelo. And thank you for your help the other night."

Angelo shrugged and gave her a small smile. "I didn't do anything. Nadine was the one who kicked ass, not me, and that man deserved it, he was a pig." He put an arm around Nadine and gestured for them to sit down at his table.

Nadine's eyes widened when he took off his shades. His left eye was swollen half-shut, with yellow and black bruising marks around the socket. "Oh my God, did I do that to you?" she asked, slamming a hand in front of her mouth.

"You sure did. Mama didn't believe me when I told her what had happened, so maybe you could talk to her. She's convinced I got myself into a drunken fight and refuses to speak to me."

"I am so, so sorry." Nadine reached out to touch his face, and he flinched when she traced his eyebrow. "I had no idea I hit you so hard, it was an accident."

"I know, and it's fine. I kind of like it; makes me look tough." He put his shades back on. "You surprised me, skinny girl. Even I got scared when I saw you beating down on him."

"Yeah, she surprised me too." Rome sat down on the chair Angelo pulled out for her and studied the man Nadine had told her about. He looked a little rough around the edges—especially with a shiner—but his eyes were friendly and his smile warm. His beanie seemed misplaced in the heat, but she figured that was part of his style as it matched the torn jeans and ripped T-shirt under the dirty apron.

"I know some people who'd be happy to hire her for muscle jobs," Angelo joked. "Anyway, it's great to have you both here. Are you hungry? What do you feel like eating?"

Nadine shrugged and smiled at him. "Whatever you recommend, the food was fantastic the other day so I couldn't wait to come back. And please join us. Or are you working?"

"I am working, but the chef is back and mama's still at home, so I'll have a beer with you before she comes in." He went inside to order food for them and came back with a bottle of red wine and a beer. "You're lucky to have a table. It's busy today as it's Sunday and the weather is warm."

"I can see that." Rome looked through the window, where crowds of locals were gathered around small tables, and more were waiting to be seated. It was quite possibly the most unromantic place anyone had ever taken her but going on the smell, the food would be great, and she felt her stomach rumbling. Everything with Nadine was an adventure, and she was enjoying every second of this strange day in which she got to see parts of Rome she would have never seen if she'd ventured out by herself or with anyone else, for that matter. "Is this your family business?" she asked.

Angelo nodded, tapping his fingers on the table while he studied Rome. "We all do something on the side because we'd kill each other if we worked here full-time together, but yes, this restaurant is the heart of our family. It's where we eat and drink with our local community, and where we come together when we need each other. The roadworkers' union meets here once a month too, and we cater for the occasional wedding." He took a long drink of his beer. "You might be the first non-local to ever sit on that chair. Most tourists feel a little intimidated when they pass."

"Why is that?" Rome didn't feel intimidated at all, but perhaps that was because she was with Nadine, who was a local herself.

He shrugged. "Don't know. Our clientele looks a little rough, I suppose."

"Or maybe it's you who's scaring them away," Nadine joked, raising her glass in a toast. "You know, the other girls from the agency warned me about you."

"They did?" Angelo threw his hands in the air and shot her his sweetest smile. "But I'm a pussycat."

"I know," Nadine said in a chuckle. "And I promise I'll talk to your mom when she gets here to explain how you got that black eye." She moved back when a man came out with a large bowl of pasta, two plates and a jar with cutlery and napkins. He smiled at Nadine and Rome, then sneered something at Angelo, which made Nadine laugh even harder.

"The chef is asking me why I'm sitting here drinking beer with two beautiful women while he's sweating in the kitchen," Angelo clarified, turning to Rome as he plated for them. "So... would it be indelicate of me to ask what is happening with the pig?"

"The pig?" Rome frowned in confusion until it clicked. "Oh, *the pig.*" Her mouth watered as she looked down at the steaming plate of mascarpone, tomato and eggplant pasta in front of her. "Right. So, unfortunately the pig is also one of my major investors. He bribed those waiters at the restaurant, and they verified his lie saying that I was the one who was drunk and that it was all a misunderstanding. The police have dropped the case and HR wants to 'mediate'," she continued, making quote marks and rolling her eyes, "so I'm not getting anywhere with them either. Since I'll be stuck in the office for the foreseeable future, and I don't feel safe around him, I have no other alternative than to sue him."

Angelo shook his head in disgust. "You know, when

Nadine asked me to follow him, I just thought she was being overprotective."

"Yeah, I didn't think he was capable of assault either," Rome said. "But I'm hoping I can help other women too, if I sue him. I'm sure this wasn't the first time he's done this." She took a bite and moaned at the silky texture and full-bodied flavor of the sauce.

"Good?" Angelo asked, a proud smile settling over his face.

"Perfect."

"More than perfect," Nadine agreed as she dug in.

"Then my job is done. I'd better get back into the kitchen." Angelo stood up and hesitated as he looked at Rome. "If you need help with anything, just let me know, okay?"

"Thank you. That's very kind." Rome stared at him as he disappeared back inside. "He's so nice. Are you guys friends?"

Nadine thought about that. "I like Angelo, but I don't know him that well, even though he's worked for me over the past few years. I didn't even know his family ran a trattoria until I met him here earlier this week, but I trust him, and I feel like he's thawing around me. He's not just all business anymore." She twirled some more pasta around her fork. "Plus, these guys really know how to cook. I think I've found my new favorite eatery."

"It's fantastic." Rome smiled as she looked at Nadine, who ate with as much passion as she did everything else, savoring every bite as if it were her last. "Thank you for an amazing date."

"I'm glad you're having a good time." Nadine reached for her hand over the table. "I wanted you to see the real Rome. All the rest, you can see from a tour bus, or by yourself in the early mornings when it's quiet in town. This is a friendly city, and I'd be devastated if Matteo ruined your stay here for you."

"He hasn't ruined anything. I still love it here." Rome locked her eyes with Nadine's and shifted in her seat as arousal coursed through her. It had been a long time since they'd had sex, and after spending the morning with Nadine, she was unable to think of anything else. "And I love spending time with you," she added.

Nadine smiled and it made her eyes sparkle in the cutest of ways. It was nothing like the smile she painted on when she was with her clients. This was real, and it touched Rome to her core. "I love spending time with you too." She stroked Rome's hand. "But our date isn't over yet."

34

"Finally, alone." Nadine moved the big plant pot further into the corner of the living room and adjusted the rug. The milkman and his son had delivered Rome's purchases and hung up the artworks for her, and Nadine and Rome had cleaned the daybed that was now in pride of place on the balcony. "I thought they'd never leave." She walked over to Rome, who was unwrapping one of the palms they'd bought on their way to her apartment. "But it was nice of you to offer them drinks, it was the right thing to do."

Rome smiled as Nadine helped her lift the big plant into the enameled pot. "It was fun. They're nice people." She stepped back to inspect her living room that was starting to look more and more like a real home and felt really happy with what they'd achieved. "Besides, I think I'm addicted to that market now, so I might need their help again."

"Smart woman." Nadine wrapped her arms around Rome's neck, and shivered at the feeling of their bodies coming together. "Do you want to try out that new daybed?" She gestured toward the balcony.

Rome's eyes darkened as she nodded. "I do."

"Come on, then." Nadine pulled her outside and sat down on the spacious chaise that was big enough to sleep on. "It creaks a little, but other than that, it's very cute." She expected Rome to sit down next to her but instead, Rome lifted up her dress and straddled her lap.

"Do you think anyone can see us here?" she whispered, shooting Nadine a sexy look.

Nadine looked through the balcony railing that was partially covered in ivy and shook her head. "No, we're too high up, but I think your neighbors might be able to hear us if they're outside." She placed her index finger against her lips and listened to the soft murmur of voices next door and on the balcony beneath them.

"Then we'll just have to be very quiet," Rome said, leaning in to kiss her.

Nadine lifted her hips as Rome ground into her lap. She took hold of Rome's behind, wanting to lay her down on the bed, but Rome stopped her.

"No. Just stay there and don't move."

Nadine wasn't used to other women taking charge or topping her, but she couldn't deny that it was turning her on like crazy. When Rome traced her lips with the tip of her tongue, it seemed impossible to suppress a moan, but she managed to stay quiet. Heavy breaths flowed between them as she brushed her lips over Rome's, then ran her hands under her dress, caressing her smooth thighs. She could feel Rome's need in her tremble, and the way her mouth finally crashed into hers, failing to linger and tease her the way she'd intended to. "I don't think I can be quiet when you kiss me like that," she said, keeping her voice down.

"Yes, you can." Rome said, locking her lips with Nadine's

again. She cupped Nadine's neck to pull her closer, inhaling deeply while they kissed fiercely.

Nadine's chest was heaving, and all her nerve endings were buzzing, longing for Rome's hands and lips. When Rome moved her mouth to her neck, she held her breath, shocked at how intense it felt. Yes, it had been a while, but she'd never thought it would surpass how she'd felt that first time with Rome. It wasn't just arousal she felt, it was an electrifying sense of euphoria, a need to feel close to her in any way she could.

Rome unbuttoned her shorts and tugged at the hem of her T-shirt, waiting for Nadine to lift her arms so she could take it off. She looked down at Nadine's full breasts in the white lace bra against her tanned skin and licked her lips. "You are so incredibly sexy," she murmured, reaching around Nadine's back to unhook her bra.

Nadine felt a twitch of lust at seeing Rome's desire for her. There was no way this woman was straight, because no one had ever looked at her like she was the last drop of water in the desert, and there wasn't a trace of hesitation left in Rome's previously shy demeanor. She closed her eyes and sank further down on the daybed as Rome pulled off her bra and then kissed her way down to her breasts, sucking a nipple into her mouth and twirling her tongue around it. "That feels so good."

"Shhh..." Rome smiled and turned her attention to her other breast while slowly lowering herself onto the concrete floor.

Nadine bit her lip, desperately trying to suppress a groan at the amazing feeling of Rome's mouth feasting on her while her hands were everywhere.

"Can I take these off?" Rome asked, hooking her fingers

under the waistband of her shorts. "God, I want you so badly."

Nadine nodded and lifted her hips so Rome could slide down her shorts, along with her panties. When Rome pushed her knees apart and settled between her legs, Nadine felt more exposed than ever, sitting out there on the balcony stark naked, soft gusts of wind blowing against her sex. The sun was setting behind the Colosseum, and even after four years, the way the light fell over the terracotta rooftops of the city never failed to amaze her. She was aware of the bright lights in Rome's apartment as the world around them slowly darkened and the balcony became a spotlight, but the flash of awareness quickly dissipated as Rome's tongue traced the inside of her thighs until she pressed her mouth tightly against her center, pulling her closer by her hips.

"Fuck!" she cried, then covered her mouth with her hand, the fingers of her other hand weaving themselves through Rome's hair. Her head fell back, and she bit her knuckle, swallowing another groan at the incredible sensations that were spreading through her core.

Rome let out a chuckle as she briefly looked up. "Quiet," she whispered again before she continued to devour her, sliding her tongue through her wet folds, then up to her sensitive clit.

Nadine bucked her hips against Rome's mouth, and tugged at her hair, at a loss for an outlet since she couldn't use her vocal cords. She pressed her lips together and started shaking as Rome feasted on her, taking her higher and higher until the pulsing between her legs intensified and her whole body spasmed. She was helpless as she crashed into her climax, the energy blasting out of her. Shuddering at the ebbing and flowing of contractions as

Rome continued, even after she'd peaked, Nadine let out a quiet moan and sank back into the daybed. "Holy fuck, Rome," she said in a breathless whisper as she wiped the sweat of her brows. It wasn't even that warm anymore, but she felt feverishly heated.

Rome got up and straddled her again, a big grin spreading across her face when she saw Nadine's blissful smile. "I think you liked that."

Nadine chuckled at her self-satisfied expression as she wrapped her arms around Rome's waist. "I did. Where did you learn that?" She pulled her in and kissed her, and realized it had been years since she'd tasted herself on someone else's lips.

"Promise not to laugh?" Rome's cheeks colored.

"I promise."

"YouTube," Rome said, after a moment's hesitation.

"Seriously?" At that, Nadine burst into laughter. "I'm sorry." She waved a hand. "But that is just too funny."

Rome nudged her. "Hey, that's not fair. You promised not to laugh. I did some research while I was home, you know, just in case..."

"Just in case what?" Nadine was unable to stop laughing, and tears were running down her cheeks.

"Stop teasing me, you know what I mean. Just in case something happened between us again. I'm a nerd; I like to know things, and..." Rome let out a deep sigh of frustration. "Improvising makes me nervous."

"That must have been one hell of a tutorial. I didn't know you could learn this from videos." Nadine arched a brow. "Or were you watching porn?"

"Eww, no, it wasn't porn." Rome rolled her eyes. "Just an informative video on how to please the ladies."

"Well, it certainly worked." Nadine gave her an

endearing smile as she pulled down the strap of Rome's summer dress to kiss her shoulder. "But now it's my turn and it's also not fair that you're still dressed and I'm not."

35

"Here. I almost forgot." Nadine reached into her purse beside the bed and handed Rome the box with the Libra perfume. "This is for you."

"Thank you. It looks so pretty, and I love the name. *Stars Aligned*; it's catchy." Rome smiled excitedly as she opened it and smelled it. "Subtle, but really good. Like it could be someone's natural scent..." She paused and breathed in the fragrance again. "But fresher, like after a shower with really great products."

"That's the idea. It just enhances your own deliciousness."

Rome dabbed some on her neck and quirked an eyebrow. "Let's see if it works." She snuggled back into Nadine's embrace and kicked off the covers, cherishing the breeze on her skin that was damp after they'd made love for hours.

Nadine buried her face in Rome's neck and closed her eyes as she inhaled deeply. "It smells perfect on you."

"Oh yeah? Well I happen to think you smell pretty perfect too." Rome rolled off her and turned on her side, resting her head on Nadine's chest. "I'm excited that it's ready but assuming it passes the consumer testing with flying colors, what happens next?"

"Do you think it's going to work, now?" Nadine chuckled. "You sound like you do."

Rome shrugged. "I'm still not entirely convinced by the star sign attraction thing yet, although you do smell delicious. Are you wearing yours?"

"I am."

"Interesting... I did notice the difference. I mean, I kept noticing your scent today. But then I was drawn to you from the beginning, so I'm biased." Rome paused, choosing her words carefully. "I think that even if it doesn't scientifically work, it will be a very commercial product, so you have to be careful with your go-to-market strategy because you'll only have one chance to launch it and this has the potential to be a huge success."

"I know." Nadine sighed as she cupped Rome's cheek, and Rome could sense her carefree façade was dropping, just like it had this morning at the flea market. It brought a lump to her throat, and she felt privileged that Nadine was now allowing herself to be vulnerable around her. "Honestly, I'm fucking scared." She bit her lip, clearly contemplating how much to share. "It's been ten years since I started escorting, and I've always had money to live comfortably, to travel and to pursue my dream of my own perfume brand. But now that it's becoming a reality, I'm completely freaking out."

"Why?" Rome pulled her in and kissed her. She felt incredibly close to Nadine in that moment as they both lay naked in each other's arms, quietly talking, and it almost scared her how much she longed to be with her all the time.

"I guess I'm not sure where to go from here. I mean, I

have a plan, sort of. But I'm not used to thinking long-term, and I have no experience in the retail business whatsoever. All I know is how to make people like me and look good. Beyond that, I have no idea what I'm doing, and I'm really worried I'm going to fuck up everything I've worked so hard for."

"You're worried about failing?" Rome caught Nadine's hand on her cheek and squeezed it. "You don't strike me as the type to be insecure at all…"

Nadine sighed. "I know. But I am. I'm terrified. I think I've been hiding behind the escort work for too long, and maybe I should have stopped a while back. The product is done, but now that it's here, it's like the real world is hitting me so hard, so suddenly, that it's frightening me."

"I know it's scary, but it's also a good thing that you'll have to stop escorting when you turn thirty. You've been hiding behind it for more reasons than just your perfumes, and I think it's been holding you back." Rome regretted the words as soon as they were out.

"What do you mean?"

"Nothing, never mind."

"Come on, Rome. You know that the most annoying thing a person can do is make a comment, then say 'never mind'".

"Okay." Rome nervously bit her lip. She didn't want to ruin their night by bringing up something that was crystal clear to her but that might not be clear to Nadine. But Nadine was right; she'd started this now, and so she'd have to finish it. "You've been avoiding emotional connections," she said.

"I have no idea what you're talking about." Nadine was smiling, but she didn't look happy, and Rome regretted ever bringing it up. This clearly went much deeper than she'd anticipated, but Nadine wasn't one to be fooled and now was the time to speak her mind.

"What I mean is, that you've been hiding behind escorting when it comes to people too," she said, dreading Nadine's reaction. "You've been hiding from love."

"Nonsense. I chose not to go down that path because it's difficult to maintain relationships while I do escort work. I don't want to have to apologize for my lifestyle all the time."

"That's not entirely true and you know it. You're scared of getting close to people too." Rome kept her voice down as she didn't want Nadine to think she was arguing with her. Nadine was the most amazing woman she'd ever come across, and although she was open and seemed to be in touch with herself to outsiders, to Rome, quite the opposite was true. "Do you have any really good friends?"

"Of course I do." Nadine glared at her, and Rome was pretty sure she was going to get a mouthful, but she mellowed and remained silent.

"Okay. Name them."

"Luca," Nadine, said after a moment's hesitation, then shook her head and chuckled. "Fine. Luca doesn't really count, so I suppose I don't have any close friends. I have acquaintances though, and I hang out with some of the other girls from the agency from time to time." She paused. "But I wouldn't consider them friends."

"See? We're the same. In all honesty, I expect you to use your job as an excuse to withdraw from me as soon as you start feeling trapped, and I've prepared myself for that," Rome continued carefully. She knew she was treading on dangerous grounds, but if they were going to make this work, they would have to be nothing but honest with each other. "Believe me; I've been through enough therapy sessions to know how this works, it's what I do, too." She bit her lip and stared intently into Nadine's eyes. "But I don't want that to happen between us. And I want you to know that I accept what you do for a living. So, if you're feeling suffocated at any point, just talk to me, okay? And I'll do the same. Relationships of any kind are hard, at least for me, so we have to talk about these things."

Nadine frowned as she processed what Rome was saying. "You sound like my Mom."

Rome shook her head and laughed, relieved that the tension between them was melting away. "That wasn't what I expected to hear, but okay."

"Maybe you're right." Nadine sighed. "Call it hiding, call it taking the easy way out, I have purposely avoided relationships. And yes, I've used my job as an excuse to avoid committing myself to a relationship with someone." She swallowed hard. "And yes, I may feel suffocated at some point, I can't promise you I won't."

"Then at least promise me you'll tell me if you do and I'll back off a little. And I'll tell you too, if I feel the same way."

Nadine nodded. "You know, you're really in touch with yourself for someone who's emotionally detached."

"I'm not so sure about that, but I've been doing a lot of thinking lately." Rome took her hand and kissed it. "I'd like to help you with your business plan."

"No, that's very sweet of you, but you've got enough on your plate as it is."

Rome placed her thumb on Nadine's lips, hushing her. "Please. I'd be so happy if you'd let me help you. You've done so much for me and well... I'm usually not one to brag, but I'm actually really good at stuff like that."

Nadine shot her an amused look. "I have no doubt you are, but..."

"It will only take a couple of nights," Rome interrupted

her. "I could come to your place after work on your days off and it will be done in no time." She really, really wanted to help Nadine and this way she could finally give something back. "Seriously, a professional consultant wouldn't be able to do a better job than me; I know my stuff."

"I love your confidence." Nadine laughed. "Okay. If you're sure you don't mind."

"Not at all." Rome traced her waist and her hip, craving her all over again. Her desire for this woman had no limits apparently, and she hardly recognized herself from the person she was before she first came to Rome. Nadine's body, her smile, her energy... She worshipped everything about her, and she was going to fight for her, no matter what.

36

"So, that's the story so far." Rome took a sip of her coffee and looked at Eliza, who had been listening intently for the past twenty minutes.

"I can't believe it." Eliza shook her head and grimaced in disgust. "Matteo needs to be punished; he can't get away with this. How can they just dismiss the case? I don't get it." She paused and rubbed her temple. "I don't want to work for someone like that, it's..."

"No," Rome interrupted her. "Please don't go there. You're working for me, not him, and I really need your help. That's why I asked you to meet me; I didn't know who else to approach and well... I trust you."

"I'm glad you told me." Eliza leaned in and squeezed Rome's arm. "Are you okay?"

"Yeah, I'm fine. Although I don't want to think about what might have happened if Nadine hadn't shown up."

"Nadine sounds like a really, really great woman. Kind of badass too, and she clearly cares about you very much."

"Yeah, she's amazing." Rome sighed with a faraway look in her eyes, her thoughts drifting back to Sunday and their

LISE GOLD

delicious marathon of lovemaking. Nadine was working tonight, and although it didn't bother her that much anymore, she couldn't help but worry about her after the incident with Matteo. "Truly amazing."

"Oh my God, you are so into her, it's almost sickening," Eliza teased. "Anyway, what do you need from me?" She waved the waiter over to order them another espresso and looked at Rome intently. "Anything, babe."

Rome gave her a warm smile. "Thanks. The thing is... if he's done it to me, there might be other women in the office who have been harassed by him in one way or another. And if there are, I'd like to find them so we can build a case against him together. I have an Italian lawyer now and he informed me it's going to be close to impossible to start a criminal proceeding against him as we'd have to get the police to reopen the case and at the moment we can't do that without any actual proof. He recommends making this a civil proceeding, in which case we're much more likely to win if I'm not the only one suing him. That also means we have to sue him for harassment instead of assault, which sucks, because I'd love to see him getting locked up." She bit her lip and paused. "On the other hand, banning him from the work floor will ensure the safety of female *Nero* employees, and it's likely there will be a payout—if we win—which will hit him where it hurts most, which is in his wallet. I don't want anyone to know what's going on though. I'm worried about jeopardizing the Carbon project, so this is a very delicate situation."

"Yes, I get that." Eliza took her time to think it over as she ran a hand through her lilac hair. She looked immensely out of place in the tourist-filled coffee shop next to the office, wearing a complicated black four-sleeved blazer and tutu combo by some obscure Korean designer she'd been raving about. "The unemployment rate is high in Italy, so even if you do find other victims, they might be reluctant to talk for fear of losing their jobs." She shrugged. "Even getting them to admit it might be hard."

"I know," Rome agreed. "But you're Italian and I've noticed you're very social and that you hang out with a lot of women from the office. I figured they might trust you more."

"Hmm..." Eliza thanked the waiter who brought their espressos over and stirred in a bag of sugar, tapping her long, lilac fingernails on the wooden table. "You're right about that, they might be more likely to open up to me. I can try, but that's all I can do."

"Trying is all I'm asking for," Rome said.

"Okay, so what's your strategy?" Eliza asked. "Civil cases can drag on for years, usually until one of the parties runs out of money."

"I know. But if Matteo's done this before, depending on how many women come forward of course, we'll have a good case. I imagine he's keen to preserve his image and would want to settle quickly."

"Of course, that makes sense. In other words, this all has to happen very quietly, without the board finding out we're asking around?"

"Exactly."

"Right." Eliza nodded. "I think that can be done. Women who haven't spoken up before won't be vocal about it now, not to their colleagues anyway. And unless Matteo has a harem of mistresses scattered throughout the departments, I doubt anyone will tell the board what's going on if they find out. He's not very liked in general."

"That makes me feel better," Rome said. "I'm suing him personally, not the company. I don't want to put people's jobs at risk over something Matteo has done."

"Good thinking. I'll let you know as soon as I have anything to report." Eliza sat back and crossed one leg over another, studying Rome. "You know, you're the opposite to what I expected you to be."

"Really? How so?" Rome asked.

"Well, for starters, I wasn't even sure if I wanted to take the job at first. The idea of working for some eco-warrior app developer seemed beyond boring and honestly, the generous salary was the only reason I got on board. But then I learned about the product, which I'm now incredibly excited about, and I got to know you..." Eliza tilted her head, continuing to look her over. "You have way more to you than meets the eye, Rome. I mean, you're beautiful, but you're also compassionate, fun, smart, fair and a great leader, and I totally get why that stunning woman is pining over you."

Rome laughed. "I don't think she's pining over me." She sat back too and sipped her coffee. "Although we're in a really good place right now."

"So, she came to her senses, did she?"

"It's a little more complicated than that," Rome said, not wanting to give Nadine's private business away. "But yeah, we're dating."

Eliza's eyes widened in excitement. "What?" She clapped her hands together. "It's official?"

"You could say that." Rome was unable to hide her blush. "At least we're trying, and it's been pretty incredible so far. She took me on the most amazing, weird date on Sunday and I'm seeing her again tomorrow night."

"You lucky devil." Eliza winked. "As I said, there's no better feeling than being in love. And you, girl, have fallen deep, so enjoy the ride."

37

"You were right. You are good at this." Nadine flicked through the forty-page file they'd worked on during the week which included distribution, direct marketing, PR, a go-to-market plan and a financial forecast, and with Rome's help, she'd even enjoyed the tedious chore she'd been putting off for months. If she'd been impressed by Rome's intelligence before, she was even more impressed now. Even in a field in which she had no knowledge, Rome was able to see the bigger picture and provide a strong strategy. Things were suddenly looking a little brighter and she had her cute girl to thank for that. They'd also written a great pitch for the retailers, which was so strong that she couldn't imagine anyone saying no to her product.

"Told you so." Rome blew her a kiss. "And it was my absolute pleasure." She closed her laptop and slipped it into its sleeve, then headed for the kitchen. "Do you have any wine? I've had more coffee than my body can handle, and I think we should celebrate." She grinned. "Aren't you the one who claims everything should be celebrated?"

"So true. And it's the first Saturday in a while that I don't have to work." Nadine got up too, walked to the kitchen and came back with a bottle of red wine. "Let's have a glass here first. But after that, I want to take you out. Are you up for that?"

Rome glanced down at her outfit, pulling a questionable face but Nadine shook it off. "No need to dress up, but if you want to, you can borrow something of mine."

"I don't think I'd do your fabulous dresses justice."

"Are you kidding me?" Nadine looked her up and down while she opened the bottle. "You really have no idea how stunning you are, do you?" She smiled when she saw Rome blushing. "I want to show you off."

Rome laughed and rolled her eyes. "And how do you propose doing that?"

"Well, in Italy..." Nadine checked the big antique clock on the wall. "It's almost show-off o'clock." She poured them both a small glass and handed one to Rome. "Are you familiar with the Italian term *la passeggiata*?"

"No, what's that?"

Nadine frowned. "Hmm... it's a little hard to explain. I guess you could say it's the principle of dressing up and going for a drink or a stroll in the early evening, when it's starting to cool down. The sun is low, and you see lovers kissing, mothers showing off their babies, and people generally dress to impress, especially on the weekend. I call it peacocking." She laughed. "It's the time for courting and flirting, for aperitifs and ice cream and everything in between as long as it involves socializing and flaunting."

"Are you serious?" Rome asked. "I didn't realize the Italians were actually making an effort at all. I've always thought that their elegance came naturally to them."

"It is natural, in a way. More natural than it would be for us, for example. But keeping up appearances is important here, so it's not entirely effortless." Nadine smiled as she took a sip of her wine and beckoned Rome to follow her to her bedroom with glass in hand. She opened her closet and started flicking through her dresses. "I take it you've never heard of the term *la bella figura* either? I don't think there's an actual translation for it in any other language."

"No." Rome was surprised at the modest size of Nadine's closet. Having seen her in some spectacular dresses, she'd expected her to have way more clothes. "Tell me."

"It's the concept of being your best self," Nadine said, taking out a black dress and handing it to Rome. "Not just in the way you present yourself physically, but also in the way you behave. To Italians, it's not just manners that are hugely important but also who and what you know, and that can mean anything from recommending the right restaurants or hairdressers, to introducing the right people to each other."

"God, that sounds tiring." Rome held up the dress and studied it. It was simple but elegant; a sleeveless cotton-silk number with wide shoulder straps and a cute peplum skirt. "But also intriguing." She took off the kimono robe she'd borrowed from Nadine, as they hadn't bothered getting dressed after their morning shower, and tried it on. "It fits me perfectly."

"It does." Nadine arched a brow as she looked her over. "Very cute, and you can wear your sneakers with it, so you won't be uncomfortable."

"I expected you to have more clothes," Rome said as she sat down on the bed and watched Nadine get dressed too.

"No, I don't need much when it comes to clothes. Shorts, jeans, T-shirts and some nice dresses, that's all. Most things I wear out on dates are provided by my agency or by clients who are trying to impress me. Although they're technically gifts, I tend to send them back the next day, so I don't feel like I owe them anything."

"That's smart." Rome took her hand and pulled her toward the bed. "You look great," she said, tugging at Nadine's jade green strapless dress. "Although I prefer you without clothes."

Nadine chuckled and leaned in to kiss her. "I prefer you naked too, but it's getting late and I want to show you off."

38

"I need you to try this gelato." Nadine pulled Rome along toward a small, artisanal gelato shop behind the market. The terracotta building was overgrown with vine leaves and nothing but an old wooden sign above the door hinted at what they sold.

"It looks super cute, but I'm so full," Rome protested. "I can't possibly eat any more after those snacks we had with our cocktails. Are you insatiable or what?"

"I am. On many levels." Nadine shot her a flirty look and stepped inside, not taking no for an answer. "Seriously, it's insanely good and we can share one."

Rome grinned as she looked over the deliciously looking selection of flavors. "You want to share your ice cream with me?"

"Of course. It's what gelato is for. It's sexy."

"Is that so?" Rome felt herself blushing when she noticed people were listening in on their conversation. A woman behind her, who obviously understood English, chuckled, but Nadine didn't seem to care. Looking at the colorful selection of creamy goodness, she licked her lips, and the unconscious gesture made Rome's heart race. It was crazy how much she longed for Nadine, and after quietly discussing the amazing sex they'd had over drinks and cicchetti whilst sitting in an adorable little square somewhere in the historic center, she realized what a one-track mind she had. "What's your favorite flavor?"

Nadine shrugged. "Depends on my mood. I'm feeling sweet today. You?"

"I like sweet." Rome pointed to a white gelato. "Vanilla, rice and dates. That sounds intriguing."

"Good choice." Nadine ordered a cone with two scoops and handed it to Rome before she paid. "The top one is honeycomb and macadamia. I think you'll like it."

Rome tried the ice cream while they walked back out onto the market square and sat down on a bench as the sun was setting. It wasn't the most famous square, and the fountain they were sitting beside was one of the lesser known of the thousands of fountains in Rome, but just like every part of the city, it was breathtakingly beautiful and utterly charming. Around them were restaurants and bars, the tables outside decked out with white linen and large bottles of olive oil. To her amusement, she was now aware of the people sitting there facing the square. They looked like they were there to be seen; all dressed up, big shades, styled hair, and it was easy to separate the locals from the tourists, who looked sunburnt and tired as they made their way back to their hotels. The condensation from the fountain cooled her skin and the mist-like tiny droplets in the air were forming an array of magical rainbow colors around them. She shielded her eyes from the low sun, took it all in and realized that this moment was pretty damn perfect. "Oh my God. You were right; this is so good," she said as she licked her ice cream and chewed on a piece of fresh honeycomb that was dripping with honey.

"Told you so." Nadine tried it too. "Mmm..."

"I don't usually share my ice cream." Rome watched her lick her lips again and fought the urge to lean in and kiss her. "And you were right; it is sexy."

"It is. And you know what's even more sexy? In Rome, we eat ice cream like this." Nadine took Rome's leg and pulled it over her thigh. Then she turned to her and flung her other leg on top, wedging Rome's leg between her own.

"Really?" Rome looked equally turned on and confused as she scanned the market square, studying the locals. When Nadine's poker face broke and she started laughing, Rome gave her a playful slap on her thigh and laughed too. "Okay, you're lying. That is definitely not how others eat ice cream here." She leaned in closer, Nadine's irresistible lips tempting her. What was happening to her? She was sitting intimately on a bench in public, sharing an ice cream with another woman and not only did it feel completely normal, she was also giddy like a teenager. "Do people have a problem with gay people here?" she asked, just to be sure.

Nadine shook her head. "Nah. Just like everywhere, there are fanatics, of course, and Italy is a pretty religious and family-oriented country so I can't imagine it's easy for young people in the countryside, but Rome's a big city and all in all, it's fine. There's a genuine appreciation for love, whatever form it comes in." She tilted her head, studying Rome as she ran her tongue through the creamy substance. "Does it bother you, sitting here with me? Like this?" she asked, patting Rome's leg.

"No, it doesn't. Maybe it would bother me if I was back home, I'm not sure. Or if people I knew saw me like this."

Nadine nodded. "Well, I suggest you try to get comfortable with it, because it's something you're going to have to live with. Not that it's a negative thing; I feel blessed to be attracted to women. God, I can't imagine having sex with men." She grimaced. "Gross is all I can say."

"Are you saying you think I'm gay?" Rome asked.

"Think?" Nadine laughed. "Honey, I'm pretty sure you are."

Rome blushed, knowing Nadine was probably right. Staring at her mouth, she saw there was ice cream on her top lip, and she knew she'd left it there on purpose as a bait to lure her in. Feeling brave, she inched closer and licked it off, and hearing the soft moan that Nadine let out left her wanting more. When she was about to lean back again, Nadine cupped her face and held her there to kiss her fiercely, and in that beautiful moment, Rome felt entirely free and kissed her back. The sun was shining on them and Nadine tasted of vanilla as her lips claimed Rome's with an urgency that turned her limbs to jelly.

The sound of laughter broke them apart, and Nadine looked caught as she looked up at a woman standing next to their bench, shouting something in Italian. She grinned sheepishly and gave her a high five when the woman held up her hand, then turned back to Rome. "Rome, this is Monica. We work for the same agency. Monica, this is Rome."

"Rome? *Che bella!*" Monica bent down to give Rome a kiss on each cheek. "That's a beautiful name for a beautiful woman." She winked at Nadine. "But I didn't expect anything less from this one. So, she'd got you all charmed up, huh? Sharing her gelato with you?"

"She has." Rome laughed. "It's nice to meet you, Monica. How do you know each other? You never actually go into the agency's office, right?" she asked Nadine.

Monica and Nadine looked at each other and shook their heads. "We've been on a couple of double dates together," Nadine said. "However, I don't actually know anything about Monica apart from the stuff she makes up when she's with her clients. Are you even a geologist? You seemed so confident talking about your stuff."

"Of course not," Monica said with a chuckle. "I just do my research, just like you. How's work been?"

"Busy." Nadine put her hand over her forehead, shielding her eyes from the sun. "A little too busy for me right now, but I only have until next February, so I tend to take the offers anyway."

"The big 3-0 approaching, huh?" Monica smiled. "Good for you. It's been quiet on my front lately, but that leaves me more time to have fun." She opened her purse and held up a flyer. "I'm on my way to meet friends for drinks at a bar in Monti. You guys want to come?"

Nadine's eyes widened in surprise. "Are you serious? We can't just crash your evening."

"Yes you can, you're with me." Monica insisted. "Seriously, it's going to be good."

"Okay..." Nadine looked at Rome, who just shrugged and smiled.

"Sounds like fun," she said, wondering why she felt so spontaneous. It was unlike her to do things she hadn't planned, but she seemed to be more open to living in the moment, lately.

"Perfect." Monica gave them a beaming smile. "We can get to know each other a little better." She pointed to a side street and tapped her heeled foot on the cobbled surface. "Come on, follow me. There should be a cab waiting around this corner."

39

"Did you just say you want to kiss me?" Nadine tilted her head and arched an eyebrow. If she wasn't mistaken, Rome was very, very much into her tonight. The way she looked at her and kept licking her lips... She didn't even realize she was doing it.

Monica and her friends had just waved farewell a few minutes ago and they were sitting in an intimate bar that was built into a hill in Monti. The cave-like setting and low ceiling made for the perfect romantic hideaway. It was a quirky place, with bookshelves full of weird books and velvet heart-shaped loveseats next to antique lamps and glow-in-the-dark coffee tables.

"I did. You look smoking hot and you smell amazing." Rome glanced at Nadine's bare arms in the simple, strapless dress. It's hard to think of anything else, to be honest with you... So, what are we doing here?" she asked, lowering her voice.

"We're having a last drink." Nadine gave her an innocent look.

Rome chuckled. "No, I mean with the perfume... are you

testing me? I get the feeling you are. I'm wearing mine and you're wearing yours and yes, I want to kiss you but then again, I always want to kiss you so it's hard to say if it's the perfume."

"No, we're just having a night out together." Nadine tilted her head as she took Rome in. The strap of her dress had dropped to reveal a tantalizing glimpse of her royal blue bra. "But it's a challenge keeping my hands to myself, with you looking the way you do."

Rome shivered when Nadine's hand gently tucked a stray strand of her hair behind her ear. She managed to keep her cool but inside, the impact of the soft touch shot through her body like a thunderbolt. "I agree," she whispered. "It's hard. I want you all the time and it doesn't help that we're sitting in a love seat together."

"Yeah. I like this love seat." Unable to wait any longer, Nadine leaned in, buried her face in Rome's neck and ran her nose along her warm skin. "Mmm... so good." She moved her mouth to Rome's ear and whispered: "But you're right; I can't tell if it's because of the perfume or because I can smell that you're turned on. It's like your pheromones are talking to me and I like what they're saying."

"Jesus." Rome let out the breath she'd been holding and tried to force back a moan. Nadine's words sent a flash of arousal through her, making her shift on the couch.

"Am I right?" Nadine moved back and locked her eyes with Rome's, leaning her cheek into the palm of her hand.

Rome nodded slowly as heat rose to her cheeks. "Yes, I'm very turned on," she whispered. They were so close that their lips almost touched, and she was dying to kiss her, but this was a public place, and she knew that if she did, she'd never be able to stop herself. It was hard to understand how her body could react so fiercely to another person. She'd always been skeptical when people talked about chemistry, but now that she was experiencing it herself, she couldn't deny its existence anymore. In fact, it was by far the most powerful thing she'd ever felt.

"God, I want to kiss you so badly it hurts," Nadine mumbled, staring at Rome's mouth while twirling a lock of her blonde hair around her finger. The silence hung between them as they both waited for the other to say something. Nadine looked like she wanted to, but nothing came out as she opened her mouth, then closed it again.

Rome decided to take the lead. "I know this is way too complicated for both of us. It's bad timing with my job, I'll be moving back to the US eventually and you make a living dating other people. It's only a matter of time before one of us gets hurt, but this force is too strong," Rome continued. "I can't fight it and I'm not sure I want to because being with you feels incredible and I want you to be mine."

Nadine swallowed hard and looked like she was searching for words once again. For someone who had a lot to say about things, she was suddenly terribly quiet. Finally, her lips parted, but instead of speaking, she took Rome's face in her hands, pulled her in and kissed her fiercely. Rome moaned as she felt Nadine's lips on hers, her tongue claiming her mouth with an urgency that left her dizzy and raging with lust. The fact that they were in a bar didn't matter anymore because she couldn't have stopped if she wanted to. She let herself be whisked away to a place where nothing mattered apart from their connection and for a moment, she forgot about Matteo, about work, and about the people around them. The thrilling sensation of their combusting chemistry set her on fire, like it was the first time they kissed all over again. Nadine took her to places she'd never been, and it felt so good. Rome ran her hands through Nadine's long hair, and she was wet and throbbing as they made out in the loveseat. Finally, Nadine pulled away and let out a reluctant sigh. "I'm already yours," she whispered.

Rome felt her heart swell, and although she desperately wanted to kiss Nadine again, she was aware of the stares directed their way. People casually turned back to their conversations when she looked around the dark room, and contrary to what she'd expected, there were no giggles or comments, as if this happened all the time. It made her remember Eliza's words—that Rome was *the City of Love.* "I've never made out in public before but today, I did it twice."

"I've made out in public many times." Nadine winked. "But it was never as nice as this."

Rome's lips curled into a smile. "Maybe we should get out of here before this gets out of hand." She stood up and took Nadine's hand without waiting for an answer. "My place? It's really close." Shaking her head, she changed her mind. "No, yours. Your bed is bigger."

40

"Ouch. I think I over celebrated," Nadine said, grimacing as she sat up in bed.

"Same here." Rome handed her an aspirin and a glass of water and got back into bed. "It was great fun though, and Monica has lovely friends."

"Yeah, I had a great time too. I don't socialize much normally." Nadine turned on her side to face her. "As I told you I don't really have any close friends. I get invites from acquaintances but I'm usually tired from going out for work all week, so I tend to stay at home when I'm off. You made me get out there and I like that."

"So you never do anything at night, your work dates aside?" Rome asked.

"Not really, apart from having dinner and going to church with Luca," Nadine joked. "You?"

"No, I just work." Rome scooted closer and nestled herself in the crook of Nadine's arm, resting her hand on her chest. "But in the weeks that I've been here, I've been out more than I have in the past ten years at home. I think Rome is good for me."

"And you're good for me," Nadine said, leaning in to kiss her before retracting with a groan. "God, I can't even move right now my head hurts so much."

"I didn't take you for a lightweight," Rome joked. "You stay here, I'll go get us some breakfast."

"Really?" Nadine looked at her gratefully. "That's the sweetest thing anyone's ever done for me."

"So no one's ever taken care of you? You poor thing," Rome said in a mock dramatic tone as she placed a soft kiss on Nadine's forehead. "Well, that's about to change. Coffee and breakfast coming up." She got out of bed and slipped into the clothes she'd worn on Friday. She hadn't been home since as they'd been working on Nadine's business plan. She wasn't at her best, but she was in a far better state than Nadine and was seriously craving the fresh pastries from the bakery she'd grown to love.

Luca came out with a garbage bag just as she was about to go down the stairs. "Here, let me take that," she said, taking the bag from him. A deep frown appeared between his brows as he stared at her, then reluctantly handed it over, clearly trying to work out if he could trust her with his trash or not. "I'm Rome." She placed a hand on her chest, then pointed to Nadine's door. "Friend of Nadine."

"Ah, Nadine." A smile lit up his face and he nodded, then rattled off a monologue in Italian. Rome made a mental note to finally start those Italian lessons she'd downloaded. Perhaps today would be a good day to do that in bed, she thought. She waved at Luca and carried the heavy bag downstairs, where the garbage truck was just driving off. "Wait!" she yelled, waving her hands until it stopped. A man stepped out and greeted her, then rolled his eyes when Luca shot off a rant from his window, waving his fist at him. He murmured something that sounded like a curse, then gave Rome a wink before he drove off.

Rome felt herself smiling, and she wondered why something as mundane as taking the trash outside made her happy. Maybe because she finally felt like she was a part of a community, however strange that sounded. She'd never been in contact with her neighbors in Portland, but the social interactions she was now experiencing in Rome touched her, even if they meant nothing. Maybe she just felt more connected to people in general here, where they smiled and greeted each other in passing, and kept an eye out for each other.

She walked to the bakery with a bounce in her step, genuinely enjoying the short trip through the beautiful alleyways. A group of nuns were waiting at the counter, laughing and joking with the baker, who looked like he was making fun of them. Again, Rome longed to speak the language, and deciding to give it a go, she opened her translation app and looked up how to order a loaf of bread and two croissants. To her surprise, the baker understood her, and although she didn't get what he said after that, she managed to work out how much to pay and even wished him a good day in Italian. Gloating with excitement, she stopped at another store to buy eggs and then moved on to the market to get fresh tomatoes and ricotta, using her app to communicate. Now that she'd finally gotten over her initial shyness, learning the language didn't seem so daunting anymore.

Nadine had taught her some fundamental phrases and how to count, to say thank you and some other polite basics, but she hadn't put her learnings into practice until now. As she walked back with bags full of groceries, she imagined herself being fully integrated by the time her job was done, and being able to communicate effortlessly, speaking the elegant language that sounded like music to her ears. And then what? Would she go back home? Continue to live her life in the US like her time here had never happened? Rome shook off that thought, because the idea of leaving Nadine made her feel sick, and she didn't want to ruin her good mood.

Back in Nadine's kitchen, she went to work and miraculously managed to whip up scrambled eggs with ricotta and black pepper. She also sliced a couple of tomatoes and added the fresh bread and the croissants onto a tray she found in the kitchen, along with two large take-out coffees from the café below the apartment.

"Here's breakfast," she whispered and felt a lump in her throat as Nadine slowly turned and opened her eyes. She took her breath away with everything she did, and even just watching her wake up was a sight she knew she'd never forget.

"Sweet, sweet Rome. You're an angel." Nadine sat up and reached for the coffee like it was a lifeline. She shot Rome an adorable smile as she looked over the food she'd prepared. "Wow. The perks of having a girlfriend are becoming clear to me now." Although she was joking, Rome could tell that it touched her from the way her eyes welled up before she looked down, taking one of the plates and avoiding her gaze.

Hearing her say the word 'girlfriend' made Rome blush, and she hid her grin behind her coffee cup as Nadine took a bite. "My first attempt at a real breakfast," she said smugly, before tasting the eggs. "Not bad if I say so myself."

"Not bad? This is amazing." Nadine squeezed her hand. "Thank you, I really mean that."

"You're welcome." Rome studied Nadine, who seemed to

have no idea what to do with her sudden emotional state, so she changed the subject. "I met Luca as I left the building and took his trash outside. He was a bit suspicious about me at first, but he chirped up when I said your name."

"Oh, you did?" Nadine laughed. "Of course he was suspicious, that man doesn't trust anyone. God, I think I'm supposed to take him to church today." She checked the time on her phone and sighed. "In an hour."

"Good thing I woke you up, then. Are you taking a cab?"

Nadine shook her head. "We're taking the scooter, it's much quicker."

"You're joking, right?" Rome tried to imagine Nadine with the eighty-five-year old on the back and raised a brow at her. "That's crazy."

"No, I'm totally serious, he's fine on the back," Nadine said as if there was nothing strange about that. "We might even be able to fit three people on my ride if you want to come. Or we can take a cab if being wedged between me and Luca freaks you out."

Rome laughed and waved a hand. "No, you go. I'm sure he's much more comfortable when it's just the two of you." She held up her phone. "But if you don't mind me staying in your bed for a little longer, I'm going to start my first Italian lesson today."

"Really? I'm impressed you're so keen to learn the language, it's hard." Nadine tilted her head and smiled as she locked her eyes with Rome's. "But then again, you're so smart that learning Italian might be as easy as pie to you."

"Don't big me up." Rome blew her a kiss. "I'm not that smart, and I have no talent when it comes to languages, but I'm sure I can remember a couple of sentences and manage the basics if you correct my pronunciation from time to time."

"That's a deal." Nadine put her plate to the side and took a sip of her coffee, then rolled over to face her again. "But if you really want to learn, you're going to have to spend a lot of time with me."

"I think I can manage that." Rome's breath hitched when Nadine ran a hand over her breasts. She caught it and shook her head as she chuckled. "If you start this now, we won't be done in an hour and you know that."

"You're right." Nadine sighed as she reluctantly pulled her hand away and got out of bed. "Will you be here when I get back?"

Rome nodded, a warm feeling coursing through her as she watched Nadine cross the room naked, searching for a towel. "I'll be waiting."

41

"Are you ready for this?" Mitch, the director of *Consumers First*, handed Nadine a file and took a seat next to her on the big, green couch in his swanky office. His company specialized in consumer product testing, secret shopper projects, focus groups and market predictions, and although they weren't cheap, they were known to be the most reliable and respected consumer research company in Europe, with offices in Paris, Milan, and London.

"I'm ready." Nadine gratefully accepted the coffee his assistant brought her, then opened the file. She'd taken an early flight to Milan and would visit some stores after her meeting, then get a flight back tomorrow. She'd never had a face-to-face meeting that wasn't escort related before and for the first time, she felt overdressed in her sharp, black suit and high heels. Mitch, who was English and had a thick accent, was wearing torn jeans and a buttoned-up pink blazer with seemingly nothing underneath. He was around her age, she guessed, and blended in seamlessly with all the millennials who were chatting and working at their standing desks in the large, open space outside his office.

"Perfect, let's dive right in." Mitch scratched his thick, blonde hair and switched on the large screen on the wall. "I just want to show you our approach first, so you can get a better understanding of how we work." He pointed to the screen, that showed a video clip of twenty people sitting behind a window. They all had microphones attached to their collar and were blindfolded. Nadine felt a surge of excitement at seeing her perfumes on the table in front of them. "What you see is a two-way mirror, like they use for police line-ups. They can't see us, although they can't see anything at this point as they're blindfolded," he added jokingly. But we can see and hear them. Sitting on the other side of the mirror are me, a psychologist, one of our employees taking notes, and a mediator, who gives instructions to one of our other employees who is in the room with the group sampling the products. We've used ten test groups, that means ten sessions with twenty people, so two hundred in total. To get a realistic representation, nine of the test groups were heterosexual, and one was homosexual."

"Interesting," Nadine said, studying the men and women in the room. The way they sat there lined up and blindfolded made it look like some obscure ritual, and they seemed a little on edge. "And they don't know each other, right?"

"No. They're also not allowed to speak at this point, so attraction to voice is taken out of the equation." Mitch fast-forwarded the video and continued. "Our lovely Nancy is now applying your perfume to the neck of each person in the sampling group. Each perfume applied matched the tester's star sign, and we then asked each of the ten women to smell the men one by one, then point to their favorite when they'd made their decision after going up and down a couple of times. After this, we reversed the process, asking the men to do the same."

"Okay." Nadine anxiously tapped her fingers on the file. Although this was the biggest moment in her eight years of perfume making, she wished Mitch would just get to the point and give her the results first.

Mitch held up a sheet Nadine had provided, that indicated which star signs were compatible with each other according to general astrology. "Now here is where it gets interesting, because to be honest with you, I was very skeptical about this," he said with a grin. "But... eighty-two percent of our total sample was attracted to one of their assigned star signs."

"Really?" Nadine's face lit up as she scanned the results he pointed out in her file. "That's good, right?"

"That's very good," Mitch agreed. Our target was sixty percent, so going on the first batch of tests, you already have solid evidence to back up your claims. He fast-forwarded the video again, and Nadine watched the people in the sample group blink against the bright light in the room when their blindfolds were removed. "Here's the point where they can see each other, simulating a more lifelike encounter. They're asked to smell each other again and verbal exchanges are still not allowed. Each of them then writes down the number attached to the chest of the person they'd most like to spend the day with." Mitch pointed to another sheet in Nadine's file. "Out of the eighty-two percent who chose one of their aligned star signs, seventy-two percent stuck to their choice, not knowing they'd picked the same person in the first place."

"Incredible." Nadine sat back, finally able to relax a little. "So we can work with this, right? Use it for my retailer's pitch and marketing material?"

"Absolutely." Mitch switched to a page with statistics on the screen before he continued. "My staff agrees that *Stars Aligned* is a very fitting name for your product and a lot of women in the office are very excited about it. They were fighting over the samples after our test day." He chuckled. "But there's also our last test, which asked our sample groups to describe the smell of the people they'd chosen, and all science aside, this may be the best claim so far."

"I'm all ears." Nadine narrowed her eyes as she studied the words on the screen.

"These are the keywords that came up before the initial blindfold test when the samplers were asked to describe each other's smell without any perfume or products. Just to clarify, we asked them not to use any soap or shampoo and just wash themselves with water before they came in that day." Mitch clicked his remote, enlarging the words 'sweet', 'spicy', 'sweaty', 'manly' and 'neutral'.

Nadine laughed as she read out some of the smaller words surrounding the bigger ones. "I see someone smells of garlic."

"Yes, we got some funny answers here." Mitch clicked to the next slide. "But then, after applying your perfume, we got very different keywords. "Attractive and sexy," he said, raising his voice. "Those were the keywords that kept coming up in the conversations." He put his coffee cup down and turned to her. "Attractive is not a common word to describe smell. Smell, as you know, is generally described using more concrete words, like sweet, musky, sweaty, floral, powdery and so on, like in the initial test."

"That's true," Nadine said, her pulse racing with excitement. "So what you're saying is their feedback after applying my perfume was emotive rather than descriptive?"

"Exactly. Here we have words like 'attractive', 'sexy',

'pretty', 'feminine', 'masculine', 'seductive', and none of them are negative. They're actually very powerful key words and all link back to the concept of attraction." Mitch tilted his head and gave her a wide smile. "So we believe this is a very, very sellable product, even without the star sign message, which will appeal to some, but others might prefer a more direct approach such as 'This will make you smell attractive', instead of 'This may help you find your soul-mate.' It all depends on the market, and we can look into that for you, if you want."

"That would be fantastic," Nadine said, feeling more hopeful than ever. With Rome's help on her strategy, she had some great tools to work with. She took a deep breath knowing she would have to concentrate on the rest of the meeting, because now, all she wanted was to call Rome with the good news. A smile played around her mouth as she pictured the woman she'd been spending most of her free time and nights with lately. The woman who had given her the confidence to finish what she'd started and to pursue her dream. The woman who had somehow found a way into her heart. She hadn't even fought it. Not really. Because she'd found that by working together, she was stronger and more creative than she'd ever been before.

42

"I'm so happy for you," Rome said, wrapping her arms around Nadine as she walked into her kitchen where Nadine was cooking up a delicious looking feast. She'd missed her while she was in Milan and had anxiously waited for Friday to arrive. "And I'm so, so proud of you."

"Thank you." Nadine smiled widely as she kissed her, then rushed over to the stove, where her tomato sauce was about to burn. "I'm beyond excited," she said, stirring the sauce. "And I'm ready to send out my pitch to the retailers. I've added in the report from *Consumers First*, and I think it's good to go now, but if you wouldn't mind casting your eye over it one more time, that would be great."

"Of course, I'd be happy to. But right now, I have other things I need to cast my eye over." Rome came up behind Nadine and pinched her ass, then chuckled to herself. Before she came here, it would have been unthinkable that she would be so crazy about anyone, let alone a woman, but now, she couldn't keep her hands off Nadine.

Nadine turned around and kissed her passionately while she kept stirring the sauce behind her, laughing at the poor attempt to multitask that made the sauce splash over the pan. "I was thinking we could go out for drinks after dinner?" she said when Rome stepped away. "I'm making melanzane and I've invited Luca over. It's not very romantic, but you know…"

"You're a total sweetheart." Rome shot her an endearing look. "I'm going to make it my mission to make Luca like me and yes, I'd love to go out for drinks after."

"Good luck with the mission." Nadine grinned. "Luca trusts no one and he's generally grumpy and hard work. Any more news from your Italian lawyer?" she asked, turning down the heat before she placed the lid on the pan.

"Yes, actually. Anton found out that Matteo already has one conviction of sexual harassment against him. It was over twenty years ago, in Japan, and for some reason there's no record of it here in Italy. The victim doesn't want to get involved, but it could still be good ammunition in court. I'm also glad Eliza agreed to help out, but I haven't heard anything from her so far. As soon as we serve Matteo with a petition, it still takes ninety days until the first hearing starts so, although it will be awful if she does, I'm kind of hoping she'll find some other women to come forward sooner rather than later. I assume he'll stay away from the office or at least from me for a while and if he doesn't, I'm hoping the HR department can make him work remotely as soon as he's been served. They insisted on arranging a meeting with a view to mediating, but he didn't show up, thank God."

"I hope so too. I worry every day you go to work," Nadine said. "And it's very nice of Eliza to help, it's a good idea to ask a local. It's not like being in the US here, where people sue each other left right and center; Europeans are very uncomfortable with stuff like that."

"I know." Rome hesitated as she looked for a sharp knife

to help Nadine slice the eggplants. "Do you mind if I invite her to come with us tonight?"

"Who, Eliza?" Nadine stared at her in disbelief, and Rome laughed.

"Come on, you can't possibly have a problem with her; you don't even know her. She's lovely and I already told you, there's no need to be jealous." She was glad to see a small smile on Nadine's face and knew she was just being over dramatic. "The thing is, she's one of the best PR people in the world and she might want to take a look at that plan of yours."

"She's in PR?" Nadine narrowed her eyes. "You didn't tell her anything about my perfumes, did you?" She was aware of her snappy tone, but she couldn't help herself. Her perfumes were her babies, and apart from Rome and *Consumers First*, no one knew about her product.

"Of course not. I just thought she might be able to help you out with some ideas to spread the word. She's got a lot of contacts," Rome continued, unwilling to take no for an answer. "Look, I know you like to keep everything close to your chest and figure things out by yourself, but the thing is, everyone needs experts. At some point you'll have to hand over certain aspects of the business and trust others to help you."

Nadine sighed as she handed Rome a chopping board and two large eggplants. "I suppose you've got a point. I'm just nervous, that's all, and I don't like being nervous."

"No one likes to be nervous," Rome said with a chuckle. "But it's going to be fine." She was glad she'd been able to return the favor for once, helping Nadine, and putting her at ease when she needed it. "You've got a beautiful product with an enchanting story behind it, and people are going to love it. All you need is advice from experts and if Eliza can help you out over a couple of drinks, why not?"

"I suppose you're right." Nadine cupped Rome's face and kissed her. "I probably need to stop being so precious about it and try to get over my fear of failing."

"Yes, you do," Rome mumbled against her mouth. "Because you're awesome and everything is going to be fine."

Luca narrowed his eyes at Rome when he spotted her at the table, but he managed a polite nod before greeting Nadine. He said something in Italian and pointed to Rome, to which Nadine yelled back at him, waving her hands wildly. The conversation seemed to get pretty heated, and Rome hadn't prepared herself for drama tonight.

"I can go somewhere else if my presence upsets him," she said as she studied the old man who looked genuinely disappointed at seeing her.

"No way." Nadine barked something else at him and took the melanzane out of the oven, then ordered him to sit down. "I told him it was you and me now, and that he'd better get used to that or there will be no more melanzane." She rolled her eyes. "God damn it, it's like having a kid."

Rome poured the wine as Nadine served the food. She slid a glass over to Luca, then held up her own. "*Salute,*" she said, looking him in the eyes with a smile, then managed to say 'nice to meet you' in broken Italian. That seemed to thaw him a little as a hint of surprise washed over his features, and he grunted and held up his glass.

"Good boy," Nadine joked as she plated for him, then shot him a wink. "Although he claims he doesn't, I'm pretty sure he understands English. There's no way he could have run a bar in Rome for most of his life without being able to communicate with tourists."

Luca shot Nadine an irritated look, and she looked back at him, raising her eyebrows.

"See?" she said to him. "You know exactly what I'm saying. Maybe we should just speak English tonight."

Nadine's comment was met with another rant in Italian, and Rome held up her hands. "Hey, hey, guys, calm down. Please speak Italian, I need to learn so I don't mind at all." She sighed as she picked up her fork, bracing herself for a long dinner. "Just pretend like I'm not here, okay?"

43

"Hey, I'm Eliza." Eliza gave Nadine a kiss on each cheek after greeting Rome. "Nice to meet you. I saw you walking past the bar a couple of weeks back when we were having drinks. That was an amazing dress you were wearing."

"Thank you. I apologize for not saying hi; I was in a hurry, but it's very nice to meet you too." Nadine put on her most charming smile as she sat down next to Rome.

Eliza looked from Rome to Nadine and back, studying them with a curious grin. "So, are you guys now dating?"

Nadine glanced at Rome, then put an arm around her and pulled her in. "Yeah, we are." She kissed Rome's cheek and shot Eliza a beaming smile. "I'm the luckiest woman in the world."

At that, Rome started blushing profusely. She put an arm around Nadine in return and tried to wipe the goofy grin off her face. "I have to disagree on that. I think I might be the lucky one." It felt great to be out together, to feel entirely comfortable about people knowing. She was immensely proud to be with Nadine, and she didn't care who knew anymore. Perhaps it was time she told her dad too, Rome thought.

"You guys are cute together." Eliza shot them an endearing look. "Not to mention, incredibly hot." She quickly held up a hand. "Don't get the wrong idea here; I'm super straight but you two are a sight for sore eyes." She fanned her face for comical effect, making the black cape she was wearing flap around her like giant bat wings. She'd paired it with a black bodysuit, and in combination with her otherworldly lilac lenses, she could have passed for someone on her way to a Halloween party. "Anyway, what are we drinking?"

"How about Bellinis?" Rome suggested. "On me, of course. I feel like celebrating, if only for the fact that I survived my first dinner with Nadine's neighbor." She beckoned the waiter over and ordered in Italian, then chuckled when she got a round of applause for that.

"What about the neighbor?" Eliza asked.

"Oh, he's just a grumpy piece of work." Nadine rolled her eyes. "And very protective over me; he refuses to share me with anyone and that's about to change." She turned to Rome. "Sorry you had to sit through that, I honestly didn't think he'd be so rude."

"Yeah, he was pretty clear about the fact that he doesn't like me." Rome shrugged. "But he seemed to mellow when I finally snapped and started being rude back to him. I guess that's the key to his heart."

"I think you're right," Nadine said with a chuckle as she sank back in the red, velvet booth and watched the barman skillfully prepare their cocktails. "I'll have a word with him, though, next time we're alone." When their drinks arrived, she held up her glass and toasted with Rome and Eliza.

"Thank you for helping Rome out with the case against Matteo. That's very nice of you."

"Of course, Matteo needs to go down." Eliza took a sip of her drink. "Someone came forward yesterday, but I can't tell you her name yet as she's not sure if she wants to take action. But I'll let you know as soon as she makes up her mind."

"So there *is* someone else?" Rome sighed, and her heart went out to whoever it was. She'd started to wonder if he'd singled her out, but that had seemed unlikely. "Poor woman."

"Yeah." Eliza shuddered and shook her head. "God, how I hate that man."

"I should have killed him when I had the chance," Nadine said, balling her hands into fists.

"No, it's not worth getting into serious trouble over him." Eliza turned to Nadine and looked her up and down. "But Rome told me you came to her rescue. Well done, girl." She held up her hand and high-fived her. "Anyway, tonight is for fun, so let's not talk about Matteo. How did you guys meet?"

"We ehm…" Rome looked at Nadine for help as she wasn't sure if she had a problem with people knowing what she did for a living. They should have discussed this before they left but she hadn't thought about that.

"We met when Rome was pitching her product to *Nero*," Nadine said, stepping in. "At the St. Regis." It was the truth, but she skimmed over the details. "We got talking beforehand, she told me about the Carbon app, and I was fascinated by her." She grinned. "So, I flirted with her and frankly, I've never seen anyone look so shocked in my life."

Rome laughed. "I *was* shocked. I'm not used to women flirting with me" She shot Nadine an amused smile. "And you weren't exactly subtle."

Eliza laughed too and turned to Nadine. "So, you're quite the charmer, huh? What do you do for a living? Are you a model or something? You certainly look like one."

"Me?" Nadine's eyes widened. "No, God, no. I'm actually a high-end escort. The dating minus the sex," she explained, wanting to get it over with. "That's why I was at the St. Regis." If Rome and Eliza were going to be friends, she didn't want there to be any secrets between them because of her, and besides, she wasn't ashamed of her job.

"Okay. That must be a pretty lucrative business to be in." If Eliza was surprised, she didn't let it show, but then again, going on her looks, this was a pretty open-minded woman.

"It is. But my contract finishes next year and I don't mind that at all." Nadine glanced down at the file and the box in her purse, deciding to trust Rome on her advice. Despite their rusty start, Eliza actually seemed like a nice woman and she was relieved that her jealous feelings had melted away as soon as she'd seen Rome and her together. There was no chemistry between them, and she felt foolish for even going there. "I'm also a perfumer, though. I've just finalized my first range of fragrances and I'm ready to launch them soon." She took the box and gave it to Eliza. "I hope you don't mind, but Rome did some digging and found out you were a Scorpio. Feisty star sign," she added with a smirk. "Anyway, here's a sample for you. Just to say sorry for possibly coming across as a little rude when we first met."

Eliza looked delighted as she studied the box, then let out an excited shriek as she opened it and held up the bottle. "It's gorgeous, thank you." She read the label, then opened the bottle and sniffed it. "I like it. It's super subtle." Narrowing her eyes, she read the printed card that came with the box, her excitement clearly growing. "Wow, Nadine, this is genius, I love the concept. Does it actually work?"

Nadine felt proud as she watched her reaction. Eliza didn't seem like the type of woman who faked enthusiasm just to be polite. "Yes, it's supposed to." She chuckled. "It's a little gimmicky of course, but according to the tests, it makes the wearer smell attractive to others, so I'm very excited about that."

"Well, gimmicky or not; even if it doesn't get me a date, this is gold. It's super cute and a perfect present." Eliza dabbed some on her wrist and wiped it off on her neck as she looked around the bar. "I'll be your test subject tonight, shall I? There are a lot of handsome guys here so let's see if they bite." She leaned in and lowered her voice. "But first, tell me more."

44

"That went well, right?" Rome hooked an arm through Nadine's as they walked away from the bar, both a little tipsy from the cocktails.

"Yeah, I had a great night." Nadine turned to meet Rome's smug stare. "Okay, I'll just say it. You were right; Eliza is a very nice woman. Fun too."

"And she's taking a set of samples to give away to celebrities at parties."

"And that. It's really generous of her."

"Imagine if just one of them tweets about it."

Nadine sighed. "Yes, that would be pretty amazing. Thank you, for convincing me to do this." She realized they were heading for her apartment, and she hadn't even asked Rome if she wanted to spend the night. "Do you want to stay over at mine?"

Rome looked up at her and smiled as the heat between them started flaring up again. "Are you kidding me? Of course I do." She hesitated. "But I'm not sure I can handle your slow teasing tonight, what with the way you're looking at me right now. I really, really want to rip your clothes off."

Nadine felt her pulse racing as she returned her flirty smile. "My cute little nerd is discovering the joys of sex." Knowing Rome wanted her turned her on like nothing else, and she was suddenly overcome with an urge to take her there and then. "How about I give you quick now and slow later?"

Rome stopped in her stride and Nadine could feel her shiver. "What do you mean?"

"What I mean..." Nadine took her hand and pulled her into a dark, private courtyard, thinking the fountain in the middle might dampen the noises Rome would be making very, very soon. "...is that we don't have to wait until we get home." She pushed her against the closest wall and kissed her hard, arousal coursing through her at Rome's soft moans. Running a hand up Rome's thigh, Nadine pressed her hips into hers and deepened the kiss, drawing another moan from her as she cupped her ass. "You feel so good," she whispered against her mouth, then lifted her dress to trail a finger over Rome's hip bone before sliding her fingers lower into her panties.

Rome gasped. "Jesus, Nadine. Maybe we should..." She swallowed the rest of her words as Nadine's fingers brushed over her clit. "Oh God."

"Want me to stop?" Nadine smiled when she felt Rome's wetness coat her fingers.

"No." Rome was squirming against her, trying her best to be quiet as Nadine lowered her hand and carefully pushed two fingers inside her. "Don't stop." Her head fell back when Nadine lifted her leg and hooked an arm under it, then started thrusting into her, hard and fast.

Rome wrapped her arms around Nadine's neck, and Nadine could feel her fisting the fabric on the back of her dress as she tensed up, breathing heavier each time she went deeper inside her. "Fuck..." she muttered.

"Shh..." Nadine said softly, as she watched Rome's lips part and her face pull into a delightful expression. Curling her fingers, she hit the spot she knew would send Rome over the edge, and she almost went there herself as she felt Rome's throbbing clit harden against her palm. It was incredibly sexy, the way Rome gave herself to her, out here in the courtyard, not caring about anything but the instant satisfaction she needed so badly. Her moans became louder, and Nadine put a hand in front of her mouth to dampen the sounds. Rome was shuddering against her other hand, her hips jerking wildly. The strap of her dress had slipped off one shoulder and her hair was a wild mess as she leaned back against the wall, slowly coming back to her senses. "You are so incredibly sexy." Nadine's voice was as ragged as Rome's breathing, and she needed a moment herself to tame the aching need between her thighs.

"And you are so incredibly talented." Rome locked her hazy blue eyes with Nadine's, her long lashes fluttering when she pulled out of her. As if waking up from a dream, she looked around, suddenly conscious of their surroundings.

"We're fine, there's no one here," Nadine whispered, putting her at ease. "And I don't think anyone heard us either." She raised her gaze skyward when a window opened above them and chuckled when a woman started yelling at them in Italian. "Okay, maybe someone did hear us."

Rome couldn't help but giggle too as Nadine took her hand and pulled her away, yelling something back at her. "I can't believe I woke her up."

"Hey, there are worse things to wake up to." Nadine

laughed as they rushed away from the courtyard and into the network of alleyways that would take them back to Trastevere.

By the time they arrived at Nadine's apartment, Rome felt restless and aroused beyond imagination. Nadine switched on music, lit some candles and opened the balcony doors to let the evening breeze in. Even after their courtyard shenanigans, her raging lust hadn't faded in the slightest, and she was desperate to get Nadine out of her clothes. She stared at her long, tanned legs in the short, navy dress, then at her full breasts in the low neckline. Rome wanted her, and she wanted her now.

Nadine blew at the matchstick in her hand, seductively swaying her hips as she crossed the room back to Rome. As if reading her thoughts, she said: "Nothing great should ever be rushed. Don't you agree?"

Rome brushed her lips against Nadine's when they were face to face. "I agree, but I'm not sure if I can avoid hurrying in this particular moment." She slid both hands under Nadine's dress and marveled at the feeling of her soft skin and feminine curves.

Nadine smiled as she raked her fingers through Rome's hair, took a fistful and pulled her head back, exposing her neck. Slowly, she trailed her tongue up the side to her ear and gently bit her earlobe. "Yes, you can."

Her hot breath and low whisper were enough to make Rome twitch in anticipation. She lowered her hands to Nadine's ass and pulled her against her hips, needing more of her. Tugging at the hem of her dress, she pulled it off, and her eyes darkened when she saw she was wearing nothing but a pair of tiny panties underneath. When had she become so entranced with Nadine's body? She longed for her like nothing else and her mouth was drawn to her breasts as if she had no control over her actions.

Nadine moaned when Rome leaned in and twirled her tongue around her nipple, then sucked it into her mouth. She traced her shoulders, her arms, and her back while she devoured her breasts, breathing in Nadine's natural scent that made her feel wild and alive. Perhaps Nadine was right. Maybe there was some connection between the stars and scent and attraction, because she simply couldn't get enough of her. "Get on the floor," she whispered.

A sexy smile played around Nadine's mouth as she kneeled down on the Persian rug in front of the fireplace and waited for Rome to join her. "What about your dress?"

"My dress will come off when I'm ready for it to come off. As you said, nothing good should be rushed, right?" Rome got down on the rug too and straddled Nadine. She leaned forward and pinned her wrists to the ground above her head. Nadine looked surprised, but the underlying desire in her eyes didn't lie; she liked it. "You just need to keep still and be a good girl," Rome teased, grinding herself into her.

"Is that how it works now?" Nadine bit her lip and chuckled, but otherwise complied.

"Yes. That's how it will be tonight." Rome bent down to kiss her and let out a soft sigh at feeling Nadine's need, seeping through their kiss. The sweetness of her lips, the urgency of her tongue and the way she moved underneath her, so sensually and animalistic at the same time, brought out a wild side in Rome. Nadine's back arched and her hands balled into fists as Rome moved her mouth back to her breasts and bit down on her nipple. Soft at first, then harder, making her gasp and writhe in her grip. Their twisting shadows danced over the

LISE GOLD

wall, distorted by the flickering candles. The precious sound of Nadine's breaths becoming heavy moans filled the room as Rome let go of her wrists and moved her mouth down toward her belly, scraping her nails over the swell of her breasts. This woman was hers and only hers, and Rome wanted her to know how deep her passion went, how much she needed her. She would swallow her whole, if only she could.

45

Rome was catching up on emails when someone knocked on her door. "Come in," she yelled, without looking up. She had the only office on the third floor, and although she spent most of her time in the meeting space with the team, it was nice to have a private room where she could concentrate.

"Hi, Rome."

Rome's eyes widened as she looked up and found Matteo in the doorway. "What the fuck are you doing here?" she hissed, desperately trying to hide the sudden surge of fear she felt at seeing him. It had been weeks since he'd tried to force himself upon her, and that she'd reported him to the police. "How dare you come anywhere near me, please leave before I call security."

Ignoring her, Matteo stepped inside and closed the door behind him. "I heard through the grapevine that you were planning on suing me, so I wanted to talk to you. I think there's been a misunderstanding."

"There is no misunderstanding." Rome waved at the door. Her staff could see them through the glass partition, and although she was sitting in plain sight, she still couldn't bear the thought of being locked up with him. She thought she'd been fine, but now that he was here, she was anything but fine. "Open that door right now and get out of here." Her hands were trembling, and she hid them in her lap behind her desk.

Matteo opened the door again but remained where he was, tugging at his tie while sweat pearled on his forehead. "Please Rome, can't we just talk about this?"

"No, we can't. Leave." She glared at him. "Now."

"I didn't mean to scare you that night, I was only looking after you." He cleared his throat and shuffled on the spot. "I'd like to apologize. I'm sorry I couldn't come to the mediation meeting with HR. Something came up but I'm available now if you'd like to go down there together. I've already spoken to them and explained the situation."

"Of course you have," Rome said with cynicism seeping through her tone. "I don't want your apology and I'm only going to ask you once more. Please leave."

"Come on, Rome. It was nothing. Do you really have to make a big deal out of this? You're about to become known as the creator of something great. Why would you ruin your career by sabotaging the company like this?"

"This is about you and what you did, Matteo. *Nero* has nothing to do with your actions. That's why I've tried to keep it quiet, but you're making that very hard for me right now. And you had your chance with HR. I was there, only because I wanted my complaint to be documented, and you chose not to show up, so you dug your own grave by pulling that trick on me. It's not going to look good on you in court." Rome met his eyes and saw anger flashing in them. Just like that night, his temper shifted within seconds and his whole demeanor changed.

Matteo straightened himself, trying to appear taller than he was. "You have no idea who you're dealing with," he whispered, glancing over his shoulder to make sure no one was listening in. "I've made your career and I can take it away just like that." He snapped his fingers. "Go ahead and sue me; you won't stand a chance. You're not just ruining your own life, but you're putting your team members' jobs at risk too. Is that what you want?"

Rome stood up and pointed at the door again, ignoring his threats. She didn't care if people could see her; she just really, really needed him to leave. Messing with her was one thing, and she was going to take him on and make him pay, but threatening her team's livelihoods was manipulation on a whole other level. "Out!" she yelled, furiously slamming her hand on her desk.

"Fine. Then you'll hear from my lawyer." Matteo held up both hands and finally started walking out, keeping his threatening stare fixed on her. "You're going to be sorry."

"We'll see about that." Rome remained standing until he disappeared out of sight, then sank back in her chair and buried her face in her trembling hands. Her heart was pounding hard in her chest and she was unable to hide how much seeing Matteo again had shaken her. It had been years since she'd had a panic attack, but she recognized the signs; the tightness in her chest and the sense of terror that gave her sweaty chills... Holding onto her stomach, she counted to four while she breathed in, then held it for four counts and slowly exhaled, repeating the exercise until her heart rate had slowed down a little. Even though she kept her eyes fixed on her screen, pretending to be reading, she knew her team had noticed something was wrong. That was the downside of a glass office; nothing was private. Of all the different scenarios she'd anticipated, she'd never expected him to have the nerve to show up in her office. She silently cursed herself for not being prepared, and for letting him get to her yet again.

"Hey, are you okay?" Lara, her assistant asked as she stuck her head around the corner. "I just heard you yell at Matteo."

Rome nodded, forcing a smile. "Yeah, I'm fine. It's nothing."

"Are you sure?" The woman narrowed her eyes as she walked in and put her hand on Rome's shoulder. "Matteo never comes up here, and he clearly said something that upset you."

"I can't talk about it right now, but I can assure you it's got nothing to do with work, so you don't need to worry," Rome said. She'd tried to keep it quiet for as long as possible as she didn't want the company or her team to suffer under the case. Matteo knew that though, and he'd just used it as ammunition. "I'm fine, really." She shot Lara a grateful look and took another couple of deep breaths. "We have a meeting in ten minutes, right?"

"We do, but I can move it if you..."

"No, absolutely not," Rome interrupted her, and gathered her things. "If you arrange the coffee, I'll set up the meeting space. Please just forget this ever happened, okay?"

46

Nadine felt a whole new sense of accomplishment as she closed her laptop after counting her orders. She'd worked hard in the past weeks, and she'd received positive feedback from retailers and department stores, and most of them were willing to buy a small sample batch of her perfumes. They were also pleased with her test-tube counter display and the majority had agreed to buy one. Her key target market included most of Europe, where she'd concentrated on the capital cities, and twelve US states. Only two months ago, it had seemed an impossible journey, but Rome had been right; the product was unique and commercial, and her marketing strategy made sense, so stores were happy to stock it for the coming season. She'd found agents for Europe and the US who would be taking over the expansion plan as soon as the first orders were in store, and she had someone working on her website and web shop, which were looking amazing and were ready to launch next week. It was all starting to get very real.

The doorbell rang, and she got up from the kitchen table

to see who it was. Expecting Luca, or the delivery of her dress for tonight, she was surprised to see that it was Rome.

"Hey, I didn't expect you here today. And so early? This is a nice surprise." She frowned when she noticed Rome wasn't her usual carefree self. "Rome, come here, honey." Nadine's heart broke when Rome started sobbing in her arms, and she held her close as she took her inside and sat her down on the couch. "What happened? Are you okay?"

"Matteo came to my office," Rome said through her tears. "I didn't think it would affect me so much, seeing him again, but I swear, I couldn't function after I'd sent him away." She shrugged. "So, I left the office and I'm sorry but I wanted to come here. I know you have to work tonight and..."

"Shh... it's okay." Nadine kissed her temple and pulled her further in. "I'm here. Tell me what happened."

"Nothing. He wanted to talk, explain the 'misunderstanding'," Rome said, making quote marks with her fingers. "I sent him away and he threatened me and my team on his way out."

"The bastard... Is he still at the office?" Nadine stood up, but Rome grabbed her wrist and pulled her back down.

"Please don't do anything stupid. I know you have good intentions, but I have to do this the right way; I can't have anything jeopardizing the case."

"Of course. I'm sorry; I don't know what I was thinking."

Rome hesitated as she looked at Nadine. "Do you mind if I stay here while you're away tonight? I don't want to sleep alone."

"Of course not." Nadine took a couple of deep breaths and gave her a sweet smile. "Don't move; I just need to make a phone call and then I'll get you a cup of tea." She walked to the kitchen where she switched on the kettle, then went out onto the balcony while she dialed the number for her agency.

"Hi Sofia, it's Nadine." She paused, wondering how to best go about this as she'd never cancelled on a client before. "I'm not feeling well," she lied, knowing there was no arguing with illness. "I was fine this afternoon, but my stomach is all over the place now. I think it might have been something I ate."

Sofia, her booker, was silent for a long moment. "You're ill? You've never called in sick." There was no genuine concern from her side, and that was no surprise to Nadine. "How do you expect me to find someone else at such short notice? This is a very important client."

"I don't know." Nadine sighed. "The dress isn't here yet, so you could have the courier send it to one of the other girls, if any of them are available?"

"But our client specifically wanted you," Sofia argued.

"Well, he'll have to do with someone else because you don't want me running to the toilet every five minutes, do you? Throwing up my food and looking pale?"

"No, we don't want that." Sofia cleared her throat. "Okay, I'll try to arrange someone else. But this can't happen again, do you understand? We already had a complaint from Louise, and this is not helping you."

"Louise lured me to a hotel because she wanted to sleep with me. I said no; it's as simple as that," Nadine argued.

"Yes, well, you know very well there are better ways of solving these issues rather than storming out. It's unprofessional."

Nadine felt herself getting angry again and she hated the feeling. She was angry at Matteo, at Louise, now at Sofia, and honestly, she was angry at herself too for letting people treat her like a puppet. "You know what? I think you need to cut me some slack, Sofia. I've worked for you for four years and never once have you had a complaint about me, apart from Louise. I solve my own issues, I'm always available and I'm always professional. Do you have any idea how exhausting that is? Smiling and pretending to be engaged all night, even if you're having a bad day?"

"That's not our problem. We're paying you a lot of money to be on sparkling form, and we expect nothing less."

"Right." Nadine took a moment to reflect on her feelings. What she really wanted was to quit, but she needed to pay her bills and she still owed money to the manufacturer for her first batch of perfumes. Even with just one date a week she'd be fine, at least until her business took off. The idea of saving up twenty thousand Euros so she could continue to live comfortably for a while in case *Stars Aligned* didn't work out was tempting, but it didn't feel right anymore. Maybe now was the time to take a leap of faith, to rely on her talent and product instead of leaning on perverts who paid her to look pretty and do with her as they pleased. She'd never had bad feelings toward her clients before, but now the idea of them picking her from a bunch of pictures on a website suddenly made her furious. Her life had seemed so normal until she'd met Rome, and she'd never second-guessed what she did for a living. Rome had given her confidence in her abilities though, and with that came a whole new sense of self-worth. And that had changed everything. Nadine closed her eyes, summoning the courage to make the biggest decision of her life. She'd make it work, one way or another. "In that case I resign," she said, and had to sit down as her legs felt shaky.

"You what?" Sofia paused. "You can't just quit. You still have jobs lined up. And why would you do that? You're our number one girl and you make a fortune."

And I make a fortune for you, too, Nadine thought, but she kept that to herself. "I'll finish the last few jobs but after that I'm done, so please take me off the system. I appreciate everything you've done for me, but I can't do this anymore."

"If you leave, we won't take you back," Sofia said sharply. "I was willing to make an exception and give you another two years after you passed thirty, taking into consideration your looks, so just know what you're throwing away."

"I'm not throwing anything away." Nadine tried to remain friendly, despite Sofia's threatening tone. "I'm starting over. And seriously, don't worry about the last jobs, I promise I'll be there." With that, Nadine hung up and walked back inside. It felt surreal, knowing she was completely independent, but she remained calm as she placed tea bags in two mugs and poured hot water over them. From now on, she'd work for no one but herself.

"Is everything okay?" Rome asked, joining her. "You're shaking."

Nadine turned to her and smiled. "Yeah, I'm fine. I've cancelled tonight, so maybe we can just chill and watch a movie together?"

"You shouldn't have cancelled for me," Rome said, looking distraught. "I don't want you to rearrange your life around me and I already told you that I don't have a problem with what you do." She bit her lip as she leaned against the counter. "I just wanted to stay here because... I don't know... I feel at home here, I guess."

"I cancelled for you because you're upset, and I wanted to be here for you." Nadine pulled her in and kissed her forehead. "And at the same time, I quit too, but I did that for me."

"You quit?" Rome's eyes widened as she stepped back to look up at her. "Why?"

"Because I don't want to do it anymore, and because you've made me realize I'm better than this."

"Hey, I never judged you."

"I know, and I'm grateful for that. But you helped me and encouraged me with my perfumes and honestly, I'm not sure if I'd have taken the leap if it wasn't for you believing in me. Putting in the work is one thing, but taking the next steps is another thing altogether. The thought terrified me before I met you." Nadine stroked Rome's face and ran a hand through her hair. "You have no idea what you've done for me, and I..." She hesitated. "I need you to know that I'm here for you, no matter what. I'll always be here."

Rome swallowed down the lump in her throat as tears welled up in her eyes. "I'm here for you too. Always," she whispered, and got up on her tiptoes to kiss her.

47

"How was work?" Nadine asked as Rome climbed on the back of her scooter.

"It was good, actually. The feedback from our test users was great, and we have a launch date."

Nadine looked over her shoulder and smiled as she handed Rome the other helmet. "Really? That's fantastic, babe."

"Yeah, I'm super excited. The board voted to go ahead, as expected. The only one who voted against was Matteo. I think it's his way of telling me he's still in control, but he failed. To my relief, he wasn't present. He was on the phone to Flavio who seemed really confused as to why he would vote against something that was looking pretty successful already."

"I can't believe that guy. If he was surprised, that means Flavio doesn't know you're suing him, right? Any news on the case?"

"Eliza told me she's getting somewhere but I don't know the details yet." Rome wrapped her arms around Nadine's waist and shifted forward. "But let's get going first. It's Friday and I can't wait to be away from the office. Where are you taking me?"

"It's a surprise." Nadine started the engine and Rome held on tight. Even though she'd been on the back dozens of times, she never got used to the speed. "You've been working so hard lately, and I thought you could do with a nice, quiet evening," she yelled as they drove off.

Rome was surprised to see they were driving out of the city, rather than toward the center. Although the *Nero* office was on the outskirts of town, she'd never explored what was farther out, always keen to get home by the end of the day. They passed industrial areas and crossed train tracks, then drove along farmland, olive groves and fields where horses and sheep were roaming, and finally passed through a medieval town with a classic Italian vibe. The ride was gorgeous and the farther they went, the greener and more rugged the landscape became. Nadine slowed down and turned into the drive of a vineyard.

"That was a long but wonderful journey," Rome said, laughing as she shook insects and dust from her dress. "Where are we? It's beautiful here." She sucked in a deep breath, cherishing the smell of nature that she loved so much. She hadn't noticed how stuffy it was in the city until they'd driven out of it, and the fresh air and the cool breeze blowing through her hair was already doing her good.

"Long but worth it." Nadine parked her scooter and joined Rome in front of the charming stone farmhouse with behind it, acres of vineyards, glowing in the low sun. "We're still in the region of Lazio, at one of the best winemakers in the region. And I hope you're hungry because we're going to have a very nice, private five-course dinner."

"Nadine…" Rome shot her a wide smile and took her hand. "That's so incredibly romantic."

"I can be romantic." Nadine gave her a quick kiss, then greeted their host, who led them around the house toward the back, where three tables were set up at the edge of the vineyard under trees in the adjoining meadow.

A lump settled in Rome's throat as she sat down and looked over the vines, planted in rows that stretched over a vast expanse of hills, with patches of wildflowers growing in between. "I don't think it gets any more idyllic than this," she said quietly. "Thank you for bringing me here."

"I've been wanting to bring you here for a while, but they only have three tables, so the wait list is long." Nadine's face was bathed in the soft light and Rome thought she looked beautiful and angelic as she allowed herself to drown in her dark eyes. Neither of them was dressed for a romantic evening, with Nadine wearing shorts, sneakers and a T-shirt, and Rome wearing her office attire, consisting of a white top and skirt, and a navy blazer, but this was not a flashy establishment and it was nice to feel entirely comfortable.

"You have no idea how much I appreciate it." Rome took off her blazer and hung it over the back of her chair, then kicked off her Converse and sighed as she planted her bare feet in the grass under the table.

The setting sun gave everything a golden hue, bringing out the deep purple of the grapes and the green of the vines. The rich smell of wild thyme that surrounded them, mixed with a faint hint from the wildflowers almost resembled church incense, and seemed to imbue the whole setting with a deeper meaning.

Their table was simply decked out with crisp fresh white linen, the edges embroidered with the vineyard's logo. A big bottle of olive oil sat in the middle of the table, next to a vase filled with yellow and purple meadow flowers and a single candle in a deep jar. There was no menu, but instead, a pretty hand-written card, listing the dishes the vineyard would serve tonight, along with their selection of wines.

"It's time to switch off," Nadine said.

"Yeah, I could really do with switching off." Rome kept her voice down as she spoke, not wanting to disturb the silence. It felt blissfully isolated, and apart from another couple sitting farther down, the only sounds came from the chirping of crickets and the buzzing of bees in the summer heat.

"You've been stressed lately, and you've had trouble sleeping because of the case. I just hate to see how it's affecting you, and I wish there was more that I could do to help."

"I'm fine," Rome assured her. "Or as fine as I can be considering the circumstances. This really helps, so thank you. It's nice to get out of the city for a little while." She rolled her shoulders and took another deep breath, the tenseness in her muscles fading already. "Michael called me from the US today. He's been talking to Anton and he wants to come over and help with the case strategy. He's very generously said he won't charge for his time and will combine his trip to include a vacation with his wife."

"That's really kind of him." Nadine tilted her head. "I thought you guys weren't that close."

"That's what I thought too, but I guess looking back, he's always been there for me, and maybe we're closer than I realized. I trust him."

"Then you should let him help you."

"I think I will." Rome smiled. "It's really nice to know I'm not alone in this. And I have you... You may not think you're doing much, but just the fact that you're there for me means everything."

"You'll always have me." Nadine kicked her shoes off too and placed her feet on top of Rome's.

"Mmm... that feels great." Rome blushed and pulled her feet back when the waiter came over with their first course of minestrone soup. He poured them both a small glass of red wine, then gave them a friendly bow and left as silently as he'd arrived. "How was your day?"

"My day was good. Not as busy as yours, but interesting." Nadine clinked her glass with Rome's and smiled. "*Consumers First* came back with geographical marketing recommendations. Italy scored the highest on the astrology angle. Even after living here for four years, I had no idea Italians spent a fortune on astrology and fortune tellers." She shrugged while she tasted the minestrone, her pleased expression giving away her excitement about its flavor. "Although I should have known; they're highly superstitious here."

"Oh yeah? What about?" Rome asked, drizzling some olive oil into her soup. It was her new favorite ingredient and she poured it over everything she ate.

"Like never spill olive oil." Nadine pointed at the small droplets on the tablecloth and chuckled. "Bad luck and misery will pour out of the bottle if you spill it."

Rome laughed too. "Right. Too late for that and thank God I'm not superstitious."

"Also, you should never hold a spoon with your left hand." Nadine looked amused when Rome quickly took the spoon back in her right hand.

"I was only stirring. I needed two hands for the task," Rome said in defense, grinning as she ate a spoonful.

"Doesn't matter. The left side is associated with the devil here."

"Is there anything else I should know, considering I've

just called bad luck upon myself and conjured the devil within a matter of seconds?" Rome stretched her legs out again and found Nadine's feet. They felt deliciously soft and comforting against her own.

"Hmm..." Nadine took a moment and frowned as she thought about her question. "Nothing that applies to you, I guess. You should never put a hat on your bed, but you don't wear hats. Most of the other superstitions are related to marriage, but you don't strike me as the marrying type. For example, if someone is sweeping, make sure your feet don't touch the broom, as you'll never get married if they do. Never sit at the corner of the table if you're not married because you'll remain single forever. Oh, and also never get married on a Friday; it brings bad luck."

"Who says I'm not the marrying type?" Rome asked, and smiled as she spotted a heart-shaped vermicelli on her spoon. She'd been seeing hearts everywhere lately; in clouds, in the foam of her cappuccino she made at home, and even in her burnt toast.

"I don't know. Are you?"

"Maybe. I've never thought about it." Rome shook her head and laughed. "Actually, I'm lying, I've thought about it plenty. I used to think it was a silly institution for people who desperately needed a sense of belonging that they were unable to find within themselves. Add to that being stuck to someone because of a piece of paper that more often than not only ends up being torn up, and I can honestly say that the idea was my worst nightmare. Also, I haven't exactly had the best example in life when it comes to marriage, with my mother taking off so I've never romanticized the idea."

"But you're talking in the past tense," Nadine remarked, studying her intently.

"Yeah, it just doesn't seem so stupid anymore," Rome

admitted. "I guess I've started to change my mind about a lot of things since I came here." She bit her lip, feeling a little shy to continue, but figured she might as well speak her mind. "I never understood the concept of falling head over heels for someone, but I do now. I understand jealousy, passion, so many things I never even got close to grasping before I met you."

Nadine seemed touched by her words, and she reached for her hand and kissed it. "Does that mean Rome is making you all romantic?" Her charming smile sent shivers down Rome's spine, and she cleared her throat, searching for the right words.

"A little, maybe," she said in a whisper. "But I think that most of all, you're the one who's making me feel romantic."

48

"Hey, what a surprise." Nadine frowned as she opened the door to let Eliza in. "Is Rome okay?"

"Yeah, she's fine. Sorry for the impromptu visit. Rome explained where you lived the other day and your name was on the doorbell." Eliza looked over her shoulder and lowered her voice as she stepped in. "Your neighbor just accused me of being possessed by the devil before he removed the cross from around his neck and held it up while he babbled something in Latin at me." She shrugged. "I only offered to help him carry his groceries upstairs as he seemed to be struggling."

Nadine shook her head and rolled her eyes. "Oh God, I'm so sorry about Luca. It must be your colored lenses, it probably freaked him out." She walked ahead into the living room. "Don't worry about him; he's harmless."

"Good to know. I was worried he might try to tie me up and call a priest." Eliza chuckled as she followed Nadine, then fell silent as she looked around. "Christ, what is this?" Her eyes darted from the ceiling to the walls and the fire-place before she scanned the furniture, her mouth gaping.

"Like it?"

"Like it?" Eliza repeated. "Can I move in with you?"

Nadine laughed and pointed to the far end of the room. "The balcony is through there. Do you want coffee?"

"Oh yes, please." Eliza lingered for another moment, looking both confused and impressed, then moved on, taking everything in as she followed Nadine into the kitchen instead. "I'm sorry but I had to see your kitchen too," she said with a sigh, eyeing the antique sideboard like she was considering stealing it.

"I'm a collector. If you're ever looking for something, I know all the best places." Nadine put two cups under the espresso machine and handed her a pot of sugar to take outside.

"Thanks, I'll keep that in mind," Eliza said as she opened the impressive doors to the balcony and sat back at the small table, looking out over the courtyard through the enormous black shades she'd pulled from her purse. "This really is a stunning place, Nadine. Is it expensive?"

"Yeah, it's pricey but worth it," Nadine said as she put the cups down and joined her. "I have my perfume room in here too, so moving would be quite a hassle. I hope I'll be able to stay here for at least another couple of years."

"Why would you not?" Eliza asked, stirring sugar through her coffee.

"It's my last night on the job tonight," Nadine said, pointing at the red gown she was wearing. "I don't normally dress like this around the house." She grinned as she studied Eliza's outfit; a lilac jumpsuit with a wide, studded belt and huge platform wedges. "Although I suspect you go through everyday life looking fabulous."

Eliza chuckled. "Yeah well, it helps me in my job. It's all about perception, right? I take it you know everything about that." She held up a hand. "I'm sorry, is this a bad time if you have to go to work?"

"No, it's fine. I have another forty minutes until I have to leave."

"Your last night, huh? How does that feel?"

Nadine gave her a wide smile. "It feels amazing. I'm a little uneasy of course, about the financial side of things, but in general I can't wait to get tonight over with. I should have quit a lot sooner."

"I'm sure it will work out for you, that perfume you gave me; I've had so many great reactions from people telling me I smell good, and those boxes you sent over will be coming with me to LA next week." Eliza leaned in and continued in a whisper. "I've been invited to Ella Temperley's birthday party."

"No..." Now it was Nadine's turn to gawk. "You're kidding me, right?"

"Nope. I don't know Ella personally but her co-star in her latest movie is a good friend of mine. He's not really big yet, but he's on the brink of breaking through and he invited me as his plus-one."

"That's so cool." Nadine bit her lip and hesitated. "But you shouldn't be dragging my perfumes with you, I don't expect you to..."

"Nonsense," Eliza interrupted her. "Work is pleasure and pleasure is work for me. I'll be talking up the Carbon app too; *Nero* is paying for my flight because it's a great opportunity to network, so it's a win-win. And if I can help you out while I'm there, that's just a bonus. I believe in your product, so I'll happily endorse you." She ran a hand through her lilac hair, then flipped it to one side. "Anyway, that's not why I'm here. After making a few discreet enquiries, I've been approached by a couple of women who have been victims of

Matteo's gropey hands in the past and I've asked them to meet me in one of the coffee shop close to the office tomorrow so that I can preserve their anonymity until such time as they agree to help with the case. One by one," she added. "They're going to tell me their story and I'm taking their details for Rome's lawyer."

"That's good news," Nadine said. "I mean, it's tragic, of course; there's nothing good about them having been subjected to his harassment, but maybe they'll finally feel like they're getting justice."

"Yes, they're very angry but also very scared about management finding out. Rome told me Matteo already got wind of the fact that she's planning on suing him, but he has no idea others will be involved." Eliza paused. "I'm here because I hadn't thought this through properly and now I have a problem. If I'm there tomorrow and someone from the office sees us together, they might start talking. Everyone knows who I am; it's hard to be incognito with lilac hair and my height."

"Yeah, you're hard to miss," Nadine said with an amused look. "So you want me to meet them?"

"If you wouldn't mind. It was silly of me, I should have considered the ramifications before arranging where to meet them, but I was so relieved to have some people approach me that I chose the first place that came to mind. And I don't have their phone numbers; only their email addresses, since they work at *Nero*, but I can't exactly email them at the office to tell them the plans have changed."

"No, I get that," Nadine agreed. "Of course I'll help. Just tell me where you want me to meet them. How many are we talking?"

"Seven women so far."

"Seven?" Nadine needed a moment because her blood

was boiling. "He's harassed seven women plus Rome and gotten away with it?"

"Yeah, but as I said, that's what I have so far. There might be more."

"Jesus..." Nadine balled her hands into fists until she felt the sting of her nails digging into her skin. "And none of them have spoken to the police or HR?"

"I don't know, I haven't asked them, but my guess is they haven't." Eliza finished her espresso and stood up. "Well, thank you very much for the coffee and for helping me out. Give me your number and I'll let you get ready or whatever it is you do before your dates. Good luck tonight."

"Thanks." Nadine grabbed one of her cards from her purse on the sideboard and gave it to Eliza. "Here, just text me the details."

"I will." Eliza hesitated before they headed back to the front door. "I just have one question before I leave, and please tell me if I'm being inappropriate."

"Sure."

"Can I please take a look at the rest of your apartment? I'm so curious after seeing your living room and kitchen that I just have to know what your bedroom looks like."

Nadine burst into laughter and waved her over as she headed for her bedroom. "Of course. Come on, I'll give you a quick tour. I think you'll like my perfume room, too."

49

"Flavio, how lovely to see you again." Nadine gave Flavio a kiss on his cheek and sat down opposite him at their table in the St. Regis. She'd been apprehensive about accepting tonight's date initially, partially because she'd already been on three dates with him, and partially because she was worried Matteo might be there and she wasn't sure if he'd recognized her that night with Rome. Rome hadn't heard anything about that though, and it had been a while since her assault, so she assumed it was fine. Besides, it had all gone so fast, and it was unlikely he would make the connection between the perfectly presented and polite woman at Flavio's side and the woman in dark clothing, sneakers and a baseball cap in the alleyway. Just in case, she'd left Angelo out of it tonight, hoping Flavio would behave himself. However, when she looked down, she realized the table was only laid out for two people. *Oh God, not again.*

"It's a pleasure to see you too." Flavio stared at her, his eyes lighting up. "I've missed you." He cleared his throat and straightened himself as if suddenly aware of his sentimental behavior.

Nadine shot him a sweet smile but didn't reciprocate his comment. "Thank you. Where are the others?"

"It's just us tonight," Flavio said, looking unsure of himself while he awaited her reaction.

"Okay." Nadine shrugged. "That's fine. Any particular reason?" *At least I don't have to sit next to him, now.* She folded the napkin over her lap and sat back.

"No, no reason. I just like your company." Flavio took the wine menu from the sommelier and continued as he scanned the list. "I tried to book you for next week too, but the agency said you weren't available anymore."

"That's right, I resigned. I'm almost thirty so it was time to give up soon, anyway. It's been fun, but I want to do more serious stuff now."

"That's a shame. Would you consider working for yourself? In the same field, I mean?"

"No, I'm afraid not." Nadine shook her head. "My escorting days are over, and this is my last night." She tried not to gloat as she said it, but it was hard to hide her excitement. There would be no more pretending after this, and no more lying to her mother. The dress Flavio had sent for her was gorgeous, and for the first time, she'd actually contemplated keeping it.

"Right." The disappointment was apparent in Flavio's expression. "You see... I'm getting divorced."

"Oh, I'm so sorry to hear that." Nadine was baffled by the fact that he was discussing his marriage with an escort, but if that was what he wanted to do, she'd play along. "Do you want to talk about it?"

Flavio sighed deeply and scratched his bald head. "My wife filed for divorce last week. She's been seeing someone else." He shook his head in disbelief and looked genuinely affected. It seemed crazy that he portrayed himself as a victim, since he'd been hiring girls to accompany him for years. He probably had girlfriends on the side too, but Nadine figured he'd never expected his wife to have affairs too, even after putting up with his own bad behavior. "Thirty years," he said regretfully.

"Thirty years is a long time. That must be difficult."

"Yes, our family is falling apart and I'm not going to lie; that's very hard. And on top of that, my business partner is being sued by our own employee," he added.

"Oh?" Nadine managed to act surprised. "What is he being sued for?"

"Sexual harassment."

"Right... That's serious. Did he do it?"

"I don't think so," Flavio said. "I only know him through the company we set up together; we don't run in the same circles. It could damage our business, even though the case is against him and not *Nero*."

"But if he did it, he needs to be punished, don't you agree?" Nadine asked. If there was a small chance that she could get Flavio on Rome's side, she would do everything in her power to convince him. She was both relieved and surprised to learn that he and Matteo weren't that close, as they'd seemed like two peas in a pod on the occasions that she'd seen them together.

"I suppose so." Flavio shook his head. "I mean, if he is guilty, yes, he should be punished." A moment went by as he pondered over something. "You've met the woman in question; it's Rome."

"Oh my." Nadine frowned and she locked her eyes with Flavio's. She had to think very hard about what she was going to say next, because if Rome wanted to continue to work for Flavio, it was inevitable that he would find out about them at some point. Frankly, she'd never expected him to bring up Matteo's case, and she hated being unprepared. "I had a coffee with Rome last week, but she didn't mention it," she continued casually, hoping he would fall for it.

"You spoke to Rome?"

"Yes, I bumped into her at the shopping mall and we got talking. Don't worry, I didn't tell her about our arrangement," she lied. "But sexual harassment, my God... I did notice she looked quite uncomfortable around him, last time we had dinner."

"Really?"

"Yes. I noticed it right away." Nadine wasn't sure how far she could go, but she decided to take a chance and continue her quest. "You're a good man, Flavio," she said without trying to sound overly dramatic. "And if it gets to the point where you have to make a difficult decision, I know in my heart you'll do the right thing."

"Hmm..." Flavio nodded. "If I get to the point where I believe he's guilty, then yes, I will. I don't want our company associated with anything like that. And of course, sexual harassment is unacceptable in general," he quickly added, then concentrated on the menu.

"I'm glad to know where you stand." Nadine batted her long lashes and put her menu aside. It was her way of letting him know he could order for her. It was her last night after all, and so far, he hadn't been a total nightmare.

50

"I'm sorry, I'm really tired. Not sure if I'm up for going out for dinner tonight," Rome said as she got on the back of Nadine's scooter. "And Angelo's place is on the other side of town. Can't we just go somewhere closer?"

"Please Rome, it's important. You'll see why when we get there."

Rome decided to acquiesce as she had little energy left. It had been a hectic Monday, and now that they had a launch date for the Carbon app, she had people approaching her all day long to sign off on budgets and press her to make decisions. It was the first time she had managed a project, and she was learning as she went along. Perhaps that was the most draining part—figuring everything out while pretending to know what she was doing so her team members kept faith in her. The case against Matteo was constantly in the back of her mind, which wasn't helping to keep her stress levels down either, and she found it harder and harder to sleep through the night as she worried the case would affect her launch even though she'd done everything in her power to keep it quiet.

She wasn't surprised to hear Flavio knew about her plans; HR would have informed him about what was going on by now, but he hadn't asked to see her yet. At some point, she would have to sit down with him and explain her side of things, but she wanted to wait until they'd filed the petition, and they could only do that once they had a complete list of the names of the women who would be suing with her.

When they arrived at Angelo's restaurant, and she saw that it was closed and the windows had been covered with cardboard, Rome sincerely hoped Nadine hadn't arranged some kind of romantic surprise for her tonight, because she wasn't in the mood to participate in a private cooking class or wine tasting right now. Still, she smiled and took her hand as they headed for the door, grateful for the woman who always lifted her spirits and made her feel confident and safe. Whatever it was, she'd roll with it, and maybe a little distraction from her worries wasn't so bad right now.

She narrowed her eyes and frowned in confusion as they stepped inside and Nadine closed the door behind her. Her first thought was that it was some kind of surprise party, from the dozens of faces that stared up at her, but the situation looked way too serious for that and it was eerily quiet, apart from Angelo, who was rattling cups and grinding coffee beans behind the bar. He looked up and smiled at her when she met his eyes, and she noticed Eliza was sitting at the bar in the back, too. The dim lighting made it difficult to figure out who everyone was at first, but soon, she started to recognize faces, and it clicked.

"Hi," she said quietly. "You're all from *Nero*." There were at least twenty women, herself, Nadine and Eliza excluded, and all of them were young and pretty. She knew some of the women by name, but they worked in different departments, and she'd only seen them in the canteen, in the elevator, or in passing somewhere in the building.

"We're with you," Eliza said, standing up from her bar stool.

Rome looked from Eliza to Nadine, who pulled out a chair and put down a coffee in front of her. "Eliza found them," she whispered, shooting her a loving glance. "We only spoke to seven women initially, but they talked to others and invited them here too, tonight. And we're all here to support you."

Rome swallowed down the lump in her throat, lost for words. "Matteo?" she asked, and her eyes welled up when everyone nodded. "I'm so sorry that happened to you." She paused and looked around the room, tears welling up as she made eye-contact with each and every one of them. "Thank you so much for coming forward. You have no idea what this means to me." Her eyes rested on the receptionist, whom she spoke to almost daily. "Maria..."

Maria stood up. "Three times," she said. "He tried it three times with me. I stopped going to Christmas parties because he gets like that when he's drunk." Rome could see Maria's hands trembling as she continued. "The last time, I said I would go to HR, but he threatened to have me fired if I did. He told me it was my word against his." She sighed. "I have my mother and my grandmother to take care of, and I can't afford to lose my job so now, I tend to just avoid him at all costs."

A girl who Rome recognized as one of Flavio's assistants stood up. "I cut my hair short because Matteo kept touching it in passing when it was longer. I never told anyone because it didn't seem like a big enough deal to report, but he actually made me feel really uncomfortable for years." She bit her lip and winced. "I liked my long hair, and I hate him for bringing me to the point that I was desperate enough to cut it. And I hate myself for not reporting it, knowing he's harassed and even assaulted others too."

"Don't hate yourself," Rome said, feeling her pain. "This is not your fault, it's all on him."

"I always call in sick when it's our annual off-site," another woman said. "Three years ago, he cornered me in a hotel corridor and started kissing me. When I pushed him away, he threatened to fire me and said I'd never find a job in this city again." She shrugged. "He never fired me, and he never tried anything after that, but I avoid him and have applied for a transfer to another floor, so I'll be sitting farther away from him, even though I love my current job."

Rome covered her mouth with her hand while she listened as everyone in the room told their story. Although she was shocked and felt for them, it also gave her comfort to know she wasn't the only one, and that they were here to help her fight the bastard who had made their lives so miserable. They would be much stronger together, and by the time almost everyone had spoken, she was more convinced than ever that they could bring him down.

The girl opposite her was the only one who hadn't said anything yet, and Rome didn't recognize her. "I don't think I know you," she said.

The girl shook her head. "You don't. My name is Titziana. I'm not with *Nero* anymore. I was an intern, in the finance department. Maria called me and told me what was going on tonight. I confided in her after Matteo groped my ass in the mail room just before my contract ended." She bit her lip and hesitated. "I thought about going to the police, but he made me believe I'd asked for it because I wore short skirts."

"Yeah, it's not the first time I've heard that tonight,"

Rome said quietly, and reached for her hand over the table. "You didn't ask for anything, okay?"

"I know." Titziana gave her a small smile. "It might be worth tracing previous interns too. The first thing he ever said to me was that he'd been looking forward to meeting 'the new intern', which makes me think he has a thing for young girls."

"She's right," Eliza said. "Matteo has an eye for either young or vulnerable women. Women with something to lose, or women he thinks he can manipulate." She turned to Rome, her lilac eyes glaring like she was about to spit fire at any moment. "Are you sure you want to sue? Can't we just hire someone to kill him? I know people."

At that, everyone laughed, brightening the mood a little.

Rome laughed too. "Believe me, it's crossed my mind. But this will be worse for him. Public humiliation, a likely divorce, a huge settlement for his wife, for you guys, who have lost out on career opportunities and promotions, but most of all, I want him banned from the office. That's what we're aiming for. Unfortunately, we're not able to sue him for assault, as most assault cases are outdated; there's a six-month cap on reporting it. I could sue him for assault personally, which would require the police to re-open the investigation, but that wouldn't help any of you, so my lawyer has suggested we go with harassment through a civil case as we have a greater chance of winning that way. I know it's not fair, but it's how the legal system works." She was interrupted by a knock on the door.

"That will be Bella, the head of HR," Eliza said, getting up to open it. "She couldn't be here earlier, said she had family commitments. I'm surprised she showed up at all, as I couldn't tell her what it was about and she was reluctant to come."

"Bella is here?" Rome looked around the room. "Are you guys okay with that?" She wasn't sure how safe these women would feel if someone high up in the company joined them, HR or not. It wasn't like Bella had done much for her apart from arrange a mediation meeting which Matteo hadn't shown up to.

"Yeah, Eliza told us she would invite her unless we had a problem with that," Maria said. "It's okay."

"Are you finally going to tell me what this is all about?" Bella sneered at Eliza from the open door. "I'm a busy woman and I don't have time for silly games." She frowned. "Anyway, what is this dump?"

"Careful lady, this is my family's dump," Angelo yelled from behind the bar.

The room fell silent again when Bella walked in, and her face pulled into a baffled expression as she put her purse down on an empty chair and looked around. Her eyes rested on Rome, who beckoned her to sit down.

"This is about Matteo," Rome said, then paused, giving Bella some time to process the scene. "As I already told you, he sexually assaulted me. But as you can see, I'm not the only one." She gestured to the group. "What you're about to hear needs to remain strictly confidential. Our problem is with Matteo personally, not with *Nero*. However, that doesn't take away that a lot of the harassment took place at work, during work hours. The company is ultimately responsible for providing a safe work environment, and none of these women have felt comfortable discussing what happened to them with your department. That's going to change right here and now."

Bella's eyes widened as she stared at the number of women sitting around Rome, her snobby demeanor dropping immediately. "All of you?" she asked incredulously.

"Yes, and quite possibly more." Rome waited until Angelo put a coffee in front of Bella, then continued. "Once I update you on everything I've heard this evening, you have two choices. You can either choose to be a part of this, or you can turn a blind eye, but if you do decide to go with the latter option, I wish you good luck fighting all of these brave women. That includes me," she said. "Because just like all these women, I didn't make it up, there was no misunderstanding, and mediation is not an option."

Bella's bottom lip started trembling, and Rome could see she was getting emotional. "My God," she whispered. "I really had no idea he was like that."

"Maybe you did, maybe you didn't." Rome shrugged. "But my lawyer, who will be representing all of us, is coming over next week to talk to everyone, and we're going to sue Matteo. I'd like the company to come out of this unscathed, or at least in the best shape possible, as all our jobs depend on *Nero*." She glanced at Bella. "Including yours."

"Of course." Bella nodded and cleared her throat. "You must think I'm some kind of monster, but I swear I had no idea."

"In my opinion, you didn't handle my case appropriately," Rome said. "But you're getting a second chance to do right by everyone else here, and we could really do with your support. The police are unlikely to investigate their cases after six months, but they can be reported to HR at any time, and you're going to document them all."

51

"You two have been amazing," Rome said after everyone had left. They were still at a table, sharing a bottle of wine with Angelo, who had prepared some food, too.

"You have Eliza to thank." Nadine squeezed Eliza's shoulder as she got up to go to the bathroom.

"That's not true," Eliza said. "Your girlfriend has been incredible, helping me with talking to them. She really has a way with people."

"I know, she's great like that." Rome turned to Angelo. "And thank you for letting us use your trattoria."

"No problem." Angelo shrugged. "A lot of secret meetings take place here. The union, my family meetings..."

Rome figured she'd rather not know what was discussed during his family meetings as she gave him a warm smile. "Well, I really appreciate it. Would it be okay if we made this our regular meeting place? I'll pay you, of course, for your expenses and some more on top, so you're not losing out."

"No need to pay me." Angelo sank down in his chair. "We're closed on Mondays anyway, so you can use this space every other Monday, when nothing's going on. I'd like to see that man go down just as much as you do."

"Thank you, I appreciate that, but we'll work something out to compensate you." Rome let out a deep sigh and took a sip of her wine. "Those women are so brave, doing this. I can't make them any promises, but I'm almost positive we can nail him, now."

"I agree, I don't think you need to worry about that," Eliza said. "It's twenty-three against one." She waved a hand and laughed. "Make it twenty-four, even though Bella has not been subjected to his gropey hands."

"Matteo would think twice before he forced himself upon the HR director." Rome shook her head. "God, that woman is one tough cookie and I can't say I like her for the way she treated me, but I did feel sorry for her when she started crying."

"I guess it's a wake-up call for her," Nadine said, joining them again. She tilted her head and chuckled as she watched Eliza nibble at the leftovers of Angelo's gnocchi. "It's good, right?"

Eliza nodded. "It's the best. Seriously the best gnocchi I've ever had. And my mama makes great gnocchi," she added, then regarded Angelo with interest. "You got a girlfriend?"

Angelo laughed and shook his head. "No."

"Why not? You're handsome, you're a good person and you're a great cook. What more could a woman want?" Eliza put her fork down and sat back, draping her arms over the back of her chair so her breasts were pointing right at him. She'd clearly tried to dress appropriately for tonight, wearing a simple black suit and high heels, but even dressed down, she still stood out with her lilac hair and colored lenses.

"If you like me so much, why don't you ask me out on a date?" Angelo said with a challenging twinkle in his eyes before his gaze lowered to her cleavage. Somehow, he'd managed to make Eliza blush, and she tried to suppress a grin but failed.

"Hmm... I don't know. I'm kind of traditional that way. I like the man to ask me out."

"You don't seem like the traditional type," Angelo retorted.

Eliza shrugged and hesitated for a moment. "You'd be surprised."

"Okay, I think it's time we get going, don't you?" Rome said to Nadine, getting up. Although the two of them would most likely be a disaster if they got together, with Eliza breaking Angelo's heart as soon as she got bored with him, they were clearly physically attracted to each other and she was starting to feel like a third wheel.

"Yes, let's go." Nadine gave Angelo a kiss on his cheek. "Thanks, buddy."

"Anytime." He looked up and shot Rome a wink. "I'm glad it went well."

"Me too," Rome gave Angelo and Eliza a quick wave. The two had switched places so they were sitting next to each other now, and they didn't look like they were planning on leaving anytime soon. "Thank you so much. I'll see you soon."

"I definitely sensed some romance there," Nadine said when they were back in her apartment. They were sitting on her balcony and she had her leg draped over Rome's lap while Rome gave her a foot rub. "That was a good call of yours to leave."

"Yeah, poor Angelo."

Nadine tilted her head and shot her an amused smile. "Why? He's a big boy."

"But he's too nice for her," Rome said, admiring Nadine's perfect pedicure. Her middle toe was a little longer than the rest and the sweet imperfection made her heart swell.

"What do you mean? I like Eliza, she's super nice, too."

"She is," Rome said, taking Nadine's other foot. "But she'll eat him up and spit him back out when she's done with him. That's just what she does."

"Maybe it will be different with him."

"Maybe."

"You're sounding awfully cynical for someone who wasn't even into women before you met me." Nadine groaned when Rome started kneading the ball of her foot. "Oh God, that feels so good."

Rome took a deep breath as she looked up at the moon. Sitting out here under the dark sky with Nadine had become one of her favorite pastimes, and although it was way past midnight, the meeting had given her so much hope and energy that she was wide awake. They were both wearing Nadine's robes after a shower and the classical music she'd gotten so used to was softly playing in the background. "You're right. I shouldn't judge her like that." Her lips curled into a smile as her fingers trailed over Nadine's foot. "Do you know your middle toe is longer than the others?"

Nadine's eyes widened, and she retracted her foot. "Hey, of course I'm aware and it's not something I enjoy you pointing out."

"But it's so cute," Rome argued, pulling it back and kissing her toe. "I love your toes, and I love the little patch of darker skin in the back of your neck that goes bright red when I touch you, and I love the beauty mark on your lower back and the way you snore softly in your sleep."

"I snore?" Nadine looked mortified. "Please tell me I don't snore."

"A little. Sometimes, when you're really tired." Rome smiled sweetly. "But I love your imperfections, and love that I know you like no one else does... I love everything about you." She swallowed hard and flinched at her own honesty. Nadine remained quiet, staring at her. When Rome looked into her teary eyes that were suddenly filled with emotion, everything became clear to her. She cursed while a million things ran through her mind. "Fuck."

"Fuck?" Nadine stroked her arm. "What's so bad?"

Rome shook her head. "Nothing. It's nothing."

"Come on, Rome, you have to say it now," Nadine persisted. "Just tell me."

"I ehm..." Rome paused for a long moment. "I think I love you." The words came out in a quiet mumble, but Nadine had heard them loud and clear. She got off the bench, went down on her knees before Rome and took both her hands.

"Rome, look at me." She waited until Rome finally met her eyes and took a tighter hold of her. "I love you too."

Rome felt a tear trickle down her cheek and shivered at the warm buzz that enveloped her. The sense of belonging she felt was overwhelming, and she started crying, shaking as she stood up, falling into Nadine's arms. She hadn't felt this in a long time. Not after her mother had left. Now that she'd uttered those words, it was like a wall had been knocked down, and she felt the need to say so much more but didn't know where to start. "You got me looking at the moon," she said through sobs. "You got me smelling things at the market, and looking up as I walk. I see things now, notice the beauty in everything around me. You got me listening to music that moves me, and I'm even more in touch with myself because of you. You opened me up. How did you do that?"

"I didn't do anything." Nadine kissed her softly and wiped away her tears. "You opened me up too, you know. I didn't plan this, you just happened to me." She paused. "I never thought I'd say those words to anyone."

"Me either." Rome took Nadine's face into her hands and stroked her cheeks. Nadine's beautiful eyes looking into her soul was all she needed. Nadine really knew her, and it felt good to be known. "I hardly dare say it, but maybe this was meant to be. I know I'm not one for astrology or any of that stuff, but this is almost too good to be true, and maybe our stars were aligned after all."

Nadine sighed as she pulled her into another tight embrace. "I have no doubt they were."

52

"So, that's the situation." Rome stood up from the table, leaving Flavio and Rob baffled. "I understand this may come as an unpleasant surprise, but I'd rather keep you in the loop, as I too, want the company to come out of this in the best shape possible. And now you also know why Matteo wasn't invited to this meeting."

"HR already informed us you were suing him," Flavio said. "And Matteo told me he expected problems a while back," he added, upon which Rob shot him a surprised look.

"Well, I hope I'll have your support, and that you'll work with me rather than against me." Rome hadn't mentioned the twenty-three other women as she wanted to protect their identities for as long as she could. The two men probably thought she didn't stand a chance against Matteo on her own, and that was fine, but she needed to know if they were decent people so she could continue to work for them.

"It's a delicate situation," Flavio finally said after much deliberation. "I suppose the judge will decide whether he's guilty or not, and if he is found guilty, *Nero* will, of course, take the necessary steps for the safety of its employees."

"I agree," Rob followed. "I don't know Matteo very well. We all have our own families and circles of friends, and apart from the board meetings and business dinners—which only happen when we're closing new deals—we don't see much of each other." He kept stabbing his pen into the table; a sign that the conversation was making him agitated. "What I can promise, is that I won't work against you, and that if he's found guilty, we'll deal with the consequences. My wife is on the board of an Italian charity for women's rights and *Nero* makes yearly donations to them. Aside from the fact that I'm personally invested in the cause because of my wife, the company is invested too, and it could make for some really, really bad press."

"I understand." Rome pursed her lips as she thought about that. "But if we work together and anticipate the bad press, we can come up with a plan of action. You, me, the HR department and the PR department. I can't talk to you about the details of the case, but I can tell you one thing for certain: you'll find out soon enough what a scumbag Matteo is, and he will be found guilty." She stood up and gave them a polite nod. "I suppose you might want to discuss this between yourselves, so I'll leave you to it. Thank you for meeting with me."

Rome walked out of the building with a bounce in her step, relieved to have gotten it out of the way. Michael would be coming over in a couple of days to meet with her and Anton, and despite the circumstances she was actually looking forward to seeing him again. Since he was reluctant to bill his hours, Rome had insisted on booking the hotel and flights for him and his wife. Three weeks in Rome in exchange for support and advice throughout the beginning of the trial was a deal they were both happy with, and she was excited to meet his wife. Michael had stood by her side from the very first day she'd tried to get her app out on the market, and even now, he was invested in the case and genuinely concerned about her. It was time that she let him in too, that she embraced new friendships and welcomed any help she could get.

A loud, flirty whistle pulled her out of her thoughts, and she laughed when she saw it was Nadine, waiting for her at the back of the parking lot. She always kept her helmet on in case one of the board members would show up, but Rome would have recognized her mint green Vespa and endlessly long legs from miles away.

"Hey!" Rome walked over to her, lifted her helmet and kissed her fiercely as she wrapped her arms around her neck. "What are you doing here?" One of her colleagues passed them and stared at them for a moment before she got in her car, but it didn't stop Rome from kissing her one more time. Kissing Nadine was like recharging her batteries; every passionate moment sparked life into her like nothing else and every time she asked herself the same question; how had she not known how good this could be? Their lips brushed lightly, then collided again with force as Nadine pulled her in and weaved her fingers through her hair. Rome didn't mind that her colleague had seen her with a woman; they could talk all they wanted, and she waved at her as she stepped away to catch her breath, wondering how Nadine made her feel so damn good.

"I just missed you, and I can tell you missed me too." Nadine smirked and licked her lips. "And I wanted to check on you, see if you were okay after your meeting with Flavio and Rob."

"Thank you, that's very sweet of you." Rome got on the back and scooted as close as she possibly could, delighted to have her arms around Nadine's waist. "But I'm okay, it went well. Rob actually doesn't seem like a bad guy and your bestie…"

"Hey, stop calling that creep my bestie," Nadine interrupted her with a chuckle.

"Okay, sorry, I meant Flavio," Rome continued, deciding to stop teasing Nadine about her last date with Flavio, during which he'd poured his heart out for hours, then told her she was the only one he felt he could really talk to. "Anyway, he seems pretty reasonable, too. Like you said; he's no saint but he's not a monster either." She pinched Nadine's waist. "So, where are we going?"

Nadine shrugged as she looked at Rome over her shoulder, her eyes twinkling with mischief. "What do you want to do?"

"Honestly, I want to go to bed. With you," Rome added with a grin, sneaking her hands underneath Nadine's T-shirt. "But first, I want ice cream."

"Ice cream and sex, huh? So demanding but I'm down for that." Nadine started the engine and sped off.

53

———

"Welcome back, girlfriend!" Nadine said enthusiastically as she put the three drinks down in front of Rome and Eliza, who had just arrived back from LA. "Did you have a good time?"

"I did." Eliza shot her a beaming smile. "It was the most amazing party. Did you see my email?"

Nadine frowned and shook her head as she sat down next to Rome. "No, sorry, I haven't checked today."

"That's fine." Eliza scrolled through her phone. "I only just sent it on my way back from LA and I know you're not a phone junkie like me." She handed her phone to Nadine.

"What the..." Nadine narrowed her eyes as she looked at a screenshot of Ella Temperley, Hollywood sweetheart and A-list actress, holding her perfume bottle next to her face as she smiled in a picture on Twitter with the caption: *Cutest present ever! Virgo perfume that makes me smell like myself but better! #starsaligned* "How?"

"I gave it to her as a birthday present." Eliza grinned. "I gave one to her girlfriend, Cam, too. She has her own yoga wear brand now, and she also has a heap of followers. I hope your web shop is live, because you're going to get a lot of orders on the back of this..."

"It went live yesterday, thank goodness," Nadine said, shaking her head in disbelief. "I don't even know how to thank you. You're going to get a bonus for this."

"Absolutely not. I was wracking my brain trying to think of a unique birthday present to give her and you gave me the perfect solution. If Ella likes it and tweets about it, that's all on her, not me. I'm just happy I was able to spread the word for you." Eliza took a sip of her Espresso Martini and moaned. "I'll tell you one thing though; LA is great, but there's no place like home. I've missed the Italian coffee, even in the form of a cocktail."

"These cocktails are pretty great." Nadine toasted with Eliza and Rome. "Thank you for doing that for me. You have no idea how much I appreciate it, and all drinks are on me tonight."

Eliza shook her head. "No, drinks are on him tonight." She waved toward the barman and manager of the small establishment they were seated in. "They just opened yesterday and I'm going to feature his bar on my lifestyle blog."

Rome laughed. "You are one crafty lady."

"Hey, as I said my mantra is 'work is pleasure and pleasure is work'."

"What happened with Angelo, last week after we left? Any pleasure with him?" Nadine teased.

"No, nothing like that." Eliza hesitated. "It was the strangest thing. The attraction was mutual, I was sure of that. So, I suggested he come back to my place, for pleasure," she clarified with a wink. "But he declined and said he'd rather take me out on a date instead. I mean, what kind of man does that?"

"The nice kind?" Rome suggested. She regarded Eliza, who seemed highly confused about the situation. Perhaps no one had ever turned down sex with her before, or perhaps no man had ever been so courteous. "So, are you going to go out with him?"

Eliza shrugged. "I don't know. A date with someone like him seems so serious, because you're right; he's genuinely nice and I don't want to hurt him; he doesn't deserve that."

"Why do you think you'll hurt him?" Rome asked carefully. "It might be different this time." She took Nadine's hand and squeezed it. "I never thought I'd love someone the way I love Nadine, yet here I am. It was different with her."

Eliza shot them a goofy smile. "True. You guys are very, very cute together." She averted her gaze and looked down at her lap, fiddling with a loose sequin on her sparkling lilac dress. "I was married once," she said out of nowhere.

"You were?" Rome leaned in and placed a hand on Eliza's arm, sensing this was difficult for her to talk about. She couldn't imagine the free-spirited Eliza who loved being in love, tied down to anyone.

"Yes, twenty years ago, when I was eighteen. I was crazy about him, completely blinded by love. I was young and foolish and had no ambitions other than starting a family back then. Not that there's anything wrong with that; my priorities just shifted."

"What happened?" Nadine asked softly.

"He got my best friend pregnant instead." Eliza clenched her jaw and balled her hands into fists. "It's not easy to get over something like that, but I moved to Rome and worked as a bartender until I figured out what I wanted to do with my life."

"I'm so sorry... that must have been horrible," Rome said, but Eliza just shrugged and painted on a smile.

She straightened her back and waved if off like she'd undoubtedly done hundreds of times. "It was a long time ago and I'm so much better off without him; those two deserve each other. I'm the one with a killer career and the world at my feet while he's still living in that tiny little factory-filled shithole and she's stuck with an unfaithful husband."

"That's true..." Nadine hesitated as she didn't want to overstep. "But just because your ex-husband was an asshole doesn't mean all men are like that."

"I know that." Eliza sat back and sighed. "Seriously, I know I'm fucked up and I'd never claim otherwise. But even knowing that the problem is with me, there will always be this little voice in the back of my mind that questions everything my boyfriends do, no matter how nice they are."

"But you might want to start giving them a chance at some point," Rome said. "Believe me, getting close to people is hard for me too, but I'm glad I finally opened myself up. And you know what? It wasn't even that hard. I think the idea of letting someone in frightened me more than the relationship itself." She shot Nadine a loving glance and leaned into her. "Unless you prefer serial dating, of course. If that's really your thing, who am I to question your love life?"

"I like dating. And I like the excitement of something new; I never lied about that," Eliza said. "But when I see the two of you together, I do wonder what it would be like to really be close to someone. To get so lucky to meet my soulmate and be able to let him in." She hesitated, then shook her head. "I don't know. I just need some time, I guess. For some reason, Angelo got me thinking and that dragged all the shit from my past back to the surface." Her drink was already finished, and she waved over the waiter. "Anyway, enough serious talk for tonight. There's only so much I can handle and I need a refill."

54

Inspiration was the greatest gift, and today, Nadine was feeling very, very inspired. She'd been in her perfume room ever since Rome had left for work that morning, and she'd completely lost track of time and life in general. It was great to be in the zone, excitement coursing through her as she got closer and closer to what she was aiming for. Carefully, she added two droplets of jasmine to the blend of oils in the Erlenmeyer flask and hovered over it as she swirled it around, taking in the harmonious scent that sung to her. *Almost perfect.*

She'd been on cloud nine ever since Rome had told her she loved her and slowly, an idea had started forming in her mind. Although there was no rush, soon she would have to start thinking about developing her next perfume, and that was exciting. This one would be much simpler to create, and she was looking forward to simple after years of research into scents associated with personality types. *Stars Aligned* was the right product for the right time, but it had taken her eight years to create the twelve perfumes. She had no desire to spend so much time on her next product, as it took the impulsiveness out of the process and with that, some of the passion she felt for her craft.

Nadine wanted to go by her gut this time, instead of by science. Fueled by her love for Rome, she closed her eyes and inhaled once more, trying to figure out if the jasmine made it better or not. Rome smelled like the sun, and she needed something warm to balance out the colder oils that she'd used to reference the scents of the forest, and the summer rain that Rome loved.

Along with the Libra perfume, Rome had been wearing the fragrance Nadine had given her before she went back to Portland a lot, and not only did it really suit her, it was also one of Nadine's proudest creations, even though she'd thrown it together on a whim. The small bottle was almost empty now, and Nadine was glad she'd written down the formula the morning Rome had gone back to the US to pack her things. It only needed to be fine-tuned.

"The sun," she mumbled as she stood up and gazed over her fragrance organ. Perhaps it needed some bergamot, or cedarwood. She was glad no one could see her working like this; naked with her lab coat hanging open. It wasn't just that she liked being naked in general, she also needed to be free of any traces of fabric conditioner, or the scent of city life on her clothes, as it was distracting. The temperature was set to a perfect twenty degrees, the lights were dimmed, which she tended to do when she was in the middle of the creation process, and music was playing full blast. Puccini's *La bohème* was her favorite opera to listen to while she was working, and she softly hummed along as she got up on the ladder and reached for the cedarwood. Using a pipette, she added a droplet to the mixture, then checked over and over before she added another and finally, a third.

After a thirty-minute break, during which she sat back

and simply got lost in the music, giving her nose a rest, she leaned over the flask again and smiled as the symphony of oils penetrated her nostrils. "Perfect," she whispered, her lips pulling into a wide smile. Sometimes it took eight years, and sometimes it took eight hours. It was crazy what love could do to a person, how it opened you up, made you feel new things, and gave you new ideas. The perfume didn't smell like Rome—at least not in the literal sense—but the association with her was remarkable. It carried her energy, her pureness; fresh and innocent but at the same time incredibly sensual and sexy.

Nadine's eyes lowered to the sketchpad on her desk, and she opened it, staring at the numerous drawings of ideas for bottles she'd scribbled down over the past week. They weren't quite right; too sharp at the edges, and too cubical. Although the designs were very elegant, they carried a hint of masculinity, and this wasn't a unisex fragrance. It was feminine, and the bottle had to be very, very pretty. Again, she closed her eyes and this time, she pictured Rome's body. Flashes of her delicious curves danced in front of her, and she kept seeing her hips. Slick, slightly rounded, inviting... Nadine realized she was getting turned on, so she opened her eyes and focused on her notepad instead, picking up the pencil that lay beside it. Yes, she would gladly release herself from the throbbing need between her legs and it certainly wouldn't take long, but first things first. Days in which she swam in inspiration were rare and she needed to get the curves down on paper before she got too distracted by fantasies to continue.

By the time she'd finished, the fourth act of the opera was over too, and rather than put on more music, she sat in silence for a long moment, staring down at the notepad while inhaling the scent from the flask. "Perfect," she whispered, studying her sketch of a droplet-shaped bottle that was narrow at the bottom and wider at the top, streamlined into a glass stopper that brought to mind the association of a slim waist. It was elegant, simple, and sensual.

Nadine let out a deep, happy sigh and suddenly felt how tired and hungry she was. She hadn't eaten all day, too consumed with her latest project, and she hadn't had coffee either as the smell was too strong and distracted her when she was working. She put the top on the flask and closed her notebook, then went back through the bookcase and into the kitchen to fix herself a caffeine shot and something to eat. Rome would be home soon and although she could hardly wait to tell her about her progress, she'd keep it to herself, just for now. This perfume would be very, very special.

55

"Hi, Luca. I'm going to the market. Do you need anything?" Rome asked in her best Italian after knocking on Luca's door. She'd had dinner with him a couple of times now, and he clearly appreciated her learning Italian as she was now met with a small smile rather than his usual grunt and suspicious stares. He wouldn't be joining her fan club anytime soon, but his comments amused her now, rather than upset her, and she'd learned how to sneer back at him.

"*Grazie, un pane per favore,*" he said, his small eyes squinting.

"A loaf of bread, sure." Rome winked at him and ran down the stairs, carrying her shopping trolley. Not too long ago, she'd made fun of people dragging the trollies behind them, but after carrying heavy grocery-filled bags up the hill time after time, she'd finally given in and borrowed Nadine's trolley that had silly cat faces printed all over it.

Rome didn't spend much time in her own apartment anymore, simply because she really liked Nadine's neighborhood and most of all, she liked being with Nadine. A month of practicing the language had paid off; she was starting to understand a little, and her confidence was growing.

The street smelled of fresh bread, the heat from the sun as it baked into the old buildings and garlic wafting from the restaurants. It was the smell of comfort, of home. She took a moment to appreciate her surroundings and life in the sweet neighborhood. Going back to the US seemed unthinkable now, and she didn't really miss anything, apart from her friend Barbara and occasionally, her father, who she spoke to on the phone from time to time. She hadn't told him about Matteo, and she hadn't told him about Nadine either. She wasn't sure why, but she suspected it was just easier to keep things to herself when it came to her father. Their relationship was very platonic and although they always had friendly exchanges about their jobs and life in general, their conversations never went deeper. Frankly, she had no idea what was happening in his life either, and that was fine.

Today, she would reunite with Michael, and she was excited to welcome him and his wife to Rome. Back home, she would have met up with him in a coffee shop or at his office, but now that she'd been living here for over four months, the Italian lifestyle had rubbed off on her, and she was excited to have him, his wife, and Anton, over for dinner for their first face-to-face meeting. She'd thought of having them over at her own apartment, but Nadine had insisted she'd invite them to hers instead, since Rome spent most of her time there anyway.

Rome wasn't used to entertaining but she was excited to cook for a group of people for the first time. Cooking had become something that relaxed her rather than stressed her out lately, and she tried to learn making a new Italian dish at least once a week. As she slowly strolled toward the market, taking in life as it passed her by, she greeted the nuns she saw almost every morning on her way to work. Saturday morning was a busy affair, as the weekend was often observed with big family dinners.

Just like most locals, she'd found her preferred stalls now and she smiled when Frederico, one of the stallholders, pulled out a bag of large, ripe tomatoes from under the counter and handed it to her. He also bagged up a large onion, some artichokes and mixed salad leaves, as she'd asked him to keep her standard order aside for her every week.

"Anything else?" he asked, pointing to the fennel. "The fennel is very, very good this week."

"Perfect, I'll have two of those, then." Rome looked over the rest of his display and was drawn to the Sicilian lemons and the huge oranges, still on the vine. "And some oranges and lemons, and anything else you recommend today." An old lady next to her interrupted them, chiding Frederico because his radicchio looked wilted. He spread his arms in apology. "I'm terribly sorry, that's how they arrived. Anyway, they're not that bad."

"Well, you should have sent them back, this is unacceptable." She took a wider stance, resting her hands on her hips. "I won't pay any more than half price for them." Rome listened in amusement as they started bickering. She'd seen the cunning lady many times, and she usually won the fight but today, Frederico was running out of patience and didn't give in. "Fine, then I'll go to my friend over there." She stormed off toward the next stall, where the stallholder hid behind his apples as he saw her coming.

"Here you go." Frederico put the produce in Rome's trolley and smiled as she paid him. "You're my favorite customer. None of that with you." He looked over at the lady who was now nagging his colleague.

"And you're my favorite tomato man," Rome said, and they both laughed as she had no idea how to say 'stall-holder' in Italian.

Opposite the market, the no-frills café was overflowing with locals, most sitting down for an espresso after their shopping, animatedly discussing life in the neighborhood. Their trolleys were next to them, colorful produce and bakery goods sticking out of the top. There was a lot of pointing and gossiping going on, and Rome chuckled to herself as she heard them mentioning the overflowing bins on the other side of the square. She didn't understand all of it, but by now, she'd heard Luca yell 'trash' and 'bins' so many times that it wasn't hard to figure out what they were talking about. She joined them and was offered a chair at one of the tables after ordering an espresso.

"I see you're starting to live like a local. I was hoping to find you here," Nadine said, joining her. Then she pointed to her trolley and laughed. "And I see you finally gave in and embraced my cat wheelie."

Rome laughed too. "Yeah well, what can I say? You were right. It's much easier." She shot Nadine a flirty look, glancing over her professional but very cute outfit. The navy slacks and white shirt looked sexy on her, and she loved the hint of cleavage, and the edge of her lace bra that was showing behind the button-down front. "You're looking snazzy. How was your meeting?"

"Great. The mall is taking a counter stand, and if it goes well, they'll expand to other stores." Nadine put her hands on Rome's shoulders as she stood behind her. "And online sales have been amazing too. I've just received my first monthly report and guess what?"

"What?" Nadine's goofy grin made Rome giddy, and she nudged her. "Tell me."

"I'll be able to pay the rent this month!" Nadine yelled, loud enough for everyone around them to hear her.

Rome threw her head back as she laughed out loud, then kissed Nadine's hand that was still on her shoulder. "Fantastic. But you do know I would have helped you out, right? I spend most of my time at yours as it is, and I'd really like to contribute."

"I know, but it feels good to pay my bills from real, hard-earned income. I never thought something as simple as paying the rent would actually make me so happy."

Rome looked up at Nadine and smiled. "Want to go home and celebrate before we start cooking?"

"If by celebrating you mean celebrating in bed, then yes, absolutely." Nadine took the trolley and exchanged a few pleasantries with the people at Rome's table while Rome knocked back the rest of her espresso.

"Hurry up, let's get going." Rome gave her a flirty wink. "I really, really like you in that outfit but I'd rather see it come off."

56

"Hey, Michael, come in." Rome gave him a hug and introduced herself to his wife Jeannie before greeting Anton, who she'd already met with a couple of times.

"It's really good to see you again," Michael said, looking around the living room. "Nice place you have here."

"It's not my apartment, it's my girlfriend's," Rome said. "She's in the kitchen, please come through." Rome noted the surprised look on Michael's face after mentioning the word 'girlfriend'.

"Hi guys, I'm Nadine." Nadine gave them a charming smile while she greeted them and gestured to the kitchen table where she and Rome had laid out a delicious spread of antipasti. "Thank you so much for coming over tonight."

"Thank you for the invite. It's good to get together, make sure we're aligned and relax a little before this endless circus begins." Anton handed Nadine the bottle of wine he'd brought. "Unless Matteo wants to settle right away, of course. He's had a lot of time to think about his mistakes and basically he knows he's fucked."

"Absolutely," Michael agreed. "But if he doesn't want to settle, this could roll on for months, or even years." He sat down and looked from Rome to Nadine. "By the way, I hope you don't mind me saying I'm surprised, but I didn't know you were..." Michael paused and pulled at his tie. "Gay," he continued with a blush on his face.

"Well, I didn't know either until I met Nadine." Rome laughed and poured them wine. "Here you go. And yes, a settlement would be perfect. To have Matteo removed from the workplace sooner rather than later, and for the employees to be offered compensation, is more than we could hope for in this instance."

"Great wine." Michael took a sip while he and his wife admired the kitchen while Nadine chatted to Anton in Italian, explaining something about the sauce she was making. "I see life in Rome has been good to you." He clumsily held up a hand and shook his head. "Apart from this case, of course."

"Yes, this city has been very good to me, and so has Nadine." Rome put a large bottle of olive oil on the table, along with balsamic vinegar and salt and pepper. They'd cooked lots of small dishes that they only had to plate or heat up, and she'd also bought some cannoli at the local bakery because they were meant to be the best in town. "Matteo has been an unfortunate exception, but I refuse to let him ruin my stay." She put on a brave face. "It's going to be okay, right? We need to win, for everyone involved."

"You have a very good case." Michael nodded confidently at Anton. "And you're in good hands. Anton's done multiple cases like yours. It's hard to find someone who's a specialist in Italy. As I mentioned, most cases of sexual assault or harassment aren't reported here, and big civil trials like yours are rare, so expect a media circus once the press gets a whiff of this."

"I'm prepared for that." Rome turned to Jeannie and winced. "I apologize, we shouldn't go straight into the case."

"Don't worry about that, it's what he's here for." Jeannie smiled. "I'm just grateful to finally have some quality time with my husband, so thank you for that. He works so hard, and we haven't been away together since our honeymoon. We arrived three days ago, and while Michael was in meetings with Anton, I've been exploring on my own and I can honestly say that I'm already overwhelmed. This city is so beautiful."

"Yeah, it really is and I'm sure you'll have an amazing three weeks here." Rome gave her a small notepad. "I've written down some nice places and directions on how to get there, in case you don't know where to start. Not tourist attractions per se, just pretty and romantic sites and eateries."

"Thank you so much, you shouldn't have. I'm sure you're very busy with work and the upcoming trial right now."

Rome shook her head as she took a sip of her wine. "It's not so bad. Work is busy, but everything is coming together and we're just preparing for the launch. And as far as the case goes, there's not much I can do. I've got these two wonderful guys who I trust with my life and other than that, I just need to show up and take the stand like the other women."

"I've spoken to all of them once more," Anton said. "And I've talked them through what to expect in the coming weeks. Or months, or years," he added, rolling his eyes. "No one's dropped out, so I'm feeling very positive. The HR department have been meticulous with the paperwork, too."

"Great. That's good to hear." Rome turned to Nadine,

who was just finishing off the sauce for the meatballs. "Do you need some help, babe?"

"No, all done." Nadine put the lid on the pan and joined them at the table. "Please, help yourselves. There will be more food out later, but I'm sure you're hungry."

Rome was surprised at how easy the social conversation flowed between talk about the trial. She'd been a little nervous as she wasn't used to having people over, but the evening turned out to be fun. Nadine was an amazing host and as the time passed and they had more wine, the kitchen filled with laughter and animated chatter. She realized she actually had a lot of shared memories with Michael, from their first year of college before he switched to law, and it felt like meeting with an old friend. His wife was lovely and so was Anton. He'd loosened up as the evening had worn on and couldn't' stop laughing when Nadine told them about Luca and all the insults she'd had to endure, and he told them about his mother in return, who had similar character traits and didn't trust foreigners either.

"Well, this was fun," he said, still chuckling as he downed the last of his espresso at the end of the night. "But I must be going now. We have a big week ahead and I need to prepare tomorrow." He turned to Michael. "Michael, it's been a pleasure. I've never worked with an American lawyer before, but your insights have been very valuable, and I understand why Rome wanted you to be a consultant on her case. I might see you in court, but if I don't, I hope to see you after we've settled at some point because I'd like to celebrate with you all."

"Absolutely." Michael shook his hand before Anton turned to Jeannie and Nadine. "Enjoy your stay in Rome, Jeannie, he's all yours now. And Nadine, thank you for the recipes, I plan to impress my wife with them. Rome, I'll see you Monday. You'll be the first to give your evidence before the judge."

"Thanks, Anton. I'll see you Monday." Rome felt her stomach drop as she said it. It was getting real now and although she wasn't looking forward to it, she'd waited for over three months for this moment to arrive. All she could do was tell the truth.

57

"Can I take my girl out for dinner now that you've seen the judge?" Nadine asked as they walked into town. "I took the liberty of booking a nice restaurant, thought it might take your mind off things." She pulled Rome against her and put an arm around her. "Unless you're tired and you'd rather go home; I'd completely understand."

"No, I'd love to go for dinner with you. I'm just so glad it's done." Rome pinched her hand and smiled. The sun was setting as they strolled along the river Tiber and passed Castel Sant'Angelo, which Rome now knew to be the mausoleum of Hadrian. The beautiful cylindrical fortress towered over them and made up for an impressive sight, lit from behind. The evening light fell on the river and made the water sparkle around the remaining cruise boats that glided along the banks. They passed Vatican City, where she'd recently spent a day exploring the various religious and cultural sites such as St. Peter's Basilica, whose iconic central dome dominated the skyline of Rome, and the Sistine Chapel where her eyes were drawn upward to behold Michelangelo's famous ceiling—the fresco of *The Last Judgement* so beautiful it blew her mind.

Surrounded by tourists until they reached the quieter streets, Rome felt like a native now, like the city was hers, too. Hearing visitors gasp as they turned corners and saw all the beauty surrounding them for the first time, like she had when she'd first arrived, also gave her a sense of pride—her heart full at the sense of being a part of it. She picked up on most conversations between locals now, and although she wasn't fluent enough to engage in complex discussions, she was getting there. Practicing with Nadine for an hour each day had helped a lot with her pronunciation, and learning how to use slang and exclamations of outrage, plus a little acceptable swearing, made the guys at the market laugh each time she tried it out on them. Just like Nadine had predicted, Rome had grown to love the city, the language, the food, the people, and if given the choice, there was no way she'd move back home anytime soon.

The restaurant tucked away in the corner of a small piazza just outside the historical center was perfect in every way, and Rome wanted to kiss Nadine for finding such a quiet spot with what looked to be great food and a warm ambiance after a stressful day.

Surrounded by leafy vines and trees, and looking out onto an old church, they had made the most of their idyllic location with dimmed lighting under canvas canopies and candles, and single roses finished off the pristinely laid out tables with white linen and immaculately polished glasses and silverware. She loved how Nadine wasn't extravagant with dates or gifts, but instead was rather thoughtful, and she always seemed to know what Rome wanted without even asking.

"It's not fair," she said as they sat down. "I'll never be

able to trump you with the places you take me; I just can't find them."

Nadine shot her a pleased grin and folded out her napkin. "Come on, I like that I can impress you. Showing you new places makes me happy."

"It makes me happy too, but I'm not going to give up trying to find gems like this." Rome chuckled. "One day, I'm going to take you somewhere in Rome you've never been, and it will seriously impress you. I just need some time."

"One day, huh?" Nadine's smile widened. "That sounds pretty long-term."

"Yeah." Rome was aware that it had come out more serious than she intended. She'd thought of them long-term, of course, but aware of their mutual commitment issues, she hadn't brought it up. They hadn't had problems so far though, and neither of them had needed breathing space, even after months of being together. It was like they complimented each other naturally and being with Nadine gave her energy and made her very, very happy. "Does that make you feel uncomfortable?" she asked.

"No, it doesn't. Does thinking long-term make you feel uncomfortable?" Nadine kept her gaze fixed on Rome while she poured them water from the jug on the table.

"No." Rome smiled at the waiter, who handed her the menu and held up her hand when Nadine was about to order wine. "Please allow me."

Nadine looked impressed when Rome managed to flaw-lessly order a bottle of red wine and enquire about the daily specials, and apart from thanking the waiter before he left, she didn't interfere. "You're getting good," she said, leaning in on her elbows.

"Thank you." Rome took off her blazer, hung it over the back of her chair and opened the top three buttons of her white shirt. "And to answer your question properly, the thought of long-term when it comes to us doesn't make me nervous. Quite the opposite; it makes me feel calm and happy."

"I'm glad to hear that." Nadine took off the polka dot scarf around her neck that she'd worn to the courthouse. It was unusually warm for September, and she rolled up the long sleeves of her navy colored knee-length dress. "Have you thought of what you're going to do after the launch?" she asked, clearly trying to sound casual. Rome could see uncertainty in her eyes, though, and all she wanted was to put her at ease. "I mean, you can run the app from anywhere after it's done, right? You could even appoint someone to take over from you."

"I could." Rome waited for the waiter to pour them wine. "But I want to stay on. I've invested too much in this to hand it over so soon, so I'm actually considering heading up a strategic team to focus on expansion. I've surprised myself and seem to be a pretty valuable leader so far, and I'm thinking of applying for a job at *Nero*, outside my ongoing contract with them. That way, they can provide me with a work visa." As she stretched her legs under the table and opened her menu, Rome noted she felt more relaxed than she had in a long time. She'd been so anxious about her appointment with the judge, and even though they might still have a long way to go, she knew what to expect now and it wasn't so daunting anymore. "Depending on the outcome of the case, of course. That's why I didn't mention the option earlier," she added.

"So you want to stay here?" Nadine seemed delighted with the news as she took her hand over the table.

"Of course I want to stay." Rome looked at her intently, Nadine's warm smile making her feel warm and fuzzy inside. "Aside from the fact that I love this city... you're here, and I love you." She ran a hand through her hair and felt a blush rise to her cheeks. "There's no guarantee that I'll get the job, but I'd definitely be the most obvious choice. Aside from that, I doubt they'll say no as that wouldn't look great on the company after everything that's been going on. So yeah, I'm optimistic."

"You have no idea how happy that makes me." Nadine held up her glass in a toast. "Here's to your future in Rome." She hesitated, then shook her head. "No, I need to rephrase that. Here's to *our* future in Rome."

"Yes, to our future," Rome said with a beaming smile before she took a sip of her wine. "I know this is technically your date, but can I order for you? I need to practice."

"Go for it." Nadine waved the waiter back. "Order anything you want. You're so cute when you speak Italian." Her eyes softened with tenderness as she listened to Rome, who chuckled to herself each time she made a mistake.

"I'm really getting the hang of this." Rome handed back her menu and studied Nadine, who seemed to ponder over something. "What's on your mind?"

"Nothing serious." Nadine shrugged. "I've just been thinking about how you don't sleep in your own apartment much anymore, and I thought it might be good if we talked about that."

"I know. It's not that I don't like it. I love it, and I'm so grateful that you found it for me, but I think I just prefer your place." Rome bit her lip and winced. "But I should really start sleeping there again, I'm constantly in your space and..."

"No, please don't," Nadine interrupted her. "I love having you around. My apartment feels empty without you and I hate waking up alone these days." She hesitated, picking on a fingernail. "But I was thinking that you might as well give up that expensive apartment. I mean, if you like my place, then..."

"Then what?" Rome asked, a smile playing around her mouth as she knew what was coming.

"Well, you might want to reconsider your official living arrangements." Nadine sounded clumsy and the blush on her cheeks was adorable.

"Are you asking me to move in with you?" Rome teased, wanting to hear her say it.

"Yes." Nadine chuckled. "Yes, God damn it. Just put me out of my misery and tell me you'll move in with me."

Rome laughed, stood up and walked around the table to kiss her on the cheek while she wrapped her arms around Nadine from behind. "Of course I want to move in with you, silly. I want to be with you all the time."

"And you don't think you'll get sick of me?" Nadine asked, squeezing her arms.

"Never. How could I?" Rome sat down again when a family of five arrived and she felt their eyes move over them. "Perhaps you'll get sick of me? My stuff taking up space in your palatial apartment?"

"No, you can put your stuff anywhere you want." Nadine held up a hand with an amused smile. "Apart from in my perfume room; I'd rather not have clothes in there."

"I know you don't like clothes in there." Rome kicked off one of her heels under the table and ran her foot along Nadine's calf. "I've seen you going in there a lot in the mornings lately, naked under your lab coat, and you have no idea what that does to me." She really needed to stop looking at Nadine like that because anyone could sense the sexual tension between them. "So, we're going to make it official? My lease runs out at the end of October."

"Yeah." Nadine caught her foot and placed it onto her lap. "What? You want me to present you with a key in a jewelry box or something?" she joked, stroking Rome's foot. "You already have one."

"No, I just wanted to hear you say it one more time." Rome was unable to stop grinning. The urge to jump up and do a little victory dance was strong but she managed to compose herself when their shared platter of bruschetta arrived. "I'm excited," she said, holding up her glass again as she pulled back her foot. "Here's to us."

58

"Sorry guys, I have to take this." Rome walked out of the meeting space, went into her office and closed the door. "Anton?" Her heart was pounding in her chest as she answered the phone call from her lawyer. Although he called her regularly with updates, it always made her nervous, and she was worried that something had gone wrong.

"Hi, Rome. Good news." Anton paused for a moment, and Rome let out a sigh of relief as she heard him flick through paperwork. "Matteo wants to settle."

"Already?"

"Yes, the judge has taken statements from all the victims, and he's been called in too. He's clearly getting jittery. Frankly, I think he knows he's fucked and wants this to be over as fast as you do."

"That's great news. What's happening now?"

"We're going to put the settlement offer we discussed before him. Hopefully he'll accept it, but if his lawyer comes in with a counteroffer, we'll have to decide if that's good enough." Anton cleared his throat. "He probably didn't expect so many victims to come forward. He might even have forgotten about some of them, so this process is a painful reminder to him of how many more could be out there. The longer this drags on, the more women could decide to take action, so I expect him to be keen to handle this fast and quietly."

"Good." Rome smiled. "I'm still going to alert the press of course, but he doesn't need to know that." She'd taken the difficult decision to inform the media if they didn't get a whiff of it themselves, purely because the world needed to know what type of person Matteo Romano was. Yes, the company might suffer, but if she couldn't send him to prison, she wanted him named and shamed and this was the only way. "I don't think he should come off lightly," she said. "But as you know, there's only one thing we all feel really strongly about and that's having him removed from the building. Whatever his shareholders decide to do with him is up to them, but the office is a no-go. If that's a problem, I don't care how long this drags on for. That man shouldn't be allowed back in the workplace."

"I know. And I'll tell them that's non-negotiable." Anton paused. "How are you doing through all of this?"

The question seemed strange, coming from him, since they didn't really have a personal relationship. "I'm okay." Rome took a deep breath. "I'm more stressed than I expected to be, but other than that, I'm coping."

"I'm sure Nadine is taking good care of you."

"She is." Rome smiled. "But she's been a little stressed herself, now that her new business is taking off, so I've arranged a nice surprise for her next week."

"That's very thoughtful of you. Please give her my best wishes."

"I will." Rome paused. "And if I haven't said it yet, I really appreciate your hard work and how invested you are in this case. It means everything to me."

"Hey, it's my job," Anton said. "I'm cautiously optimistic that we'll have this settled soon, but let's see how it plays out."

"Whatever it takes. Keep me posted." Rome looked over at the meeting space, where her team was gathered. There was no way she was going to let the ten women there, nor any of the other women in the building, be subjected to Matteo's advances.

"I will."

Rome walked back to her meeting and gave Eliza a quick reassuring thumbs up, letting her know everything was fine. "Right", she said, settling back into leader-mode. "Where were we?"

"The launch party," Eliza reminded her.

"Of course." Rome grabbed her notepad and sat down on one of the recliners, pulling her legs up underneath her as she chewed her pen. "The party of the century," she added with a chuckle. "We have to be conscious of what is served. Everything we offer has to have the lowest carbon footprint possible, within reasonable limits of course, and the venue needs to match that. So think organic wine makers, vegan chefs, and a suitable location with public transport nearby. I know you guys are creators and not necessarily the users but still, you represent the Carbon app, so think about what you'll be wearing, too. No fur, of course, preferably sustainable brands, and make sure the wait staff is dressed sustainably, too."

"There are a lot of abandoned warehouses in Rome," a girl from the marketing team suggested. "They have great acoustics because of their height, and we might get permission to use one of them. I've also looked into a couple of hotels with Green Key certification."

"Great thinking." Rome pointed her pen at her. "Check their availability and let me know what our options are. It needs to be smart enough for the celebrities on our guest list, though, so make sure it's either weirdly spectacular or super smart. The board will only sign off if they think it will lift the company's image; we're doing something good here and that needs to be reflected in the media."

"You keep mentioning the media," Jonathan said. "I don't understand why you're so worried about that; we're launching a fantastic product, so I don't get why you think they'll be desperate to criticize what we're doing." He looked genuinely confused as he leaned in and stared at her. "We're not doing anything wrong here."

Rome took a moment and sighed as she realized it was time to tell her team what was going on. They needed to be prepared for the inevitable media coverage that would surround Matteo just as much as she did, and now was as good a time as any. "There's something I have to tell you," she said, looking around the room. "It might impact our launch, but then again, it might not." All eyes were focused on her now, and she was pretty sure she'd be able to hear a pin drop the room was so quiet. "It's about Matteo."

59

"**G**ood morning."

"Hey." Nadine smiled as she turned to Rome and inhaled the smell of coffee. "Thank you, honey. That's just what I needed." She sat up and glanced at the clock on the nightstand as she took a sip, wondering why Rome was still here. "Why haven't you left for work yet?"

"I thought I'd take a day off." Rome hiked up the cream-colored negligée she was wearing and straddled Nadine. "We've both been working so hard lately, so I thought it might be nice to spend a day in bed together."

Nadine grinned and rubbed the sleep out of her eyes, then ran her hands under the satin fabric and slipped them around Rome's hips to pull her closer. "I like your thinking." She licked her lips as she eyed the sexy little number Rome was wearing, the outline of her hard nipples telling her she had nothing underneath. "Is that new?"

"Uh-huh." Rome leaned in and kissed her lightly on the lips while she ran her hands through Nadine's hair. "Do you like it?"

"Very much." Nadine pushed Rome into the mattress and rolled on top of her. "Can I take it off now?"

Rome chuckled as Nadine grabbed her wrists and brushed her mouth with her lips. "Wait, not yet. I have a surprise for you." She sighed in delight at the feeling of Nadine's weight on top of her. "As much as I like that you're naked right now, there's something next to the bed that I want you to wear for me. I'd give it to you in person if I wasn't pinned down."

Nadine laughed too, let go of her and shifted to look over the edge of the bed. She raised a brow as she picked up the beautifully wrapped present. "Is this going to be some kind of role-play? I didn't know you were into that."

"Just open it."

Nadine carefully unwrapped the present and felt her heart swell as she took out a crisp, white lab coat with the *Stars Aligned* logo embroidered on the chest. "Oh, Rome, this is beautiful." She tried not to cry, because it was by far the sweetest and most thoughtful present anyone had ever given her.

"Do you like it? I had it made out of a highly durable anti-bacterial fabric with some kind of softener, so it will be more comfortable."

"I love it. But why did you do that?"

"Just because I love you. And you needed a new one."

Nadine stood up and put it on. "How do I look?"

"You look hot." Rome winked. "I prefer it unbuttoned, though." She pointed to the hallway. "I hope you can forgive me, but I sneaked into your lab and put some stuff in there too."

"You did not." Nadine narrowed her eyes in mock anger. "I might have to punish you for that."

"Go and have a look first. Then, if you still want to

punish me, I'm all yours," Rome said as color rose to her cheeks. She followed Nadine into the living room and through the opening in the bookcase.

"My God..." Nadine switched off the ventilator and walked over to her desk, where a pile of branded notebooks were laid out next to a branded pot with beautiful silver pens that matched the color of the logo. On the wall hung an illuminated white neon sign of her logo and next to it a large monthly planner. "This is incredible. When did you do this?" She ran her fingers along the new white sideboard situated underneath the neon sign that now held enough space for her test-tubes, scales, pipets and other lab paraphernalia.

"I had some guys come in yesterday, while you were out getting groceries. That's why I didn't want you going in there last night. Don't worry; they didn't touch anything." Rome smiled. "Now that your business is off the ground and you can afford to stay at the apartment, I thought it would be nice to give your workspace a makeover. I did some research into what you might need, but if I missed anything, let me know and I'll order it for you."

Nadine wiped at her eyes as she looked around again, taking it all in. "That must have been so much work." She couldn't begin to describe how touched she was, so she simply closed the distance between them and wrapped her arms around Rome. "I love you."

"Mmm..." Rome closed her eyes against Nadine's shoulder and held her tight. "I love you too." She looked up and kissed Nadine's cheek that was wet from her tears. Knowing Nadine was uncomfortable with being emotional, she unbuttoned her lab coat and pointed to the desk. "Go and sit in that chair."

Nadine felt a twitch at seeing the fire in Rome's eyes. "Why?"

"Because I have one last surprise for you."

Nadine sat back, a flash of heat shooting between her legs when Rome got down on her knees and crawled over to the desk. She moved slow and seductively, cat-like, her hips swaying each time she put one knee in front of the other. The negligée crept up, baring her thighs, and one of the straps slipped off her shoulder.

"You have no idea how sexy you look," Nadine whispered. A gasp slipped from her mouth when Rome crawled underneath the large desk and spread her legs apart.

"You look pretty sexy from this angle too," she said in a sultry voice.

Rome's warm breath on her sex made Nadine buck her hips, and her hands clamped around the armrests of her chair, her knuckles turning white as Rome ran her tongue along her lips. It felt incredible, and despite being more turned on than ever, she fought to keep her eyes open, the sight of Rome under her desk and between her legs too arousing to miss.

Rome pulled her forward until she was sitting at the edge of her chair and twirled her tongue around her clit, then sucked it into her mouth so hard that Nadine shot up. She felt the need to wriggle, but Rome held her still, and as she dug her nails into her hips, Nadine's body tensed up.

"Please don't stop," she begged when Rome pulled away and looked up at her with a teasing smile.

"Open your top drawer," Rome whispered, and waited for Nadine to do so.

Nadine's lips parted as she picked up the small, egg-shaped purple device. "I didn't know you were a toy girl."

Her voice was shaky, as she was so close already and desperate for Rome to continue.

"I'm about to find out if I am." Rome held out her hand. "Give it to me." She smiled when Nadine shifted in her chair while she handed it over, eager for her to use it. Leaning in again, she ran her tongue down along Nadine's lips until she found a pool of wetness. She darted her tongue inside her and switched on the vibrator, then placed it where Nadine needed it most.

"Fuck!" Nadine jerked her hips as a climax of enormous proportions washed over her. She closed her eyes and gave in to the deliciously warm feeling, her mind vaguely registering her own moans and Rome's mouth on her that didn't stop pleasing, even though she could barely take any more. When she came down, she realized her hand was in Rome's hair, pushing her face hard against her as she shuddered. "You make me crazy," she said through ragged breaths.

"And you make me wild." Rome pulled herself up and sat down on her lap, her hair a mess as she licked her lips. She put an arm around Nadine's neck and kissed her so passionately that Nadine thought she might drown in the kiss. When Rome pulled back, her eyes were dark and hazy and her chest heaving, giving away her own arousal. Grinning, she studied Nadine, who was staring at her, open-mouthed, for once, entirely lost for words. "Did you like that?"

60

"Rome, there's someone from the press here. She wants to speak to you." Nadine came out onto the balcony, where Rome was catching up on her emails on Saturday morning.

Rome looked up and frowned. "What? How did she know I was here? I don't even live here, technically."

"No idea. Do you want me to let her in, or shall I say you're busy? She's from *La Repubblica*, so it's a big one."

"Perfect, that's the one I wanted." Rome closed her laptop and stood up. "No, I'll go down and have a coffee with her somewhere public, I don't want to let strangers in here."

"Want me to come with you?" Nadine took Rome's hand as she walked past.

"Sure. Unless you're busy?" Rome squeezed her hand. "I'm glad I told the team last week; I wouldn't want them to find out on the news." She bit her lip and winced. "Although Anton briefed me, I have no idea what I'm doing, and I've never dealt with press before."

"That's okay, you just need to tell her the truth," Nadine assured her. "But it might be nice to have someone with you." She pressed the intercom button and told the woman that Rome would come down, then stepped into her sandals. "Don't you need to get dressed?"

Rome laughed as she looked down at the kimono dressing gown she was wearing. "God, I'm all over the place this week. Waiting for the settlement to be finalized is so stressful; I'd forget my head if it wasn't attached." She rushed into the bedroom and quickly put on a pair of black slacks and a T-shirt. Her hair was still wet from her shower, and her eyes looked sleepy, so she covered them with a pair of Nadine's big, dark shades. "No pictures today, that's for sure. But I have permission from the others to get everyone together for a picture at some point this week, so she'll be able to use that. Most of them are happy to be interviewed, too."

"I bet she won't believe her luck. They usually have to scramble for stories like this one, and women rarely speak up about sexual harassment," Nadine said.

"Exactly. And after the settlement she'll have another story, to keep the momentum going. Hopefully by then, everyone will know what a piece of shit Matteo is."

They both chuckled quietly when they came down and found Luca and the journalist sitting on the edge of a wall in front of the building, engaged in a heated discussion about the mayor. Rome expected Luca to sneer at the journalist as she broke up the conversation, but instead, he gave the woman a sweet semi-toothless smile and wished her a good day.

"It looks like my grumpy neighbor finally approves of someone. That alone, is worth a story of its own," Nadine joked before she and Rome shook the woman's hand.

"Hi, I'm Matilda. Thank you so much for meeting with me. I tried to get hold of you at the office last week, but you weren't at your desk, so I figured the weekend might be better for you."

"Yes, I've been very busy." Rome didn't ask how she'd tracked her down. It was important for this woman to take a liking to her, because perception was everything in this case. "Is it okay if we have a coffee here?" she asked, pointing at one of the free tables under Nadine's apartment. "Nadine is my girlfriend, by the way, I'd like her to join us."

"No problem." Matilda had a curious look in her eyes as she looked Rome up and down while Nadine got the drinks. "You're different to what I expected. You look much younger in real life than the pictures on the *Nero* website."

Rome shrugged and smiled. "Well, I'm kind of small, so that might have something to do with it. I assume you're here to talk about our case against Matteo Romano?" She was secretly relieved that the journalist was a woman. Matilda was in her fifties, she guessed, and didn't look like she took crap from anyone. The deep grooves between her eyebrows told Rome she was suspicious by nature, but her eyes were friendly and open. She was casually dressed in jeans and a blouse, and her short, dark hair was combed back. A pair of black-rimmed glasses balanced on the tip of her nose as her eyes widened a little, snapping to attention.

"Our case?" Matilda swiftly produced a small device from her bag. "Is it okay if I record this?"

"Sure, no problem."

"Great." Matilda switched it on and started firing off a monologue about the location, the persons involved, and the time and meeting place as if she were running a police investigation. "So, you said 'our' case. I was under the impression this was your case. It's very hard to get information regarding a civil case, but I was tipped off by an anonymous source." She leaned in closer, resting her chin on her fist.

"Yes, it's concerning myself and twenty-two other women." Rome could tell Matilda was excited by her revelation, even though she was trying very hard not to show it. "Most of them still work at *Nero*, one has left." She paused. "I'd also like to clarify that this case is against an individual, not the company."

"And the twenty-two other women would agree with you on that?"

"Yes."

"And is there any chance I could speak to these other women to verify your story?"

"Yes. Most of them have given me permission to give out their details. It's hard to stay anonymous in a scandal, so we'd rather speak up and get the real story out there rather than have people speculating. I was waiting for someone from your paper to show up."

Matilda tilted her head. "If it makes you feel safer, I've been a journalist for twenty-seven years and I don't speculate."

"That helps," Rome said, and smiled as she looked up at Nadine, who came out with their cappuccinos. She took a deep breath and sat back, blowing into her cup. "So fire away. What do you want to know?"

61

Nadine stopped and picked up a vase, examined it, then put it back down again.

"Fifty Euros," the dealer said. "The best Italian craftsmanship."

Nadine raised a brow at him and let out a sarcastic chuckle. "Are you serious? It's obviously fake."

"No, it's not. It's a genuine Bitossi."

"It's made in China, is what it is," Nadine said, picking it up and showing him the small stamp on the bottom. Her lips pulled into a smile as she watched him blush. "And if that was real, you could have charged over a thousand, so get your information straight before you try to rip people off." She felt a little sorry for him and pointed to a vintage postcard with an Italian restaurant scene. "But I'll take that one if you promise to give me a fair price."

"Okay. One Euro." He shook her hand and Nadine gave him an indulgent smile, letting him know there were no hard feelings.

Porta Portese market was busy as she and Rome scanned

the stalls for treasures. She'd bought an antique ring and a small, silver jewelry box and Rome was currently haggling over a brooch she wanted to buy for her friend Barbara. Listening to her broken but extremely passionate Italian made Nadine laugh because Rome could put Moroccan souk traders to shame, throwing in a random curse here and there, making the stallholder cry with laughter. She eventually settled on a price that was a little too high for her liking, but it was just for fun, after all, and the brooch was unique and a perfect gift.

"Barbara likes dragonflies," Rome said, holding up the antique dragonfly brooch so it shimmered in the sun.

"Have you spoken to her yet? Or to your father?"

"No. Barbara is busy enough as it is with her kids, and I'll call my father next week, or whenever I feel like it."

Nadine stopped in her stride and turned to Rome. "Rome, I know you two aren't that close, but it's your father we're talking about. I'm sure he'd want to know if his daughter is suing someone for sexual harassment."

Rome pursed her lips and sighed. "Honestly, I don't have the energy right now. I just want to do things that take my mind off the case because I can't stop worrying about the other women involved. They've put their careers on the line for me and I need this to be worth it, for them."

"It will be. But still, I think he should know."

"Please drop it." Rome tilted her head and glared at her. "I don't want this to be our first fight."

"Okay, I'll stop bringing him up." Nadine gave up and put on her shades. She didn't want to fight either. "Ice cream?"

"Thank you." Rome's expression softened, and she took her hand. "And yes, I'd love an ice cream. You always know the way to my heart."

They followed the market to the exit, walked underneath the ancient city gate and continued to the gelato shop by the river, from where they would walk back to Nadine's apartment. This had been their Sunday ritual lately. An early visit to the flea market, then ice cream for breakfast before they picked up Luca for church. Rome was growing on him; she'd made him smile on multiple occasions but he still refused to admit that he liked her, and that amused them both. Nadine and Rome had fallen into an easy life together; enjoying the simple things and living every moment they were together to the fullest. Their nights were passionate, their mornings sweet, and although Rome was a little on edge right now, she tended to push it to the background, pretending everything was fine. Nadine wasn't sure if that was the best way to handle things, and her mind went back to Rome's friend and father once again, wondering if she should get involved anyway.

"What do you want?" she asked as they joined the back of the queue.

"Anything you feel like, I'll share," Rome said, pinching Nadine's waist.

Nadine put an arm around her. "Okay, I like that. Should we get a pastry for Luca while we're here?"

"He doesn't deserve it if you ask me, but sure, go ahead," Rome joked as she looked up at her. "Just to be clear, I'm not getting on the scooter with him again. It's highly awkward being wedged between the two of you, not to mention illegal and dangerous, the way you drive."

Nadine chuckled. "Come on, it's not that bad."

"Seriously, Nadine, it's awful. This guy hates me, and he's literally got his arms around me, cursing all the way to church. And then he grunts at me some more throughout the service for leaning back too far and accuses me of trying to kill him."

"He doesn't hate you, the fact he argues with you tells me he loves you." Nadine laughed even harder now. "But sure, I promise you there will be no more awkward rides and we'll take a cab. I don't want to go without you; it's too much fun to hear the two of you bicker. Finally, it's not me who's getting yelled at all the time anymore."

Rome nudged her. "It's not funny."

"It so is." Nadine pulled her in and shot her a loving smile. "I never thought I'd say this, but I'm going to miss that man."

"I'm going to miss him a little too," Rome admitted. "He taught me the best swearwords, even though they were directed at me. When are they picking him up?"

"Next month. I spoke to his son yesterday."

"What will happen to the apartment?" Rome asked.

"I'm not sure. Why?" Nadine regarded Rome, who seemed to be in deep thought all of a sudden. "Do you want to be neighbors? Because I meant it when I said that I love having you in my space."

"No, I want to move in with you, I have no doubt about that. It's just that..." Rome bit her lip as she hesitated. "If it comes up for sale, then I'd certainly be interested. The location is fantastic and although his apartment is a little worn-out, it still has all these amazing original features, like yours, and it would be a fantastic investment. I could easily afford it now." She met Nadine's eyes and shrugged. "You might be in a position to buy yours too, soon."

Nadine's heart did a jump at that. She'd never thought about buying the apartment she lived in before, just because she'd always assumed that she wouldn't be able to afford it. If her business kept running the way it was now though, it was definitely something to think about. She suddenly had visions of amalgamating the apartments to make one huge, joint home, but just like Rome, she didn't dare voice it. "That's true," she said, then gave the woman behind the counter her order. "You've just given me a lot to think about."

62

"Happy?" Nadine asked as they left Anton's office. Rome had been asked to come in to finalize the settlement.

"Very." Rome smiled. "Having Matteo banned from the company's premises, combined with public humiliation, was exactly what I wanted. It's the next best thing to having him sent to prison."

"And don't forget about the settlement. A hundred thousand Euros for each claimant. That's a substantial amount... times twenty-three." Nadine frowned as she did the math. "Two point three million. Ouch. That must have hurt. What are you going to do with your share?"

"I don't want it," Rome said. "I'm donating it to the women's rights charity Rob mentioned in our meeting. I spoke to his wife just now, and she's delighted."

"That's very generous of you."

"It's the right thing to do. It was never about the money for me; I just wanted him out of the office so the women working there can feel comfortable again. And as far as his other victims are concerned; most of them could really do with the money and I'm very happy for them. Salaries aren't exactly high in Italy unless you're at the top, like me, and they deserve a break after everything they've been through."

"I think it's time to raise a glass to acknowledge your victory, don't you?"

"Yeah. I didn't want to organize anything before the settlement came through because I was afraid to jinx it, but now it's definitely time to celebrate. Any ideas on what we can do?"

Nadine was already ahead of her. "Hmm... I do have an idea, actually. Why don't you come with me; I want to show you something." She raised a brow when Rome stalled. "Come on, it's right over there."

"That place doesn't seem nearly big enough to hold thirty people," Rome said as she regarded the restaurant at the edge of the river with only a handful of tables outside. It was very cute, with red roses growing up against the sand-colored wall and red cloths draped over the small tables, but she wanted to invite the other women too, and celebrate with them. Her eyes narrowed as she suddenly spotted a familiar figure sitting at one of the tables and a strawberry blonde-haired woman in a deep purple sundress sitting beside him.

"Dad?" Rome slammed a hand in front of her mouth, and she gasped when she saw it was Barbara sitting at the table with him. "Barbara?" She glanced up at Nadine but was too overwhelmed to ask questions before she stormed toward them both to give them a long hug. "What are you guys doing here? Together," she added with a chuckle.

"Your wonderful girlfriend contacted me," Barbara said. "She told me what had been going on with you, and she thought you could do with the support today, no matter what the outcome of your settlement was. Why didn't you tell me? I had no idea."

"Neither did I. Nadine called me too," her father said. "So, Barbara and I came together." He took Rome into another hug. It was strange, because Rome and her father had never been physically close, but she let him, knowing they both needed it today more than they would ever admit.

"I'm sorry I didn't tell you." Rome sighed against his shoulder. "I just had so much on my plate, and I didn't want you guys to worry about me on top of that."

"You should have told me." Her father stepped away and put his hands on her shoulders. "You didn't even tell me you were in a relationship."

"We don't talk much in general," Rome said quietly as she shrugged.

"I know, and I'm to blame for that." Her father's expression softened, and he gave her a smile. "But these are big things and I want to know what's going on in your life. You're all I've got."

Rome felt her eyes well up at his words and she swallowed hard as she felt her bottom lip tremble. "I'm sorry."

"It's fine, we're here now." Her father looked emotional too, but he composed himself before he nodded to Nadine. "We met with Nadine this morning, after we arrived. You're lucky to have someone who cares so much about you."

"Yes, I feel really lucky." Rome put an arm around Nadine and pulled her in.

"You can imagine how nervous I was to meet both your father and your best friend," Nadine joked. "I hope you're not angry with me for doing this behind your back."

"Not at all. Thank you." Rome shot Nadine a loving look and clasped her hand.

"We thought we could have dinner here together?" her father said. "Catch up, just the four of us?" He grabbed the two extra glasses on the table and poured wine for Rome and Nadine. "Apparently, Nadine has arranged something for later."

"I'm not sure if I can handle any more surprises." Rome shook her head again as she looked from Barbara to her father and back. It felt surreal to have them here, and she was pretty sure nothing could have made her happier.

"I've invited the other women to Angelo's restaurant for drinks later. Anton is calling them now to update them regarding the outcome, he'll be joining us too, along with Michael and his wife as they're still here. And Eliza, of course."

"You're amazing."

"She is. I get it now." Barbara gave Nadine a wink. "I was telling Nadine how you were swooning over her when you were back home, packing up your things."

Rome blushed profusely and covered her face in her hands. "Oh God, that is so embarrassing."

"No it's not, it's cute," Nadine argued.

"I don't think I've ever seen Rome blush before," her father said. "You must be something. I had no idea you were even gay, Rome." He hesitated as he regarded his daughter like he had just seen her for the first time. He wasn't being judgmental, just curious. "But from what I understood, you didn't either."

"I didn't realize until I met Nadine. It was kind of like being struck by a thunderbolt; she just happened to me."

"I can see that." Barbara laughed. "It takes a lot to sweep you off your feet." She sat back and her expression turned serious. "So, you're happy with the settlement?"

"I am."

"Do you want to talk about it? About what happened?"

"No. Maybe later, but not now." A glimpse of sadness passed over Rome's face but she then smiled. "How long are you staying?"

"One week," her father said. "It would be great if we could spend some time together, but if you're busy, I totally understand. You're a workaholic like me."

"And I'm staying for ten days," Barbara added. "Ten wonderful days just by myself. No screaming kids, no nagging husband. Just me, the sun and the city." Her eyes twinkled with joy. "And my bestie."

Rome smiled, thinking how much fun this was going to be. "In that case, I'm going to take a week off. I'd love to spend some quality time with you both and I'd also love for you to get to know Nadine better." She took a sip of her wine and turned to Nadine. "My lease is up soon, and I'll officially be moving in with her."

Barbara and her father stared at her in surprise. "Are you serious?" Barbara asked. "I'm happy for you; don't get me wrong, but you're not one to do anything on a whim."

"I'm not doing this on some random impulse." Rome shrugged. "We've known each other for a while. Almost six months, if you count our first meeting, and it just feels right, you know? But I get what you're saying; the old 'me' would have needed years to make a big decision like that. I've changed, I guess."

Barbara nodded slowly as she glanced at her with a curious look in her eyes. "I can see that. You have a glow about you."

"Yeah, well, I have the city and Nadine to thank for that. Just wait and see; ten days here will make you appreciate life in an entirely new way."

"I believe you." Barbara held up her glass in a toast. "In that case, we have two things to celebrate. To love, and to justice."

63

"Your friends are very nice." Rome's father joined Rome at her table in Angelo's restaurant, after introducing himself to everyone.

"Yes, they're wonderful women." Rome nodded to Angelo, who was serving Aperol Spritz from plastic cups and handing out finger food wrapped in pieces of faux newspaper. "And so is he. I feel blessed to have met so many amazing people since I moved here."

It was far from a fancy affair, but she couldn't have wished for a better place to end the day and to be thankful that they would never have to see Matteo again. Barbara was talking to Anton, her lawyer, and Matilda, the journalist, who Nadine had also invited. They were laughing as they clinked their cups together. The article Matilda had written had now been published, and there would be a follow-up tomorrow. It had sparked other publications to do the same, and with that came the expected media storm, plastering Matteo Romano's name all over Italy's newsstands. His name was tainted, and Rome could imagine him sweating and praying that no one else would come forward. He had a long, impressive résumé, and there was no doubt that he'd harassed women in previous companies he'd worked at.

"I'm glad you found your place in life. And I'm glad you found love." He paused and looked down at the empty cup in his hand. "I know I've never said this before, and I'm very sorry for that, but I need you to know that I'm proud of you, Rome. I'm so incredibly proud. What happened to you when you were younger—when your mother left—was horrible, and I probably didn't deal with it the right way, especially not when it came to you."

"It's fine. I know you were hurting, too, and..."

"No, wait, Rome. I need to say this," her father interrupted her. "You are the strongest person I know, and I wish I could take credit for that, but I can't. You've accomplished so much at such a young age and knowing you did that all by yourself makes me sad. I should have been there for you, but you never asked for help. Not even financial help. Barbara told me how you'd struggled for years." He took a deep breath and continued. "Promise me you'll call me next time you need help, okay? I'm your father and I'm here for you."

Rome nodded, doing everything in her power not to cry. *Not tonight.* "I will," she whispered. His words meant everything to her, and it felt like a weight had been lifted from her shoulders, like the air had suddenly cleared. He was right; she'd never asked him for anything. Going through life entirely alone was the only way she'd been able to function, but she'd learned it was okay to get help, and that only relying on herself wasn't a guarantee for a stable life, or happiness. She was glad to see Nadine approach as she had no idea how to continue their conversation.

"I like your father." Nadine handed them both another drink and placed a soft kiss on Rome's temple. "He's no-

nonsense, to-the-point and very smart, like you." She gave him a wink.

"And I like your partner," Rome's father said, and shot Nadine a goofy smile, still emotional from their conversation and a little tipsy from the cocktails. He rarely opened up or let his hair down, and Rome realized it was the first time they'd had a drink together. They'd drifted apart over the years and perhaps it was time they got to know each other again. "Is partner the correct term?" he asked, clumsily shuffling on the spot.

"Partner is fine." Rome gave him a pat on his shoulder, still not entirely sure how to interact with him. The week ahead would surely take away some of the distance between them and Rome was looking forward to some free time with her father, Barbara and Nadine. There was no way she could express how grateful she was to the woman who was responsible for two of the most important people she loved and had missed, being here tonight. She'd clearly already charmed the hell out of her father, and it was almost amusing to watch him interact with her, all smiles and laughs.

"What's going on over there?" Nadine gestured to the corner of the room, where Eliza had sneaked behind the bar. She and Angelo were standing close together while she helped him make more drinks, and she giggled as he whispered something in her ear. They were an unusual pair; Eliza slightly taller because of her platform shoes, outrageously dressed in something that looked like a black version of a wedding dress, and Angelo in his torn jeans and old T-shirt, his shaggy hair sticking out from underneath his beanie that was permanently attached to his head. But the way they looked at each other made total sense, and Rome put an arm around Nadine's waist as they stared at them.

"I don't know, but they look good together and there's definitely some romance in the air tonight."

"Rome..."

Rome turned around and narrowed her eyes, surprised to see one of *Nero*'s board members standing behind her. "Rob? I didn't expect..."

"I apologize for just showing up," Rob said. "That's my wife over there, she's just saying hi to your lawyer. She's very grateful for your donation and she wanted to meet you in person. Anton called her regarding the transaction and told her you guys were having a little get-together here." He hesitated. "I hope my presence doesn't put anyone off, I just wanted to show my support. We won't stay long."

"No, it's fine." Rome gave him a warm smile. "Thank you for coming and I'd love to meet your wife." She looked around the room, noting some curious glances as the other women spotted Rob. "I can only speak for myself, but at the end of the day, we all have to be back at work tomorrow and continue with our roles and responsibilities, so I'd say it's a positive thing that you're here to show your support. It might take away some of the awkwardness going forward."

"I really hope so." Rob cleared his throat. "Flavio sends his regards. As you can imagine, he was in two minds about coming along tonight, and just like me, he wasn't sure if he would be welcome. He's got a lot on his plate at the moment... we both do," he added. "But he wishes you the best and asked me to tell you he's looking forward to continuing working with you."

"Thank you, I appreciate that." Rome saw his eyes widen as he spotted Nadine, and quickly stepped in to clear the air. "This is my father, and you've already met Nadine. Nadine and I bumped into each other at a shopping mall after we had dinner together, and we got talking." She shrugged and smiled as if it was no big deal that Flavio's alleged girlfriend was here. "And now we're dating."

Rob greeted Rome's father, then frowned and looked from Rome to Nadine and back. "You're dating?" Although his confusion was mildly amusing, Rome didn't flinch.

"Yes. Flavio knows about it, so don't worry about him. We're actually moving in together. Weird how things can turn out, right?"

"Right..."

Nadine saved her from having to explain further by taking Rob's arm and guiding him toward the bar. "It's so great to see you again, Rob. How about we go get you a drink? Anyone else?"

Rome shook her head and shot her an adoring smile. The music was turned up and the laughter and animated chatter in the room grew louder, making her heart swell. There was a wonderful sense of support and comradery among them that Rome had never experienced before. She wasn't a loner anymore, she was a part of a community, of this wonderful group of women who had helped her to create a safer work environment. She had new friends, who she cherished, and she was a part of the neighborhood she lived in, and of the city she loved. But mostly, she was a part of Nadine, and Nadine was a part of her.

64

"Shall we take the scooter?" Rome asked as she closed the door behind her. "I think I can manage not to crease my dress, if I'm careful."

Nadine looked at her phone and typed something in, then shook her head. "No, let's walk. It's a nice evening."

"But we're going to be late and I'm wearing heels..." Rome frowned as she glanced at Nadine's screen. "Hey, what are you doing there?"

"I'm recalculating my carbon output," Nadine said with a grin. "I've already managed to reduce my carbon footprint by twenty-nine percent this month, so I don't want to ruin my efforts by driving tonight."

Rome rolled her eyes and laughed. "Come on, I'm starting to regret ever inventing that app."

"But I want to show your colleagues how well I've done," Nadine protested, her eyes widening as Rome took her purse and searched for the key to her scooter.

"Zero-point-zero-one percent is not going to make a difference to how impressed they are going to be," she said, placing a soft kiss on Nadine's cheek before she got on and

LISE GOLD

beckoned her to hop on the back. "You're amazing and everyone will see that." Rome was aware of how out of place they looked on a scooter, with her wearing a long, navy blue silk off-the shoulder gown and Nadine a sparkling black jumpsuit, but a taxi was not an option in the rush hour traffic and despite Nadine's protests, she certainly wasn't going to walk anywhere in her designer heels.

N*ero* had gone all-out for the Carbon app launch party, giving Rome and her team everything she had asked for and more. It was a month after the soft-launch, which meant they were able to share initial live-time results with their guests on a big screen they'd placed in the middle of the grand hall of the Savoy. So far, the app was already widely used and proven to be a successful tool in making consumers more mindful about their choices, and as expected, they liked to share the results, which had led to more downloads and card orders. Rome was delighted with the reactions from collaborating companies, the general public and the key opinion leaders they were working with, and the free advertising from celebrities who had been endorsing it on their own accord was invaluable.

"This is unbelievable." Nadine said, gasping as she looked around the beautifully decorated space. Over six-hundred people dressed in formal eveningwear were parading around the hall and surrounding areas, among immaculately dressed waiters, journalists and the *Nero* team. Champagne was flowing, canapés were being served and on the stage at the back of the hall, a jazz band was playing old tunes. "Wait, is that...?"

"Uh-huh." Rome took her hand and felt herself shaking. Even though she'd known what to expect, it was overwhelming, and the thought of getting up on that stage and speaking in front of everyone made her feel instantly nauseous. A famous Italian actress—one of the VIP's who had accepted the invite, along with a handful of other international stars—was leaning on one of the standing tables, talking to Flavio. "Want to meet her?" she asked, raising her voice in an attempt to sound confident.

"My God, Rome. Not yet, I've got helmet hair." Nadine stopped and brushed a hand through her dark locks, then turned to her. "How do I look?"

Rome took her hand and licked her lips while she looked her up and down. "You look scrumptious and even though this is the biggest night of my life, I really wish we were alone right now. You know? Just for fifteen minutes," she added with a chuckle.

"Really, fifteen minutes?" Nadine pulled her in and shot her a sexy smile. "Well you are the most beautiful woman here tonight, and I couldn't be prouder to be by your side. Are you nervous about your speech?"

"Yes." There was no point lying about that; Rome had been running around like a headless chicken all day, doing nothing in particular. She'd practiced her speech over a hundred times throughout the week, but even if it went wrong, it wasn't going to define the course of the Carbon app's success. "I'm so nervous, I think I might throw up any moment."

"Don't worry babe, you're going to be amazing," Nadine assured her. "But you might want to delay the throwing up part, because Flavio is waving you over."

"Oh God." Rome laughed and was grateful for Nadine holding her clammy hand. She'd always been good at staying composed but being here and realizing this was all her doing was like being thrown into the deep end all over again. She'd been on good terms with Flavio and Rob since the settlement, and although some of the employees had decided to leave after receiving their pay-out, the majority had stayed. "Please don't let go of me tonight."

"I'm right here, honey, and I'm not going anywhere."

Rome painted on a smile as she greeted some of her team members while they slowly worked their way through the crowd. She'd become a high-profile figure in Rome, after numerous newspaper and magazine interviews, and even a TV appearance, and as a result, sexual harassment in the workplace had been a trending topic on social media. Being an introvert at heart, Rome didn't necessarily like that all eyes were on her right now, but she was very happy with the growing awareness around the topic, and proud to be a part of such a change.

Several weeks had passed since the settlement, and Matteo had been expelled from the office and from inter-acting with *Nero* staff in general. He was in the process of buying himself out, and Rome suspected his funds were drying up as more and more cases came to light. The HR department had worked with his victims to compensate them in their own way by creating a more open culture when it came to reporting sexual harassment, and the PR department's hard work had ensured *Nero* survived the scandal. Tonight's launch would help with saving their image too, and Rome was pleased that the company was now open to invest in green start-ups, building on her success.

"Flavio. Congratulations," she said, greeting him and his movie star table companion.

"I believe I should be congratulating you instead; this is your night. Good job with the launch, it looks great and it's been going very well for us so far."

"Thank you, I'm very pleased with the results, too." Rome turned to the woman next to him. "This is my girlfriend, Nadine. She's a big fan of your work." Seeing Nadine blush was a rare sight and incredibly cute, and she focused on Flavio so Nadine would have a chance to talk to her.

"I heard you two recently moved in together," Flavio said, shooting Nadine a quick glance. He was clearly still a little hurt after learning Nadine was gay, but there was no bad blood between them. They hadn't told him the whole truth, and intended to keep it that way.

"Yes, we have. And I'm in the process of buying her neighbor's house. Now that I'll be staying here, there's no reason why I shouldn't invest. Nadine will be buying her own apartment too, and we're thinking of converting them into one big home. It's exciting."

"That sounds exciting indeed." The band stopped playing, and Flavio flinched as a technician moved the microphone stand to the center of the stage causing a loud beep to echo through the room. "I think that's our cue." He looked at his watch. "I'll get up there and announce you. Good luck."

Rome gave him a nod and felt her stomach turn. "I'm on," she whispered to Nadine, and shot her a quick smile before she followed Flavio to the front. Her hands were shaking as she pulled her notes from her purse and stepped onto the stage after Flavio said a few words to introduce her. Staring over the crowd, she took a moment to compose herself. It felt daunting, but she reminded herself that they were with her, and not against her.

"Thank you, Flavio, and thank you everyone, for being here tonight to celebrate something very special with us," she said, hoping the nervous tremor in her voice wasn't obvious. "The Carbon app and card are not only a product and service, they're a movement. A collective of people willing to make small changes in everyday life, and as a result, big changes will happen. I want to thank you all for caring, for supporting us and for endorsing this movement. As you can see on the screen, the half-million current users have already saved the equivalent of a forest after cutting down on the purchase of paper towels and switching most of their correspondence from paper to digital, and simply replacing their lightbulbs to energy saving ones, has had an effect similar to removing a hundred thousand cars from the road. Imagine what we could do if the whole world started doing this. But you were the first, and you should be very proud that you got to stand at the beginning of a positive revolution because we're making history here." She paused. "If there's one thing I've learned over the course of the past months, is that we're much stronger together. A very special person taught me that." Rome locked her eyes with Nadine, who was standing in front of the stage, looking up at her. Seeing the tears in Nadine's eyes, she took a deep breath and continued before she got too emotional to say another word. "I used to be a loner. I liked being a loner. But things have changed because I've realized we're all a part of something bigger, whether we want it or not. And as a part of this planet; a country, a city, a community, or even a neighbor-hood or a household, we have a responsibility to make better choices. For ourselves, and for the next generations." She cleared her throat and looked out over the crowd once again, then turned to the group of journalists and photogra-phers like she'd been instructed to do. "So, thank you, again. Let's start a new chapter." She shifted her gaze to Nadine. "Together."

The applause that followed made Rome burst into tears, but she didn't care. Almost blinded by the flashes from the camera's, she searched for her handkerchief in her purse and chuckled in relief as she wiped her tears. Although she'd dreaded being up there, she gave herself a little more time to appreciate the love and support in the room, because she knew there would never be another moment like this.

EPILOGUE

"Merry Christmas, beautiful." Nadine pulled Rome in as they met up in town after Rome had finished her last day of work for the year. The city was glowing in brightly colored lights and the abundance of Christmas decorations made every little street seem even more enchanting than before.

"Merry Christmas." Rome got on her tiptoes and pulled down Nadine's scarf before she kissed her. "Looking forward to some time off?"

"I certainly am. What about you?"

"Honestly, I can't wait. I'm loving my new job and all the challenges that come with it, but I'm also tired." Rome smiled. "Two whole weeks spent with no one but you is a dream come true." She put an arm around Nadine as they started walking. "I'm excited to see the St. Peter's Square Christmas tree; it's supposed to be spectacular."

"It will be spectacular." Nadine gazed over the snow-covered streets and took a moment to reflect on how lucky she was. Just over a year ago, she'd been walking the same route, alone. She'd been happy and content, or at least she thought she was happy, back then. After seeing the tree, she'd rushed home and gotten changed for her 'date'. Most girls at the agency didn't work over Christmas, so she'd been extremely popular, even though generally, business wasn't carried out over the holidays in Rome. She'd had one-to-one dinners with rich, lonely men who wanted someone to accompany them, then enjoyed a glass of wine by herself after she got home. Now, she had the love of her life by her side, she was a homeowner, and she ran a successful business. Frankly, she was astounded by how much had changed for her this year.

"I never expected to have a white Christmas here." Rome sighed in delight as they passed a small stall selling nativity figurines.

"It's not common, but I've experienced snow over Christmas once before, since I moved here."

"Well, I feel blessed to see the city covered in snow, it's magical." Rome paused. "I never cared much for Christmas —in fact, I tended to avoid it—but now I'm looking forward to Christmas Eve Mass at St. Peter's Basilica, a big, Roman lunch on Christmas day, classic Christmas carols at the Auditorium, and visiting all the beautiful churches at night... I can't think of a better place to spend Christmas than here."

"No Santa Claus though," Nadine joked. "Can you live with that?"

"I don't need anything. All I need is you." Rome smiled. "But I'm sure *La Befana* will bring you something if you've been a good girl."

"Really? Did you get me a present?" Nadine smirked.

"Of course I got you a present. In fact, I got you a whole set of presents to try out in bed later."

Nadine arched a brow as she bit her lip, her mind

already consumed with fantasies. "You know me so well." The fire in Rome's eyes made her want to take her home right away, but she had plans for tonight, and they were big plans.

St. Peter's Basilica came into sight as they turned onto the long, wide road leading up to the square, and they both stopped for a moment, staring up at the huge white basilica and Bernini's columns, beautifully lit up. At the front of the square, next to the four thousand-year-old Egyptian obelisk, was an enormous Christmas tree, its hundreds of lights casting a magical glow over the snow-covered square. The closer they got, the more aware she became of how awe-inspiring it was. Nadine had walked here many times at night, but she never failed to be amazed by the vastness of it all. The huge arcs on either side were like two benevolent arms embracing her, making her a part of something larger than herself.

Rome let go of her to look at the nativity scene next to the tree, and as Nadine buried her cold hands deep in her pockets, she felt the box she had placed there earlier—the enormity of what she was about to do making her heart jump.

"This is so beautiful." Rome let out a deep sigh and joined her under the tree, where more people were gathered, admiring the sight. She turned to Nadine, her eyes narrowing as she studied her. "Hey, are you okay?"

"Yeah." Nadine locked her eyes with Rome's and noticed her hand was trembling as she handed her the present. "This is for you." Keeping it a secret for so long had been incredibly hard but she'd wanted it to be perfect before Rome saw it for the first time.

"For me?" Rome smiled sweetly, tears shimmering in her eyes as she studied the rectangular box wrapped in simple, silver paper. "I haven't had a Christmas present in years. My father always sends me a gift card," she added with a chuckle in an attempt to hide her sudden emotional state.

Nadine waited nervously for her to unwrap it, and a wave of relief washed over her when she saw Rome's expression. First surprise, then utter delight as she read the name of the perfume, printed in a Roman font on the white box.

"Rome..."

"Yes, named after you, of course. Not the city." Nadine managed a smile, but her stomach was doing summersaults. She'd never been so afraid in her life. "It will be in stores next year, and just to put your mind at ease, it's all made out of recycled material. Go on, open it. You were the inspiration behind it."

"Wow, this is so awesome. I can't believe you named your perfume after me," Rome said through tears as she opened the box and pulled out a beautiful teardrop-shaped frosted glass bottle with a slim neck and glass stopper. She took the top off, put some on her wrists and inhaled the heady aroma. "I love it. It smells like that perfume you made me when we first met. Only better." Her bottom lip was trembling as she looked up to meet Nadine's eyes. "Thank you. I can't believe you did that for me."

"That's not all..." Nadine drew her attention to the bottle. "There's something hanging around the neck."

"Oh, it's a little dark here, I thought that was part of the design." Rome chuckled through her sniffles as she studied the sparking embellishment hanging from a silk ribbon wrapped around the bottle. Her eyes then widened as she realized it was a diamond ring. "No..."

Nadine held her breath, cursing the long silence that followed as Rome slipped it off the ribbon and held it up against the light of the tree. "Is this...?"

"Only if you want it to be." Nadine took the ring while Rome removed her glove, then put it on her finger. "I'll totally understand if it's too soon, or even if you don't want it at all. I just want you to have it."

"No... I do." Rome's lips pulled into a wide smile as she stared at her hand, then at Nadine, as if she couldn't believe what was happening.

"Really? You want to marry me?" Nadine let out an elated shriek, lifted Rome up and spun her around. "Are you serious?" She asked as she put her back down and took Rome's face in her hands.

"Yes. I'm very, very serious. Nadine Costa, I can't think of anything better than to be married to you."

Nadine basked in happiness as Rome gave her a long and lingering kiss that swept her off her feet. Despite the cold, she felt warm and clammy; the culmination of nerves and excitement getting the better of her.

Rome pulled out of the kiss and looked around as applause broke out and she noticed tourists were filming them. They both laughed and Rome waved her hand, flashing her ring at their cameras. "We're getting married!" she yelled, then flung her arms around Nadine's neck.

"I love you so much," Nadine mumbled against Rome's mouth as she kissed her again. The vast expanse of the night sky twinkled above their romantic backdrop, the universe seemingly celebrating with them. Their stars had aligned and there was nothing more perfect in the world than loving Rome.

I hope you've loved reading *The Scent of Rome* as much as I've loved writing it. If you've enjoyed this book, would you consider rating it and reviewing it on www.amazon.com? Reviews are very important to authors and I'd be really grateful!

ACKNOWLEDGMENTS

Writing a novel takes a lot of work, and I couldn't have done this without Claire Jarrett, my editor. Claire, thank you for your invaluable feedback throughout the process. I love our smooth working relationship that will hopefully last for many, many more years to come. I'll just keep on writing :)

Laure Dherbecourt, thank you for always being so flexible last-minute. It's a pleasure working with you, and I'm sure we'll get to meet in person one day!

Also, thank you Bella (what a great name!), for advising me on the workings of the Italian legal system. I've kept it as simple as possible so I wouldn't mess up ;)

Fatima M, thank you so much for sharing your personal experiences with me. It was super exciting to learn about the life of a high-end escort.

ABOUT THE AUTHOR

Lise Gold is an author of lesbian romance. Her romantic attitude, enthusiasm for travel and love for feel good stories form the heartland of her writing. Born in London to a Norwegian mother and English father, and growing up between the UK, Norway, Zambia and the Netherlands, she feels at home pretty much everywhere and has an unending curiosity for new destinations. She goes by 'write what you know' and is often found in exotic locations doing research or getting inspired for her next novel.

Working as a designer for fifteen years and singing semi-professionally, Lise has always been a creative at heart. Her novels are the result of a quest for a new passion after resigning from her design job in 2018. Since the launch of Lily's Fire in 2017, she has written several romantic novels and is currently working on 'The Compass Series'.

When not writing from her kitchen table, Lise can be found cooking, at the gym or singing her heart out some-where, preferably country or blues. After living in Amsterdam and Hong Kong together and getting married in Spain, she and her wife have finally settled in the UK with their dogs El Comandante and Bubba, and their cats Kanye, Lil' Tittie and Extra Sweet.